A requiem f

by Joyce C

Joyce Collinson

Published by David Hetherington and Sketchnews
Copyright 2013 Joyce Collinson
ISBN-13: 978-1484846292
ISBN-10: 148484629X

Synopsis

Professor Joy Hetherington, a delightful eccentric and one of the 'old brigade', finds herself enmeshed in a terrifying series of events as she innocently goes about her academic business with unbounded enthusiasm.

This captivating novel is set at a time of momentous transition in Oxford, as the old regime of learning in the late 1970's gives way to the new. A powerful entity from outside is hell-bent on destroying this ancient city using any means available. It is a tale of murder, mystery and espionage that comes alive with the rich and timeless tapestry of college life in the city itself as the background.

Acknowledgements

to my editor,
Dr. Jean Woodward

to Frances Fyfield
for literary direction

to Anne McHardy
for technical assistance

Cover sketch of Oxford skyline,
by Joyce Collinson

In memory of

*Sir Richard and Lady Southern
and Mary Drewett*

Table of Contents

Chapter I - **An unexplained death**
Chapter II - **Tangible evidence of foul play**
Chapter III - **Doom and disaster imminent**
Chapter IV - **Enter Madge Spragnell**
Chapter V - **A body in the well**
Chapter VI - **Escape from an assassin**
Chapter VII - **The mills of God grind slowly...**
Chapter VIII - **Haunt of the Grey Monk**
Chapter IX - **Balloon**
Chapter X - **Demise of the greengage tree**
Chapter XI - **Big wheel and the Gallopin' 'Orses**
Chapter XII - **Tudor and Elizabethan style**
Chapter XIII - **All the fun of the fair**
Chapter XIV - **A raffle draw, a brawl and drugs haul**
Chapter XV - **Drug squad reviews the case**
Chapter XVI - **Mynah bird talks to the police**
Chapter XVII - **Wedding bells**
Chapter XVIII - **Treasure trove of ancient documents**
Chapter XIX - **An engagement and a party**
Chapter XX - **Drink, food and a 'bombe surprise'**
Chapter XXI – **The villain revealed**
Chapter XXII - **Foiled by infiltrators**
Chapter XXIII - **Police conclude their account**
Chapter XXIV - **On to the next tutorial**

CHAPTER I

'Dainty fine bird, who art encaged there,

Alas, how like thine and my fortunes are ... '

The First Set of Madrigals and Motets of 5 parts

Orlando Gibbons 1612

Professor Trondheim picked up her brass telescope and shuffled painfully to her bedroom window. Not much fun to be eighty-nine and housebound, with an agile mind and a frail body.

One of the few pleasures left in life was to sit at her window, high up looking out over Port Meadow on the edge of Oxford, and survey the world through her ancient German telescope, the only surviving relic of her husband, who died in Auschwitz.

It was really quite remarkable what one saw sometimes!

Such incredible goings-on! Especially if one focused a bit nearer home; say, for instance, at the back windows of the houses in the next street across the long back gardens of North Oxford.

The things people got up to!

Most extraordinary! In particular, the antics of one young man in the attic opposite, who spent most of his evenings all alone, dressing up in women's clothes and admiring himself in the mirror! Very interesting; and yet he looked so respectable usually, pedaling off to college on his bicycle every morning, as though nothing was amiss.

Ah, well! Professor Trondheim twiddled her telescope and peered westwards over the meadow.

It was a beautiful late summer evening.

Lazy tongues of blue smoke curled upwards from bonfires on Trap Allotments beyond Aristotle Bridge. A heron flapped languidly over Binsey Village on the other side of the Thames, boats dreamed along the waters, and a high-fly jumbo-jet made vapour-trails for Canada in a sapphire sky turning orange for sunset.

A movement below in the next garden distracted the old lady. Ah, yes! It was Joy Hetherington, surrounded by her cats, hanging out her washing.

Very curious! Every day, without fail, it seemed, she hung out endless pairs of drawers (usually in conjunction with other washing, of course). Elise Trondheim caught her attention and waved a greeting. "Hello, Elise," called Joy. "What can you see today with your telescope?"

"Wass?" said the old lady, who was practically stone-deaf. Joy patiently repeated the question until finally she got through. "Oh, many fine things I can see today: but nothing very exciting or unusual."

"I should watch for the B-52," called Joy. "It's floating around doing something or other."

"V.2!"

Elise Trondheim was confused by this terrible thought.

"No, dear. B-fifty-two." (Oh how she dearly wished she had not embarked upon this conversation! Very exhausting.)

"B-fifty-two. It's something very special which is meant to stop us all blowing ourselves up. It looks like something out of Ezekiel's description of aeroplanes prophecy - rather like a jumbo-jet only more so."

Joy stood back and surveyed her washing with satisfaction. A good west wind and a dry night should do the trick.

The memory of the B-52 filled her with sudden sorrow.

"Poor Melody," she mused. "How much could one grow to love something so silly as a common green budgerigar - noisy little brute that he was!"

It had been six months before that a young student lodging in her house had asked her to look after this extraordinary bird during the long vac.

"I'm off to Tunisia - I'll only be away for a week or two" the girl had said. "Here's his bird-seed, and he never comes out of his cage, so he's no trouble" - and never returned.

Joy Hetherington, a Professor and a Lancashire sheep-farmer's daughter, hadn't much time for cage-birds. "You won't be away long, will you, dear?" she had said to the girl, "I don't know a thing about birds in cages. I'm only used to the wild variety."

Howbeit, no luck; she was left with the bird. Joy eyed the poor creature uneasily, shivering in a corner of its cage. It looked ill and wouldn't eat. She put the cage in her study by the window, so at least it could see out into the garden.

What a terrible life, to be confined for ever to a metal cage; most unnatural. Moreover, she was quite sure it would soon be slaughtered by one of the cats when they realized that there was a real live twittering bird in the house.

The message soon went round of course, and there was an attentive queue of feline beings on the window-sill and outside the study door on the very first day.

They were all half-wild strays anyway, mostly having been left behind by departing students, as is regrettably a common pattern in Oxford, with its large visiting population, so for these cats, the chance of a tasty dinner was quite irresistible.

The bird was completely silent on the first day; it didn't appear to eat anything and cowered on its perch, trembling. However, on the second day the silence was suddenly rent by an almighty screech. Joy dashed into the study just in time to see the act of attempted execution.

The cage and stand rocked wildly, as little stray tabby - who had got in somehow - took a flying leap from the floor, landing neatly on top, rather like something out of a cartoon film. The unfortunate bird raced around inside the cage, terrified, as tabby grimly clung on with all claws. Feathers flew everywhere.

There was a moment of total horror as the cage completely disintegrated, jettisoning its entire contents on the sofa - perches, bells, mirror - bird.

Joy froze completely.

The cat and the bird lay stunned and perfectly still, side by side on the sofa. The cage was on top of the cat and the bird lay, eyes closed, on its back, panting faintly - and surely dying. As Joy put out her hand to pick up the bird, it suddenly came to life with another blood-curdling screech, and scattering feathers everywhere, again, fluttered squawking loudly under the sofa.

Joy threw tabby out after making sure that she was uninjured and then tried to find the bird. It was no good. It must have got up into the springs underneath; and there it remained - for a whole week! She knew it was still alive somewhere inside the sofa, as she put bird-seed and water underneath and there were occasional sounds of pecking and the odd flutter and chirrup.

A week later, Joy entered the room and was astonished to see the bird perched on the window-sill chattering away merrily to other birds out in the garden.

The window was wide open, but Melody made no attempts at all to go outside, and that was how the situation remained. Melody spent all his waking-hours running up and down the window-sill, chattering loudly to his new-found friends in the garden, yet never once attempting to go out through the open window! He was absolute death to concentration, as Joy ruefully explained to her friends. Birds of all varieties came and sat on top of the garden shed in considerable numbers to talk to this extraordinary budgerigar. He was a source of wonder to everyone; particularly a visiting ornithologist, who declared he had never heard of anything like it before and why on earth didn't it flyaway like any normal bird?

Melody was particularly interested in aircraft, but displayed no interest at all in those colourful air-balloons which silently drift across the summer skies of Oxford.

V.C.10s coming in to Brize Norton were his particular passion. He would jump up and down on the window-sill and fly round the room in elaborate figures-of-eight with sheer excitement as they passed low overhead. Joy concluded that he thought they were large birds of some kind.

However, he was terrified of the B.52.

Joy stuck his battered cage together with tape and string, and Melody eventually even deigned to go into it sometimes; but usually only just for quick snack or a nap. He evidently preferred his window-sill as living accommodation. She even got him a new cage, but he totally ignored it.

The cats gave up their vain attempts to get him. Instead, they would sit in a row outside the study door or out in the garden beneath the open window, teeth chattering with frustration, attempting mass-hypnosis on the bird, willing him to come within catching-distance. But he had learnt all about cats the hard way and wasn't having any of it. Instead, he drove them completely demented by screeching at them in an endless barrage and zooming down in sudden aerial displays, until in the end they gave up and went away.

Melody was also an excellent burglar-alarm, and a useful asset in this respect; for many strange characters wandered about St.Julie's Road and this peculiar area adjacent to Port Meadow. Peculiar, possibly, because of the immediate transition from city to country in just a few yards.

It is a curious quality of Oxford that it has countryside and the things of nature coming into the very middle of it from all sides; and there is, therefore, a kaleidoscopic mixture of several elements; the jumble of the dreaming spires and university, the city, meadows and waterways; all combine to bring the qualities of life which belong to them, together - in a kind of uneasy centrifuge, making Oxford what it is: painfully unique.

The number of unsavoury people who inhabit the place would be lost in a bigger city, but in Oxford they seem numerous. Some sleep rough on the dumps and roam the meadows and their periphery at night, and St. Julie's Road occasionally has its spasms of late-night fracas and the odd burglary. So Melody was a great asset, for the least unusual sound would provoke him to immediate shrill squawks. He saw off occasional intruders in the back-garden during the small hours in this way.

Joy reflected sadly upon his death. Fred, her blind stray tabby, missed him terribly, for he was the one who had had full value from the bird. He would sit for hours, listening to Melody's entertainments, purring loudly, and whiskers a-twitch.

The usual pattern went thus. Melody would make the occasional sortie over Fred's head and they had a little game of catch, as the bird fluttered like a sparrow-hawk as near Fred's nose as possible. The cat would flash out a paw sometimes - and once or twice very nearly scored a direct-hit. All things considered, it was a good friendship they had.

The B52 had really excelled itself the day Melody died, with its deafening roar and awe-inspiring low-passes overhead.

The budgerigar had gone utterly berserk, shrieking all day long until Joy felt she might strangle him if he didn't shut up. He did, eventually, and rather suddenly.

Joy went into the study wondering why he was so quiet. He was nowhere to be seen; perhaps he had at last flown away - blessed thought! However, after a search, she found him quite dead under the sofa.

He lay on his back, eyes and beak wide open, wings neatly folded, with a look of abject terror on his face. He looked as though something had literally frightened him to death.

Joy took him out to bury him in the flower-bed, feeling unaccountably sorrowful. The cats came along to the burial, and she let them sniff the tiny corpse, but they simply shook a paw and walked off, showing no further interest. Evidently he was not worth eating.

The house seemed dreadfully quiet afterwards, and Joy toyed with the idea that maybe she ought to get a dog to replace him.

The ornithologist commented that possibly he had indeed died of fright by the sound of things, for he was such a healthy young bird with plenty of life in him. It was all very sad. Professor Trondheim inspected the burial via her telescope and agreed with the verdict.

"Most likely! That thing is awful. It should not be allowed in the sky: schrecklish!"

During rehearsal with her madrigal consort that night at St. James' College, Joy mournfully retailed the sad tidings and Lady Westhoe suggested that they should sing Orlando Gibbons' 'Dainty fine bird' as a requiem.

The glorious setting of the Presidential Drawing-Room lent solemnity to the occasion. They sang beautifully: 'Dainty fine bird, who art encaged there; Alas, how like thine and my fortunes are---'. Their voices interwove gracefully in the lovely melody: 'Thou liv'st singing, but I sing and die - I sing and die'. The final cadence softly floated away across the quad in a gentle pianissimo. It was very moving.

"It's strange," said John Spry, "How there's a madrigal for every occasion."

"Indeed, indeed," added Professor Peterson, looking over his half-glasses. A ripple of laughter went round the room.

"You needn't laugh," poor Joy riposted with dignity; "I am most upset. We have such weird people roving around the place. My bird was absolutely outstanding as a watch-dog at night. I feel most insecure without him!"

"Believe me; we have even more riveting things to offer in Museum Road," retorted John Spry. "The other day, in broad daylight, my doorbell rang. I opened the door and there stood a man with a knife pointing straight at my chest!"

The choir gasped, "What on earth did you do?" asked Caroline Grieve. "Shut it quickly," replied John, "And rang the police."

"Brilliant thinking," said Professor Peterson.

With that, choir practice disintegrated in loud laughter.

This was simply because John Spry was possibly one of the least likely people to whom this kind of dramatic event would ever happen, and to think of him reacting so fast was improbable.

John was a sedate young man of twenty-eight; an archaeologist. He possessed the great gift of never seeming to be in a hurry.

Well built and fair, with a short beard and gold glasses, behind which twinkled steel-blue eyes, he had a delicious sense of humour and a beautiful smile but could also present a most solemn demeanour when he wished - as befits all distinguished academics.

The choir discussed the down-swing in the quality of life in present-day Oxford.

"Well," said John, "I maintain things have never been the same since that thunderbolt hit the scaffolding round Keeble Chapel this summer."

"Not to mention the other one which just missed Magdalen Tower by inches, and ended up sizzling in the river just over the bridge where the punts are," commented Caroline Grieve.

"Quite so," said John, "I feel that this may be a judgement on the city. God's angry. Probably missed only because there was less than half a tower at the time, as they hadn't yet finished rebuilding it."

"Anyway," said Caroline, "London must be in disfavour too, because a short time afterwards on the same day, one hit County Hall fair and square. I've got a friend who saw it from her office window on the other side of the river. Quite spectacular, she said; made an enormous bang."

"Probably meant for the Houses of Parliament and missed," said John looking thoughtfully into his madrigals.

"One poor undergraduate in the library at Keeble was blinded completely for a while by the flash," said Lady Westhoe: "He was sitting by the window and it struck the scaffolding just outside. He was very lucky not to have been seriously injured, I would think."

When rehearsal had finished, Joy and Brenda Page-Philips crossed the quad together, stepped through the tiny door within the main gate and stood outside in St. Giles', discussing life in general and Oxford in particular, as they unlocked their bikes.

"I suppose," said Brenda, looking into the distance towards St. Giles' Church, "That in my work, I see Oxford as it really is."

"Really? What then? Joy struggled with her combination bicycle-lock in the gathering dusk. "Why on earth don't they have luminous numbers on these wretched bike-locks? How on earth can I find 4377 in the dark?'"

Brenda patiently waited; and watched the afterglow. Really, it was almost a green sky at this time of year - and the evening star! Quite breathtaking; a vivid jewel over the church tower.

They walked their bikes as far as The Lamb and Flag, but it was packed out, so they gave up the idea of a drink there.

Continuing on towards St. Giles' churchyard, they stopped at the war memorial and looked back down St. Giles'. The mediaeval front of St. James' College tucked away down on the left-hand side had a welcoming and homely air about it - in spite of its ghosts, some forbidding, some not; and its long history, with none but the most distinguished academics as its graduates over the centuries.

Brenda continued: "At a place like Botticelli's we are bound to attract everybody who is anybody. I suppose it's inevitable. If we were in London or somewhere, it probably wouldn't be the same at all. Here we are, hidden away in an Oxford back-street - we're really only a cottage industry, you know - yet we have the very highest international reputation for clothes. Kings, Queens, film stars, racing drivers you name it, they all come to Botticelli's. And yet what is so lovely about it is that all the local people come-along too: shop-girls, housewives, usually dragging their husbands along as well. All come with a real intention of trying something on with a view to purchase, and no matter who they are, everybody gets exactly the same treatment. Nobody stands around ogling the famous. It's all very friendly and ordinary. This city really is a great equalizer, isn't it?"

They agreed the point and parted, Brenda pedalling off up the Banbury Road to play darts at the Rose and Crown, Joy taking the Woodstock Road to join her friends at her local pub, The Jolly Sailors, by Aristotle Bridge.

The pub was busy. A large number of foreign students from the English language schools were in possession of the saloon bar, and happy laughter and jocular shouts in various foreign tongues drifted across the courtyard.

Joy went round to the public bar where serious darts was in progress and the locals were in occupation.

She spied her nephew Mark at the bar. He had, as usual, sorted out for himself the most attractive of the foreign students to talk to; she was a particularly beautiful Scandinavian. It really was most amusing to watch him at work with his great charm and good-looks.

Come to think of it, that spell in the Marines had done him no harm at all; he was now so self-assured. It had made a man of him. Oddly enough, he never spoke much about his experiences during that period. He seemed to have spent a good deal of his time out of the country, sometimes returning with a fine sun-tan after a tour of duty abroad, but he would never be drawn, except to say that travel broadens the mind, and that the Far East is interesting, but too hot.

Voluble exchanges in Arabic from the saloon bar lent an incongruous air to the tranquil scene. Silence and concentration enveloped the darts-match and the bar-billiards and small groups of local people talked quietly of parochial matters: the allotments, the prospects for the next boat-race, St. Giles' Fair - soon to take place, St. Julie's Church roof-repairs, or the current goings-on at the car factory.

Dick Ballard sat alone with his dog in the far corner by the bar-billiards table, contemplating his pint of bitter.

The young King Alfred-the-Great would be a good description of his looks, with his long fair hair and beard. He was, in fact, from an ancient village hidden away up on the downs near Wantage where Alfred had been, and he looked so like the statue in Wantage Market Place that it was quite uncanny.

However, the pork-pie hat stuck fair and square on his head and the horn-rimmed spectacles somewhat spoilt the image.

His dog, Hugo, was the most remarkable animal. He should really have been a wire-haired fox-terrier, but somehow he had come out as an all-black half-Airedale with foxes' ears.

He was a wonderful hunting-dog and kept Dick's stew-pot well supplied, for Dick loved rabbit stew, being a countryman.

Also, the rabbits and the odd duck came in very handy as a boost to the economy, for Dick was out of work, so Hugo really earned his keep with zest, as he adored his master with a love that was the envy of all who saw them together.

Professor Trondheim knew their movements very well, and would make a special and painful effort to get out of bed at dawn on fine mornings, simply to follow their expeditions with her telescope, until at length they vanished into the rising mist far away over by Medley Bridge, Hugo in front, nose to the ground, question-mark of a tail aloft, zig-zagging ahead, following those most lovely scents known only to dogs.

The old lady knew nothing about Dick - except that he lived somewhere nearby in St. Julie's Road. She dearly wished she could attract his attention somehow and talk to him.

It was such a lonely life up here. One saw so few people, except at a distance, and he looked so nice, going out over the meadow every day. Such a happy existence - a man and his dog. Where did he go, this man with the flowing-beard and the funny hat? Sometimes he would not return until dusk, for she would often sit all day at her window, watching events on the meadow and keeping an eye on Medley Bridge to see when he came back. She was always so pleased when he came into focus, usually carrying a heavy bag over his shoulder, his dog dancing on ahead, playing chasing-games with the horses grazing over by the river.

He had the purposeful and confident stride of the countryman, she observed; perhaps he worked on a farm over towards Wytham somewhere. This was a possibility.

She asked her daughter Erica about him, but she provided no information at all on the subject - except to say, with an air of distinct disapproval, that she thought he was maybe, "One of those people at number 45" - whatever that meant.

Erica was at the best of times uncommunicative, being almost a recluse. She seldom went out, but when she did, she always dressed like someone about to undertake a polar expedition, no matter what the weather; winter or summer.

Her beautiful ash-blonde hair was completely obscured by a black woolly tea-cosy affair, which was rammed so firmly on her head that one only saw a face south of the eyebrows and the ear-lobes, so to say. An equally awful black woolly jumble-sale coat completely enveloped her excellent figure from chin to shin, and to finish off the ensemble, a pair of best quality heavy-duty Wellington boots took care of the bottom end of the anatomy.

She always carried a hefty walking-stick – or perhaps it was a Bavarian shepherd's-staff, people had speculated about this and there was some disagreement about what it actually was; but it looked quite useful as a weapon: perhaps it was a sword-stick.

To keep the world even further at bay on her sorties out over the meadow, she had, plugged into one ear via a long lead a transistor radio and cassette machine of large proportion, which hung from a shoulder-strap.

A formidable sight she was, frowning firmly at the ground as she walked on at funeral pace, looking at nothing and acknowledging nobody.

Joy, contentedly digging her allotment one day as Erica passed, asked her what it was that she listened to so intently on these excursions.

"Bach?" ventured Joy. "Beethoven?"

"Of course not; how unconstructive!" retorted Erica scornfully, "It is my language course."

Joy enquired which language.

"Serbo-Croat and Welsh, naturally; what do you think?" muttered Erica with a frown and strode on, clearly not pleased by this interruption.

Joy felt somewhat crushed.

Professor Trondheim watched her daughter from the window during these peripherations. They were not close, Erica and herself, she reflected. Erica was so withdrawn. It was almost as though they were strangers. They seldom saw one another, even living in the same house. Erica, though now nearly fifty was still a beautiful woman, and yet she totally rejected the approaches of even the most charming men who had crossed her path over the years.

She seemed to be completely obsessed by her researches into the origins of language. For some years she had been preparing a book on the subject and every conceivable kind of social consideration seemed to have got totally obliterated by this obsession. She did not seem to need people at all. It was so sad. Such a beautiful woman, with so much to give, yet so isolated - an iceberg, one might say, and really very selfish too.

The old lady secretly doubted whether the book would ever be finished, for she had never been shown any of it in all the years it had been in preparation.

Surveying the meadow as Erica made her progress towards the dumps in the Wolvercote direction, Elise Trondheim noticed a small figure in the bushes by the ditch which ran alongside the path. She focused her telescope as accurately as possible and got a good look at the face of the young man she saw there. She had seen him before once or twice going through Trap Allotment gate; usually in the early evening at twilight, disappearing in the direction of the dumps, but this time it was earlier in the day.

He appeared to be examining something close to the ground. He was very small; a neat and trim figure, with long black wavy hair and a fine aristocratic face with a small black moustache. His sallow complexion was accentuated by the Prussian blue velvet jacket he wore.

Probably a botanist looking at some particular wild species of flora. He spent a long time in that particular spot, then slowly moved off in the direction of Medley Bridge following the usual route of the young man with the beard, who had gone that way earlier.

He kept his head down all the time as he walked, and was evidently searching for something in particular which must also be very tiny, for he would occasionally crouch down and delicately separate the short meadow-grass with his fingers.

He did seem, however, to be somewhat furtive in his manner, for he frequently looked back as though he thought somebody might be watching.

The old lady did not see him come back. Perhaps he was not a creature of regular habits, like the young man with the dog.

She really must ask Erica more about this place, number 45, when she next saw her, but it was most difficult to catch her; she came and went like a phantom from the basement.

For mother and daughter, they might as well be on different planets for the amount they saw of one another.

At night, in the summer-time of the year, Elise Trondheim sat at her window - for hours sometimes, with the lights off, of course. From twilight until the early hours was possibly the most interesting time to view the world through one's telescope.

How strange it was that people often didn't bother to draw their curtains at night in summer.

Next door to the young man who liked to dress up in women's clothes, lived a man and his wife. It must have been his wife, Elise, surmised, since they had three children and a dog and two cats. On warm summer-nights they would prepare for bed the curtains open, quite unconscious of the fact that they could be seen across the back-gardens through the telescope of Professor Trondheim.

The young man, though completely naked, would always wear his spectacles. It was so amusing. He had really a very fine physique - although he was evidently an academic - for he would often walk around the bedroom reading aloud to his wife from a book as she lay in bed, listening intently, and occasionally offering a comment. He never wore pyjamas - very strange. From the way he moved around and the eloquent gestures he made, it must be Shakespeare, the old lady concluded.

It all went to prove that some young people had other ideas in their heads apart from their sex-lives, she thought with approval.

The sky was marvellous to watch at night. Even here in the city, the stars were wonderful. The Milky Way was often quite distinct and the Plough was a constant friend in the sky, moving round in a majestic circle overhead as the seasons progressed. True North seemed to be a variable, according to the time of the year, which was curious and interesting.

There were, of course, other lights in the sky, besides the stars. High-altitude aeroplanes blinked silently across the heavens; and sometimes the most astonishing shooting-stars flashed through the night. Quite awesome. One realized how small one was when one saw such things. Once or twice burning satellites had passed overhead, burning themselves out in the most wonderful firework-display. And all accomplished in complete silence. One waited for the mighty bang which ought to accompany the stunning visual impact, but it never came.

When she saw Joy Hetherington in the garden one day, the old lady asked about number 45.

"What is this place, number 45, of which Erica speaks?"

"Ah!" said Joy, leaving the washing-line and coming to the garden-wall, "You mean our local house of ill-repute!"

She lowered her voice.

"Some very odd people live at number 45 and there are mighty strange goings-on there. The police are always appearing outside - especially late at night. How do you know about it?"

"Erica told me of this place. I wanted to know about the young man with the black dog; she thinks he lives there. Do you know of him? He has a long beard and glasses and a pork-pie hat."

Joy leaned on the wall and teased tabby with a twig.

"Ah, yes, of course. You mean Dick Ballard! A lovely man. He has an allotment next to mine - comes from near Uffington Castle on the Downs. He's not working at the moment, so far as I know, so he's probably off hunting and things when you see him. His dog Hugo is a wonderful retriever, marvellous at catching rabbits; so quick. You would adore Dick. He is a real, 'Old Berkshire', and so refreshing to talk to; so much country-lore in him. What he doesn't know about the things of nature isn't worth knowing, as they say."

Elise Trondheim asked about the young man in the blue jacket, but Joy did not recollect ever having seen him.

She also guessed he could be a botanist by the description of his activities.

However, she was soon to meet him in somewhat unusual circumstances.

Always recalling her father's sheep-farming background, it was instinctive in Joy to seek peace of mind - in all the hurly-burly of Oxford - in solitude, at dusk; looking westward to the Cotswolds across Port Meadow, thinking often of the family farm on the windy high Pennines.

'Twilight it is: and the far woods are dim,

And the rooks cry and call.

Down in the valley, the lamps and the mist,

And a star over all -'

John Masefield's marvellous words always echoed in her mind.

Having learnt the poem by heart (and, incidentally, large chunks of, Hiawatha; such agony!) in detention at school, it had truly stuck firm.

She stood, as usual, in the gathering dusk, just inside the allotment gate, hypnotized by the afterglow in the western sky, and watched the Canada geese take off in stately formation from the river for their evening constitutional. This took the form of a kind of circular-tour of Oxford, happening on fine nights at precisely the same time. Not time as the clock-goes but time as the sun-goes, as it were.

The sun would slowly disappear in a wonderful final burst of glory over Wytham, and two or three minutes later the honking would begin as the geese prepared for take-off down on the river.

First, there was the honking of many voices, followed by the whirring of a thousand powerful wings in the quiet of twilight. Then, like a squadron of aircraft, they would rise in perfect formation, an inverted, 'V', following the line of the river, turning left over the old castle mound and then slowly circling over the city two or three times, their leader honking incessantly.

Finally, they would return, making a perfect landing on the river again to settle down for the night.

Totally mesmeric - a wonderful experience, simply to stand perfectly still and absorb it all. The whole episode took over half an hour from beginning to end, and as they returned it was practically dark.

Joy remembered how she had stood outside St. Mary the Virgin by the Radcliffe Camera one summer night after a concert, and had been surprised to see a great flight of Canada-geese pass low over the spire, honking as they went. Now she knew how this came to be.

Whilst standing alone one night in this curious dream-sequence, she became aware of a slight movement by the ditch outside the allotment-fence. It was nearly dark, but her eyes had become accustomed to the conditions and she could now, 'see in the dark', as most country-bred people can.

She felt there was somebody or something there.

Was it a fox?

She stood perfectly still and waited.

There were, of course, many tramps and other people, too, who came that way at night, but they were normally going somewhere; i.e., the dumps to sleep overnight, or perhaps walking over to Binsey for a drink at the Perch. Cattle and horses moved around also, but this was something, or somebody, behaving in a stealthy manner.

Was it a poacher? - this was unlikely, as there was little to poach around the allotments at night.

She waited.

As the movement came nearer, she made out a small figure crouching close to the ground, evidently looking for something.

She held her breath and tried not to move as the figure passed by. Luckily he did not see her as he slowly moved along, and she realized that this must be the young man who had been described by the old lady as the possible botanist.

She could see the pale, handsome face and long dark hair, the small stature and the dark jacket.

She let him pass without interruption.

What on earth was he doing, scrabbling-about by the ditches? She was to find out a few days later.

Time to do some digging. Evening was the nicest time to go over to the allotments to work. A particular atmosphere surrounded the area as evening approached, somewhat ghostly, but so peaceful.

Not everyone found it peaceful, however.

Many local people found it too eerie to go over alone in the evening. Some said there were ghosts. One very level-headed woman said she was quite sure her dog saw ghosts at a certain spot just over the railway-bridge, for he would not pass a particular place at a certain time in the evening, but stiffened and growled, the hair on his back bristling with fear, and this in an open area of the meadow with nobody in sight.

She maintained that he definitely saw something, as he would go perfectly rigid and watch something move across the path from left to right. She herself saw nothing.

There were also well-attested stories of the sound of cavalry coming from the meadow along Aristotle Lane and up Polstead Road; turning left towards Woodstock. This event always took place in the middle of the night.

Some people claimed to have been wakened by the sound of distant hooves and the clank of metal and harness. Going to the window, they would look out to watch for the approaching riders, but they saw nothing as the ghostly cavalry thundered past.

As she picked courgettes and spinach, Joy reflected upon these things. She herself felt none of the unease which others had experienced whilst alone there.

Come to think of it, though, she did not ever recollect seeing anyone else working on their allotments much after sundown.

Perhaps people thought of the tragic suicides which happened from time to time at the railway-bridge, or - more likely - they had better things to do than watch the sunset and the geese in flight.

It was by now nearly dark and she couldn't see well enough to do any more. She straightened-up slowly.

Oh! Such a stiff back from too much bending. She started suddenly with surprise at what she saw, her heart banging against her ribs.

"Hey!" she exclaimed, "You startled me!"

There, standing not four feet away was the elfin-figure of the young man with the long dark hair, standing quietly watching her. How long he had been there she had no idea.

"Ello, Miss," he said cheerfully. "I see you the other night over 'ere. Thought I'd come and say how-do-you-do." He made a little bow to her.

They talked for quite some time and he told her all about himself. It was as though he was shedding great burden as he told the story of his life.

As he spoke, he kept looking back over his shoulder, as if someone was watching him, although it was by now quite dark and this was therefore unlikely.

His was a heart-breaking story. No family, no job, no home, and all this achieved by the age of 23 - and in trouble all his life, from his own testimony. However, he was quite cheerful about his misfortunes.

His name was Cledwyn, he said, and although his accent was faintly Liverpudlian, he said he had been born and reared in South Wales, but had, 'moved around a lot'.

He was at the moment sleeping rough on the meadow, but sometimes he would stay with Dick Ballard, "at No. 45 - for a clean-up," as he put it so nicely.

Joy put her tools away and they walked back to The Jolly Sailors for a beer. Good beer went down very well after a bout of hard work on the allotments.

She looked at her young companion closely.

He was astonishingly clean and tidy for a lad sleeping-rough.

His face was so familiar somehow, and yet she knew she hadn't seen him before. Such aristocratic good-looks, and yet so small in stature, but completely in proportion and clearly very fit, in spite of an irregular life.

No doubt he didn't eat properly, as seems common with people who live-rough. He chain-smoked as though his life depended on every puff.

Whom did he look like? She couldn't think of it at the moment, but she knew it would come to her eventually.

At the pub he told her what seemed to be a very tall story; he said he was, 'mushrooming' on his expeditions over the meadow! Although to be quite honest, he did seem to know everything there was to know about mushrooms. He knew the botanical names of all the species and, which was most interesting; he knew their ancient alchemistic properties. His face lit up as he talked with great animation about this subject - really most stimulating. He was a delightful character.

Next day in the garden, while hanging out the inevitable washing, Joy looked up and saw Professor Trondheim trying to catch her attention.

"Hello, Elise, what's the matter?" she called.

"Ach so!" said the old lady, "I have seen something very unusual in the sky!..."

"Unusual?" Joy said, "What?"

The old lady, leaning precariously out of the window, said earnestly, "I have seen something strange in the sky last night, and I don't know what it could be..."

Was it an aeroplane or a shooting-star or something?"

(Really, it was all just too exhausting! The old lady was getting very deaf and, please God, don't let her fall out of the window!)

"Just a minute, I'll come round and see you, Elise!"

She went next door quickly, to ensure that a catastrophe would be avoided, and let herself in with, 'the key with the red string', as it was known. This key was kept in a small cat-proof wooden box in the porch. The box had been put there for deliveries of fish and other tasty tit-bits, which domestic animals love to pilfer if they get a chance.

It was really a very neat design, being a box on legs with a drop-flap and a firm cupboard-catch; totally paw-proof.

It might seem a little strange to leave the front-door key in such an obvious place, but that is how things are often done in Oxford; whimsical like the White Knight.

Upstairs in her room, the old lady sat by the open-window, telescope at the ready.

She was practically snowed-under by newspapers and magazines. They were everywhere; on the floor, on the desk, on her bed, in fact anywhere that a space could be found. All were spread open at some particular item of interest and neat red lines were drawn round articles of special-note, for Professor Trondheim was an avid reader.

She was a remarkable old lady; a fine German face with snow-white hair and gold half-glasses. Her steel-grey eyes were bright and clear in spite of her great age. It was sad to see her so frail in body.

A formidable intellect. That had been said of her many times, for her achievements were renowned in the world of psychology. She had known all the great men in this sphere in earlier-days, and could talk first-hand about the people who are household-names in the subject.

She sat in her old leather wing-back chair facing the window. It was touching to see the limitations of her world. She had arranged it so that her chair was as close to the window as possible so she could sit with her elbows on the sill; just the right attitude for holding a telescope comfortably for long periods. Her desk was close by and everything else she needed near to hand.

"Ach, there you are," she said. "I see you are hanging out your washing again. I feel the world is normal when I see your underwear on the line! When one is alone so much, one attaches importance to such small things. It is a kind of contact with the outside world."

They laughed about this and then the old lady explained about the unknown, 'thing in the sky' as she called it.

"It was after dark and the stars were wonderfully clear. Suddenly, in the darkness I saw a huge flame like a large candle. It appeared suddenly and disappeared after a short time. It is quite inexplicable."

They decided it couldn't have been a flying-saucer, but came to no satisfactory conclusion on the subject.

Joy saw Mark later at the Jolly Sailors and mentioned the strange light in the sky, as they played darts. He shrugged his shoulders.

"Can't think what it could be - Oh damn!" he exclaimed, missing a double 20 to finish the game. "Doesn't correspond to anything I know that would be night-flying."

Joy gleefully finished with a double-one. Distraction was a great advantage-maker in darts. She tried to look penitent about the double.

Mark continued: "Could have been a flare of some sort, I suppose."

Peter Rumbold, the local garden-centre man, ventured that it could have been an air-balloon, perhaps, but this suggestion was firmly pooh-poohed by Mark, who said it was very unlikely that it would be night-flying.

"Far too difficult," he said, "Probably hit a pylon or something."

At the Jolly Sailors there were many interesting people who passed through - and there were the regulars, of course - but sadly, not so many nowadays; and occasionally the odd person would appear who was a total enigma.

One such was a man in his mid-forties, who came in two or three times a week. He would buy his beer and sit in a corner doing the Times crossword. He never spoke to anyone, except the barman, and concentrated completely on the newspaper.

An intriguing character, clad from head to foot in black leather with an American-style peaked-cap. He had a lean and handsome face and close-cropped red hair. Nobody knew anything about him except that he went home along Hayfield Road on a mini-bike.

Conjectures about him varied. He could be a tutor it was supposed - but the black leather uniform affair and peaked-cap didn't go with the image: and it wasn't motor-bike wear either - it was too lightweight. Also he always wore a particular kind of shoe, rather like a police-shoe, but in very nice leather. It definitely looked like part of a uniform.

He couldn't be a policeman, though, or a detective. Just didn't look right. Far too individual in appearance. He stuck out a mile.

Peter Rumbold thought he really ought to be a spy.

Everybody agreed that this was a very satisfactory idea. It was about time Oxford had a greater share in the spy industry, as Cambridge seemed to have had a monopoly so far.

Next morning, Joy went to Peter's shop for some plants and during the exchange of ideas and advice on gardening Cledwyn passed by with a jaunty step and a cheery wave of his plastic bag.

It was full of something which looked like an evil-mixture of weeds and compost. Not very nice.

"What is that stuff he picks on the meadow?" Joy asked. "He says it's mushrooms - I don't believe a word of it!"

Peter, a young man with a delicious sense of humour, roared with laughter.

"Don't you know? It's quite true, of course. That's just what they are!"

He laughed again. "Mind you, he must know his stuff to be sure of recognizing the variety. If you or I tried to eat them, we'd probably be dead after the first nibble, having picked the wrong sort. They're the famous magic-mushrooms; a highly prized psychedelic trip-maker. I hear that one little mouthful of those wicked-looking little toadstools - and you freak out completely - just like an L.S.D trip. Apparently you just go completely mad for a while.

"The little monkey," said Joy, "I'll bet he sells them to his friends. Really, I don't know what young people are coming to these days."

"By the way, how about some millet-spray for your bird?" said Peter, "I've just got a fresh lot in."

A wave of peculiar misery overcame Joy for a moment.

"Oh no! Alas and alack - speak not of my beloved bird! He's dead!"

She related the sad tale.

"Ah, well," said Peter, "A short life and a merry one! Pity though - I specially got the millet with you in mind. He was such a character, that bird. Fancy never flying out of an open window! Oh by the way, speaking of magic-mushrooms and all things mysterious - here's today's funny-story. You see that mixed bird-seed?" He pointed to a large sack by the pony-cubes and dog biscuits.

"Well, one of these lads - like your friend Cledwyn - comes in occasionally and buys a small amount. I know for a fact he hasn't got a bird, as he lives-rough, too; so I made a few enquiries - and guess what? Certain imported seed has cannabis mixed in with it, as it's so common in some countries, apparently (or so them wot knows sez) and, of course, the birds love it! Anyway, this lad sometimes buys half-a-pound of bird-seed and plants it here and there, down by the railway and the dumps, where nobody would notice it, and sometimes he strikes lucky and gets your actual cannabis-plant! It's a very lovely thing, it seems, long slender leaves and beautiful flowers, or so I'm told."

Joy was thoughtful.

"Do you know," she said, "I think we had some around the back-gardens hereabouts a couple of years ago. My next-door neighbour Harriet Spinster is a botanist, and she mentioned one day that there were some very interesting and unusual species of flora growing wild around our back-gardens. She didn't volunteer what they were; however, I noticed by my compost heap a rather large plant with unusual flowers. It was nothing common that I recognized, but it seemed quite happy in its sunny situation and was decorative. It didn't grow again the next season, though. The bees liked it.

The other strange thing was some simply gorgeous poppies which suddenly appeared round about the same time. I found a whole patch of them growing in a sunny corner, tucked away at the bottom of my herb-garden. I always did have little Icelandic-poppies dotted about the place, but nothing grand like these.

They still seed themselves and come up in ones and twos, but nothing like they grew that season. Harriet had a good look at them and said they were a most interesting variety, but didn't say which, so I got that marvellous French book on herbs - and there it was! 'The Mediterranean Opium Poppy' - Papaver Somniferum. It came to me later that they might possibly have been planted by that rather funny fellow who used to come to my house. He was slightly weird, long hair, pale and underfed-looking, glazed-eyes and an absent manner, and that rather sloppy speech which seems to go with the drugs-image. He was studying chemistry, I believe, and was the boy-friend of a nice young lassie who lived with me for a while. She was perfectly pleasant and respectable, but he seemed quite the reverse. Most odd. He used to spend hours roaming around at the bottom of the garden in the evenings, talking to himself. He smoked the most awful-smelling cigarettes, too. Filled the whole house with a fearful stench.

One evening at the pub, I was talking to a policeman about those silly drugs they all experiment with, and he laughed like a drain when I described the smell - which I concluded to be hashish. I said: "If you could imagine about 20 pairs of dirty policeman's socks, having been worn for 2 or 3 days non-stop on the beat in hot-weather, then being left in a plastic bag for a while to mature, then having been thrown on a particularly smelly bonfire in the garden when it was really going well, stand over it and take a deep breath - that's the smell!" The poor man spilt his beer in a fit of the giggles; he said it was a fair description.

As for cannabis, I don't know if the smell is worse or better. That's the other stuff which used to linger round the place. Essence of stale, sweet and oily-mothballs in grandma's closet. Absolutely vile, gets into everything."

Peter Rumbold interposed gently at this stage to say that in fact hashish and cannabis were really much the same thing, but Joy dismissed this with an airy wave of the hand, saying "I think I prefer smelly old tom-cat spray any day."

By this time a small queue had begun to form in the shop and there was considerable laughter over the conversation.

Everyone, however, was agreed about the nuisance-value and peculiar behaviour of drug-takers. Particularly disturbing at night.

That evening, Peter and Joy found they were paired in the darts mixed-doubles at the Jolly Sailors, so they arranged to meet in the public bar at 7.30pm. for a short practice together.

As is often the case in Oxford, after a perfectly lovely day, the heavens opened and a mighty downpour suddenly drenched the city without any warning.

Ah, well, it would definitely have to be the Welsh tweed cape and the awful old tweed hat for the walk down to the pub. Both were incredibly waterproof, but only fit to be worn during the hours of darkness, for the tweed was, to put it nicely, loud. It was bright green and orange, pink and yellow patterns woven throughout, strongly reminiscent of ancient Celtic-runes. The hat was even worse; bright yellow. An upturned pudding-basin with a wavy-brim, but magnificently waterproof. They were in fact jumble-sale leftovers from Joy's Cancer Research Elizabethan Day at St. James' College the year before. Much too good to go to the rag-man but perfectly unwearable during the hours of daylight.

As she left the house she saw Professor Pyper from the house opposite standing out thoughtfully in the pouring rain, lightly clad in a pullover and slacks. The professor and his young family had recently arrived for a sabbatical year from Sydney - such pleasant and easy-going people.

"You'll catch your death of cold, Professor!" she called.

He laughed.

"At Wyong, where I come from, we haven't had rain for over a year. It's a beautiful experience!"

"Everyone to his own taste!" she replied, and walked on in the deluge, leaving him standing there in his front-garden under the dripping lime-trees, looking at the dramatic double rainbow in the darkening western sky.

She paused at the life-size crucifix at the corner of St. Julie's Road outside the church and watched the afterglow over Wytham Woods. The sky was blood-red for a moment, then alizarin-crimson, going purple - then deep-blue as night approached.

She turned the corner and the welcoming lights of the Jolly Sailors and the sound of music and laughter greeted her.

The pub was full to capacity and there was scarcely room to get to the bar for a beer.

There, of course, was Mark, comfortably ensconced at the bar on a high-stool with a young Nordic beauty in close attendance.

Cledwyn sat in the far corner by the billiard-table with a girl-friend. They both looked thoroughly miserable and were clearly pondering some deep-seated problem. Cledwyn was, to say the least, damp in appearance. His hair was so wet that it clung to his face, and his blue-velvet jacket sodden. His suede-boots were thick with mud.

The girl-friend, a comforting soul was offering him loving advice of some sort, whilst trying to dry him out a bit over the radiator and wipe his wet face with a handkerchief.

"Probably been freaking-out on the dreaded mushrooms," said Mark, with a nod in their general direction. "Maybe he fell in the river!"

The darts-match was exhilarating.

The whole place was completely enveloped in a Dickensian fog of blue cigarette-smoke. A joy to smokers, no doubt - and agony for those who don't; smarting-eyes and an acrid stench, conducive to much coughing and spluttering. Why was it that pipe and cigar-smoke were quite pleasant to the non-smoker, and cigarettes (sauf gauloises et gitanes, naturellement) so awful?

The hubbub increased as the end of the match approached, with much shouting, laughing and ribaldry in the true Oxford tradition.

"Last orders!"

The ear-splitting shout reverberated round the pub from end to end.

The stentorian bark of Tony, the barman, made everyone wince, as usual.

"Of course, his brother is a sergeant-major in the army," Mark mused. "And there is, you know, a legend that he can be heard in Australia."

A breathless hush overcame all as he continued: "A student from Melbourne who lives just up the road was making a tape to send home to the family one night recently, and apparently Tony's shout came through loud and clear in the background. The boy's mother asked by return what on earth was this, "Last orders" and, "Time, gentlemen, please."

The peals of laughter which greeted this tale were almost eclipsed by Tony's final shout of the evening.

"Roight, now, ladies and gentlemen! Can Oi 'ave your glasses, please? It's way past toime!"

The round speech of old Oxfordshire was beautiful, notwithstanding the deafening delivery.

Joy and Mark were the last to leave. Mark picked up her brolly and she went to the coat-rack for her cape and hat.

They weren't there.

Mark looked in the saloon bar; no luck.

"That's funny," he said, "Who'd walk off with your awful old cape and hat. Must be mad! Bound to be a joke. We'll probably find them hanging on a lamp-post or something."

They walked together as far as the crucifix at St. Julie's Church and stood on the corner talking for a few minutes.

The storm had been a short one, and the night was now beautiful; that indescribable freshness of the English night after rain. A gentle warmth came up from the earth, filling the air with the sweetness of the scent of wet leaves and grass.

But it was a little chilly, suddenly, as a light breeze sprang up from the west.

"Must go, dear," said Joy, with a slight shiver.

Going into the house, she thought how much she missed the loud chirrup from Melody which always used to greet her when she came home. He didn't even bother to untuck his head, but would simply call out in his sleep. Funny old bird!

She slept uneasily that night, jerking awake two or three times, thinking she heard him give his alarm-call, long drawn-out urgent sounds delivered on one insistent monotone - no mistaking their meaning - fear! fear! fear!

A strong pot of tea in the morning revived the drooping spirits. Another lovely day. She went out into the back-garden in her dressing-gown with a mug of tea.

The early-morning dew made elaborate lace patterns everywhere and invisible cobwebs became visible for a while with their dewy decoration.

They were everywhere, in a myriad of shimmering rainbows. And what enormous distances little spiders could navigate! Silken threads stretched for what must have been miles in spider terminology, from tree to tree across the garden. A magic-moment in the freshness of early morning.

The washing, hung out overnight, was wet with dew and smelt wonderful. It was that marvellous smell which is unique to something which has been hung out soaking-wet, and slowly begins to dry in the early-morning sun.

Thinking of Professor Pyper, she laughed involuntarily and wondered what clean-washing smelt like in the early-morning in Australia; it must all be dry in ten minutes with the heat. No time for sweet dampness...

Silly thought!

Several cats appeared as she stood, thus-musing, by the garden-wall, as though summoned by some invisible force. All they wanted was breakfast presumably, even after a night of mouse-catching!

She looked up at the old lady's window.

That was odd. The window was wide-open and the light was on. The old lady was sitting at the window, her head tilted to one side, as though she were asleep.

"Curious," thought Joy. Professor Trondheim was never an early riser. Something must be wrong. She called out. No movement. Clad as she was, in a dressing-gown and slippers, mug of tea in one hand, she ran next door and let herself in with the key from the box, remembering that Erica was away and the old lady was alone in the house.

She mentally prepared herself for the worst as she sped upstairs. After all, she thought, the old lady was eighty-nine.

She tripped over the cord of her dressing-gown as she got to the first floor landing and fell headlong. In that instant she noted that the landing was slightly muddy. Mrs. Badger, fastidious as ever, kept the whole place impeccably clean, so this in itself was odd.

This thought was immediately lost as tea spilt everywhere. Her favourite mug from St. Alban's Abbey with the picture of King Offa inspecting the building of it, smashed to pieces by the bedroom door.

Irritation, anxiety, regret, the mental preparation for an emergency; all these things passed through her mind as she got up and went into the room.

She stopped suddenly, just inside the door, transfixed by the atmosphere. Stillness, silence. Death.

She stood for perhaps thirty seconds behind the still-figure in the chair before she moved forward. A curious feeling of reverence came over her. The old lady sat, as usual, facing the window, back to the door, in her wing-back chair. Only the top of her head was visible, resting against the right-hand wing.

Joy went round to look at her, mentally steeling herself, for she had seen much death and disaster in her lifetime, but it was always a new experience to look upon the face of the dead, especially those whom one had known well in life.

An ice-cold charge of shock ran through her, for what she saw was not peaceful as she had expected.

Professor Trondheim was fully-dressed and sitting more or less upright, but the look on her face was quite uncanny.

Her eyes and mouth were wide-open and she looked shocked, as though she had seen something alarming.

The telephone was close at hand, and Joy automatically dialled Mark's number. Mercifully he was there, but was not pleased to be roused so early. However, he consented to come straight round.

She then rang the doctor, who said he would come as soon as possible.

Mark viewed the body.

"Hmm, she does look a bit-off, doesn't she, poor old girl! Perhaps she saw Old Father Time up there coming down to get her!"

"Oh, Mark! Don't be flippant!" Joy was affronted. Men! Really!

"Well, honestly, come on, aunt - she did have a damned good innings, you know. You mustn't get sentimental."

The arrangements were all made very smoothly. Professor Trondheim had organized her departure from this world very efficiently. Everything was quite straightforward.

The doctor came and went at speed. In the middle of a mini flu-epidemic as he put it. Very trying.

Mr. Key, the affable undertaker, arrived promptly when called.

"Oh, yes," he said, looking approvingly at the old lady, "She had everything beautifully organized to the last detail. I have all my instructions. She often used to ring me up for a chat and to make sure I hadn't forgotten all the finer points.

Cremation. No flowers. She even prepared her own obituary for the papers. All very tidy. Most businesslike she was. Typical German."

He took the body away, and Mark and Joy were left to shut up the house in Erica's absence. She had left no address, so Joy wrote her a letter and left it on the hall-table for her return.

"Not that she'll be interested. Probably won't even notice the old lady's gone unless we tell her!" There were no other relatives to notify, so there was nothing further to be done. Very depressing.

"Better switch off the immersion-heater and things," said Mark, and went off downstairs to lock all the windows and doors.

Joy looked dolefully around the bedroom, with its snowstorm of newspapers and magazines.

Mark came back upstairs.

"O.K., aunt. Everything's under control. Now don't get morose, let's lock-up and go!"

Joy followed him reluctantly as far as the door. She stopped suddenly.

"No, Mark. Wait a minute. There's something wrong about all this!" She thought for a moment. What was it that didn't ring-true? She looked around the room.

"I know! There's no telescope! It's gone!"

CHAPTER II

'See what maze of error and labyrinth of terror...'

The first set of English Madrigals to 4, 5 & 6 voices

George Kirkbye 1597

Mark groaned.

"Oh, no! I knew it was all too good to be true! Here do I come home to Oxford for a few months' peace and quiet before going back into the international maelstrom - and what happens? Auntie Joy drags me into something yet again!"

They searched the whole room from top to bottom for the fatal telescope, but it was, of course, not there.

They pondered the matter.

Joy pointed out the dried, muddy footprints on the landing and Mark had a closer look. "Tennis shoes or something similar. About size nine, I should say. So the old girl had a visitor last night! A man!"

They remembered how it had rained hard for a while in the evening, but had cleared up quickly, and the night and morning had been fine - hence the muddy prints.

"God," said Mark, "I'm starving! My stomach is desperate for breakfast. I wish you'd made this earth-shattering discovery a bit later on in the day!"

Joy promised bacon and eggs in due course as a bribe, and so the detective-work continued.

Mark carefully searched the back-garden below the old lady's room for the telescope.

It might conceivably have fallen out of the window.

However, he drew a blank, and went next door for the promised breakfast.

They ate out in the garden, as it was another perfect day. Mark tucked in with a will. Two eggs, bacon, mushrooms and tomatoes, four rounds of toast, plus two large pots of strong tea.

"Beautiful," he said. "Why do English breakfasts taste so good - outside in the sun, especially."

Joy had little appetite. She was filled with an unease, which made her restless.

Somehow, she felt the presence of the old lady up at the window trying to tell her something. She didn't dare look up in case she saw a ghostly face.

Mark was thoroughly fed up with the whole business, so it was wiser not to press the point any more. However, she did manage to discuss with him the things that troubled her most about the old lady's death.

First, the disappearance of the telescope. He had no ideas about this at all. It was a fine antique; a real collector's piece without doubt, and well worth stealing - but nothing else was missing, as far as their cursory inspection could confirm. The silver, and there was a lot of it, was all there in the glass cabinet, and the old lady's handbag lay untouched by her chair. Her purse had a fair amount of money in it, and her cheque book and cards were intact. His gold watch, still going, was on the desk by the telephone, and her keys next to it.

Nothing at all seemed to have been disturbed. Everything was as usual.

But, there was the look on her face.

Mark dismissed this as unimportant. After all, there were no signs of violence, she had simply died from natural causes, sitting in her chair.

"Old age. She just ran out of breath."

Joy did not share this opinion, but said nothing.

The muddy footprints on the landing. That was certainly a mystery, as it was always polished like a mirror. Mrs. Badger, the gimlet-eyed, would not tolerate even a speck of dust anywhere. She was like some kind of dirt-exterminating laser beam.

The old lady never went outside the house at all; indeed, she could not have got downstairs even to answer the front doorbell if anyone had rung. Anyway, she had tiny feet.

Most certainly, nobody would have been in since the morning when Mrs. Badger brought the shopping and did the cleaning.

This was a worrying point, especially as the footprints were of men's sports-shoes of some kind.

No one except Erica, Mrs. Badger and Joy Hetherington knew where the spare door key was kept, so this was a complete mystery.

"But not enough evidence to make any kind of case out of," said Mark, munching a triangle of hot toast and butter with great relish.

"It's just not worth worrying about. Forget it. Let the old lady rest in peace. Got any marmalade? Tell you what - we'll go to the crematorium and see her on her way. Will that make you feel any better? At least we'll be giving her a good send-off. I don't suppose anyone else will be there."

And so it was, as Mark had prophesied.

Erica, it appeared, was in America, studying something or other to do with Red Indian languages and wouldn't be back for at least three months, so there were precisely the two of them in the congregation; the chaplain and organist augmenting the grand total to four.

As the coffin slowly slid out of sight to the strains of ghostly electric organ music (molto vibrato e misterioso), Joy began to feel truly desperate. There went the evidence! Sliding away sedately through the curtains to the furnace... The whole thing was totally, completely, utterly and absolutely wrong. She was disconsolate and agitated.

They went outside and Mark lit a cigarette and inhaled deeply.

"God, I needed that!"

He looked out over the green fields towards Beckley. After a moment's deep thought he turned and said with a positive air, "Now look, Auntie Joy, forget it! She's gone."

Even as he spoke, the crematorium incinerator rumbled quietly and the chimney -somewhat reminiscent of Vesuvius - belched a sudden spurt of pale smoke into the bright sky.

"See, there she goes - in a puff of smoke. Now, just forget it completely. Erase it from your mind. There is absolutely nothing more that can be done. She's gone and that's the end of the matter. Think positive. She's happier out of it. Life must have been a terrible burden for her. It can't have been any fun being so much alone, and so very frail - plus a crackpot for a daughter. Forget it!"

They drove slowly back down Headington Hill into the city. Really, on its day, Oxford was truly lovely: the colleges, cream and gold in the mellow sunshine against a backcloth of bright blue sky. The trees were turning gold, too, for the approach of autumn. Quite idyllic.

That night, Joy had the most appalling nightmare she had ever experienced in her life.

The old lady's face, coming out of the darkness, ghastly white with that horrific expression - and her voice urgently pleading in German - Please! Please! Please!

And suddenly there was Melody too, looping the loop and flying his figures of eight, shrieking his alarm-call: "Fear! Fear! Fear! Fear! ..."

She jerked awake suddenly, feeling quite ill, and actually screaming inside, as sometimes happens in nightmares. Three-thirty a.m. God! How was she ever going to get through the night!

When in doubt, make tea.

Mercifully, little tabby and a friend appeared on the kitchen window-sill asking for early breakfast. How wonderful animals were to have about the place! Undemanding (except for food and strokes, etcetera) and such good companions in time of need.

As dawn approached, Joy now knew in her heart, beyond a shadow of doubt, that it was murder. She was quite convinced. No wavering.

Someone had got in and killed that defenceless old lady. Why? Why? - and even more alarming, who? ... And more baffling still, how?

The evidence was destroyed. The old lady's body was now ashes on the crematorium rose-garden, she supposed. What was to be done?

Mark had said it all. It was too late. Professor Trondheim had gone up in the proverbial puff of smoke.

Despair. Frustration.

What to do? She could think of nothing.

Somewhere, possibly near at hand, a murderer was quietly laughing, safe in the knowledge that they had got away with it completely.

But was that the end of the matter?

Fate was to take a hand in a most unexpected way.

Mrs. Badger had said she would keep an eye on the house until Erica's return. After all, she had been looking after the Professor for nearly forty years and she felt she had,"an obligation" as she put it. In any case, she would most certainly stay on to, "do for" Miss Erica, as she had, "no idea at all" when it came to doing housework and things like that. Her mind was definitely tuned to higher things.

Joy met Mrs. Badger outside the house, and they compared notes on the situation.

"Tis a shockin' business," said Mrs. Badger, casting a fearful glance heavenward. "Oi don't know wot to think, Oi'm sure! Miss Erica shouldn't never 'a went to America, an' the old lady 'ad 'a bin all roight. She shouldn't never 'ave ought to 'a bin left on 'er own loike that. Twas a terrible cruelty an' no gettin' away from it!"

Mrs. Badger was also uneasy about the unexplained footprints. She had, since the funeral, "Bottomed the 'ole 'ouse" in her own words, and there was absolutely nothing missing apart from the telescope.

"Oo'd want a daft thing loike that any road. Now if it 'ad 'a bin the colour telly, you could understand it!"

The desk, which contained all the old lady's private papers, had not been touched, she said, and the Professor's jewel-case was in there, quite intact - "pearl necklace, emerald brooch an' all."

As she spoke, the lace curtains at the drawing-room windows of a house across the road trembled slightly.

"There," she said, "That's Miss Dacre, at it again she is. Really, 'ow she 'as toime to make 'erself a cup 'o tea, Oi don't know. She spends 'er 'ole loife glued to that winder. Wot ever is she after this toime?"

A small disembodied hand appeared through a gap in the curtains. It beckoned them with a rapid motion. Evidently the matter was urgent.

"Oh, dear, oh lor'! Now we'll never get away - and Oi've got work to do!"

Resigned, they walked across the road to Miss Dacre's house, smiling politely as they approached - hopeful for a quick getaway. They were to be disappointed, howbeit.

The front door flew open with a bang as they went up the garden path to the house.

"Oh Chroist Church bells!" said Mrs. Badger. "Now we're for it, Oi reckon! Battle stations boy the looks o' things!"

Miss Dacre's mini-Pekingese shot out of the doorway like a rocket - representing the advance-guard, snapping and yapping menacingly round their ankles, just to get them into submissive mood, as it were. They stood meekly side by side, smiling hopefully at the dark interior of the house.

Miss Dacre appeared suddenly, like the demon king, on the doorstep.

"And just what is going on, I'd like to know?" she announced in a high soprano, to the whole street.

Mrs. B. and Joy looked blank.

The ensuing tirade made them wince. There was nothing to do but stand firm and grin and bear it, while gritting one's teeth, so to speak.

Why hadn't she been told? she proclaimed. Really, one might as well be living on an oasis in the Gobi Desert as in St. Julie's Road! One's old friend of forty years' standing dies; and nobody, but nobody even has the decency to say a word about it. Why, the first intimation one had at all that something was wrong was the arrival of Mr. Key to take the body away! Really, what was the world coming to?

This harangue continued for several minutes and eventually Joy did manage to mumble a word or two apologetically about it all having been a terrible shock for everyone, and so sudden - no warning at all, in fact; and what with Erica being away, etcetera.

"No warning? No warning?" hooted a wrathful Miss Dacre. "You must have known there was something wrong! Professor Trondheim must have looked off-colour when you went in to see her that evening!"

"Went in to see her?" Joy and Mrs. Badger looked at one another mystified. They both had that same eerie feeling. Something ghastly was afoot.

"Yes, yes! I saw you -I saw you!" She pointed an accusing finger at Joy. "I saw you come up the road in the rain and go into the house! You must have known all was not well. You didn't stay long either, did you? I saw you rushing off down the road not fifteen minutes later! That poor, poor old lady, left to die all alone!"

They were both stupefied by this barrage. Mrs. Badger mouthed silently "whatever is going on?" Joy, speechless, shook her head slowly in total perplexity.

"Miss Dacre," she said feebly., "I didn't go near Professor Trondheim that night at all. I was at the Jolly Sailors all evening."

Miss Dacre was beside herself, and did a little dance of righteous indignation on the doorstep. She puffed up visibly. She seemed suddenly much bigger than her usual tiny stature.

"What a terrible lie, Miss Hetherington! How can you say that? I saw you! I saw you quite distinctly; even though it was dark and raining. You came up the road in your waterproof cape and hat and went into Professor Trondheim's house. I watched you go in. I thought something was wrong! You came and went so quickly. I know, you simply didn't want to be bothered with that poor old lady! We old people just don't matter. We are just thrown on the scrap-heap and nobody cares if we live or die; it's a perfect disgrace!"

With that, Pongo, who had been constantly growling at them, shot back through the open door with a parting salvo of vicious snaps and mini-pekingese yaps and Miss Dacre slammed the door in their faces with a majestic flourish.

Mrs. Badger and Joy looked at one another in complete horror.

After a moment or two, speech returned.

"Mrs. Badger, shall we go across to the house for a minute?"

They went back to the Professor's house and decided on a plan of action. After considering the full story of Joy's stolen cape and hat, and piecing this together with the appalling things they had just heard about the old lady's visitor dressed in this garb on the night of her death, they agreed that a thorough search should be made at once for some clue - anything which might possibly give them a lead, before they went to the police. After all, with no proper evidence, there could be no case. It was all like some bad dream; the kind where one runs after something and it is always just out of reach beyond the outstretched fingertips.

"Not that you'll foind anythin' much. Oi did clean straight through the 'ole place, remember. Can't be too careful. Especially when there's been a death in the 'ouse!" said Mrs. Badger. "Oi even washed down all the paintwork so if there was anythink loike fingerprints, they'd be gorn."

This was not very encouraging. Nevertheless, they went upstairs to the old lady's room. They stood, perplexed, in the middle of it. It was a strange experience to see everything exactly as usual - except for the bed, which was, of course, stripped off. The old lady's chair was in its usual place at the window.

Really, they did seem to have come to a dead end. There was just nothing to go on at all... or was there? Wait a minute! Something was different!

All the newspaper snowstorm had disappeared!

"Mrs. Badger, what about all the newspapers and magazines? Have you thrown them out?"

"Wot?"

Mrs. Badger secretly thought this was a funny kind of question; after all, whatever kind of importance could a load of old newspapers have? But she thought for a while and then said, "Well, 'tis quare you should say that, 'cos Oi would 'a done normally, but Oi stacked 'em all up over yonder by the paper-bin under the desk. You see, Miss Trondheim an' the old lady used to 'old a sort of a koind of a conference every now and again about certain things wot they read in the papers, an' that. They used to put red loines round articles and swop 'em round from one to t'other about once a month. Could 'a bin about anythin' - current affairs, cookin', weather forecasts - any old thing they fancied. There's a 'ole stack of 'em 'ere, waitin' for Miss Trond'eim to 'ave a look at when she gets back from where-is-it."

Thus informed, Joy now resolutely decided she must follow her intuition and read through the whole pile, tedious and time-consuming though it might be.

Mrs. Badger disappeared to tidy up the garden and Joy began the marathon read, for there must have been at least a hundred newspapers and magazines with red lines squaring off items of special interest on most pages.

Generally, the main themes seemed to be politics, the world situation and a great deal about stocks and shares and things of that kind. Very boring. Quite a lot of rings round psychology articles, and a fair bit about astronomy and space exploration...then suddenly; ah! here it was - 'Unidentified Flying Objects!' She jumped up and threw open the window. In her head rang loud and clear the old lady's voice, "Something strange in the sky."

"Mrs. Badger, Mrs. Badger!"

"Whatever is the matter, Miss Hetherington. A startled Mrs. Badger dropped the garden fork with surprise at this sudden eruption. Cats disappeared in all directions.

"I think I've found a clue!"

"O dear, o lor'! Just wait a minute and Oi'll come on up."

Really, it was a bit much, she thought, as she washed her hands under the garden tap. It would have been much better to have found nothing at all and let the old lady rest in peace. But that was life; nothing was ever simple and straightforward, was it?

As she got to the front doorstep, she was met by a newspaper being triumphantly waved in her face through the open door.

"Look! Look! I knew we'd find a clue somewhere! There is some fishy business going on after all. I knew it!"

There were several articles on UFOs in the papers and magazines and all were ringed with double red lines. In the professor's handwriting, in red ink, were little comments in German, such as 'significant', and 'vertical flame' and 'rocket launch?'

"Mrs. Badger, that's it! Something to do with UFOs or something she saw from the window at night with her telescope. I remember now, she mentioned it - and she was very concerned about what she saw, 'something strange in the sky', she said."

Mrs. Badger nodded politely, but privately thought the whole thing was getting to be too much, quite honestly, but didn't like to say so. She did suggest, however, that it was time for a nice cup of tea, and went off to Joy's kitchen to make some.

"Well, moy dear," she said, returning with the tea-tray, "Oi know it's all very interestin' an' that, but wot's it got to do with 'er doyin' so sudden loike?"

"Exactly so, Mrs. Badger, we don't know yet; but I know in my bones that's why she died. She saw something, and whatever it was led to her death. It wasn't natural causes. I must get hold of Mark if he's around. As yet there isn't much to go on, but I think there is quite enough to show that there is some kind of monkey-business going on. Who took my cape and hat? Why? How did they know about the spare key? They must have got in that way, I'm sure. Why impersonate me? It just doesn't make sense. I shan't rest until I know the truth for the sake of that poor old lady."

She settled down again at the desk to read on through the pile of papers. Nothing more of interest came to light, and she heard Mrs. Badger call "Cheerio" up the stairs as she went, slamming the door firmly. The house was silent, unearthly quiet, and she became unpleasantly aware that she was alone in the building.

As she sat, quietly reading, a sudden spasm of unaccountable fear seized her. Totally illogical.

Not being a fearful type, and of hardy Lancashire stock, she did not 'frighten easy' as the dialect has it.

It was broad daylight, with sunshine, fluffy cumulus clouds and blue sky through the window, and there was old Mrs. Graystone sitting out in the pleasant warmth of the afternoon sun surrounded by her roses, knitting happily - and yet, notwithstanding this vision of normality, Joy was actually afraid, and for no accountable reason, an uncomfortable cold chill prickled her spine. But it was so stupid!

She went to the window and leaned out on the sill, to say hello to Mrs. Graystone. A cheery wave back gladdened her heart and she felt better. She returned to the desk, but left the window wide-open to represent some sort of contact with the outside world and pleasant things. It also helped to dispel that curiously oppressive atmosphere which pervaded the room.

She sat down again and idly turned over the next newspaper.

My God!

A bolt of fear went through her. She felt quite sick.

Horrors! There it was! She stifled a scream. An ugly footprint clearly defined, defaced the Telegraph crossword. It was made by some kind of man's sports shoe - about size nine, one would think.

Panic seized her, and she fell over the chair in a desperate effort to get to the telephone quickly and ring Mark, feeling terribly afraid. A murderer might well be very close at hand - horrific thought!

There was no reply from his number.

She left the house immediately, taking the disturbing piece of evidence with her. That footprint was indeed alarming; terrifying, in fact, for it represented violation and death.

What was she to do? Call the police? No, not yet; there just wasn't enough to go on.

The best thing to do would be to get hold of Mark as quickly as possible, and get some constructive advice.

There was still no reply from his number. Where could he be? He did have the rather disconcerting habit of disappearing suddenly. She dearly wished his smiling face would appear at the window as it often did. His was a very comforting presence. Maybe he would be at The Jolly Sailors in the evening; she would go early and wait for him.

Unhappily, no one had seen him. Michael Walters, his next-door neighbour, thought he might possibly be away for a few days, as there was no sign of him about the house. Michael was a thoroughly reliable type and a great friend, always willing to lend a hand in time of need - truly kind, and Joy decided to confide in him.

After listening intently to the whole story, Michael commented that there certainly seemed to be a strong case for investigation. He smiled ruefully.

"What a pity there is no corpse for examination, so it can never really be properly established how the old lady died. But, for my money, you must in any case, get hold of some kind of firm evidence before you contemplate going to the police. I wonder where the telescope is, for instance? That could give a good lead.

Now, really, that is a most intriguing thing! Maybe our unfriendly intruder has an irresistible passion for telescopes! A secret telescope hoarder! Like people who collect tea-caddy spoons or riding-crops!

You know, it's something I have never understood - this passion for collecting just one particular kind of object. Now-stamps I can understand; even matchboxes! But some people are quite extraordinary - like squirrels or magpies. They do hoard the most peculiar things.

Take Mrs. Blatchforth at No, 9, for instance. She's got about twelve television sets, two in every room, or thereabouts, and all in working order! Most extraordinary! And, she has a formidable collection of lawn-mowers; indeed, one of them ought to be in the Science Museum, in my opinion! They don't all work, of course, but there they are, rows and rows of them, all lined up in the garden shed, like tanks ready for battle!"

The conversation was getting decidedly silly, and they both laughed. A good laugh did make one feel better.

"But seriously," continued Michael, "I would guess our unknown visitor simply saw the nice, shiny brass telescope lying there, took a fancy to it, and pocketed it. People do the strangest things, you know, even in times of stress. He probably took it almost without thinking what he was doing. Anyway, my advice to you is, try not to worry about it and don't let it get on your nerves. One possibility is that nothing more at all will happen, and this will become yet another of the great unsolved mysteries of darkest North Oxford. In fact, it would be much the best thing if the whole business faded quietly away. But if more evidence should happen to turn up - then act - that's my advice."

He agreed that the whole thing was most unpleasant but that perhaps something would eventually occur to clarify matters.

Prophetic words indeed, as subsequent events were unhappily to prove. Joy was uneasy. Her student lodger upstairs was away for a few weeks on an archaeological dig in Greece, and for the first time ever, she was not happy about being alone in the house. Solitude had never worried her, for she had learnt to be self-sufficient after the tragic death of her fiance in youth. She had learnt to be alone, and in any case, there were always the animals around the place for company, but now she dearly wished she had a large dog. She would feel a lot more secure at night.

If only Erica Trondheim would come back, it would make her feel easier in mind. And, Mark being away too - it was all a little unnerving. She felt very isolated, somehow; and in a curious way, that she was being watched by some unseen eye. A quite inexplicable feeling, but very strong indeed.

"Don't get neurotic," she told herself, sternly, but the feeling persisted. She slept uneasily again, jumping awake at the slightest sound in the night.

The following day a great urge overcame her to clear her mind with some strenuous digging on the allotment. That potato patch really needed a good going-over and it was about time that it was done properly.

She went over in the afternoon, pausing on the way at the stables to talk to the horses. Walking on along the lane towards the level crossing and Trap gate, she passed the college dumps on the right.

A most extraordinary collection of rubbish was visible through the bushes behind the wire fence. Three-piece suites, old television sets, washing machines, mountains of bottles, comics and magazines, old shoes and clothes of all varieties, prams, broken dolls and toys. In fact nothing at all to do with colleges, for rubbish of every kind was cheerfully dumped by all and sundry over the wire fence - in spite of the stern official warning notice threatening unpleasant recompense to all unauthorized dumpers of refuse.

Joy ruefully smiled to herself at the sight of the incongruous collection of objects. All forms of wildlife lived happily in this extraordinary muddle. A great variety of birds, and rabbits by the dozen, rats and mice, and several big healthy cats living wild, as the hunting was so good for them there.

Thus musing, she watched the progress of a grey squirrel as he darted up and down a horse-chestnut tree. He seemed fully aware of the fact that he had an audience. Evidently, he was quite a character this squirrel, for, fixing her with a bright eye, he laid on a most delicious private entertainment. He leapt backwards and forwards from a big tree to the overhanging branches of a willow tree nearby, performing a kind of trapeze act specially for her, jumping repeatedly from one bough to another, sometimes pausing to see if she was still watching his acrobatics.

Suddenly he disappeared under an upside-down sofa, which was rotting away in the bushes, then quickly emerged again carrying a large nut in his paws. With this, he did a little juggling act for a few moments, pausing again to make quite sure that he still had his audience's attention, and then disappeared under the sofa.

His little head popped out suddenly from the other end and he put on a wonderful display of peek-a-boo, appearing and disappearing like lightning from different hidey-holes under the sofa.

The grand finale was very funny indeed. Joy thought he had perhaps become bored and gone away, as there was no sign of him for some considerable time, but suddenly he re-appeared on top of the sofa, popping up like the genie in a pantomime, carrying in his mouth a large piece of dry toast! It was almost bigger than he was. All that could be seen of him was a large square slice of toast, a nose and whiskers over the top, a bright pair of eyes and two intelligent ears pricked forward.

Joy could not keep silent any longer; she roared with laughter. The squirrel promptly scampered off with his piece of toast, startled by the noise, and she watched him disappear into the bushes beside the sofa, delighted by his wonderful display.

However, her laughter died instantly.

With profound shock, she spied, rolled up tightly and thrown well into the bushes with the general collection of old tin cans and rotting clothes and furniture, the hideous green tweed cape which had been stolen from the pub that fatal night.

She was stunned and simply stood open-mouthed, not yet quite able to absorb the full implications of what she now saw.

The squirrel appeared again close by on a high branch with his piece of toast, which he began to nibble delicately. This little demonstration was accompanied by much juggling and jumping up and down, but she was now unable to enjoy this delightful show.

She stood quite still, with her eyes riveted to the lurid tweed pattern, which was as yet not dulled by the wet and the insidious mould, which now permeated the material.

The sinister implications flooded through her mind in a sudden torrent. A confused kaleidoscope of memories flashed past in vivid visual sequence; perhaps it was for seconds, perhaps for much longer. It all seemed to be happening in a realm outside the sphere of time. It was, in any case an experience which was to be imprinted starkly in the forefront of her memory like a brand; instant, shocking, real, with everything magnified. It was all so appallingly clear now. The jigsaw puzzle was falling into place. The pattern of events now resolved into something hideous, like the jangling colours of the tweed cape lying there in the bushes before her; unseemly, repulsive, unwholesome.

"Something strange in the sky ..."

"I saw you, I saw you! ..."

"Fear, fear, fear!..."

Those voices called loudly again to her, Professor Trondheim, Miss Dacre, Melody's urgent alarm call.

She felt sick.

Steeling herself, she did the thing she most dreaded. To pick up the cape was going to be a traumatic experience, but it had to be done. Being the only tangible evidence in this incredibly confused business, it would have to be examined for some kind of clue to the meaning of the affair.

She climbed gingerly through the broken wire fence. Mercifully, gardening gear was good protection against the hazards ahead. Heavy Wellington boots and slacks were a great help, for the broken glass and brambles were murderous. Maybe this was what it was like crossing a minefield? Every step was an agony.

She reached for the cape. A bramble cruelly slashed her face, drawing blood. Slipping on some wet wood, she fell on top of the sofa. How weird the smells were in the dumping-ground! Primaeval scents, not at all what one would expect from recently jettisoned things.

An eerie feeling pervaded this place. There was a strong smell of sweet decay and the scent of deep woodland bowers. Several patches of lovely wood-mushrooms and toadstools were dotted around. She recognized Helvella Lacunosa and Helvella Crispa, and something over there in the distance, which might possibly be Otidea Onotica.

There were other species, too, that she didn't know at all and would have to look up in the book. This was undoubtedly Cledwyn country!

These thoughts passed rapidly through her mind as she reached out again for the cape. This time she made contact, but it was so heavy with the wet that it rolled soggily open when she lifted it up. Out fell the awful yellow hat, screwed up like a dishcloth, soggy and quite mildewed. Tiny frogs, little spiders and leatherjackets scurried frantically away as they were disturbed.

Ugh! The whole thing was repugnant.

Draping the wet cape over the sofa, she reached for the hat in the tangle of brambles. Picking it up by the brim, she shook it with a shudder of distaste.

Something instantly sprang out of it, as though alive, and landed on her foot. She screamed involuntarily.

A hideous face grimaced at her from the ground. She felt terribly giddy and lost vision for a moment. An unbelievably shocking and uncannily life-like rubber mask grinned at her unseeingly with unmistakable mockery.

It was quite horrific; a kind of witch's face, covered in gruesome warts, and one side of it had the appearance of having been horribly injured, as though acid had been thrown at it, and the flesh burnt away. Leather-jackets ran in and out of the eye sockets and mouth to make the thing even more bizarre.

So, that was it. Professor Trondheim had indeed been frightened to death. How very cruel.

She could picture the whole thing quite clearly now. The old lady innocently peering through her beloved telescope at the friendly lit windows across the back garden. Meanwhile the front door opens, shuts, and feet come up the stairs.

"Hello, is that you Joy?"

As she painfully turns around in her chair, she sees a familiar cape and hat in the shadows at the bedroom doorway.

"Ach, how nice to see you, my dear. Come in! What a pity about the rain. It came so quickly. I hope you are not too wet."

The figure approaches, and as it comes into the pool of light from the little desk lamp, she sees...

Horrors! That was how it was, without a doubt. She had simply died of fright.

The murderer hadn't even needed to lift a finger, probably, to accomplish his evil task.

Suddenly, Joy was no longer afraid, simply angry, furious, in fact. She herself had been used as an unwitting instrument of murder. That was the only way one could describe it. Indignation rose in her breast.

How dare they do such a vile thing? She vowed there and then to find this wicked person, no matter how impossible the task might seem.

She took the evidence home.

By the crucifix at St. Julie's Church she stopped suddenly. What about the telescope? Where was it? She must go back and search for it. If it was there, then there would be presumably enough evidence to give to the police with a view to an investigation. There might even be some fingerprints of interest. That was an exciting possibility! She felt somewhat uplifted and decided to put the cape, hat and awful mask in the potting-shed to dry out.

No - better peg them out on the washing-line first to get rid of some of the evil stench of mildew.

She pegged out the cape and hat, but put the mask on a shelf in the potting-shed, high up where she didn't have to see it every time she went in. That really would have been too much - like walking into the Chamber of Horrors and seeing those ghastly severed heads!

Then she returned to the exact spot in the dumps where she had found the evidence and searched a large area round about very thoroughly for the telescope. No luck.

Bitterly disappointed and feeling very frustrated, she decided to call at Mark's house and see if she could find out where he was. Again, she drew a blank. The house was all shut up, with windows fastened, as though he intended to be away for a while.

She peeped through the letter-box and saw a fair amount of post on the floor in the hallway, confirming that he had gone away, and there was no milk on the front doorstep, so presumably he wouldn't be back today.

On the way home, she called in at Peter Rumbold's shop. Yes, he recalled that Mark had mentioned that he would like some things for the garden in a week or so, and had made an order. That was a couple of days ago, at least; so not to worry - wherever he had gone, it wouldn't be for long, one would guess.

She told Peter briefly what had happened and he was sympathetic, but shrugged it off as being yet another of those potty things which only seem to happen in Oxford.

"After all, the place is bursting at the seams with eccentrics and nut-cases of all types," he announced discomfortingly as she left.

"Have a talk with Michael Walters about it. He'll be at darts tonight. He always comes up with bright ideas. Maybe there's quite a simple explanation. Personally, I shall miss the old lady because she was always such a wonderful customer. Always liked the best and was quite prepared to pay for it - one of a dying breed."

He gave her a cheery wave as she went off up the road. Dick Ballard approached with Hugo from the opposite direction, with an empty sack over his shoulder. Hugo led on ahead as always, tail aloft in the usual question-mark.

"Hello, Dick, off hunting?"

"Well," said Dick, "Oi thought we'd have a little wander over Binsey an' see wot there is about. Moight come across summat."

Hugo clearly had a strong message that "Summat" was indeed about and made loud woof-woofs to get a move on, dancing backwards and forwards in the direction of the meadow in little urgent forays.

"E knows, any road," said Dick over his shoulder. "Cheerio, now! There's a couple o' pheasant over yonder 'as got moy name wrote on 'em, oi fancy moy chances today!"

Presumably, it didn't matter whether pheasant was either in or out of season to him. All was fair game, most likely!

As she walked home, Joy remembered how tame and silly pheasant were up on the Berkshire downs round Sparsholt and Childrey. Just carry a handful of corn or sunflower seed, and they would come to you, so trusting, for slaughter, just as they did when reared by the gamekeepers to be hand-fed. It was all a bit unfair, this game business to please man's Epicurean fancy, but the human race must go on - or so they say! She remembered in a flash of complete clarity a depressing lecture by an eminent anthropologist on the future of mankind, who had said, in summing up: "But of course life must go on" and someone had murmured wearily-close by "Oh really? Why?" Amusing, really, if one thought about it. No - ironical - that was the word, and it was a valid point. She reflected on the un-niceness of the human race.

In general, for instance, animals and other creatures of nature were more civilized and reasonable in their behaviour. They stuck rigidly to the rules of their kind, a pecking order being always strictly observed and families being reared in an orderly fashion. Any rogues were usually pretty quickly got rid of.

Thinking of the grim tale of Professor Trondheim's demise, she reflected bitterly that there was one rogue she would dearly like to deal with.

When she got back to the house, she observed Miss Dacre's curtains quiver gently. A row of four cats and two dogs were waiting at the gate, all sitting neatly in a row, cats on the wall, sedately out of the way of the dogs, and the latter, tails a-wag, sitting to attention in the gateway, hopeful for some interesting tit-bit, no doubt. Strange how they always knew when one would return. Interesting, too, that the cats could maintain quite a good relationship with the two visiting dogs - as long as they kept just out of reach of Sally the beagle!

Iffley, the gorgeous Persian Blue - another left-behind cat, sat solemnly on top of the high gatepost. She as yet didn't trust anybody much, for she had been shunted around so much in her short life. Passed from hand to hand, as it were, and finally left with Joy, who regarded this as her good fortune, for she was a truly beautiful animal with the very nicest nature. She was also an excellent hot-water-bottle at night; her great warm shape occupying most of one's bed (if she managed to sneak into the bedroom without being seen).

Her great trick was to hide in the shoe-cupboard in the evening and then quietly land on one during the night, purring gently. However, overall she was quite co-operative about bed-sharing; at least she would allow one room to turn over occasionally, reasonably unhindered. A most accommodating cat!

After feeding the animals, Joy took a cup of coffee out into the garden and sat in the mellow late summer sun, quietly working on her notes for a lecture to be given in a day or two.

The cats arranged themselves around the garden in suitably warm and sunny spots, dozing gently; occasionally twitching an ear or a whisker if a bee or some other bold intruder passed nearby, the odd paw flashing out deftly at hovering flies or midges, as opportunity offered. Iffley sat like the Sphinx, on the high wall dividing Joy Hetherington's garden from the Trondheims', her great golden eyes blinking sleepily in the sun. However, she was completely alert in spite of her somnolent appearance, for if a butterfly or something else on the wing fluttered within a few feet, she would come to life in a trice, leaping up in enormous jumps to attempt a catch, then subsiding instantly into perfect repose. Strange animal! The complete aristocrat - a perfect lady, who would never be drawn into a fight or be rude to the other common cats. If they greedily pushed in when she was being fed (she was a 'little and often' cat) she would politely sit back and wait until they had finished so rudely eating her dinner, and then quietly wait to be fed in peace. Joy's cousin Jayne had said of her once; "She really is the most beautiful animal. As big as a dog and enormously fit, and yet she spends as much time as possible sleeping and preserving herself. It's almost as though she is saving herself up for something, you know ... some great act of heroism or some terribly important event."

They giggled at length over this ridiculous thought, but the rather unkind laughter was later to be superseded by feelings of total admiration and gratitude for the noble heroism of this remarkable cat, - and wonder at the truth of Jayne's unwitting prophecy.

As Joy sat working on her notes, subconsciously she became aware that something was not quite right about the garden. Looking around, she could see nothing amiss, but felt that something was wrong.

As the sun began to move towards the west, and the shadows lengthened, she went indoors and prepared to go down to the Jolly Sailors to look for Michael Walters.

This business was all very tiresome and was now bothering her greatly. It was a bit like fighting a feather pillow. Most unsatisfactory. She put on her jacket and took a last look at the back-garden. Really, the flower borders were lovely and the trees turning gold with their ripening fruit "orient and immortal," like the poet Traherne's wheat. It was all so peaceful and she couldn't think what was wrong.

CHAPTER III

'...the judicious sharp spectator is,

That sits and marks still who doth act amiss...'

From: 'What is our life? a play of passion.'

The First Set of Madrigals and Motets of 5 Parts

Orlando Gibbons 1612

To her immense relief Michael was there when she got to the Jolly Sailors, thoughtfully sipping his pint. He had actually succeeded in engaging the mystery man in conversation, and he had just furnished him with a vital clue to the crossword.

After the darts match, they managed to find a quiet corner of the public bar, and she told him in as much detail as possible all that had happened.

He listened intently, stroking his short auburn beard reflective.

"It is a most extraordinary affair, I agree. All very fishy. If you don't mind, I think I should walk back with you now and we'll have a look at the evidence and then consider the next move."

Joy was very relieved at this suggestion, and they walked back through the balmy night to St. Julie's Road.

"I've got some brandy, so how about coffee and liqueur?"

"Excellent idea," grinned Michael.

"If I put the study light on, so you can see what you're doing, would you bring in the cape and hat from the washing-line?" called Joy: "While you do that, I'll get the coffee percolator going."

Michael went off down the back-garden for the evidence and the coffee percolator was set up. "Hmm, Kenya Peaberry, I think," mused Joy, and ground it fine.

As the percolator began its work, it crossed her mind that Michael seemed to be an awfully long time outside in the garden. She called out of the kitchen window: "Michael! Are you all right? Found it? The washing-line is between the potting-shed and the greenhouse at the bottom end... mind the gooseberry-bushes!"

His reply was not immediate.

"Yes, I'm O.K. ... just! I've found the washing-line all right, and nearly decapitated myself on it in the process. But there's nothing on it! If my throat doesn't recover from the fracture and impedes my beer-drinking, I'll sue for damages!"

For Michael, with the most placid of natures, this was a strong statement. He sounded cross.

Joy was horrified.

"Just a minute," she called. "I'll bring a torch."

Going quickly down the garden and tripping in the process over little Tabby, who shot out from the herbaceous border, evidently wanting to join in the fun, she arrived at the washing-line breathless. Michael was standing there, his trouser-leg firmly impaled on the cultivated blackberry. Very nasty. She stopped dead, shocked by what the powerful beam of the torch revealed. Michael stood patiently in the pool of light, trying to disentangle himself from the vicious blackberry thorns.

"Ouch!" he exclaimed, and sucked his hand as they sprang away, drawing blood.

"Nasty little so-an-so's!" he muttered.

Joy was so preoccupied by the alarming sight of the empty washing-line that she couldn't even offer an apology.

"My God!" she said, aghast, "Everything gone... the cape-the hat-and all my underwear!"

"This is ridiculous," said Michael, slightly mollified by the excellent coffee and liqueur, accompanied by the finest Suchard orange chocolate.

"My cousin Jayne's speciality," said Joy, "She always brings the same thing and it's delicious for this kind of occasion."

Goodness knows what the brandy was; Joy didn't know where it came from: it had been in the cellar for donkey's-years and the label was unreadable, but it was wonderful - as is the Oxford tradition, of course. Things simply appear from some forgotten archive and are always first-class.

"Personally," Michael said, turning his glass round against the light, "Knowing you, however potty the whole thing may seem it's probably all true! But most people would say, "The woman's crazy, it's all a figment of her imagination'."

Joy, looking dismally at the late-night news on television and the current disasters in the world, said: "Well, it may all seem quite mad - but what could be madder than that," indicating the television screen with her brandy glass.

Michael nodded in agreement.

"Tell you what," he said, "I'll come back tomorrow morning before work and we'll see if there are any clues to follow up. You never know - there might be something."

Although she did not share his optimism, she was mightily relieved and they arranged to meet before nine o'clock the following morning.

Statutory mugs of tea in hand, they proceeded to the bottom of the garden to assess the situation.

"Michael - it's very kind of you to bother like this," she said. "I feel such a fool. All these horrid things happening and not a shred of evidence to prove anything."

"Never mind," he said, sipping his tea, "You never know, something may turn up."

They inspected the washing-line. There were several pegs lying on the grass beneath. This was not right, as they were always put back in the peg-bag in the laundry-room downstairs after use, and never left out. Of course there were no footprints, as the area around was grass. Michael picked up about twenty pegs.

"Could be straightforward theft, of course," he reflected, straightening up, "But I very much doubt it. After all, who would want a few items of underwear and a mouldy cape. No, I think they wanted it to look like ordinary theft. I also think we're dealing with an amateur here, myself. It's all a bit clumsy, isn't it?"

Joy suddenly remembered the mask and wondered if it was still on the shelf in the potting-shed. No, it had gone too, of course. Nothing else had been touched.

They retired to the garden seat with their tea and Michael considered the situation as it stood.

Looking across the pleasant back gardens at the houses opposite, he observed that living in St. Julie's Road was very much like living in college. The general layout was somehow similar. All the back-gardens made a kind of huge quad, subdivided by garden walls, and the large houses looked down on this open area, so that it really was a very public place in spite of the feeling of seclusion and privacy, which was simply an illusion created by the numerous trees and bushes dotted around. In fact, everybody could see exactly what everybody else was doing with no effort at all. There were literally hundreds of windows looking down silently on to this central quad.

Michael's opinion, therefore, was that whoever had done this thing could clearly observe Joy's movements with no trouble at all from some vantage-point nearby. It could be anybody whose windows overlooked the area. They might even be watching now!

They looked around at the blank windows. It was strange to think of all the activity which must be going on inside the houses and yet the windows revealed nothing. There seemed to be no movement at all. Simply odd sounds, little snippets of conversation floating through open windows here and there, and screams and shouts from the Convent school playground at the Woodstock Road end.

Joy commented that she felt sometimes that she was being watched and the feeling was not benign.

Michael nodded. "That follows," he said.

"And with no evidence at all to prove anything," she continued, "I shall not from henceforth be able to rest easy in my bed! Do you think this unpleasant person will come after me now?"

Michael thought not. After all, she herself hadn't seen anything strange in the sky, had she? So presumably, there was no need for action.

"Goodbye now," said Michael, "See you later, no doubt."

He stopped and turned at the gate.

"Oh, by the way - you have got some evidence - the footprint! You haven't thrown it away, have you?"

She laughed and said no, she hadn't thank goodness; as dear Mrs. Badger had not rejected it as rubbish yet; so the newspaper was still tucked away in the study.

He turned again outside the gate.

"And of course, you have the all-seeing Miss Dacre as your chief ally!"

He nodded in the direction of the quivering curtains across the road. They twitched irritably and a muffled yapping began backstage.

"Ally?" Joy pulled a face from the doorway, where she was well out of Miss Dacre's line of vision.

"Oh yes," said Michael, "She is your number one witness. Now she, bless her, really could be in danger. She actually saw the villain in the flesh. If he finds out, then there really could be trouble!"

Uttering these uncheering words, he departed with a jaunty wave. Joy reflected that the only comforting thing about this nasty possibility was that horrid little Pongo would most certainly give the villain a good run for his money, should he attempt to harm Miss Dacre. Being a vicious little brute, he would most certainly find the Achilles heel of the unknown intruder - quite literally!

She looked across the road with a fixed smile, and the quivering curtain subsided immediately and the irritable aggravated yapping ceased.

Returning to the back-garden with her lecture notes, she settled down to a good morning's work.

The madrigals of Claudio Monteverdi... she became lost in deep thought, transported to Venice. If Monteverdi had been alive today, no doubt he would have made a fortune as a writer of pop music; such an astonishing gift for thinking up catchy tunes - and those wonderful cross-rhythms! For instance, one need only think of the Nisi Dominus from that magnificent sacred work, the Vespers of 1610. What a marvellous modern tune for a pop-group to have fun with! She laughed aloud, and then told herself not to be frivolous.

After working on with absolute concentration for an hour or so, she became aware of something bothersome in the back of her mind, rather like some kind or psychological mosquito. Concentration flagged. She felt irritable.

Looking up briefly, she felt a sudden sharp pang of unease, a strange chill feeling. She was being watched. Quickly glancing round at the blank windows, she perceived no movement. God! This was awful!

Collecting up her papers and books, she went quickly indoors and then pedaled off to the Bodleian Library and enjoyed a peaceful day's work forgetting everything else. It was the sense of threat that was so unsettling at home. What was to be done? Where was Erica Trondheim? Do hurry up and come back, Mark! It was so eerie, being alone in the place. If Petronella would only come back from the dig in Greece! Noisy as they were sometimes, young students were a great comfort to have about the house.

In the evening, she went to the allotment to continue her autumn digging. Passing through Trap gate, she talked to the horses, munching thoughtfully at their hay in the stable-yard. It was all so peaceful. There was something truly marvellous about being with horses! A feeling of comfort and well-being.

Leaning on the gate, she went into a kind of mesmeric state of abstraction for some considerable time. The only sound to be heard was that of the horses munching and the odd flutter and chirrup as birds settled down for the night.

A slight rustle in the bushes and the crack of a twig brought her out of her reverie with a start.

Turning in the direction of the sound, she found herself looking directly at the spot where the bundled-up cape had been thrown by the sofa. She felt suddenly chilled by a spasm of unease. The horses also reacted. They all looked towards the same spot, ears pricked forward. They did not like what they sensed. Arnold, the white gelding, whinnied loudly and the others became restive. This noise and movement obliterated any further tell-tale sounds from the bushes.

Joy stood her ground, although her impulse was to run. She saw nothing, but she knew, as did the horses, that somebody was watching. The horses, quick to sense danger, told her clearly that whoever it was had no good intentions.

She remained standing quietly by the horses, but there were no further sounds from the dumps. The animals settled down again, snorting gently as they resumed feeding.

Uneasy, but determined to get some good digging done before dark, Joy crossed the railway-line, pausing to look back momentarily from the higher vantage-point of the level-crossing for signs of life in the dumps. There was no movement at all.

The allotments were deserted and she worked methodically for about an hour with fair concentration, but could not ignore that curious pang of disquiet in the back of her mind. As twilight came, instead of the usual feeling of peace and tranquillity of spirit at the sight of a lovely evening sky, she felt jumpy. The Canada geese began to honk from the river preparatory to take-off, and she straightened her back to watch the ritual flight.

"Oh - Cledwyn!" She started violently and dropped her fork with shock.

"Cledwyn! Whatever is the matter? You startled me! I do wish you wouldn't creep up on me so quietly!"

Cledwyn stood in the shadow of her shed door and he looked afraid, but this was a sensation felt rather than seen, as it was now getting dark, and she could only dimly discern the shape of the slight figure and the pale handsome face in the shadows.

She sensed fear and not just her own - his also. He put his finger to his lips and waved his other hand up and down in violent motion.

"For God's sake, Miss, keep your voice down," he said in a hoarse whisper.

"Cledwyn - what is it?" she said rather loudly, in what she hoped was a firm teacherly voice, remembering her early post-graduate days teaching in London.

Cledwyn danced up and down silently in the shed doorway, sending her the most urgent semaphore messages in a sort of pantomime.

"Miss - please! Keep your voice down! Please - please - don't come down here late on your own, it's not safe!"

"What?" she said, incredulous, but with a strange feeling of inevitability, as though it had all happened before, like precognition or someone waking from a dream with a half-memory of what has been so vivid in sleep and then is quickly lost in the doings of everyday.

"For God's sake, Miss, be quiet!" He seemed quite desperate. "If you want me dead, keep shoutin'!"

She stood stock-still and quite silent, transfixed by the bald statement.

"You been good to me, Miss," he whispered: "You 'elped me get myself sorted out an' I don't feel so mixed-up no more - so it's my turn to 'elp you now. You must keep away from 'ereabouts at night for the next few days, an' everythin'll be all right. Please, please, Miss, just do it for me!"

With that, he vanished into the bushes by the gate without a sound. There was not even the crack of a twig to betray his movements thereafter.

Alarmed, Joy picked up her tools and made quickly for the top gate which gave access to the meadow. Much better to go back along the open path and over the railway bridge where there might be friendly strollers, rather than go over the level-crossing and through the dark stable-yard, where unbenign spirits might lurk. Too risky. Fear made her feel quite sick.

She stopped on top of the bridge and looked down over the tangle of bushes and trees below. There was no movement, but in any case, in the twilight it would be difficult to spot in the dark blur of the undergrowth.

She made for home, cautiously casting a glance at the dumps as she passed Trap Bottom gate.

The lights of The Jolly Sailors showed comfortingly over Aristotle Bridge. The amiable chug of a holiday barge surging underfoot greeted her as she crossed this battered edifice.

Articulated lorries had wrought their unhappy work by straddling the hump-back too low, and had damaged the parapets on both sides, going to and fro from the industrial area, but the bridge stood valiantly still, a testimonial to the sturdy building of earlier times.

Calling in at the saloon bar, she ascertained from Michael Walters that Mark was not back, but did not mention the disturbing business of Cledwyn's warning. Better mull it over for a while. The whole thing was most upsetting and she dearly wished it would all go away and that peace of mind would return. However, this was evidently not to be.

As she pondered over the alarming developments of the evening, it occurred to her that her own bedroom was exactly on the same level as the old lady's, so she went up and stood at the open window. She didn't put on the light, but stood looking out over the back-gardens and beyond the houses into the darkness.

The meadow itself could only be discerned as a black void edged by a tiny necklace of lights from the villages of Wolvercote to the north and Binsey to the west.

The stars were vibrant and the sky deepest blue velvet. There was no moon. Aircraft winked silently across the heavens at great height. The old lady most certainly did have a marvellous vantage-point for quietly spying on the world - especially at night. For instance, Mrs. Graystone was clearly visible in her sitting-room on the ground floor, as she watched television with her large ginger cat happily ensconced on her lap. She had not drawn her curtains at the French windows and a pool of light illuminated the lawn, brilliant green like a billiard-table.

Strange how so many people didn't bother to draw their curtains at night in summertime. One could derive much entertainment from simply watching the happenings within the lighted windows. Lights came on and went off at intervals and one had an instant cameo of people's lives.

A gentle plop at her elbow brought her out of her reverie as the large warm shape of Iffley landed neatly on the window-ledge beside her. She purred loudly and said "Waouw?" with an upward lilt. She never used the common British miaouw, but always said, quite distinctly,"Waouw!" (Evidently, this must be the Persian equivalent). Her other words were, "Rrrrrrrr!" delivered on a long high-pitched note somewhere about C above middle C. (This usually meant "I'm here, come and chase me," etc.) and, "Waouw - waouw - waouw!" declared in rising emphatic tones on B flat (molto marcato), which usually indicated that something was wrong, or that she was requiring sustenance or attention of some sort, i.e. strokes or tummy ticklings. She was a most original and endearing character.

They looked out together into the darkness, Joy, solemnly musing upon the unhappy events of recent times, and Iffley no doubt thinking deeply about catching mice and things as she stared hard at the dark garden below.

Could it be, as Michael had suggested, that one of those many windows was being used as a lookout? And if so, which one was it? There were so many. If one sat here for days and nights on end, it would be very difficult to spot anyone watching.

Who was this unknown person - and why the ill will? Why must she keep away from the allotments as Cledwyn demanded with such urgency? Could it be that some black-magic rite was to be performed there? This seemed to be about the only thing which would fit the bill. But no - it was much too near the town, and surely it was by tradition only ancient sites and graveyards which were used for this kind of activity.

Although, on second thoughts, the business of the cape and the hideous mask could have some connection with such things. And, of course, the fact that the old lady had been most certainly frightened to death.

Yes, indeed, there was a faint glimmer of light here. Perhaps it had something to do with witchcraft. Oddly enough, if this should prove to be the case, then she was not so worried, for she herself was a direct descendant of one notorious witch whose end had been particularly unpleasant. Strange happenings of that order held no terrors for her, for she felt free of that world. She had often been told that she had "the sight"(by those who presumably had it themselves) but she had no interest whatsoever in such activities, simply regarding the whole idea as pitiful and sad. Much healthier to stick to the sober Christian ethic.

"Something strange in the sky..." - a familiar voice sounded in her head and the dead face of the old lady was once more vivid in the darkness; as though she had materialized for a moment; then the image faded and the clear night sky came back into normal focus.

"Waouw-waouw-waouw!" announced Iffley emphatically, jumping down from the window-sill with a loud thump.

"Hungry?" asked Joy.

"Waouw!" replied Iffley, with an affirmative downswing of a semi tone and led the way downstairs to the washroom in the basement, where dinner was normally served.

After a small snack, she sniffed round the washroom uneasily. She seemed unhappy.

"What is it, Iffley?"

"Waouw," she replied, vigorously applying her nose to the crack in the door, urgently wishful to depart.

"Really, you are being such a silly girl! What's the matter?"

She opened the stairs door and Iffley shot upwards like a rocket, shaking a back paw in disdain as she ran.

Soon after, she found Iffley on her bed in that sphinx-like posture which seemed to mean complete abstraction from the world and absolute contemplation.

She affected deep slumber, front paws neatly tucked in the arms-folded position - but the giveaway was the dark frown and the odd twitch of an ear.

Oh well, cats were funny things - or "quare," as they say in Oxfordshire. Best to ignore her and get to bed.

But this simple operation in itself presented problems, for Iffley had firmly planted herself in the middle and wouldn't budge.

Eventually they managed to negotiate terms and she graciously allowed Joy approximately half the bed.

It proved in any event quite difficult to get off to sleep because of the anxieties and turbulent thoughts which cascaded through her mind, but the discomfort of having so little room to move in bed made things intolerable. Iffley seemed to double in weight somehow when she was in this kind of mood, and however much she was pushed away, she simply re-established her former position again without appearing to move at all.

Eventually, in the small hours, Joy drifted off to sleep.

Horrid nightmares again plagued her dreams. Once more, the old lady's face came and went, luminous in the darkness, pleading and agonized. The hideous mask grimaced once more, becoming animated, vilely contorting into extremes of ugliness and wailing a maniacal shriek of mockery and derision.

"Waouw, waouw, waouw!"

Iffley came into the dream, her face close to Joy's.

"Waouw, waouw, waouw!"

She struggled to the surface of her consciousness, drugged with sleep.

"Go away, Iffley!" She pushed her off violently and with this became aware that she was not dreaming. The cat was in reality trying to waken her. She had been knocked off the bed, but would not be deterred, jumping determinedly back straight on to the pillow.

"Waouw, waouw, waouw." The call was urgent.

But the door was ajar and she could go out if she wished, so why all the fuss? Joy literally fell out of bed, feeling quite stupefied. There was a curious smell in the air.

Putting on the light, she saw Iffley at the door with her nose in the place where the door met the jamb. She looked back in desperation, her great golden eyes filled with dismay.

"What is it, Iffley?"

Joy opened the door and Iffley shot through like a rocket, making straight for the landing door to the basement, running backwards and forwards, to and from the door with great urgency.

Joy followed her, tripping over the cord of her dressing-gown in her stupor.

An evil smell of oily burning drifted up from the darkness below. She fumbled for the light switch, jerking fully awake at the sight of a black pall of oily smoke hanging like a thick canopy in the air. Iffley ran on ahead downstairs, looking quickly back, with alarm clearly written across her countenance. She showed no fear of the dense black smoke, which filled the lower hallway.

Following on rapidly, Joy was at once choked by the fumes. She ran back to her room and soaked a towel in cold water, using it as a makeshift respirator.

Blinded by stinging tears as the smoke and searing heat overwhelmed her, she dashed downstairs once more in an attempt to locate the source of the burning. It flashed through her mind that dear Iffley must be choking, too! The wash-room door was ajar and this brave and beautiful cat stood by it to show her where the fire was.

But of course! She was so near the ground that the smoke did not affect her. It hung visibly from chest-height to the ceiling, but the ground level was as yet still clear. Clever cat!

In the darkness and the fog of dense smoke, a fire blazed in the washroom. She put on the light and was horrified to see the old gas stove in the corner alight, one ring blazing full-on.

The old battered pan in which she soaked her dirty tea-towels in a strong mixture of bleach and detergent prior to a good boiling, stood on top, well ablaze, the contents cinders. Moving like lightning, she instinctively threw open the window, and using the wet towel, with a Trojan effort, threw out the pan and its fiery contents into the rockery.

The bottom of the pan glowed red as it lay on its side, hissing and incinerating the Aubretia upon which it lay. Steam rose in warm clouds and sparks floated up lazily into the night sky.

Desperation in the emergency had made her act swiftly. Now she lay across the window-sill coughing and feeling horribly sick with the fumes and shock - and the slow and horrifying realization that someone had tried to kill her.

Iffley landed neatly on the window-sill alongside and watched the red glow and drifting sparks from the smouldering pan.

Again the sickening feeling of threat overwhelmed her. Whomsoever it was who had done this must have come in by the basement door; it was all too easy. The bolt had never worked properly and in any case, the changes in the weather made the door stick, so it was difficult to close at the best of times.

Thank God for dear Iffley. Melody, would once, of course, have seen off the intruder long before he got into the house, with his piercing shrieks. No one would have stood a chance of getting near the place. It was ironical that she should have been protected by a budgerigar! How she missed that infuriating little bird.

Someone wanted her dead. But who would believe her? Worse still, was she simply going mad? Had she indeed left the pan on the stove and let it burn dry?

The stark facts, however, were now horribly clear. She had very little proof and no witnesses to any of the incidents which had taken place so far. No one else had seen her with Cledwyn when he came to warn her. There was no way to prove the theft of her clothing from the washing-line and the mask and the cape were gone.

The only thing she could prove was that she was at the Jolly Sailors when Miss Dacre saw her impersonator go in to the old lady's house - or could she? Upon reflection, this could be quite difficult to establish, as she had in fact slipped out for a breath of fresh air twice to Aristotle Bridge, and had spent a few peaceful moments watching the holiday narrow-boats tie up for the night, and a blue and red air-balloon drift gracefully across the evening sky. She had also seen the tail-end of the language schools' football match - an uproarious affair.

The appalling truth slowly dawned as she leaned across the window-sill, gasping for breath. Nothing which had happened so far could be proven to be an unlawful act. She was entirely on her own in an increasingly alarming situation. Meanwhile Iffley, who had been sitting next to her on the sill, uttered a definitive "Waouw, waouw," and thumped down on to the washroom floor.

The air had by now begun to clear and Joy surveyed the room. The cat ran to the stove and back again and she noticed that it was still alight. She speedily switched it off. The heat in the room was intense, so she opened the side door which led to the garden steps and returning to the washroom, spied her paraffin can by the stove.

This was not right. It was normally kept outside with mops, brooms, buckets and lawn — mower, under the lean-to which covered the garden steps, and she would never have left it, under any circumstances, by the gas stove. Furthermore, the cap was off, and a paraffin-soaked rag lay across the top, actually touching the stove, which was very hot indeed.

Very cunning. A well-arranged accident had been set up. This much was quite clear.

"Ach, Gott! What is this awful smell?" proclaimed a loud Teutonic voice. Joy, startled, turned to the basement window with a mixture of feelings, astonishment and relief predominating.

"Erica! Thank God you are back!"

The riposte was immediate and strident.

"Of course, you stupid woman! What else? One can't stay away from this crazy place for ever, unfortunately. Really, Oxford is a madhouse! America is peace compared with it."

The voice came from the darkness outside in the back-garden.

"Are you trying to burn down the house especially for my welcome? The moment I go away, everything becomes chaotic! Why are people so irresponsible and so completely stupid?"

Joy smiled. She was well-used to the tirades of abuse which Erica generally employed as a substitute for kind words, or any display of affection or friendship, so she was not too disconcerted.

Peering out of the window, her eyes became accustomed to the darkness and she perceived a figure clad in a long white robe, rather like a roll of limp mutton-cloth, in fact.

Erica could be dimly discerned standing at the top of the rockery, clad only in this curious garment, which was almost transparent. She looked very much like Callas as Lucia di Lammermoor in the Mad Scene, except for the lovely ash-blonde hair which cascaded down to her shoulders, half pinned-up, half loose. She had the wildest eyes with a quite livid gleam, and was altogether an alarming apparition with which to be confronted in the small hours, but Joy, certainly, was immensely relieved.

Perhaps with Erica's return some sense would now come out of this extraordinary business. It was indeed an incongruous situation, to find that one could derive some kind of comfort from contact with a person whose automatic response was always to repel. It was all most unnatural.

Perhaps she had been emotionally hurt in some way when younger. This might account for her curious reactions. However, one must be thankful for small mercies. At least she was back and no matter how uncooperative, perhaps might be able to assist in making some sense of the matter. Perhaps she would be able to impart some information about the old lady which might possibly cast light on the circumstances which had led to her death.

But now was evidently not the time to ask. Erica was in a furious temper - demented with rage would be a more accurate description. Thank God, it was the middle of the night, so there were mercifully no witnesses to this astonishing spectacle but Joy herself.

Erica was not in the slightest bit interested in any kind of explanation about the fire, but simply strode up and down the lawn proclaiming a loud oration to the night sky. Shakespeare must have been a strong subject with her, for the performance was well worthy of consideration as a possible hitherto unknown fragment from the Tempest - yes, definitely the Tempest.

Doom and disaster were obviously imminent - and Erica was doing her best for them. The see-through mutton-cloth nightdress billowed and swirled round her as she paced up and down. She looked very impressive and rather alarming.

Now who was she like? Ah yes - that was it. Queen Boadicea, as portrayed in that fine sculpture at the end of Westminster Bridge. All she lacked was the chariot with the scythes on the wheels to mow down the enemy - and of course there were no daughters clustering round her. Possibly this was an important factor, for Erica, after all, had never had any children.

What a pity that her personal drive did not relate to something positive and outward going, like that of the ancient British Queen. Erica simply did not care tuppence about other people or their needs. Everything was internalized; she was totally introspective. Her personal requirements were all that mattered in the whole world. Everything and everybody else could go hang.

For example, the fire and its cause and result were clearly irrelevant to her. The only thing that mattered was that Erica's private world had been encroached upon in some way and this could not be tolerated at all.

By this time, there were three cats in attendance to watch the spectacle. Little Tabby appeared through the ferns in the rockery and sat quietly gazing at Erica's antics with an expression of wonder.

Iffley sat comfortably at Joy's elbow on the window-sill. Scherzo, the timid black tom, peered out from his safe hidey-hole under the water-butt, and blind Fred scrabbled about at Joy's feet, listening intently, and then stretched up on his hind-legs to reach the window-sill. They were all clearly mystified by the performance.

It finished as suddenly as it had begun, with Erica disappearing offstage left and failing to return, so the enrapt audience was left waiting for a re-entrance which never came.

Joy and the cats remained looking out into the darkness - or was it now first-light? There was already a dim glow in the eastern sky.

Looking up carefully and leaving all the downstairs lights on, Joy wearily returned to bed and slept, exhausted, until late morning, comforted by the thought that Erica, crazy as she might be, had returned and would in effect act as a kind of unwitting watch-dog. Her very presence would act as a deterrent and without doubt put off the unpleasant character from coming readily to the house again.

CHAPTER IV

'Consture my meaning.'

Canzonets to Four Voices

Giles Farnaby 1598

Pedaling off to college later in the day, Joy stopped at Michael Walters' office in St. Giles'. Luckily, he was free and they had a good half-hour together.

Michael, genial as ever, listened patiently to the synopsis of events and finally summed up exactly as she had expected. Swivelling his chair round in order to look out over the broad avenue of St. Giles', he sat for a while, elbows on armrests, fingertips delicately touching, in that particular attitude akin to supplication which is often unconsciously adopted by academics and their ilk when deep in thought. He smiled a rueful smile.

"As we've agreed before, you and I know it's all true and there is most certainly much skulduggery and dirty work going on, but any independent observer hearing this extraordinary tale might easily say (and, by the way, it's with all due respect that I say this, cruel though it may sound) - 'Oh, a typical potty academic. She's got a wonderful imagination; probably had too much to drink and must have left the stove on herself- it's all in her mind', etc. etc.'"

Joy nodded miserably in agreement.

"And, worse still, quite honestly Erica is going to be no help to you at all as a witness to any happening. It's well known that she's quite mad and completely unreliable. One of Oxford's great eccentrics."

Joy nodded again, defeated.

"If only Petronella would come back from the Greek dig, at least I'd have somebody else in the house. I would have thought she'd be back by now - and she's such a character too; always bubbling about the place, usually with lots of boy-friends in and out all the time. That alone ought to put off our unknown friend, I would imagine."

Michael agreed with a smile. "Yes, she's a vivacious little thing, isn't she? Makes me wish I were ten years younger! By the way, where's Cledwyn since the fatal warning?"

"That's what troubles me most; he's completely disappeared. He's basically such a sweet boy, you know. He does deserve a chance to make something of his life. I would love to see him settled, with somewhere comfortable to live and someone to look after him. He seems so lost and utterly vulnerable - drifting about the meadow searching for his mushrooms, living rough and sleeping anywhere."

Michael gazed into the distance, deep in thought. A flag fluttered gently on the top of St. Giles' Church bell-tower and church and college clocks struck three - all at completely different times. It must have taken about two minutes for them all to accomplish this feat.

He turned back to face the desk.

"One thing is quite clear to me in all this. It's drugs which must be at the bottom of the whole business. And what is more, I believe it's no small operation. I feel sure the old lady stumbled across something big and had to be got rid of quickly."

Again he paused, and swivelling his chair round to face the window, once more sat silent for a few moments.

"Tell you what I'll do. I think it's now time for a quiet word with the C.I.D.. Inspector Vardon is an old friend of mine so I think I'll have a private word with him. Nothing official. Just to sound him out and see what he thinks. Perhaps we'll have a quiet chat over a pint and a game of darts at the Royal Oak - just leave it with me for a while."

Joy felt this as an enormous relief, freeing her from the anxiety of puzzling over the inconclusive affair and enabling her to forget it for a bit. Michael would deal with it. She was quite confident of that, and what a joy it was to have such a good and reliable friend to lean on in time of need.

In any case, in a few days' time she would have to go to Vienna to examine that ancient music manuscript which had recently come to light, so it was a comforting thought to know that Michael was taking a practical interest and would no doubt come up with some solution to the whole beastly business. He was always so thorough in everything he undertook, bless him.

Mrs. Badger was just leaving on her antique bicycle as Joy got home. She wobbled to a halt and stepped down from the high saddle. Her bicycle was an early vintage Oxford model and these are now, alas, so rare and usually handed down through families. Very few remain, for collectors have mostly snapped them up and the rest have no doubt rusted away with old age.

This one was what might be called a younger sister of the penny-farthing in its stature; the original sit-up-and-beg bicycle, with enormous wheels on a huge black frame and a curious

concave bend in the lady's cross-bar - specially designed for stepping down elegantly, notwithstanding the encumbrance of the long skirts and voluminous petticoats of Edwardian days. The back wheel was criss-crossed with ancient strings from the hub to the mudguard - an ingenious skirt-protector, and the high handlebars gave to the frame not only the appearance of quite extraordinary height, but also of great elegance. Mounting and dismounting required a skill somewhat akin to mounting a horse, needing particular expertise in balance. The basket attached to the handlebars was full to overflowing with shopping, and a large bunch of red roses was perched precariously on top, held in position only by the neck of a large bottle of scotch on one side and an inverted bunch of carrots on the other.

"Mustn't drop that, else!" she said, indicating the Scotch with a nod. "Moy 'ubby, 'e'll go mad! That's 'is treat to 'isself this week. Got to 'ave summat to keep you goin', ain't yer, kid?" - with a saucy wink.

Looking at Mrs. Badger, you saw plainly that she and the bicycle were made for one another. Both were large and stately and had a distinctly aristocratic air. Until she opened her mouth and spoke in the Oxfordshire vernacular, Mrs. Badger could easily have been mistaken for a dowager duchess. She was very tall and well set-up, a Wagnerian soprano in build, with ample bosom and an erect carriage. Her snow-white hair was immaculately groomed. A fresh English complexion, bright blue eyes a-twinkle with country humour, expensive gold-framed glasses and the most tasteful clothes made her an attractive as well as an impressive figure.

"Oi've 'ad a terrible toime with 'er ladyship this mornin'," she said, inclining her head slightly towards the Trondheims' front door, but keeping her eyes firmly fixed on St. Julie's Church roof, so as to give nothing away to any unseen observer.

Miss Dacre's curtains twitched irritably. Evidently, she was having difficulty in interpreting the meaning of the conversation.

"Walkin' up an' down loike a caged toiger, she is. Still got 'er noightie on at this toime o' day! Summat to do wi' you settin' the 'ouse on fire an' troyin' to gas 'er an' all - summat o' that sort. Sobbin' an' croyin' summat shockin', she is - crocodile tears o' course. If you ask me, Oi think she needs treatment, meself, moy duck - or a good man - one or t'other." Mrs. Badger sniffed a deprecating sniff and fixed the church roof with a look enough to kill it.

"Not enough to do, she 'asn't. Stark ravin' bonkers, Oi reckon. She don't care a tinker's cuss about the ol' girl doyin', not the sloightest bit interested, she ain't. Oi tell you wot, moy gal - if Oi'd of 'ad a daughter loike 'er, Oi'd a' chucked meself in the canal years ago."

Joy quickly explained about the fire, trying hard not to give away too much to Miss Dacre. Pongo could be heard yapping furiously in the background.

"Well, Oi dunno. Oi think as it's all daftness meself, but Oi personally don't disbelieve a word you say. Oxford's a mad'ouse these days. Probably some lad 'oose been a'sniffing' this 'ere glue or summat o' that sort. Gawn off their 'eads, these young 'uns. All this studyin' an' layin' about oidlin'. No good for 'em faint. Ought to get out an' do a bit o' muck spreadin' and get diggin' some 'taters. That'd soon cure 'em! ... Oh, Chroist Church! 'Ere come that Mrs. Spragnell - Oi'm off!"

She departed at speed with a grimace and a hasty wave, wobbling dangerously as she took off with her precious cargo.

Joy groaned and made as sedate a dash as possible for her front door, pretending not to have seen Madge Spragnell approaching at speed from the direction of St. Hugh's College.

Madge, wobbling along much more dangerously even than Mrs. Badger, perched on an incredibly tiny folda-bike and laden with even more shopping (if indeed, this were humanly possible) called "Coo-eee!" as she determinedly pedaled directly across the road at Joy, missing the Wolvercote bus by inches.

Too late! Joy was ambushed. She looked around in desperation, but there was no escape.

As Madge wobbled to an abrupt halt at the gate, everything which could fall open, or get dropped, or fall off the bike did exactly that - including Madge herself, who landed in a kind of untidy heap over the iron gate, the contents of her enormous handbag cascading everywhere. It was quite astonishing how much there was in it and a great mound of things piled up both on and around Joy's feet. It was a kind of lucky-dip selection, rather reminiscent of the contents of the bran-tub at the church fete earlier in the month.

Pencil-sharpeners, bangles, a pencil-torch, lots of keys, rings with fancy ornaments dangling from them, ear-rings (mostly odd ones, it appeared), packets of peppermints, any amount of raffle-tickets and bingo cards, an incredible number of eye-shadow pencils and lipsticks, and even a small, powerful magnifying glass of considerable vintage.

"Thank goodness - that's where it is!" announced Madge, spotting it in the pansies, "It's the General's, and he is really cross with me for losing it. Oh, look! there's my potato-peeler! I lost that, months ago! However did it get in my handbag? Most extraordinary!"

"Now dear," she announced, "I simply must talk to you."

She propped her bicycle against the garden wall and it immediately fell down with a resounding crash. The lights fell off and disembowelled themselves in the process, bulbs, batteries, reflectors, etcetera, rolling in all directions. Astonishingly enough, nothing seemed to have got broken in all this chaos. She picked up a box of eggs and opened them and they were quite intact! as indeed was all the rest of her shopping, which was scattered all over the pavement, but seemed quite undamaged, notwithstanding the fact that much of it was quite fragile.

It took the pair of them some time to collect everything up, as oranges, tomatoes, onions and the like had rolled to a far distant place under the privet hedge and down the rockery. Joy retrieved a box of dog-biscuits from the birdbath, which, mercifully, had no water in it, and hoped that all was now well.

"My dear, do you know, I'm always doing it - and nothing ever gets broken. Isn't it extraordinary?"

Joy agreed that it certainly was.

"Now, where are my glasses, dear?"

She fumbled about her person for them without success. After a brief search, they were found dangling from the rosebush by the gate.

"What a good thing I got that long chain for them when I was in the States. Such a good idea to hang them round one's neck, isn't it? Saves so much trouble looking for them under cushions and things, and they do seem to get sat on so much!"

She put them on and they promptly fell off; she tried again and succeeded in perching them precariously on the bridge of her nose. However, the earpieces were not correctly positioned, and they began to slide slowly off again as she fumbled with her diary.

"Now, dear, I've got a date for you - hold on while I find it. Oops!"

She dropped the diary and Joy dutifully retrieved it.

"I really must change these glasses, dear, I literally can't see a thing with them!" She fumbled again and found the date.

"Ah, yes, dear; here we are. Now," said she with an air of great moment. "You remember my bazaar, don't you?"

"Bazaar?"

Joy searched her memory for some recollection of this event. A glimmer of something in the back of her mind brought to light a sudden vision of a sort of rugger scrum, which took place in the church hall earlier in the year, involving much strife over coveted items of jumble.

"Yes, yes, of course, my famous Christmas Bazaar. Now come along, dear, you can't have forgotten, surely? I had you all knitting socks for that dreadful earthquake. Only it wasn't socks they wanted - it was blankets in the end. But I'd lost my glasses, so I thought it was socks. Anyway, they eventually went to the Sally Army, so at least they went somewhere, and that was all right."

An airy wave of the hand dismissed this altogether trivial point. She stopped suddenly in mid-stream and looked sharply at Joy.

"Are you listening, dear? No, no, I can see you're not listening! Now come on, dear - concentrate! This is a matter of life and death! Concentrate with me!"

Emphatic enunciation accompanied this final admonition. Joy opened and shut her mouth in a vain attempt to affirm that Madge Spragnell had her complete and undivided attention but she was given no chance to speak. The torrent continued.

"Now, what I want you to do is this. It's really quite simple - even a child could do it!"

What was meant to be an engaging smile, displaying a glittering array of gold fillings, dammed the verbal tide for a brief moment. She looked rather like a shark with its mouth open ready for the kill. This image was reinforced by the fact that she looked down sideways at Joy with a curious leer, exactly as a shark might do. It was a quite uncanny resemblance.

As she resumed, she was unstoppable, and Joy was reminded, not for the first time, of a galleon in full sail riding the waves over all other unfortunate craft in her path.

In figure, she was tall and commanding, very curvaceous and youthful in build for a woman approaching seventy ("I've always had a good corsetier, my dear. Costs money, but pays dividends - in the long run!") and she was involved in absolutely everything important and respectable on the Oxford circuit. As a do-gooder, she was formidable indeed. If there was a committee to be on, Madge was on it, and of most she either was, or had at some stage been chairman. She had the knack of being able to bulldoze anybody into doing anything she wanted. Equally, she could also bulldoze them out of the way if they represented any form of obstacle to her proposals.

Strong men wilted before her, in particular her distinguished and long-suffering husband, General Rupert Spragnell, a mild-natured and lovable man, who simply said yes to everything she demanded so as to avoid any confrontation, however trivial. "Line of least resistance, my dear chap," he had commented to a fellow-officer at a regimental reunion. "Be strong on the field of battle, but always show the white flag at home - complete surrender at all times. It's the only way to keep a happy marriage like mine intact, don't you know!"

Joy's cousin Jayne had once remarked, after Madge Spragnell had suddenly descended on a lightning visit one afternoon: "Hmmm, tremendous presence, but not quite out of the handkerchief drawer, I would think."

Perhaps it was something to do with the vision of the blue hair, the purple or lime-green trouser-suits, the magenta and shocking-pink silk blouses with voluminous sleeves, and the festoons of beads and bangles which drew this comment from the rather non-committal Jayne.

Artificial eyelashes, thick mascara and lilac eye-shadow were also inevitably part of Madge's daily attire, and the general effect was dazzling, but conceivably a little vulgar. "My dear, I would feel so undressed without my eyelashes," she had been heard to say whilst consulting her image in a hand-mirror in order to make adjustments to her mascara.

She had also confessed in a weak moment (after several large pink gins in the Playhouse bar) that she came from an old theatrical family and that they had known Marie Lloyd intimately. How had the General ever got in tow with her? But this remained a mystery. Jayne conjectured that it might have been one of those legendary stage-door romances figuring in Edwardian novels, and the General as a young subaltern had fallen madly in love with a gorgeous chorus-girl. It was an intriguing possibility.

"Now dear, you know it's St. Giles' Fair soon, don't you?" Madge broke into Joy's little reverie with a regal wave of a hand heavily be-ringed with the largest of diamonds and other glittering stones. A kaleidoscopic flash of brilliant light incorporating all the colours of the spectrum passed inches from Joy's nose. The fingernails appeared to drip purple nail-varnish.

"Wake up, wake up, dear! This is desperately important, you have simply no idea - you and your darling little choir are going to be responsible for saving thousands of lives!"

"Are we?" Joy faltered, mystified.

"Yes, yes! Now listen carefully, dear! All you have to do is this. As I said before, even a child could do it."

A row of cats had gathered on the garden wall, settling down amiably to watch the performance. Iffley, sitting by the bicycle, which had somehow managed to remain upright, was very interested in Madge's shopping; obviously fish, judging by the delicate twitch of the nose and whiskers.

Madge continued, acting out the scene expertly in a kind of mime as she spoke. Joy idly watched Iffley out of the corner of her eye.

As the cat became more interested in the fragrant scent from Madge's bicycle basket, she seemed to grow imperceptibly taller. She sat, like the long, thin Egyptian tomb-sculptures of cats, extending herself upwards without appearing to move at all, until in the end her nose was just level with the thing which interested her most in the basket. She blinked her golden eyes sleepily and smiled an innocent cat-smile at Madge Spragnell.

"Now, I have approached the powers that be and of course they are simply delighted to co-operate with me in my proposals."

She smiled graciously at Iffley, who was of course giving Madge her rapt attention.

"All you have to do, my dear, is this," repeated Madge grandly.

She was clearly pleased with the receptive attitude of her audience. Joy silently observed Miss Dacre's curtains not only twitch, but actually open an inch, and an eye appear, fixed balefully on Madge Spragnell.

"Simply dress your choir up in those adorable little costumes you wore for the Elizabethan Day at St. James' - you know, with the ruffs and everything - and stand in front of my display and sing those pretty little madrigals and things which always go down so well with the tourists." More hand-waving accompanied this. She was evidently conducting an invisible choir with a considerable amount of rubato. - "And it'll all be marvellous!"

"Will it?" murmured Joy faintly.

"Yes, yes, of course!" declared Madge emphatically and swept on, "There's no doubt whatsoever in my mind..." She dropped her diary yet again, this time scoring a direct hit down the drain in the gutter outside the front gate _ She absently watched it disappear, doubtless to be lost forever in Oxford's unique drainage system.

"Oh bother! Ah well, there we are then. People will just have to ring me up if I'm not somewhere when I should be, and that's that. Now don't forget, dear, I'm depending on you utterly! Be there! St. Giles' Fair! Bye-eee! I'll be in touch. Don't forget...," she carolled, wobbling violently away towards Kingston Road, "I'm depending on you!"

"Bye-eee!" returned Joy, by now feeling rather weak. She looked down.

"Iffley! What have you got there, you naughty cat?"

Iffley was well settled on her haunches under the privet hedge, intent on her own business and masticating with great relish a pair of juicy kippers and an Arbroath smoky. She chewed away quietly with epicurean-delight, the other cats waiting humbly behind her in a queue, according to pecking-order: Scherzo, the timid black tom, Smiley, the longhaired tabby (who had been Smelly until he was tamed and neutered), blind Fred, son of Smiley, and finally little Tabby (grandmother of all of them) sitting some way off. She was a nervous little thing and always waited until last for food.

Joy picked up a tube of toothpaste from beneath the privet hedge and took a quick look down the drain outside the gate.

She smiled, as Miss Dacre's whole face appeared, incredulous, at her window. At the sight of the drain inspection, curiosity had overcome discretion.

Peering down into the darkness below, Joy spied the diary floating in its red plastic cover on the murky waters. That was definitely one thing she was not going to fish for. Three of the cats joined her, also looking curiously down the drain. "Rats," she teased, and they looked up at her, ears laid-back, in either earnest expectation or pitying disbelief.

Miss Dacre evidently thought that Joy was quite mad. However, a cheery wave had the desired effect. The curtains snapped shut in response. Pongo's yapping ceased.

It was time to pack a few things for Vienna. The trip should only last about a week, so no need to take many clothes. Mrs. Badger would feed the cats and keep an eye on the place - must bring her a nice present back, a liqueur or something; that would go down nicely with Mr. Badger too.

As she considered these matters, a dilapidated car with an extraordinary amount of luggage and camping gear on top drew up with a loud screech of brakes and a cheery toot on the horn. What was on top of the car gave the impression of being about the same size as the car itself.

Four sun-bronzed faces grinned and the doors flew open, disgorging Petronella and her friends.

"Hallo! We're back!"

Checking the impulse to call out in mingled relief and delight, Joy said simply, "So I see - how lovely to see you all looking so well!"

A happy reunion followed with much laughter over the joys and travails of archaeological work - the glorious climate, the awful food, the extraordinary tedium of sorting, cleaning and tabulating pottery fragments in hot, stuffy tents, when a swim in the sea was the tantalizing prospect outside. The remarkable and unexpected finds, the disappointments over supposedly certain locations, which after much painstaking toil produced no firm result, but nevertheless the utter exhilaration and fun of the whole venture. And, oh dear! the car - poor old Bessie! The breakdowns (usually in the middle of nowhere, or in some obscure and tortuous mountain pass - surprising what can be done to repair a car with a piece of elastic!) and the comic situation in the nether regions of Yugoslavia, where one didn't speak a single word of the language, so the whole thing became like a piece of classic Jacque Tatti! And that flock of goats! Unforgettable. It had been the smell which woke everybody that morning, and there they were on top of a mountain, with a breathtaking view, and surrounded by hundreds of remarkably friendly and appallingly smelly goats!

"We managed eventually to persuade our four-footed friends to go so we could pack up the camping gear, but the smell stayed with us for days! Simply nobody wanted to know us! And have you ever tried explaining why you smell so vile to people when you don't speak their language?"

Finally, the present. Where was it? Somewhere buried in the boot, they thought. After much rummaging it was found at the bottom of everything. Yes, there it was, within the rim of the spare wheel, a very large bottle in a cellophane box. A most extraordinary bottle!

"Oh dear," said Petronella in dismay. "We forgot to declare it! Thank goodness, customs didn't bother much with us. I suppose we looked so poverty-stricken and disreputable in our clapped out old Morris Oxford!"

"Not forgetting the smell!" said one of the boys with a wicked grin. "It's still with us, you know."

She gave the bottle to Joy, with an affectionate hug. "Now don't drink it all at once - it's absolute mother's ruin!"

Joy inspected it cautiously. It was an elongated Greek temple in design (more or less bottle-shaped) with built-in caryatids all round the body, supporting a decorated cornice at the neck, whereon were written the mystic words:

'ΓΑΛΑ ΑΠΟ ΤΟ ΣΤΗΘΟΣ ΤΗΣ ΑφΡΟΔΙΤΗΣ'

"What does that mean?" asked Joy. "My modern Greek's awful. I'm afraid."

"Light the blue touch-paper and retire immediately," said one of the boys solemnly.

"I think it's actually meant to be The Tower of the Winds," said Petronella, thoughtfully turning the cellophane box round and scrutinizing the bottle inside.

"Anyway, if you take a look at St. Pancras' Church in London next time you're going to the British Museum - you know, the Regency church on Euston Road - the caryatids are identical and the bottle is exactly the same shape as the tower, so, I'm sure it's meant to be a replica. As you know, the design of the church is based on the Tower of the Winds and other things on the Acropolis; but I'll look it up just to make sure."

"Ingenious," said Joy, "What is it?"

"Ouzo," grinned one of the boys. "One sniff and it blows your brains out. We ran out of petrol in Yugoslavia and we seriously considered using it for fuel, but we decided against it; better to walk several miles for petrol than end up on the moon powered by an advanced fuel-injection system."

"It's lethal," said a muffled voice from within the car - "But incomparable."

A tousled head of bright red hair appeared over the roof. A screwdriver was brandished overhead in triumph.

"Hooray, my whisky's intact!"

The whole company made its way to the other side of the car. The owner of the red hair had prized off the driver's door-panel inside the car, to reveal two bottles of Glenmorangie, ingeniously wedged within a selection of French newspapers- providing insulation.

"Bruce! How could you?" exclaimed Petronella, truly scandalized: "What if Customs had examined our stuff?"

"Aye, well now; for us Scots good whisky is our religion, so anything goes. That's nothing - watch this!" He rummaged around in the boot and eventually located a water-carrier at the very bottom.

"Voila!" he announced, taking off the cap with a flourish.

"Well?" said Petronella, "What's so wonderful about brackish old French water from the Bois de Boulogne camp-site?"

"Just get a whiff of that!" he directed with a cheeky grin.

Petronella extended a wary nose over the open neck of the container.

"My God! What on earth is it? Paint-stripper?"

"Vodka!" he declared triumphantly: "Three whole gallons of a delicious nectar fit for the Gods on Olympus tay sup!"

"Deus omnipotens!" said Joy, "How can you live so dangerously?"

He laughed. "Very easily. Where I'm going, it will all be living dangerously. I'm away to Australia next month to work on a big new mining project. You've got to be tough and learn to survive. I'm just practicing. You have to live by your wits out there, and after all, I am a MacGregor, ye ken!"

"Ah, yes," nodded Joy with reverence. "A name to conjure with!"

After unloading the contraband, during the course of which further interesting bottles were unearthed, Petronella declared that they must all have a thorough clean-up before going off to Brown's for that much longed-for delicious meal, which had been the talk of the journey for at least a week en route.

"We can't go to Brown's smelling like goats!" Petronella was emphatic. "A hot shower, followed by a sheep-drench of some suitably delicious smell from my scent archives in the bathroom, and away we go."

"Mine's Chanel No. 5," said Bruce MacGregor with a leer, performing an instant balletic pirouette with breathtaking art.

Laughing, they departed upstairs for the ablutions.

Ah, well, normality had returned to St. Julie's Road. Life would now resume its usual pattern.

The students were so refreshingly carefree in their attitudes. Life was fun, and they communicated a warmth and happiness which made one feel good. They simply refused to be weighed down with life's problems, and yet they were totally responsible. Very touching.

Joy then made her final arrangements for the Vienna trip and Mrs. Badger agreed to feed the cats. Petronella was such a delightful scatterbrain that it would have been quite futile to ask her to do it.

Michael Walters was persuaded to keep an eye on the greenhouse and water the allotment brassicas, for after the recent dry spell they were looking rather limp.

Michael had commented that it was a curious fact that England could not survive for any length of time without a liberal dousing of rain. Other countries could manage without for years, quite literally, and yet any dry spell longer than a fortnight, and we were practically in drought. Very strange!

So a few days later, on a crystal-clear morning, Joy boarded a flight for Vienna.

The aircraft took off towards the west and as it banked steeply and turned south, for a brief moment she caught a glimpse in the distance of the Thames valley and the verdant hills towards Henley and Oxford. She thought of her brother's lovely half-timbered mediaeval manor-house nestling peacefully in the Berkshire Downs beyond, and felt a sudden curious pang of regret at leaving.

However, this feeling was soon dissipated as the aircraft crossed England's coastline. The channel below was a glorious deep-green and the surf creamed gently on the golden sands at the shore. Europe lay sprawled invitingly in the distance.

From the description of the manuscript she was going to examine, it sounded as though it might just conceivably be an unknown Heinrich Schutz. It was a long shot, but what an exciting possibility!

Such extraordinary style; such marvellous music! She settled down happily for the flight in anticipation of great things and the delights of Vienna, that most evocative city.

CHAPTER V

'Drop, drop, slow tears...'

First strain of song 46

Orlando Gibbons 1583 – 1625

Two days later, and still no rain. Michael eyed the cloudless skies and decided that now was the time to do the allotment watering.

And it was a pleasant chore. A quiet walk along Aristotle Lane on another golden evening, preceded by a quiet pint at the Jolly Sailors, outside on the terrace.

Swallows and swifts darted urgently overhead, weaving fantastic aerial patterns as they fed on the wing, building up strength for the long flight south to Africa which would begin quite soon. Such astonishing speed, while uttering their shrill, high call, and so inspiring to watch.

Another riotous football match was in progress on the recreation ground. Two language schools were playing in the grand finale - the last match of their term, and the wonderful antics of both footballers and exuberant spectators were a delight to see. Dancing Brazilians in affectionate embrace wove happily along the touch-line. Serious Arabs, jubilant Iraqis and volatile Latins of all varieties, a multitude of tongues in happy chorus, cheered on their teams.

Michael walked on, crossing the railway bridge, then paused to survey the pastoral scene, the meadow, the river, Binsey and the hill beyond. Looking over the dumps, he noticed a wisp of smoke from a camp-fire in the undergrowth: old one-legged Willy and his friends setting up home for the night, with plastic sheeting draped over the low bushes, making an effective tent for the overnight stop.

Two or three dogs ran snuffling around the immediate periphery of this dwelling, led by Dick Ballard's Hugo, the master rabbiter. He appeared to be hot on the scent of something really worth catching.

Dick stood amiably chatting with the men sitting around the camp-fire. He had his bag over his shoulder. Evidently there must be some game worth pursuing over towards Binsey, for he was pointing towards the Perch and clearly, by his gestures, whatever it was over there was a big one!

The men nodded enthusiastically as they passed round the cider bottle. Perhaps Dick would bring them back a rabbit or a duck for their stew-pot; this was wedged on the fire and steaming gently. They sat round it in a ring, forming a picture of almost primaeval poverty, but at least they had a plentiful supply of fresh vegetables purloined from the allotments a few yards away!

It was indeed a lovely evening, marred only by a few mosquitoes, the giant Port Meadow variety and a unique species. Tough Australians had blanched at the sight, declaring that

Oxford's mosquitoes rivalled any of their own native champion' varieties, not only for size, but for viciousness too.

Professor Pyper had in fact declared Oxford to be a swamp quite soon after his arrival in St. Julie's Road, and this was regarded by indigenous Oxonians as informed opinion, for was he not after all a most eminent naturalist? He also sported several honourable battle-scars from his encounters with these fiendish insects on the meadow, as if to prove his point!

Michael walked on thoughtfully through the Trap top gate, proceeding up the broad green centre-path towards Joy's allotment. There he found Percy Chadlow bending lovingly over his prize pumpkin, offering it tender words of encouragement.

"If 'e don't win at Wolvercote Show," he said, "Oi'll walk to Carfax tower!"

He straightened his back and looked at the western sky. Then he lit his pipe and puffed slowly with deep enjoyment.

"Well now, soon be St. Goiles' Fair come September and the noights be already drawin' in again!"

They stood together in peaceful silence, each man thinking his own thoughts in the stillness of the evening.

Eventually Michael said he'd better be getting along to water the thirsty brassicas before dark.

"Water-table's very low," said Percy. "Nip down to my well over yonder if you don't 'ave no luck. Oi've got a a pump an' a water-butt alongside. Just pump up the water to fill 'er up

again when you've done. Save you 'aulin' up from the well. They goes very deep, you know.

'Tis a back-breaker pullin' up a bucket on ten foot o' rope boy'.

Michael found Joy's well down by the gate to the meadow.

He took off the top and looked into the darkness below. There was something a little chilling about looking down a well, a curious feeling of the ancient and unknown, with the dank, cold smell of enclosed earth and water, set in ancient stone.

He saw nothing.

Normally, one would see one's face reflected back, which would give some idea of the depth, but it was getting towards dusk, so it was impossible to judge the water-level by visual means.

He found the bucket, with its attached clothes-line knotted at intervals of a foot or so, and dropped it down the well to the length of ten notches and waited for the splash.

However, there was simply a dull thud as it landed on something solid. "Drat," he said, then hauled up the bucket and tried again, with the same result.

He peered down into the darkness. No, nothing to see at all. Either it was dry, or there was rubbish or something down there. He gave up and went along to Percy's well.

Water weighed very heavy indeed when carried for more than a few yards or so. It took about twenty buckets to do the job properly and Michael mumbled a few private oaths into his beard.

Percy said he would scoop out the other well in the morning. "Probably full o' muck an' sludge, Oi expect," he declared. "But not to worry. There's always a chance o' foindin' a bit o' treasure trove round these 'ere parts. The Romans an' such was very fond of 'oidin' their valuables down wells. Didn't 'ave no banks - an' 'twas the safest place in them days, Oi suppose. Best stuff ever found 'ereabouts - Roman silver dishes t'was - come up out of a well bein' dredged up at where-is-it, Oi believe." He pointed south towards the Berkshire Downs in the distance to indicate "here-is-it."

"The feller wot got it out got thousands o' pounds treasure-trove 'e did. Bought 'isself a lovely little small 'olding wi' the money. Oi could just do wi' that meself!"

Michael gave him thumbs-up, wished him all good luck, and departed gratefully to the Jolly Sailors, whose lights twinkled invitingly over Aristotle Bridge.

There was of course some foundation for Percy's optimistic speculations. After the sack of Rome, those who left these islands, temporarily, as they may have thought, to defend their distant homeland, did not necessarily return to Britain, and such precious things as they might have buried provisionally in the ground for security until their expected return still lie largely undiscovered; as was also the case with subsequent orders of society, particularly during the dark ages, when much marauding took place in Britain and the only secure hiding-place would have been a secret hole in the ground.

The following morning, bright and early in the dew, Percy took his scoop, which in appearance was rather like a gigantic soup-ladle and removed the top of Joy Hetherington's well. He peered hard down into the depths but saw nothing, and therefore concluded that it must be thoroughly silted up.

Tina, his little Jack Russell terrier, having - as was her usual ritual - dug up a potato, was running up and down the path with it in her mouth, pretending it was a rat. She killed it several times, tossed it in the air, and then chewed at it viciously, growling menacingly as she did so.

Carefully lowering his scoop, Percy felt a soft thud as it hit something solid, a few feet down the well.

He poked around a bit to see what he could dredge up, drew out the scoop and found that it contained nothing: no water, no silt, no debris.

"Damned thing," he muttered, and hanging over the side as far as he could safely do without falling in head first, concentrated hard until his eyes became accustomed to the darkness below.

After a few moments he did see something.

It was a face - a still, waxen face, And it was not a reflection of himself. It was the face of a young man: so silent, so motionless - so dead.

"Chroist Church!" said Percy, and nearly fell forward to join the face in the well. His feet left the ground for a moment with shock, but he held on and recovered his balance, dropping his scoop on to the dead body below.

"God Almoighty!"

Percy was well-used to death and disaster, for he had seen a great deal of it in his lifetime, having fought in some of the great campaigns as a young man with the Desert Rats.

Even so, he was quite transfixed for several moments by the horrific sight below.

Tina whimpered at his feet, sensing that something was wrong. Looking up, she turned her little head from side to side in deep concern. Percy looked down.

"All roight, old gal," he said. "Take it easy now; worse things 'appen at sea."

He leaned again over the side of the well. There was an ominous creak as the superstructure took the strain of his weight. He was a tall, well-built man and for his years was "as fit as a flea," as he had said of himself many a time.

Looking down into the dark hole once more, he saw the face more clearly this time. The head and shoulders were just below the water-line - hence the thud and no splash.

Percy took his gas-lighter and flicked it on to high flame, bending down again over the edge of the well.

The flaring light illuminated the ghastly scene and gave it a yet more eerie effect, imparting an illusion of movement to the corpse, which appeared to twitch slightly in the irregular light of the flame.

It was an optical illusion, of course. He was quite dead.

"Poor sod," breathed Percy. "'Ow in God's name did you end up down yonder? Wot a terrible way to go!"

He looked more closely at the face. No, he didn't know this lad at all - never seen him before - at least, not that he remembered. But then they all looked the same, these students, or whatever.

Nice-looking lad, even in the solemnity of death, lying there in the water; long, dark hair and an aristocratic kind of a face, with a long nose, but rather swollen up from lying in the water.

"Wot a waste," he thought out loud, Wot a waste of a loikely lad!"

Tina growled and picked up her potato. She'd had enough of this tedious business, so running off down the path, she tossed her potato high in the air, yapping expectantly at Percy to come on and give chase.

"All roight, gal, let's go an' get the bobbies to fish out this poor owd lad."

He reverently put the top back on the well and stood silent for a moment. It wouldn't be right to leave the body uncovered - wide open for the world to see.

It never entered his head at all that this young man might possibly have been murdered. He didn't even give it a thought, for there had been many a death over the meadow, some accidental - drugs overdoses, suicides, and other kinds of end, including people who occasionally fell down wells, so the other possibility did not so much as cross his mind - that there might have been foul play in this instance.

But that was a queer thing now! Wotever was 'e doing at Miss' Hetherington's well? E didn't 'ave an allotment, so wot was 'e after?

Percy called the police and told them all he knew; which was not a great deal, except that Miss Hetherington was apparently away, but perhaps Mr. Walters might be able to offer more information on the matter. He then left them to their gruesome task of recovering the body.

Walking away, he heard a voice say in the distance:"I know this lad. He's been sleeping rough over the dumps with old Willy and his mates. Magic mushrooms were his speciality, I recall. Name of Cledwyn - quite a character this boy!"

"Come on Tina, let's dig them spuds," said Percy, not taking in the significance of what the policeman had said, being rather deaf.

Percy threw Tina's personal potato high in the air and she deftly caught it with an acrobatic, twisting leap off the ground. Clever little dog, and so beautiful, too. Percy's pride and

joy, and a perfect specimen of her breed.

"Wot on earth was 'e doin' up yonder at the well, Tina? One thing, for certain, old gal, 'e won't be tellin', that's for sure."

Percy bent his back to the task in hand. It was a perfect day for digging potatoes: shimmering blue sky and a fresh breeze - should dry them off beautifully in no time. Get 'em sacked up boi evenin', no trouble.

It was a long time before the body was taken away. Percy had dug five pole of potatoes before the quiet cortege finally moved off through the top gate.

"Wot do you think to it, then?" he called to the last of the departing policemen.

The policeman shrugged his shoulders.

"Hard to say, really. Poor old lad. He was known to us as a vagrant, and he tinkered around with drugs, apparently. But we shan't know much more until they've examined him properly. No signs of violence, anyway."

He waved goodbye and Percy surveyed his potatoes drying nicely in the sun.

"Tis a quare old loif, Tina, gal," he said to his little dog. She wagged her stub of a tail expectantly, looking up at him with her head tilted to one side.

"Blow this for a game o' soldiers - let's go an' 'ave a jar at the pub, old gal, whoile they spuds droies off a bit."

At the bottom gate by the level crossing he noticed a small transparent plastic bag full of small toadstools and compost lying in the long grass. He thought no more about it and walked on, Tina running resolutely on ahead, with the potato firmly clenched in her teeth.

CHAPTER VI

'Weep, weep, mine eyes, my heart can take no rest.'

The Second Set of Madrigals to 3, 4, 5 and 6 parts

John Wilbye 1609

Michael was staggered at the woeful news, which was related to him by a young policeman who came to see him at the Office.

Being at the time quite snowed under with rather complex paperwork, the very last thing he needed was this unhappy distraction: howbeit, the Oxford police, so well known for their relaxed and gentlemanly attitude, made the encounter rather less unpleasant.

Michael was very sad about the pitiful end of Cledwyn as he told the policeman in a general statement about the matter. Drugs: the anguish of our times. The destruction of personality, the sordid life-style, the abusive and violent behaviour of the unfortunate addicts, the sorrows of their families, and finally, perhaps, at the personal level, the ultimate sorrow for this poor lad - such a waste of a life. Michael spoke of all these things in a kind of sad soliloquy. A young man of great potential with nobody to guide him in life and see to his basic needs. That was Cledwyn - a boat without a rudder, and his final tragedy, an ignominious death.

With regard to information about Cledwyn's movements and his associates, Michael knew very little. He had been a casual customer at the Jolly Sailors, sometimes with a girlfriend, but mostly alone. He roamed the meadow a great deal, apparently, and had befriended Joy Hetherington not long back. She had intimated that she was very concerned for his welfare as he appeared to be living rough somewhere round the dumps, and was resolved to help him in some way before winter set in. She would no doubt be deeply shocked at Cledwyn's death and the manner of his going, when she got news of it, and particularly about the well. The whole thing was completely bizarre. There were, after all, two or three others on the allotments, so why choose hers to get drowned in? If, indeed, drowning should prove to be the cause of death when the post-mortem results were made known.

Michael commented that he had intended to have a chat with Inspector Vardon about some rather odd things which had been happening to Joy Hetherington, but hadn't yet got round to it. He just wondered if there was some connection with this curious business. He sketched in as briefly as possible the background of the strange events in and around St. Julie's Road. The policeman smiled discreetly at the incident of the theft of the underwear from the washing-line.

"Sounds a bit like a student prank at first hearing, doesn't it?" he said.

After he had gone Michael turned round in his chair and gazed thoughtfully at St. Giles' church tower. Oxford had always been known for its weird and wonderful goings-on, but frankly he felt uneasy about the situation at St. Julie's Road. There was something very unpleasant about it.

Joy Hetherington was, without a doubt, a scatterbrain in some respects, slightly eccentric too, perhaps, but Michael was fairly convinced of the authenticity of her story. She was a practical woman in many ways and would not, he felt sure, ever have left the gas-stove on and the paraffin close by like that. And now there was the affair of Cledwyn. No: it all smacked of something nasty.

He resolved to contact Inspector Vardon immediately.

Petronella, meanwhile, was settling down happily once again to the Oxford routine. It was fortuitous that Joy was away, because that meant, of course, that one could throw a party or two at the house without being a bother to anyone.

She was quite alone for a while and this was a great luxury in itself after the cramped conditions on the dig, not to speak of the incredible journey! It was fun to be with the crowd but it was a marvellous thing now to extend oneself in simple ways like wandering quietly round the house and garden in a dressing-gown and having breakfast on the terrace alone (except for the cats!) with the Times to read. Simple pleasures, but so relaxing.

Then to do one's washing in the Hoovermatic and hang it all out on the line - so nice to see it all bleaching in the morning sun and blowing gently in the breeze. Ah well! There was no doubt a housewife lurking inside all of us somewhere, just waiting to get out.

Petronella had also dealt with Bruce's jeans, which had been absolute agony to get clean. Really, he seemed to spend his whole life sitting in puddles of black engine oil! Quite awful! He was very lovable but absolutely incorrigible. Perhaps Australia would knock off some of the corners. Time and the bush would tell, no doubt.

Next morning Petronella awoke refreshed. She had unwound. Bruce's jeans were reasonably clean; her own washing was nicely sun-bleached and dry, and the cats were all quite happy to have her back, sitting around the garden in comforting attitudes, up the apple tree, on walls and window-sills, all smiling blandly in approbation. Now it was time to get things together about the work done in Greece. Petronella made her plans.

First, a good day's hard slog to get some of the paper-work sorted out. Then she must think about a party! After all, Bruce would shortly be off to Australia.

Perhaps a buffet supper and - weather permitting - a disco on the back lawn? Fancy-dress party, of course, with a prize for the best - a nice bottle of wine, or something. She had better make sure to pack up at midnight, knowing North Oxford. The very thought of Erica Trondheim throwing a fit about noise and things was enough to make one expire! Really, what was the matter with the silly woman?

Petronella rang round and everybody was enthusiastic. Day after tomorrow? Fine! About 7.30? Great! Bring a bottle? Excellent! She totted up the figures. Say about 30 people in all. No trouble there. But the food! Oh dear, that would be an expensive item!

However, come to think of it, Joy had said that Petronella must take anything from the allotment if she needed it, as courgettes and other things should be harvested if they were to come on again afterwards. So, that was it - an enormous ratatouille! A couple of roots of potatoes for a gargantuan salad, with hard-boiled eggs and things tossed in Hellman's mayonnaise. There was plenty of fresh garlic in the kitchen and masses of onions and tomatoes on the allotment, and green peppers, too, as a matter of fact, so with a few anchovies, mushrooms, capers and things, plus paprika, black pepper, lemon juice, etc. - there it was: magic! And yes, fresh herbs from the garden, too. No trouble at all. Voila! We have a feast!

Petronella sat and wrote her definitive list of things for the party and to her delight found that she would only need to buy about four items from the shops. All the rest would be free from the allotment or the garden. On reflection, Prof. H. was not such a bad old stick after all. She had her moments. A fuddy-duddy in many ways, but kind and generous in practical things.

The archaeological work went very well indeed. The jigsaw would eventually fit nicely together and Petronella was quietly confident that she might even ultimately pull off a decent D.Phil, into the bargain, with any luck!

Better go over to the allotments before dusk and get the vegetables for the party. She eyed the western sky apprehensively whilst preparing to go. Even as she watched, menacing purple-black clouds obscured the sun in a frantic scurry. A blustering wind sprang up without warning, hastening their advance. By the look of things, Petronella was in for a soaking. Damn! The only feasible time to go over to Trap ground was the present. The following morning would be too late. There was far too much to be done in preparation for the party. The locking-away of all Joy's precious bits and pieces alone would take an age, for example. There was so much: the collection of a life-time. Quantities of fine Staffordshire pottery (oh dear, why was it so ugly? or perhaps gauche, or even primitive were better words to describe it?) Particularly appealing but yet so crude, was the Robert Burns dark blue-glaze figure on the drawing-room mantelpiece. Compared with the sophistication of eighteenth century Bow or Chelsea, or any fine pottery of that age, Staffordshire was cartoon-like in style, somehow, with no refinement at all, one might say, and yet a kind of beauty in its very crudeness, like the people who made it, the doughty people of Staffordshire, basic, solid, rough, even, with no nonsense, but nevertheless lovely.

Ah yes, better lock away the Edinburgh crystal glasses, too, for safety, and those two family miniatures - just the sort of thing which might disappear during a party!

Oh no! She looked out of the window. The storm had begun with a violent squall. The lime trees; in St. Julie's Road blew wildly, lashing their branches back and forth in the wind and rain. The sky darkened rapidly. Petronella shivered with apprehension. There was nothing else for it. She must go at once to the allotments. The weather was evidently setting in for the night by the look of things, for the sky showed that there was worse to follow. Better dress accordingly. Joy's ancient waterproofs would be the best thing.

Going to the Victorian coat-rack in the front hall, Petronella selected her attire. One of Joy's awful old tweed hats, a long cape and a large pair of Wellingtons - not forgetting three or four plastic bags and a cutting-knife.

Thus arrayed, she went off reluctantly down St. Julie's Road, crossing Aristotle Bridge in the driving rain. There was not a soul about.

Petronella trudged on. She felt rather like something out of a Count Dracula film as the wind gusted and blew the cape in dramatic swirls around her. What a nuisance the boys were not around. They seemed to have the knack of not appearing at times like this when they were really needed!

She passed through Trap bottom gate and squelched along the lane towards the stables. Everything was blowing wildly, bushes and trees straining, sheds rattling. All seemed animated eerily at the height of the storm. A sudden spasm of fear shot through her very being. Quite unaccountable! She stopped involuntarily. How stupid! Go on, Petronella! Gathering herself together, she walked on. Stopping at the gate to the level-crossing, she looked back. There was nobody to be seen; only the driving wind and rain lashing everything into a wild frenzy.

The storm would soon abate, however, for a blinding flash of golden light cut underneath the black clouds in the western sky, heralding the end of it. Another fifteen minutes or so, and It would all be over.

"Crack."

A bullet passed an inch from Petronella's left ear with a deafening high-pitched whistle, and sped on to infinity over the level-crossing behind her.

The shot came from a position in the thicket on the dumps and very close at hand.

This was a moment she was to remember with crystal clarity for the rest of her life; for she had been kissed in an instant by death, and then let go.

"Hey, man, what's going on?"

A voice shouted urgently from the railway bridge over the line. Three heads appeared simultaneously over the high parapet. At that very moment, the rain ceased and the wind dropped.

Petronella could not speak. She looked up with her mouth open. No words came.

"Get down! Get down! Somebody's shootin' at ye!" shouted the voice. "Hold on - we're coming down!"

Petronella crouched down low as bidden, behind the cover of some blackberry bushes, as the voice from the bridge continued, addressing the unseen marksman in ringing stentorian tones.

"Right, now, you miserable hound, why don't you go and shoot yourself and do us all a favour? We're coming to get you - you trigger-happy Sassenach!"

A red-headed figure in a blue tracksuit, leapt, commando-style, over the fence at the end of the bridge and slid at speed down the steep bank, followed by two other figures in similar garb. He ran towards Petronella.

It was Bruce, accompanied by two friends. He uttered a deafening warlike Scottish whoop as he approached, shouting further words of withering discouragement at the felonious person hidden in the dumps.

"Stay down," he whispered with great urgency. He crouched down alongside Petronella and was swiftly joined by the other two.

"Petronella! I thought it was you, somehow! That murderous idiot shot directly at you from close range. He meant to get you! That's no hunter after rabbits!"

They all crouched in a huddle behind the dense cover of the blackberry bushes by the gate.

Petronella was so shocked that she was still quite unable to speak, but simply shivered miserably, her head on Bruce's shoulder.

"Keep still, everyone. Look and listen," whispered Bruce. For what seemed an age, they crouched motionless, watching for some tell-tale movement within the dumps.

There was none.

The Worcester express roared past a few feet from them. The driver sounded its klaxon several times as he saw them huddled together by the line, and looking up, they caught a fleeting glimpse of his face as he looked down in concern for a second from his high cab, way above them.

Bruce, telling them all to stay put, climbed back up to the bridge again to make a quick survey of the dumps from that high vantage-point. He spent several minutes looking out over the whole area, and then quickly descended the steep bank again like a mountain goat, in deft skips and jumps.

"Not a sign of the miserable skunk: he's scarpered," he announced angrily. "Let's go down to the pub and ring the police."

Petronella, by now recovering from the shock of this truly bad experience, talked about it as they walked back together. Curiously enough, her first concern was for the party catering. That was most certainly the end of the exotic ratatouille and potato salad for the morrow; no doubt about that. It would have to be simply cheese and things. Under no circumstances whatsoever was she going back alone over to the allotments ever again. She had often heard the legend about the whole area being spooky and from now on as far as she was concerned, it was probably true. It was weird. She just wasn't going back, and that was that and all about it; certainly not alone, anyway.

Walking back along the lane together, they reflected upon the incident.

"For myself, I have the distinct conviction that someone really did take a deliberate potshot at me. It just came out of the blue, totally unexpected - quite terrifying!" Petronella shuddered. "The noise was astonishing. Just like the Concorde passing your ear, and accompanied by a kind of swishing sound. I didn't realize at first, but when I did, I was petrified!"

"Aye," Bruce said, "That shows just how close it was. It must have missed you by a whisker, no more. That was no poacher after rabbits, as I said before - and it was not random shooting by a novice either - of that, I am quite certain. What's more, it wasn't a shotgun; it was a rifle - and a powerful one at that. One single shot; nothing before, nothing after! He meant business!"

Petronella was aghast.

"But who would want to kill me? And how did they know it was me anyway - all muffled up in those dreadful old waterproofs of Prof. Hetherington's?"

"That's a point," commented one of Bruce's companions thoughtfully. "All we heard was one hell of a sharp crack below us as we ran up to the top of the bridge and saw you down by the gate all alone, standing like a stuffed duck, if you'll pardon the expression. It was obviously a pretty near thing."

Bruce smiled ruefully and gave Petronella a reassuring hug. The walked on amicably in silence. The setting sun blazed a golden farewell to the city as it sank behind the dark mass of Wytham Hill.

"D' ye ken what I think?" Bruce stopped on top of Aristotle Bridge, turned and looked at the sun as it slowly disappeared in a Turneresque display of crimson and orange, with a sky of

palest green behind. I believe our unfriendly sharp-shooter thought you were Joy Hetherington. Somebody must want to rub out the old girl for some reason. That's my honest opinion, for what it's worth."

"Oh Bruce - come on! The poor thing! She's just a nice, well-meaning old don, bumbling along happily doing her thing in mediaeval music. Who could possibly want to harm her? It's ludicrous."

"I dinna ken," said Bruce, "But I'd take a bet on it."

They rang the police from the pub, drank a welcome bitter-shandy and waited for the patrol car, which appeared in due course. Two young policewomen stepped out of it and Bruce, declaring this to be his lucky day in a quick aside to the others, went across to explain the matter to them. They were friendly, listened attentively and inspected the area where the shooting took place. Of course, they said, no shooting was authorized on the dumps by the college, but inevitably there were fairly regular reports of such things happening. It was mostly youths with air rifles, after rabbits and so forth; indeed, recently there had been reports of extensive poaching of swans on the river, and police patrols were in operation, but with such a large area to cover, it was difficult to keep a comprehensive surveillance.

Vandals, inevitably, were numerous. However, a special watch would be kept for a while around the dumps for any further shooting.

Over a soothing game of bar-billiards, Bruce said how ironical it was practically to get one's head blown-off without warning, and yet there was very little that could be done to prevent it in the final analysis. He commented that it could only happen in Oxford.

Petronella agreed vigorously. It would be a long time before the sound of that startling crack and deafening whistle were to dim in her memory.

Michael Walters, standing at the bar with Peter Rumbold and overhearing the conversation, raised his eyebrows but said nothing.

Peter, interpreting the message, shrugged his shoulders, drank up and departed with a cheery wave.

"Must get on to Vardon about this business," thought Michael. Time was the problem. So much to do that it was hard to fit things in. But it really must be done. The whole thing was getting decidedly silly. Somebody definitely had it in for Joy Hetherington. Why? It was very curious and definitely unpleasant.

Petronella's party was a riot. Dozens of people came, bringing drink in abundance. No one seemed to care much at all that there was no exotic food as planned. Bread, cheese and pickles, and a couple of large quiches, which Petronella had made in the afternoon, went down very well. Inspecting the arriving bottles, Bruce decided that he would knock up his amazing "Mickey Mouse punch," as he called it. This mysterious beverage consisted of one bottle of everything in sight, including - sacrilege! two bottles of Joy Hetherington's homemade elderberry wine, which was several years old, a bottle of her beetroot port and a variety of things from canisters and storage jars in the kitchen storecupboard sprinkled liberally on top of the liquid.

Petronella watched uneasily as she perceived dried yeast, mixed spice, ginger, candied peel, powdered nutmeg, glace cherries and the like casually thrown into the cordial without any attempt at all to measure the amounts.

She said "Ugh!" with distaste as a pint of bottled Guinness was poured in. Already the colour of ox-blood boot polish, the liquid slowly turned into a turgid sludge rather reminiscent of Thames estuary mud - Leigh-on-Sea at low tide, for instance. It smelt rather like it, too.

"Bruce! That's disgusting. It looks quite evil. I'm certainly not going to drink any. No! For God's sake don't put that in!"

Petronella snatched a carton of paprika from his hand as he held it thoughtfully poised ready to sprinkle into his strange concoction.

He picked up the garlic powder speculatively. She took it quickly from him and slammed the cupboard door, standing defensively against it.

"No, Bruce. I suppose you'll be putting curry powder in next."

He picked up the tea-pot, shook it and found it to be half-full of cold tea. He poured it into the punch with a flourish.

"Fantastic," he declared with rapture, on tasting the mixture: "But I do think the colour could do with a little improvement."

He searched the cupboard at length and eventually found a tin of black treacle.

"Oh no!" said Petronella with horror, "Not that, Bruce. It'll taste absolutely vile!"

She tried in vain to get the tin off him, but he would not be deterred. He poured in a large quantity and stirred it vigorously with a wooden spoon. After a short while, the mixture began to bubble and froth like a witch's cauldron. It looked simply dreadful and turned quite black and nasty, like flat Guinness.

"Perfect," he announced, with an air of great satisfaction, tasting it with relish. "Come on, have some, lassie!"

"Not likely," said Petronella. 'What are you doing, Bruce? Just come out of there!"

He had dived literally head first into the, deepfreeze. After rummaging around for some time, he emerged triumphant-with a half-gallon container of vanilla ice-cream.

"Voila!" He declared.

"You can't have that, Bruce! Put it back at once - it's not mine! What on earth do you want it for, anyway?"

"Och, away, lassie! It's an essential ingredient, and the old girl will never miss it in any event!"

Petronella threw up her hands in despair and followed him, resigned, as he bore his awful punch and the ice-cream upstairs to the party. People were arriving in droves, and the drawing-room was by now quite full. Most were in fancy dress and there was much laughter over some of the costumes, which were, to say the least, inventive.

"Let me assist you in your task young fellow," said a convincing Sherlock Holmes, accompanied by a tubby Dr. Watson in Derby bowler and tweed jacket with plus-fours.

Sherlock Holmes solemnly assisted with the setting-up of the punch bowl and ice-cream. He looked very good with deerstalker and meerschaum pipe, which was lit and going well. Clouds of blue smoke filled the air with a delicious aroma.

"What's in it, my dear chap?" he asked engagingly, between puffs. "Arsenic! Looks absolutely disgusting! Do we drink it - or polish the floor with it, old man?"

Dr. Watson tentatively sniffed the foaming liquid with suspicion. He - or rather, she - for it was in fact a girl in quite effective disguise, polished her monocle and adjusted her walrus moustache, declaring that nobody in his right mind would touch it if he wished to survive the evening.

Count Dracula also inspected it and announced with a vulpine leer, that he would personally be quite happy to drink the beverage in the regrettable absence of any good fresh Christian blood. It would make a reasonably good substitute, judging from its appearance and smell.

Lord Nelson approached, examined it, telescope to his blind eye, and murmured dubiously, "England expects" etc., "Splice the mainbrace" and "Any port in a storm."

Bruce was undeterred and solemnly got on with the business of serving his punch. He filled 30 glasses about two-thirds full of the concoction, and then carefully floated a large spoonful of ice-cream on top of each one. After a moment, the drink took on the appearance of Irish coffee.

Batman was the first to sample the drink. He picked up a glass declaring, "Death or glory! Stars and stripes for ever!" and took a mighty swig. Robin, supporting him with great concern, exclaimed "Holy cow!"

"Well?" asked Petronella, "What's it like? Will you live?"

There was a moment's silence as Batman absorbed the alcoholic shock-waves.

"Absolutely astonishing! It's magic! What an amazing drink! It tastes just like..."

"San Izal?" asked Robin.

"No indeed, my dear fellow," said Sherlock Holmes, thoughtfully sampling the remarkable brew, then holding his glass to the light, "Strega with Pernod. It's superb!"

Thereafter the party took wings and Petronella, though suspicious to the last, eventually tried some and found it not only quite delicious, but also highly intoxicating: to which fact a thumping headache the next day bore infallible witness.

Several of the men had come in drag, and created riotous diversions with their outrageously funny attempts at feminine behaviour. Their disguise was so complete that two or three of them were quite unrecognizable and there were vain attempts to get their wigs off to find out who they really were. Their girl-friends had done a fine job with their make-up, which was so good that no one at all guessed correctly who was who. They staged a most effective handbag-fight during the dancing on the lawn in the back-garden, ending up in a tangled heap on the ground, muscular legs in fishnet tights and high-heels flailing the air, bottoms up!

This was altogether too much for Erica Trondheim, who put in one of her rare appearances to shake a fist over the garden-wall, shouting hysterically that the whole world had apparently gone completely mad, and were there no sane people at all left in Oxford? Was she herself the only one?

As this outburst was completely ignored by the assembled company, entirely absorbed in the riotous goings-on in the garden, Erica - by now in a frenzy of rage - began to throw rotten apples at the bodies writhing on the lawn.

"Stop! Stop at once or I call the police!" she screamed.

With that, there was complete disorder, with everybody joining in the mock fight. Several people were quite dramatically strangled, and died beautiful deaths on the lawn. Some, actually coming back to life for a short time, staggered about uttering appalling groans and died again. The death-throes were remarkable to see. Finally, Count Dracula swept menacingly towards Erica, arms raised, cloak swirling, fangs revealed ready for the kiss of death. He made strange blood-curdling noises as he approached.

She fled with a scream and did not return.

"Well, that's got rid of her!" said Bruce with satisfaction. "The miserable old crow, do you know, I don't believe that daft old biddy has ever laughed in the whole of her life?"

"Quite, quite mad," observed Sherlock Holmes, puffing gently at his pipe. "What do you say, Watson, old chap?"

Thumbs in her waistcoat, Dr. Watson nodded sagely: "Nothing a good man couldn't cure," she said, completely forgetting her role.

It took only a very short time for anyone who had drunk more that two glasses of Bruce's punch to get exceedingly merry, and thus the party became progressively livelier. As midnight approached, Petronella was increasingly uneasy about the neighbours' reactions to the noise, meaning the reasonable people in St. Julie's Road, not, of course, Erica Trondheim. She therefore sought out Sherlock Holmes and got him to organize the fancy dress competition to wind up the evening.

Someone had brought a splendid bottle of Moet et Chandon, which she had contrived to abstract from the incoming bottle-donations, and this would make an excellent first prize, and her own Niersteiner Domthal would be a reasonable second prize, with a small box of chocolates to accompany each. She even managed to rustle up a third prize, a large box of chocolate nuts, which had been a gift to her and of which she was not over-fond, so this seemed a fairly adequate selection of prizes.

The costumes were all extraordinarily good and some of them extremely funny. Even Bruce, who normally scorned such frivolities, had eventually conceded, and having raided Joy Hetherington's wardrobe, had found a kilt and presented himself as Rob Roy MacGregor. A kitchen knife in his sock served as a dirk and a travelling rug he had unearthed upstairs did duty as a plaid, the result being quite effective, even though the tartans were all wrong (Hunting Stewart travelling rug and Black Watch kilt!). He looked splendid, with his flaming red hair and cobalt blue eyes.

The first prize went by unanimous consent, to a hefty giant, a rugger blue well over six feet tall and enormously broad, who came dressed as a baby. He was clad from head to foot in a yellow track-suit with the hood up. A huge home-made dummy and a very large teddy-bear added the final touches and the effect, though so simple, was very funny indeed.

The second prize had to go to either Batman and Robin or to that redoubtable pair, Sherlock Holmes and Dr. Watson. Each duo had gone to such lengths to get their costumes exact in every detail that it was hard to choose between them.

Sherlock Holmes was perfection in dress and personality and Dr. Watson, in reality a pretty and curvaceous blonde, was immaculately attired and convincingly padded round the middle. Across this paunch, over the waistcoat, was festooned a handsome gold chain with a splendid fob-watch, which she consulted frequently. Her incredibly realistic walrus moustache, which had the unfortunate habit of tilting to one side and wobbling violently as she spoke, in spite of a stiff upper lip, had the assembled company in constant fits of laughter.

However, Batman and Robin took second prize in the end for sheer ingenuity, as they had devised their effective costumes from the simplest materials. Batman's hose consisted of two pairs of his girl-friend's stocking-tights, worn one over the other for the sake of opacity, with a pair of ladies' briefs on top, a tight jersey and an old curtain as a cape, ankle-wellies and a toy Batman plastic mask completed the outfit.

Robin was kitted out in the same utilitarian way, and they were an impressive sight as they affected the stylish poses of the famous pair.

As the prizes were presented, a further diversion was engineered by the drag-ladies, who were protesting volubly in high soprano tones that they had not been given a prize and that the whole thing was a fix. They minced about in a convincing fit of feminine tantrums and a further handbag fight ensued during which poor Sherlock Holmes and Batman were practically debagged as a gesture of protest. Things were definitely getting out of hand, so Petronella got the baby to maintain order while she dashed inside to find something with which to placate the irate ladies.

After a quick rummage through her personal toiletries she found a small bottle of scent she didn't like, a can of awful hair-spray and some heavily scented toilet water, and hurried back with these to the garden, just in the nick of time, for a riot was rapidly developing. Sherlock Holmes had nimbly climbed to the top of the old Bramley apple tree to escape, and poor Batman, quite desperate, was cornered by the greenhouse and in immediate danger of losing his briefs. Robin had prudently fled over the garden wall until the skirmish subsided.

Order was restored for a moment or two as the three ladies gracelessly snatched their prizes. There was considerable argument over who should have what, and then they promptly drenched everyone within range with the perfume and sprayed the entire company with some awful hair lacquer.

"Who on earth is the tall one?" asked Petronella. "He's absolutely improbable."

No one knew. He wore the shortest mini-skirt, black fishnet tights and the very highest high heels with ankle-straps, a black lace see-through blouse with a daring padded bra beneath, and a tiny 1930s pill-box hat (with veil) over a long blonde wig. He was a handsome fellow, with a craggy athletic build and fine muscular legs. The whole effect was really rather stunning, for in some curious way he contrived to carry off the feminine image quite convincingly. His make-up had been expertly applied. False eyelashes, elaborate mascara and silver-speckled eyeshadow gave him a highly seductive look, enhanced by a most tasteful touch of silvery-bronze lipstick.

By now, the laughing onlookers had had enough and they wanted revenge. A short skirmish ensued, during which two of the 'ladies' were stripped practically naked. They screamed "Rape!" of course.

However, the tall one was more difficult to catch. Deftly fending off a fine rugger-tackle by Robin, he shinned up a drainpipe and managed to get as high as the first floor. There he hung precariously for several minutes before Bruce had him nicely.

Running upstairs, Bruce threw open the bathroom window and grabbed him neatly round the middle, uttering a wild Scottish whoop of triumph. After a brief struggle, Bruce dragged him through the window. He then carried his captive downstairs over one shoulder, protesting and kicking furiously.

Despite the disparity in size and build, it was clear that Bruce had the upper hand in the matter. He did not hold a Judo brown belt to no purpose. He had a firm lock round the man's waist, and obviously the young man did not like it at all and wriggled wildly, doing his very best to escape. However, he was unceremoniously dumped on the back lawn and stripped like the others.

As the wig came off, Petronella said, "Good Lord, Jasper - it's you!"

Jasper was not pleased at the summary unmasking and managed to make his escape, displaying as he ran off a mixture of petulant anger and embarrassment.

"No sense of humour at all," observed Dr. Watson sorrowfully

"Stupid twit," said Bruce.

"I'm surprised at him - he's normally such an old sobersides" said Petronella. "I would never have thought he would go in for anything outre like drag! I always assumed his only interest in life was the sex-life of the heron, or whatever it is he's working on. He never talks about anything else. He's just so boring with it. "Hidden fires," said Sherlock Holmes, puffing thoughtfully at his meerschaum. "I wonder where he got the clothes. Oxfam? I don't think he bothers much with girl-friends, to go on the borrow."

"Och, forget it," said Bruce, surveying the wreckage of the party, "Let's clear up the mess - and hae a dram!"

"No more drink left." Petronella examined the empty bottles mournfully.

"Oh no?" Bruce winked and produced a flask of whiskey from somewhere under his plaid.

Petronella was quite insistent that she would not now stay alone in the house at night while Joy was still away. She was very nervous, so Bruce, Holmes and Watson all stayed for what was left of the night. It was in any case nearly first light by the time all the debris had been cleared away. However, there was an odd feel to the house in some way, as though someone was watching: it was quite pronounced and Petronella was not at all happy after the events by the railway line.

CHAPTER VII

'Alas, and ay me, ay me...'

from 'Too much I once lamented.'

Songs of 3, 4, 5, and 6 parts Thomas Tomkins 1622

Michael Walters meanwhile had managed to pin down Inspector Vardon and they met at the Royal Oak for the proverbial pint and game of darts. They spent a pleasant hour together and the inspector listened with interest and a flicker of amusement to the story of the curious goings-on. The theft of the directoire knickers from the washing-line was in any event guaranteed to evoke a twinkle of mirth.

Of course, he said, Michael would no doubt appreciate that there was very little comment he could make about the affair. He could only listen to the story of the events and keep them in mind for possible future reference, as it would seem that there was no firm evidence to go on at the moment. It was, however, an interesting tale. It would make quite a good plot for a detective story! The air of mystery, for instance, the untied ends and inconsequential happenings.

As for the other matter, the unfortunate death of Cledwyn, that of course was a different kettle of fish altogether. The body was with the pathologist at present and nothing much could really be said or done yet, except for basic routine enquiries. However, it would be a good idea to talk to Joy Hetherington on her return from Vienna, for the body was, after all, found in her well and she might be able to cast light on the matter in some way. Michael expressed his relief, remarking that he would hate anything unpleasant to happen to the old girl. She was one of Oxford's minor eccentrics. It did most certainly sound a potty kind of story, but he felt uneasy for her, as though some unseen force of ill-will was dogging her.

The inspector smiled and promised to keep an eye on things. The darts had been best out of three for a pint and Inspector Vardon, concentrating, took the last game, finishing with a deft treble sixteen - bullseye.

"A well-earned pint, my dear Inspector," said Michael, fetching the foaming tankard from the bar, "Two to one to you!"

A card from Vienna next morning cheered up Petronella no end.

"Having a wonderful time," it said: "And eating far too much delicious schnitzel. Disappointment over the manuscript. Charming music, but certainly not the work of the Master. Pity! How are the cats? Back on Friday with luck! J."

"O hooray!" thought Petronella, "Thank God for that!" She hadn't seen much of the cats, but they were all alive and kicking around the back-garden, leading their usual sybaritic lives, blind Fred peacefully asleep in the airing-cupboard as always.

Thank goodness, she would at least be able to talk to Joy directly about the nasty experience and find out if there might be some truth in what Bruce had said about it. She must make sure that he stayed with her until Friday. This would also give her an opportunity to get him organized for his departure to Australia. He could bring all his stuff over and she would supervise his packing, making sure he threw out all his rubbish, i.e. old socks and jeans, etc. He had simply no idea - quite impossible! It would be so sad to see him go, but that was Oxford: like a transit camp. She was going to miss him terribly. People came, lived the life of the city with passionate zest, then disappeared. Strange place, really.

She would take him down to the market on Wednesday and get him some T-shirts and socks and a couple of pairs of decent trousers for dressing correctly when socializing. She really must make a list.

Mrs. Badger did the complete song without words about the state of the place when she came to feed the cats. She glared balefully at the washing-up in the kitchen sink as Petronella made coffee for the recumbent forms huddled up on sofas, swathed in blankets. She looked askance at the rubbish sticking out of the kitchen waste-bin, and expressed her disapproval with a loud sniff and a twitch of her aristocratic nose. Inspecting several cardboard boxes full to overflowing with empty bottles of all denominations, she took off her glasses, polished them vigorously, and putting them back carefully on the end of her nose, pushed them up slowly with a forefinger until they arrived at the bridge in the desired position.

"Well, Oi don't know wot the world's a-comin' to, Oi'm sure," she said with an air of complete disdain. "Twas never loike it in moy day, that's for sure!"

Petronella smiled apologetically and forbore to ask what it was that was never like it in Mrs. Badger's day, although she would have been quite interested to know. Instead, she suddenly bethought herself that maybe Mrs. Badger might know something which could cast some light on the mysterious happenings by the railway line.

She made tentative enquiries as they drank coffee together in the kitchen. Mrs. Badger had mellowed somewhat by this time and listened intently to what Petronella had to say, looked over the top of her glasses with a keen eye, nodded and said:

"Tis a quare thing altogether, moy dear. In the first place, Oi was of a mind to think as Miss 'Etherington was a-romancin' over it, but not no more, Oi ain't. Some moighty quare things be goin' on, an' Oi believe as somebody 'ereabouts be up to no good whatsoever!"

"Good gracious!" said Petronella, upon hearing the tale, "What an extraordinary business! Trust Prof. H. to land right in the middle of something weird. Do you know, I've got a curious feeling she's somewhat prone to finding herself in rather odd situations. From what she's told me - just odd little snippets of her experiences, she does seem to have had a most extraordinary life - really most exciting."

"But wot Oi 'aven't told you, moy dear," said Mrs. Badger, leaning forward, "Is -," she paused, to add impact, "That Oi was just now down at the Post Office Stores, an' Percy Chadlow was stood there in the queue, a-tellin' that Mrs. Spragnell as that young drug-addict wi' the long 'air 'as bin found drownded in Miss. 'Etherington's well on the allotments! 'Ow about that then?"

There was an unmistakable note of triumph in her voice as she delivered the verbal coup-de-grace.

"Good grief!" gasped Petronella, "How perfectly frightful, Mrs. B!"

"Well, one thing's for sure," Mrs Badger leaned forward again. "It can't 'a bin as Miss'Etherington 'ad a brainstorm an' shoved 'im in, 'cos she's out o' the country in foreign parts. So, that's Number One. An' Number Two is this: whoy did 'e drown 'isself in 'er well? 'E could 'a chucked 'isself in the canal wi' no trouble at all. 'Tis only twenty yards away, 'an a good lot bigger for jumpin' into. An', look 'ere, moy gal - wot if 'e 'ad' a-got stuck 'alfway down the well an' only got 'is legs wet? 'E could 'a bin dangiin' there for days, an' nobody moight not never 'a knowed a thing about it, loike the Chamber of 'Orrors - entombed! It don't bear a-thinkin' about, do it, gal?"

Petronella, somehow managing to keep a straight face solemnly agreed: "Yes, it does sound all very fishy indeed - sorry-that wasn't in the best of taste, was it?"

By this time, the recumbent forms were stirring and yawns of impending wakefulness arose from beneath the blankets.

Mrs. Badger sniffed in disapproval, but softened slightly as Bruce's tousled red head appeared slowly over the back of the nearest sofa.

"Coffee?" asked Petronella. Bruce groaned and disappeared again under his blankets.

"Oi do 'ope as nothin's got broke," announced Mrs. Badger, glaring at the waking bodies: "T'was never loike it in moy day, loike Oi said afore."

She darted a quick glance around the room and noted the absence of Joy Hetherington's personal priceless artifacts, such as the irreplaceable Staffordshire figure of Robert Burns, so beloved of her great-grandmother, and various other objects.

"No, nothing," said Petronella chastely.

"Well, Oi must be on me boike, as they say 'ereabouts," said Mrs. Badger, snapping her handbag shut with an air of finality. "Now, Oi think as you should get Miss 'Etherington to go down to St. Aldates an' get the police to sort summat out about this business, 'cos Oi don't loike the look of it one little bit, Oi don't! Now don't forget, moy gal, you just get it movin' along, 'cos it ain't roight, it ain't.'"

With that, she departed, turning back in the doorway to wag a monitory forefinger. Petronella frowned, thoughtfully looking out across the gardens to the meadow.

"She's right, yon owd lassie," yawned Bruce, surfacing somewhat painfully. "The whole thing stinks like ..."

"Spare us, dear boy," said Sherlock Holmes, raising himself up gingerly on an elbow from his couch: "No gory details, please!"

"What on earth was in that punch?" enquired Dr. Watson, "I feel terrible!" She really did look quite green.

"Och away, lassie," said Bruce: "It's good for ye; finest black molasses - better than porridge - almost!"

"Ugh!" Petronella shuddered at the memory of it, and particularly at the thought of porridge, which she loathed.

"I suspect we shall have trouble with Erica over last night. There's bound to be a flashback sometime soon. She won't let us get away with it so easily. I rather think there will be a further skirmish. Poor Prof. H. is bound to get a broadside when she gets back from Vienna."

"Och, forget yon stupid old Erica wifey - she's daft," said Bruce, emerging again from his blankets. Petronella was just a little irritated.

"It's all very well for you, Bruce; you don't have to live next door to her. She's quite mad, you know - and thinks nothing of running up and down the road at two in the morning in a see-through nightie when she's in the mood, screaming her head off. The irony is, nobody takes any notice, but it's quite unnerving to witness. Usually she claims it's a man who's been chasing her, or something."

"Wishful thinking?" said Dr. Watson.

"Hmmm, that seems to be a singular quality of this part of North Oxford," said Sherlock Holmes, sipping his coffee.

"There's any amount of peculiar behaviour going on in this really rather respectable area and no matter how outrageous, nobody pays the slightest attention to it. Do you remember that poor crazy girl who used to stand on the corner all night moaning and gazing at the moon? Quite extraordinary. Drugs, I would think. She was a regular fixture, then after about a year, she simply disappeared overnight and was never seen again. Most peculiar!"

Petronella nodded. "Yes, it does seem so sad to think that once upon a time Oxford was full of the most marvellous characters, true eccentrics who were really fun to know and who added lustre to the place. But the terrible tragedy is that nowadays they have been largely replaced by a sordid collection of disreputable creatures who are just drop-outs with a high nuisance-value. It's so very sad. The whole trouble seems to be that Oxford is too tolerant; it always has been - and it's being taken advantage of!"

"Aye," Bruce soliloquized in a quavering voice, "Would this world were such as we: sae sage, sae guid, sae g dy-g dee...!"

"Oh shut up, Bruce! You are a pain!" Petronella smothered him with a pillow. "You know jolly well what I mean. I'm being serious."

Muffled expostulations came from beneath the pillow, and she let him go with a fond kiss.

"Now, come on, everybody: let's get the place cleaned up. It's chaos! Just look at it! You know how fastidious Prof. H. is. If she saw it now, she'd have me out on my ear in five minutes flat..."

She stopped short as there was a thud from the front hall. It was the door banging open and a voice called "Thank you" to an unseen taxi-driver.

"Oh, my God! It's her! She's back! Oh no!"

Bodies flew in all directions, desperately trying to bundle up clothes and get out through the French-windows to the garden. Only Bruce remained completely calm. He stood, clad only in vest and underpants, calmly folding his blankets; no retreat for him. The others froze as the door slowly opened, to reveal a tired Joy Hetherington. It crossed Petronella's mind that Vienna must have been amused at the vision of the old tweed suit and the ghillie hat, complete with trout-flies. And yet there was a touch of elegance in the dark-blue cashmere turtleneck-sweater and fine Liberty silk scarf knotted artistically at the throat.

"Oh, hello, dears! How's everything?"

They stood politely in a row, en deshabille, as she continued:"I came back early. Very lucky to get a seat on the plane. Pity it's not Schutz - But... I found something else! Absolutely marvellous! Something which I know beyond a shadow of doubt (in my mind, that is) is a missing part of that lovely Gibbons thing in St. John's library.

"You know it..." She sang a snippet of something plaintive which seemed to be all about sorrow, pain and eternity, then disappeared upstairs with her luggage.

They stood looking at one another with raised eyebrows, but before they had time to consider the next move, the door opened again and her head appeared round it.

"By the way, dear, where's Robert Burns?" she asked, fixing Petronella with a straight look.

"Top shelf - airing-cupboard," murmured Petronella faintly.

"Oh" - excellent, excellent! Well, must have a bath." And off she went again.

It didn't take long to set the place to rights and Robert Burns was once more restored to his rightful-place on the mantelpiece.

"Aye," said Bruce, looking at him with approval, "Now there's a man for ye. His values were definitely in the right place, but a true Romantic nevertheless. D'ye ken he wrote: 'O gie me the lass that has acres o' charms: O gie me the lass wi.' the well-stockit farms.' And in the next breath he says: 'O my luve's like a red, red rose ..'"

"Aye, man," interjected Sherlock Holmes. And he also wrote: 'The best laid schemes o' mice an' men gang aft agley.' So shall we gang awa' wi' a' stealth after having been caught in the act so nicely, lads and lassies?"

Petronella caught Joy briefly later on in the day and spoke of the affair of the shooting and the death of Cledwyn. Joy was incredulous and deeply shocked. She would get in touch with the police at once.

The police were most helpful and arranged to send someone round first thing in the morning.

The next priority was to seek out Michael Walters at the Jolly Sailors and talk the matter over again with him before seeing the police.

Petronella volunteered to come down about nine o'clock to hear Michael's comments.

Jovial laughter and loud music could be heard, coming from the saloon bar, as Joy walked down. A happy crowd of overseas language students were celebrating the end of their course. Four diminutive Japanese girls caught the eye, sitting demurely side-by-side, smiling that particular Japanese smile from ear-to-ear and drinking - incredibly - whole pints of Guinness from large beer-mugs. They each wore T-shirts with 'Oxford,' printed across the front, blue-jeans and high-heels. They looked practically identical, almost like quads, for their glossy black hair was trimmed in exactly the same way, shoulder-length with a deep fringe to the line of the eyebrows. They were indeed a delight, happily ensconced behind their pint mugs, putting up an elegant Geisha hand to cover a giggle, and speaking that particular brand of clipped English which is the exclusive province of the Japanese, peppered with a great deal of "Ah, so!"

Uncomfortably wedged in a corner beyond them, the mystery-man in black leather wrestled with his crossword. He was frowning in deep concentration. Michael was there with a group of Arab students, talking about cricket, judging from his gestures, and they appeared mystified as he described l.b.w. to them, using a bar stool as the wicket. In due course, Joy managed to attract his attention and they found a corner to sit down and talk.

Petronella soon appeared, accompanied by Bruce, and together, all four of them put the pieces in place. The story as it emerged was not a nice one.

Where was the evidence? As before, there was none - except for one footprint on a newspaper; one cremated old lady: some stolen washing, and a young man in the mortuary: added to which there was the rifle shot and a pan on fire. The whole thing was ludicrous, and yet it all stank, "O'rotten haddock," as Bruce crudely summed up.

Peter Rumbold joined the group and remarked that for his money it had to be drugs at the bottom of all this. It was the only thing which could possibly account for all the inconsequential events.

"I guess," said Peter, looking in his dreamy way at the bar-billiards match: "And it's only a guess, mind you - that somebody panicked and made a terrible mess of everything in consequence. A proper bull's-foot, as they say. And..." He looked into his beer-mug and swirled its contents round slowly in the bottom of the glass: "was then dealt with." He drank down the remaining beer with satisfaction. "Light and bitter, please, Tony!" he called, holding up his glass above the crowd.

"Dealt with?" Petronella looked up at Peter quizzically.

"Yes - erased."

"Cledwyn?" Joy, chilled; remembered bleakly his urgent words of warning and sighed a sigh of profound sorrow.

Peter nodded and relapsed once more into his dream. They sat quietly in all the hurly-burly of the pub. Not even the continuous noise of the jukebox, the laughter of the students or the distraction of darts, dominoes or bar-billiards broke into their quiet thought.

"And you..." Peter indicated Joy with his beer-mug: "Know something - or rather somebody thinks you know something, and so you've got to go as well, to put it rather bluntly."

Joy and Petronella looked at one another, eyebrows raised.

'However, fear not," continued Peter; "Tomorrow will reveal all. The police are not stupid. Though the mills of God grind slowly, yet they grind ..."

"Exceeding small!" Bruce finished the quotation with an air of triumph. "Possibly Robert Burns' finest words!"

They all spluttered into their beer at this jest and the sorrowful spell was broken.

"I must say, I am intrigued, though, by the light in the sky seen by the old lady," said Michael.

"Probably only a helicopter or something going over to Brize Norton."

"No, Bruce." Joy shook her head emphatically. "She said it was like a candle. She was quite positive about it."

Bruce had the last word again. "I know, it was a distress signal! A Very-light from the Oxford boat-race crew, sinking during night-practice on the river!" They looked at him askance.

"But seriously, now, I don't believe she saw anything particularly important, in fact. She was after all a very old lady, remember. She simply probably simply thought she saw something. I'm inclined to think that she died of natural causes and she had nothing at all to do with any of these peculiar happenings. Maybe poor old Cledwyn buried some drugs on your allotment, and the secret of where the cache is died with him. Perhaps the villains are afraid you'll find it before they do - you've got to be stopped from going over to dig until they find it; hence the pot-shots!"

"Oh, this is all so depressing!" Joy was irritated. "Come on, darts, anybody? Doubles?"

There was still no sign of Mark. Michael confirmed that he had not yet been home and Joy confessed she was worried.

"Not even a post-card to give any indication as to his whereabouts. Quite infuriating, especially at a time like this when he's really needed. He is a naughty boy. I do wish he'd come back!"

Happily, Bruce would definitely be staying for a few days, as arranged by Petronella, to get him sorted out for Australia; so, thankfully, there would be a man about the house for a while.

In the morning, Joy told the complete tale, as accurately as possible, to the police. Petronella added her piece to the jigsaw of events and Bruce told of his experience of and personal opinion about the meaning of the shooting incident.

Joy had rather expected the whole bizarre story to engender some flicker of amusement, not least because the saga of her stolen underwear really did sound rather comic. But no: everything was taken quite seriously and searching questions asked about times and places. Detailed descriptions of events and even personal conjecture about the meaning of these events were requested.

They also paid a visit to Miss Dacre and spent quite some time with her, going carefully over everything she had seen. She was, unhappily, quite damning about Joy, being utterly convinced that it was she who had gone to see the old lady on that fateful night.

"I saw her, I saw her!" she repeated vehemently: "She left that poor old lady to die all alone! Nobody cares a jot about us old people. It's a perfect disgrace!"

The parting words of the police to Joy and Petronella, though their purport was alarming, brought them at least some comfort and ease of mind. There were certainly suspicious circumstances surrounding the death of Cledwyn, and there was clearly cause for concern about, and investigation into the strange events in St. Julie's Road. Whether or not there was any connection between those things remained as yet unknown, but the whole matter would be subjected to careful scrutiny and they would be in touch,

Later that day, as it looked like rain, Joy thought she had better bring the washing in. Iffley, in sphinx-like posture, inspected the proceeding from the top of the garden-shed, and little tabby watched from a high bough of the old apple tree. How peaceful it was down here at the bottom of the garden. The area had once been the old Leckford Monastery orchards and the ancient well was still there, filled in, of course, and now an attractive rockery. Perhaps, thought Joy, it might be a good idea to excavate it; after all, there were so many old bits and pieces continually coming up in the earth around it, notably some Spanish fourteenth-century bottle glass, ancient door latches and hinges, the odd coin, and even fragments of Roman pottery and red tiles and several stone-age small arrow-heads, beautifully fashioned, as well as what was possibly the most touching find - an early metal toy aeroplane, circa 1920, in perfect condition, propeller and wheels intact.

These tranquil thoughts were rudely interrupted by the advent of Erica Trondheim, whose face appeared, contorted with rage, over the garden wall. She glared at Joy and hissed like a snake:"Are you completely mad? Are you quite crazy?" and promptly disappeared. Simultaneously the cats fled. They did not like Erica Trondheim in the least. Somewhat bemused, Joy returned to the house. Petronella's head popped out of her window upstairs.

"What was all that about?"

"Goodness knows! Apparently I'm completely mad - or so she tells me."

Petronella looked rather guilty.

"Oh dear, oh dear! I knew there would be some kind of come-back over the party!"

She came downstairs and explained about the ragging of Erica during the festivities.

Joy agreed that it was unfortunate, but as Erica was inclined to erupt even at the subdued clatter of a teaspoon, there really was no point in too much heart-searching over the matter.

Petronella then came up with an uneasy thought. Could it be that Erica was behind any of the strange happenings? The fire episode, for instance? Who could tell? She was, after all, quite mad enough to do anything. It was certainly food for thought, anyway. She gave Petronella the creeps, and that was a fact.

Joy confessed to sharing this feeling about her. She was quite weird. However, they agreed that it was essential not to get neurotic about the issue. They must try to forget it for the moment; everything was getting too involved. The police were the ones to deal with it.

CHAPTER VIII

'Come, gentle swains...

Adorned with courtesy and comely duties...'

Madrigals to 5 and 6 voices

Michael Cavendish 1601

Madge Spragnell floated past on her bicycle a day or two later, pursued as at other times by the Wolvercote bus. She waved and wobbled violently, as was her wont, and yet again disaster seemed imminent.

Her attempts to stop were neatly foiled by the bus, which made loud menacing noises with its engine, at the same time emitting a sort of heavy breathing sound resembling an angry bull, gathering speed as it closed in on her from behind, rather like a scene from a silent film, with noises off.

"Can't stop dear! Don't forget! Be there! I'm depending on you ...!"

The message was quite clear. If the instructions were not obeyed to the letter, there would be hell to pay later. Oh dear, what was one to do? Ah well, when in doubt, yield - it was the only way with Madge and her projects. The matter would have to be broached at choir-practice on Thursday, for St. Giles' Fair was to take place not very far hence.

And so it was mentioned, very tentatively, and - as was only to be expected - met with firm rejection by the choir in a unanimous "No!"

"Ridiculous idea! And in any case we'd simply never be heard over the awful din of the fair!" said Caroline Grieve. "A complete waste of time and effort."

John Spry polished his glasses. "Well, it would be true to say that nobody would hear much, but we would certainly look rather good, especially with St. Giles' Church and the graveyard as a background. Quite mystical."

Brenda Page-Phillips looked out over the quad at the statue of the King. "She has a point, though, your Mrs. Spragnell. If you dress people up in period costume, singing madrigals and things, and put them in that particular setting, something quite unexpected could happen. The vital spark of inspiration could ignite, and ghosts might walk, even! It would most certainly capture the public's attention - and a good deal of money could conceivably roll in for the charity. There's nothing like an unusual visual spectacular to draw people. It could be quite exciting. Imagine; the frenzy of the fair, and this tiny oasis - a little vignette of history by the churchyard. A sort of time capsule."

Joy thoughtfully nodded in agreement. "Yes, if we could only raise a quorum, say four voices; that would do. Anything to avoid the wrath of Madge Spragnell! You know what she's like. We would simply never hear the end of it if we didn't do it. We needn't sing much - just enough to attract people to her stall."

And so it was agreed. John Spry nobly volunteered, entering with zest into the spirit of the occasion, and commenting that after all it didn't matter if one looked a fool, as it was all for a good cause, but complete disguise was absolutely essential. Brenda Page-Phillips decided that she would also give it a try and would wear one of her own splendid Elizabethan creations. Encouraged by such boldness, Professor Peterson then followed suit, saying that academic gown, climbing breeches and a ruff would have to do as his garb. So, with Joy as soprano, that was a quartet.

Lady Westhoe offered to watch from a discreet distance and send suitable telepathic messages of support, taking up a position somewhere near the giant Ferris-wheel (which was always situated conveniently near the college gate) in case for some reason escape should prove to be immediately necessary.

"What will your Mrs. Spragnell be offering to the madding throngs by way of merchandise for this eleemosynary event?" John enquired.

"Oh, the usual thing, I imagine. Bric-a-brac, books, preserves, high-class jumble-" this evoked some smiles -"Pot-potpourri, and of course the famous lavender bags, and the inevitable raffle - or tombola. She really does get the most astonishingly superior prizes. I often wonder where on earth they come from. Oddly enough, though, the first prize is always a huge teddy-bear, with quality goods like whiskey and wine as secondary prizes. It's curious, but she seems to set great store by her giant teddy-bear as an eye-catcher for the raffle, as though it means something special to her."

"She probably thinks everybody in the world has hosts of grandchildren to give such things to," said Caroline Grieve, "The eternal matriarch."

John Spry laughed. "I can just see her going round the town wearing all the tradespeople down for donations of bottles and things."

"No," Brenda Page-Phillips shook her head, "Definitely not! They probably see her coming, grab the nearest thing and rush out to meet her, breathing great sighs of relief when she goes out of the door - quick turn-round job."

"A subtle variation on the protection racket," said Caroline Grieve: "Ingenious."

"Precisely! A well-known technique. People like Mrs. Spragnell know how to pick their victims. They have a nose for it" Said Brenda.

"Shall we sing?" Lady Westhoe twitched her music slightly. "It's getting late. After all, it is nine o'clock."

The college clock had just begun to strike. It struck seventy-three, for the original number of undergraduates, in order that present members of the college should be reminded to pray for the repose of their souls.

Lady Westhoe looked out over the quad at the clock over the chapel door. Its benign golden face glinted in the soft evening light. The baroque swirls of the scroll carvings in the surrounding stonework gave it a smiling look.

"You know, that clock is beginning to show its age somewhat."

She looked at it affectionately. "It's getting a tiny bit senile, we think. It behaves perfectly normally until five, and then starts to go haywire."

"Haywire?" Professor Peterson raised his eyebrows.

"Yes, it strikes the hours and quarters quite normally until five, and then it begins to accelerate, gathering speed on the strike every hour, until by eleven it's worked itself up into an absolute frenzy.

Twelve is utterly indescribable. At midday it doesn't matter so much because during the day nobody notices much, of course, but if one is unfortunate enough to be awake at midnight, the suspense is killing. One simply lies awake, worrying oneself to death about how it's going to behave during the small hours. Rather like having an elderly relative in the place, who's got to be listened out for in the night, lest there should be a mishap of some sort."

Talk, however, continued on the subject of the college, which had been founded in its present form by King James I, and which had had strong Royalist connections during the Civil War. King Charles I had visited it when he stayed at Christ Church at the time of the Siege of Oxford, and as was the case at St. John's, which stands close by in St. Giles'; his ghost sometimes walked in the college.

There were other apparitions, too. Monks were often seen crossing the quad and walking in the ancient cloisters, for the heart of the college was the original monastic buildings, to which further quads had been added in the sixteenth and seventeenth centuries. Most of the ghosts were benign, but one in particular was not.

He was known as the Grey Monk. His appearances were few but always unpleasant. He was renowned for materializing in the middle of the night and triggering off the highly sophisticated electronic alarm system which guarded the archives of ancient manuscripts and other priceless possessions of the college: the superb Van Dyck of Charles I, the exquisite tapestry woven by the ladies of the court to while away those tedious hours of the Siege; and the undisputedly genuine night-cap, night-shirt and bedsocks of Charles II, left behind after a Royal visit to a Gaudy student event in 1669. Also a lady's nightdress beautifully embroidered with oranges, bananas and pineapples, thought to have been left behind at about the same time, owner unknown.

The college rugger team had suffered worst at the hands of the Grey Monk. Fresh from a glorious victory, having trounced the champions, they had returned to college one dark winter evening exulting in triumph. They had come through the college gate in victorious procession, muddy and wet from battle, and had chaired their captain across the Great Quad. Passing through the small archway to the darkness of the King's Quad beyond, they had been confronted by the Grey Monk, cowled and menacing, apparently coming straight towards them from the direction of the ancient cloister. They had - to a man - run, terrified, back to the porter's lodge in the main gatehouse, and would not under any circumstances be persuaded to go back without an escort. Eventually Lady Westhoe herself had gone with them, assuring them that it was probably all in the mind, and that it was best simply to ignore it and it would go away, and so on.

However, notwithstanding this reassurance, morale had been severely undermined and they had lost all subsequent matches in that particular season; for them a most unpropitious encounter with the ghost.

Lady Westhoe's philosophy about the spectral manifestations was simply to regard the paranormal as a part of life's rich tapestry, and not to pay too much attention to it, otherwise it might conceivably become a nuisance. The only personal objection she had to sharing her house with the various ghostly beings was, that they were inclined to leave doors open.

She didn't mind feet tramping round the place, or even passing close by her chair in the Great Drawing Room with no visible body to accompany the sound of feet; but to leave the doors wide-open was just a nuisance, especially in winter. The draughts were awful and heating costs were high enough already without that.

Sylvia Westhoe and Joy had sometimes compared notes on the subject of ghosts, and Joy mentioned that by an odd coincidence, her brother had quite recently had a parallel experience with unexplained open doors at his ancient home. The family were aware of three ghosts around the house: a sad little girl, seen only by the children, but sometimes heard by the adults, moving about upstairs; a forbidding woman in a long dark dress, seen only fleetingly on the top landing during the night, and an active poltergeist, which seemed to derive great enjoyment from throwing the children's toys around the nursery with enormous zest. Curiously enough, nothing ever got broken, although the crashing and banging was exceedingly alarming.

However, the family had worked out a method of dealing with this, violent spirit. When the manifestation got too bad, they would simply stand at the foot of the spiral staircase and shout:

"Be quiet and go away!" And it worked for a while, that is to say, for a week or two. Then the noises would start up again, quietly at first, but gradually rising to a crescendo over the ensuing month.

The business of the open doors was also uncanny. A new central heating system had recently been installed at great expense and was ceremoniously switched on for a trial run one chill September night. It worked perfectly, and warmed and comforted, the family retired to bed in the happy expectation of a joyful awakening in the morning to a cosy house. Their black Labrador, Dodger, was fast asleep in his basket by the hall radiator. Joy's brother, Alexander, locking and bolting all doors and windows downstairs, went to bed a happy man, and all was peace.

At about half-past two in the morning the whole family awoke, frozen. An icy blast gusted through the entire house, rattling every casement window and light fitting. Pictures fell off walls and papers blew around everywhere.

Switching on the lights, Alexander went downstairs, fearing the worst, i.e. burglars. He called the dog. No reply. Downstairs in the hall he was confronted by a strange sight. Every door and window on the ground floor was wide open, but with all locks, bolts and catches still in the locked-position! Dodger was fast asleep in his basket, curled up snugly nose in tail, and quite undisturbed, although normally he was a wonderful guard dog. Nothing was missing and there was no sign of a break-in. The whole thing was a complete mystery.

Over breakfast, the family discussed the matter at length and eventually arrived at an astonishing conclusion. One of the ghosts didn't like the central heating and had staged a protest!

However, mercifully it hadn't happened since, so they crossed their fingers and simply hoped for the best.

In conclusion, Joy, smiling ruefully, mentioned the incident of the fiery pan and the paraffin can in the basement. Could it perhaps have been staged by some unknown resident spirit? For there didn't seem to be any reasonable explanation. But could ghosts move heavy objects and light gas stoves?

Sylvia Westhoe told her in reply the following story. Relatives of hers in Wiltshire had experienced the friendliest of hauntings, which still continued. Every time the family went out for a walk together they would return to find the kettle on the kitchen stove, full and just coming to the boil. Never boiling - but just about to do so! All they had to do was to brew the tea and this they always did, and then said "Thank you" to the ghost.

CHAPTER IX

'As Vesta was from Latmos Hill descending, she spied...'

Madrigals of 5 and 6 parts

Thomas Weelkes 1600

For some years, Joy had been privileged to make what might possibly be described as a sort of Mulberry Benedictine from the college mulberry trees, which had been thoughtfully planted by the King at the time of the foundation of the college.

This excellent brew was simply a concoction of fallen and well-rotted mulberries from the lawn round the trunk of the tree; the more squishy and mildewed the fruit, the better the brew, which was then made up to Mrs. Genery-Taylor's formula, as described in her famous wine-making book, but using double the amount of fruit and sugar, with the addition of cold tea. Then, upon completion of the wine-process, after about a year, half a bottle of vodka was added to each gallon. The result was always truly astonishing. A most distinguished semi-liqueur, pale pink in colour and highly intoxicating, even after only a year in maturation. Goodness knows what it would have been like in ten years. Regrettably, none had ever survived that long for anyone to be able to assess its potential.

Six bottles were presented every year to the President of St. James', Lord Westhoe, a brilliant and charming man. Outwardly, he exhibited a decorous and solemn image, which was sometimes even forbidding; thus his mercurial wit and unique sense of humour, when manifested, always took everyone completely by surprise.

The time of the mulberry harvest came just before St. Giles' Fair, and Joy was duly notified by Lady Westhoe that they were beginning to fall nicely and were rotting well. The best of the fruit was, of course eaten as a seasonal epicurean delight at dinner parties in the President's lodgings and, as tradition demanded, was served with whipped cream and a generous dash of Drambuie.

So, armed with plastic bags and several buckets, which hung from her bicycle like decorations on a Christmas tree Joy arrived at the appointed hour at St. James', making her way through the high wrought-iron gate and proceeding via the Royal Quad to the President's garden, where the mulberry trees grew. As she approached, Lady Westhoe leaned out of a mullioned kitchen window on the ground floor of the north wing and waggled a silver tea-pot speculatively.

"Tea in half an hour?"

Joy smiled and nodded in appreciation, beginning the back-breaking task with a will, for Lady Westhoe's teas were always something to look forward to, as she was a marvellous cook for both savoury and sweet dishes. Her home-made scones and tea-cakes were indeed something to remember and soliloquize about later. And, when tea was taken outside in this setting with the background of the vast velvet lawns and the wonderful herbaceous borders, the pleasure was all the more memorable. And yet, in spite of all its grandeur, historical renown and great fame as a place of academic learning, St. James' was so homely. It had often been said that Lady Westhoe made it so, for Westhoe hospitality was a byword in Oxford.

The silver tea-tray was a welcome sight, borne by Lady Westhoe to a large rustic oak table set in the middle of the lawn's expanse.

"Do you know, this is the first time I've had a moment to sit down since I got up at half-past six this morning," she said with a sigh of relief, sinking gratefully into a comfortable garden chair. "Quite honestly, it will be a blessed relief when term begins again. The summer vacations are absolutely hectic in college nowadays; so many resident conferences and things. Very interesting, but utterly exhausting. Roll on, October!"

The tea was perfect; a delicate mixture of Earl Grey and a pinch of Lapsang-Souchong. The flavour was delicious, especially when combined with the taste of hot scones and unsalted butter with just a trace of raspberry jam.

They sat for a while in amicable silence, enjoying the afternoon sun, which slanted across the lawn and warmed the ancient stone walls, whereon blew a solitary salmon-pink antirrhinum in the lightest of warm breezes.

"Probably the direct descendant of the one on Trinity wall which Newman wrote about so eloquently."

Joy nodded towards Trinity College, which lay not far distant. Vertue, the college cat, appeared, landing neatly on top of the wall close by the antirrhinum. She was nearly the same colour as the flower, a pale golden-ginger. She settled down, gimlet-eyed, to watch the tea-party.

"No food for you, Madame - you've had plenty today from the college kitchen!"

Vertue, pretending complete disinterest, flashed a paw at a passing bumble-bee and missed.

At that moment, low in the afternoon sky, over the high wall behind her there slowly appeared a multi-coloured air-balloon. It floated lazily into view and seemed to hover almost stationary over University Parks, for there was very little wind.

As they sat, idly watching its progress, the balloon moved almost imperceptibly nearer and eventually appeared to be poised directly over the edge of the college grounds.

"I know," said Sylvia Westhoe, emerging from her reverie, "Call him down and we'll give him some tea."

"What? Really?"

"Oh yes, we've had them here before. Great fun! Go on, stand up and give him a wave with something. Here, take my hat."

Laughing, Joy obliged and crossing the lawn, she waved the straw hat vigorously above her head. As she did so, with her mind's eye she had a sudden vision of the situation in reverse. How strange it must be, looking down on Oxford from up there, to see this curious sight. There was no doubt that he must be able to see them quite clearly. Two lone figures seated at a tea-table in the middle of a vast expanse of green sward, with the college laid out behind, a patchwork of green velvet and soft golden stone quadrangles. For amid all the hurly-burly of the city, with traffic and people moving restlessly like ants around the central shopping area, lay these calm oases of green and gold, like some kind of animated chequer-board, but which could be seen only from a celestial vantage-point, such as the air-balloon.

He hovered overhead, somewhat uncertainly, it seemed, looking down on them from his bird's-eye view.

"Wave again," said Sylvia Westhoe. "He'll catch on in a minute."

"He doesn't quite know what to make of it, I think," said Joy, picking up the tea-pot and a cup and holding them aloft, miming the pouring of tea. "Probably thinks what a frightful fool he would look if he landed and then found we hadn't been inviting him down after all. Fancy landing in a heap on the President's lawn only to find yourself not wanted. How very embarrassing!"

Even as she spoke, there was a brilliant flash of flame as the pilot ignited the gas-burner to make height. A subdued roar followed a second or two later.

Joy was quite transfixed, for she instantly heard the voice, loud and clear, as though the old lady were there beside her: .".. Something strange in the sky ... like a candle..."

Rooted to the spot, she watched the balloon rapidly ascend and drift away east over University Parks.

So, that was it! It had after all been an air-balloon which Professor Trondheim saw that night, without a shadow of doubt. Joy now knew that this was the answer to the puzzle. But what on earth (or rather, in the heavens) had they been up to, floating over Port Meadow after dark?

Leaving St. James's quickly, she called in on Michael at his office and told him of her revelation.

"Well," said Michael, somewhat dubiously, "You could well be right, Joy. An air-balloon it might have been, but it may possibly signify nothing at all. Simply an innocent air-balloon, minding its own business, coming down to land somewhere. Maybe he'd been blown off course or something, who knows?" Joy was sorely disappointed by his reaction. Her conviction that the air-balloon was up to no good was very strong indeed.

"Well, I think he was looking for something." She looked hopefully at Michael.

"What - in the dark?" Michael shrugged his shoulders and raised a quizzical eyebrow. Then he smiled, not unkindly at her evident deflation.

"Never mind, here's a bit of positive news for you, howbeit not very pleasant. The inspector has been in touch with me again. A thorough investigation will be made into Cledwyn's death. They are not satisfied that the way he died was quite as straightforward as it may appear. I hear that the pathologist confirms that there was indeed a drugs overdose, but how the poor lad came to end up in the well concerns them greatly. It looks as though he didn't just fall down it in a drugged stupor."

"How do they know that?"

"Well, first of all, he was the right way up - which in itself is odd. When people fall down wells, they normally go down headfirst, of course. And poor old Cledwyn was nicely planted the right way up."

"Good lord!" said Joy, aghast.

"And secondly, he was already as dead as the dodo when he was popped in. He didn't drown."

"Well, I'll go to t'foot of our stairs!" Joy reverted to the old Lancashire dialect with the shock of this awful piece of news.

"The poor, poor boy! If only I'd known a bit more about him, I might have been able to help him in some way." Michael smiled again, kindly, but slowly shook his head.

"Not with drug-addicts, my dear. It's not so easy to help them. They don't necessarily want to be helped. They live to serve the drug. That's their life, and there doesn't seem to be any way out - except in certain cases, of course. The exception proves the rule', as they say. But that's only my opinion. Other people who are better informed may have rather different views."

Thoroughly depressed, Joy made her way home, bicycle laden with buckets of mulberries.

She was just not in the mood for winemaking, but it had to be done. Propping up Mrs. Genery-Taylor against the food mixer, she read the recipe and began to pick the mulberries over.

The telephone rang. Oh no! What a pest! Probably only one of Petronella's boy-friends, anyway. She decided not to answer it, but it rang and rang. Eventually she gave in and with hands stained crimson made her way to the hall, dripping mulberry juice on her precious Wilton carpet as she went. Oh damn! It stained so terribly and was quite impossible to get rid of. Truly irritated, she picked up the 'phone.

It was Mark, affable as ever. "Mark, dear, where on earth have you been?" Her relief was unutterable. However, she berated him at length for disappearing so adroitly at a time when there had been so many horrid things to contend with.

His response was to make light of it, but also to commiserate. He had had long experience of Auntie Joy's disasters over the years, but somehow things had always seemed to work out all right in the end, notwithstanding perils in the interim.

He mentioned that he had been in Europe on business, but would be at home in Oxford for the meanwhile, so she was not to worry. All would be well. Now, to think about some more pleasant diversions: how would she like lunch at the White Hart at Wytham on Saturday? Game pie! and pheasant were now on the menu, as the season had begun. And, by the way, he would be available to lend a hand at that charity 'do' of Madge Spragnell's. He would rattle a tin or something. (He had a winning way with people and always took large amounts of money at events of this kind.)

Pleased at the prospect of the epicurean delights of the White Hart and comforted by his return, Joy acquiesced. She was truly fond of her nephew, and it was difficult to be cross with him for long. He had great charm, even though he was somewhat elusive.

Mrs. Badger, meanwhile, was out in the garden next door, beating the life out of the Trondheim stair-carpet; which she had hung out over the garden wall, and was attacking vigorously with the ancient Trondheim carpet-beater. Loud thumps and great clouds of dust assaulted the senses. Several cats appeared over walls roundabout and settled down to watch this curious human activity. They looked truly surprised.

"Oi dunno," Mrs. Badger muttered at Joy: "The only toime as Oi gets anythin' done is when Miss Erica's out on one of 'er walks. Can't get a thing done when she's about. She's everywhere - just loike a bloomin' vulture she is, 'anging about. Complaini' an' carryin' on. Tis shockin', 'tis. 'Ave you 'eard the latest?" Joy confessed that she hadn't heard the latest.

"Well, Oi tell you, not a word of a loie, moi dear - she says as 'ow you was tryoin' to murder 'er - just loike you did the old gal!"

Mrs. Badger stopped her thumping and sneezed with the dust.

Joy sneezed too, and in between sneezes said wearily that this was the last straw, it really was.

"She's quoite mad, you know. Ought to be took orf away up yonder." Mrs. Badger nodded in a southerly direction, presumably indicating Littlemore Hospital up on the hill.

"Never you moind, Miss 'Etherington. Tis an ill wind? as they say. Just look wot Oi found when Oi took up the stair carpet." She fished in her apron pocket, producing a variety of objects such as clothes-pegs, matches, safety-pins, and even the inevitable potato-peeler, and finally found what she was looking for. It was a coin, or at least it looked like one.

"Now, Oi think it's a clue!" Mrs. Badger announced with emphasis.

"A clue?"

"Yes. "Ere, take a look."

She handed it to Joy over the garden wall. It was a largish coin of bronze appearance and looked Celtic. Joy turned it over. No it wasn't. It was a coat-button! The image portrayed on it was that of a horse, rather like the one cut into the hillside at Uffington Castle, segmented in design.

"Of course!" she exclaimed: it was her own button from the Welsh tweed cape! It held the cord-loop fastening in place at the throat.

Mrs. Badger nodded sagely. "Oi thought as you moight reckernize it! Oi knew straight away wot it was when Oi see it! It was under the carpet tread at the top o' the stairs boy the Professor's room. 'E must 'a lawst it when 'e wen' up to froighten the old lady that noight. You can give that to the police now, along wi' that footprint on the newspaper - that's proof, that is!"

Joy agreed. The button, she recalled, had in fact still been on the cape when she last wore it to go down to the Jolly Sailors on that fateful night. She remembered fastening it because or the sudden gusts of wind and blustering rain which made the cape flap open so much.

"Mrs. B. - you're right! At last, we have something to show. I'll get in touch with the police straight away!"

The response was immediate, for after being transferred through several extensions, she was soon speaking to the inspector himself, who was kind and conciliatory, but direct. He confirmed what had already been intimated by Michael. Yes, indeed, the whole matter was being taken very seriously and the objects in Joy's possession would be carefully scrutinized, even though they might not have any bearing on the main issue. He himself would like to see her personally about the case, which was most interesting. Would some time today be convenient?

He arrived within the hour. Looking out of the window as he approached the house, Joy thought that he could be of farming stock, for in appearance he was very much like many of the farmers she had known around the county. Tall, and strongly built, with the fitness of a rugger-player, dressed in tweed jacket, pullover and twill, trousers he came up the drive with a brisk and business-like gait.

Coffee? No. Then quickly on with the day's business. He didn't stay long, but in the short time they talked, every point was comprehensively covered. He took no notes, but simply asked questions then listening carefully to the answers; mostly asking about Cledwyn, but also about other things - the basement episode, the shooting by the dumps, and the affair of the impersonation, the theft of the washing from the clothes-line and the disappearance of the telescope. When told the tale of the strange light in the sky, he did not comment, but simply looked thoughtfully out of the window and nodded. It was all most reassuringly professional.

He then went across to Miss Dacre, who opened the door before he had even rung the bell. Pongo shot out and snapped at his ankles.

Joy watched from a front window and cringed at the thought of what Miss Dacre was probably saying. She made some lively gestures as she talked to the inspector, which spoke volumes. The accusing finger was pointed directly at Joy's front door, accompanied by hostile looks.

Soon the inspector came back, said his goodbyes and took away the footprint on the newspaper and the cape button.

"Just in case," he said, "You never know."

Joy began to feel depressed. Her spirits wilted and an uneasy thought crossed her mind. Perhaps the inspector thought she was just a little mad. In spite of Mrs. Badger's enthusiasm over the famous clues, a footprint and a button didn't represent much in the way of evidence, and Miss Dacre would no doubt have said some pretty damning things. She really did not like Joy at all. If only that wretched telescope would materialize with a nice set of incriminating fingerprints on it - that really would be a help!

But it was time to think about something else. She really must keep Madge Spragnell happy and sort out some music for this 'do' of hers at St. Giles' Fair. There was simply no end to Madge's tiresomeness, but one had to admit in mitigation that she always achieved great results as a charity fund-raiser. In ancient times she would have been tailor-made for the role of master of a team of galley-slaves, cracking her whip across their bleeding backs and driving them on with unbounded enthusiasm - hers, not theirs! She had such stamina herself, and simply had no thought at all for anything or anyone else. Only the immediate object in view, like the donkey and the carrot. Better make sure she got her carrot, and a nice juicy one to boot and then to hope for an interlude of peace for a short while thereafter, possibly even till Christmas, when she would no doubt expect Joy and Co. to stand out once again in the driving sleet in the Cornmarket, singing carols to the frozen populace in order to raise funds for her next project!

It was decided at their practice that they should sing a set of twelve simple madrigals, throwing in a few well-known old English folk-songs for good measure. After all, nothing much would be heard over the general din of the fair, so it really wouldn't matter awfully what they sang. The visual spectacle was the important aspect, so "Greensleeves," "Early one morning" and other well-known songs of that kind would be the simplest things to do, with "Now is the month of Maying" (although a bit late in the year, as John Spry observed), "The Silver Swan," and "Fyer! Fyer!," which the choir regarded as old pot-boilers suitable for the uninitiated to listen to. As Joy remarked, "After all, the madding throng won't hear much. They'll simply see our mouths open and shut, and our gorgeous costumes. That should fetch in the money, with any luck."

There was cynical laughter at this, for glorious indeed, they might look, but the way in which this appearance had been contrived was, to say the least, ingenious in its economy and improvisation.

Brenda Page-Phillips' costume, for instance, was breathtakingly beautiful. She looked stunning, like something straight out of a Nicholas Hilliard miniature. But from what had this marvellous costume been fashioned? Two moth-eaten old curtains and a worn-out bedspread! And the head-gear? Great-aunt Mildred's ancient blue velvet tea-cosy, skilfully adapted to make a charming Elizabethan hat.

"Surprising what you can do with other people's rubbish," had been her comment at the costume preview before Elizabethan Day at St.James' the previous year, as she turned critically before the mirror in the President's Great Drawing-Room.

This year, Lady Westhoe (having nobly relented and deciding to sing after all) appeared, resplendent in green silk, through the far door to the North Wing, at the costume parade for Madge's forthcoming event. She queued patiently with other members of the choir, for a look in the long mirror.

"Thank God no one will recognize me." She breathed a sigh of relief, carefully scrutinizing herself. "Really, I look just like a stuffed sofa - or Hamlet's mother - one or the other! I shall most definitely not wear my glasses, and that should clinch it - though I shall be as blind as a bat, of course." She gingerly adjusted her pearled head-piece.

"Lovely dress! What's it made of?" Brenda approached the impressive green silk creation with respect. "Such marvellous material...!"

"Ah yes. Well now, it's made from an old parachute which belonged to my father. Found it in a trunk up in the attic. He flew in the '14 - '18 war, you see, in one of those things made of paper and string. You know -" She made a movement with her hand in the air, which described perfectly the unstable flight of the early aeroplanes.

"Very fine silk," said Brenda. "Incredibly durable. It must be well over 60 years old, then. Quite, quite lovely."

Lady Westhoe looked out over the quad at the ancient mulberry tree, eyeing it affectionately. It was so arthritic, so aged, so venerable - yet still so fruitful like the Psalmist's wife. There was, after all, a purpose in planting mulberry trees within monastery precincts in former times. Fruit and wine and silk. A most useful and beautiful tree, she mused.

Her musing ceased abruptly as Caroline Grieve appeared, looking very aggravated indeed, attired in some curious garb which seemed to be a cross between the dress of a mediaeval kitchen scullion and a rather dishevelled milk-maid of some bygone era - as though she had been dragged through a hedge backwards behind an irate cow!

"I do so hate dressing up - can't stand it!" She took off her mobcap and threw it on the floor with a petulant gesture.

"What on earth are you supposed to be?" Joy was aghast.

"Oh, don't ask me! My daughters took me over and dressed me in their combined bits — and-pieces. Anyway, I've emerged as a Tudor milk-maid - according to them. I was supposed to be an Elizabethan lady in the first instance, but somehow it hasn't come out quite right!"

"A milk-maid?" Brenda enquired politely. "Did they sing madrigals?"

"Quite frankly, I neither know nor care. I'm heartily fed up with the whole business anyway." Caroline went quite pink with vexation. "I really don't know why we keep on doing these stupid events at all. It's that wretched Madge

Spragnell and her charity projects. Just so exhausting! That woman ought to be banned. She's a pain!" Heads nodded sagely in agreement; a pain she surely was.

Meanwhile, the men had come in, quietly suppressing a smile at all this display of feminine emotion.

"My word!" Lady Westhoe's voice was filled with admiration.

"Gentlemen, you look simply splendid!"

And indeed they did. With a swish of scarlet, Professor Peterson came in first, wearing academic robes and jauntily waving his black velvet hat. John Spry followed in graduate's black, gown - over a grey turtle-neck sweater. The ruff at the throat provided the authentic touch. He wore grey climbing breeches buckled at the knee and long vivid orange socks.

"Very fetching!" Brenda Page-Phillips laughed a mercurial little laugh. "Not quite in period, those breeches, but you certainly do look the part - even in suede ankle-boots!"

"How's this for a clever touch?" John fished in his pocket and dangled a heavy silver medallion on an equally heavy silver chain. He dropped it quickly over his head with a flourish and centred the medallion carefully on his chest.

"Lord Mayor of Oxford, 1542," he said, with a smile of self-satisfaction. "I pinched it from my girl-friend's wardrobe."

"Don't you dare lose it, or you really will be in the dog-house! It's very nice." Brenda laughed again. "Isn't it disheartening how the men eclipse us every time? We spend hours toiling with a needle, getting our costumes together and yet, in they walk, wearing everyday things, and outshine us completely!"

"Yes, don't we look grand?" Professor Peterson twinkled over his half-glasses, thoughtfully stroking his goatee beard.

"I did think that I should perhaps come as Cardinal Richelieu, but it also occurred to me that it might seem just a little pretentious. However, wouldn't you agree that there is an astonishing likeness to the Van Dyck. The profile, perhaps?"

He turned his face to the window, one finger under his chin. Joy threw a cushion at him. Fielding it neatly, he put it back on the sofa with a wag of the finger, saying, "Now, now, girls, let us not give way to ignoble emotions such as jealousy. Most unseemly!"

Meanwhile, Brenda, casting an appraising eye over the disconsolate Caroline as she stood miserably by the casement window, rummaged in her bag-of-tricks and produced a long roll of Velcro stick-on gold braid.

"Eureka! There we are: I thought I'd brought it. Come hither, Caroline, me dear, Cinderella shall indeed go to the ball!"

Cinderella, disbelieving, came meekly forward to Brenda, who stood in the middle of the room with her tapestry bag wide open on the floor. Rather like Madge Spragnell's bag, it seemed to have an endless number of things in it. Pairs of scissors of all sizes, from large pinking shears to the tiniest pair of fine scissors, surgical style and lethally sharp. Pieces of velvet, large and small, were there in abundance, in lovely colours, with yards of old lace curtaining and rolls of gorgeous braiding in every conceivable subtle shade.

"Where did you get this? It's marvellous!" Joy tugged at a piece of material poking out of the tapestry bag.

"Well, I believe it is, in fact an ancient Chinese silk tablecloth. I got it at the Animal Welfare Shop in Summertown for 75p."

"Whatever would we do without Oxford's charity shops?" Lady Westhoe mused, stroking Vertue, as she sat on the window-seat watching this strange human activity in the Great Drawing-Room. "It's quite unbelievable what turns up, you know. Recently, I went to look for some parts for my old hand-mincer. It belonged to my grandmother, so you can imagine how obsolete it is - and not only did I find the parts I needed, but I also came away with a veritable treasure as well. It was at the bottom of a box of jumble. Sir John Stainer's own hand-written notes for a music lecture he gave here in Oxford many years ago. So interesting."

"Not about the Crucifixion, I hope?" Professor Peterson pulled a long face. "One of my pet hates as a chorister! My trouble was I was far too advanced as a boy and so winsome with it! - notwithstanding the pea-shooter under my surplice and the sticky sweets! Only the very best in music for me: just the early stuff. Well, as far as Purcell, let's say. Mind you, 'Fling wide the gates' is a bit of a romp - I'll give you that. Great fun."

He struck a Victorian attitude, hand on-chest, and then thundered in a stentorian voice (molto vibrato): "Fling wide the gates! Fling wide the gates! Fling wide the - fling wide the - fling wide - the gates!" He sang all the parts expertly and played an invisible organ, deftly pulling out the stops and coaxing an invisible swell-box to give of its best. He also conducted an unseen choir.

"How about that, then?"

He turned, perspiring, to his silent audience.

"Riveting, utterly riveting!" murmured John Spry.

Thoughtfully considering himself in the mirror, he shook his gown around him and gave a quick twirl - almost a balletic pirouette in its preciseness.

"Hmmm, definitely a throwback I am."

"To whom, dear boy?" enquired the Professor, with a quizzical look over his half - specs.

"Lord Mayor of Oxenford, wasn't it?"

"Why, no: John Donne, of course! Just look at the demi-profile. Exquisite; and the perfect goatee beard!"

"Not forgetting the gold 20th century jet-set glasses and the wrong colour hair. John Donne was dark, you know," mumbled Brenda through her mouthful of pins, deftly disguising Caroline's waistline with a bum-roll (nylon tights, stuffed into a single stocking under her skirt).

"Men, peacocks all!"

Caroline sighed a deep sigh as she spoke.

"I know that I shall never ever look like anything but a sack of potatoes tied with string round the middle, no matter how hard I try to look chic. I do get so fed up!"

"It's your age, dear!"

"Really, John, you are a pain sometimes!"

This time Joy scored a direct-hit with a cushion in his midriff.

"Ouch, Madame! Mind me codpiece!"

There was a discreet tap at the door, and a head appeared round it. It was Livia, the President's housekeeper.

"Your Ladyship, Lord Westhoe present' ees compliments to the choir, and please weel you all join'eem een the President's garrden for a glass-a-wine when you all ready een the costumes."

Her delicious diction was a joy to hear.

Livia, rotund, small, dark-haired, delightful Portuguese, could not suppress a vivacious smile.

"You look-a-lovelee! Please to come in the garrden: thank you." With a little inclination of the head she departed.

"Shan't be two ticks," Brenda mumbled again through her mouthful of pins. She tugged and pulled at Caroline's dress, a tuck here, a pleat there. Many pins went into the good work.

"Don't dare sit down in it until I've sewn up the alterations later," she warned - "Could be painful!"

John Spry grinned mischievously.

"Like sitting on a porcupine!"

Brenda smiled a restricted smile, applying her Velcro gold braid at speed, some in straight strips down the front of the skirt, some down the front of the bodice and some along the sleeves.

The end-product was beautiful.

"Looks absolutely authentic!"

Lady Westhoe admired the finished article.

"You look exactly like a particularly fine Holbein portrait, Caroline!"

Brenda discarded Caroline's mob-cap.

"Can't possibly do anything with that, I'm afraid."

After a quick re-arrangement of Caroline's long auburn hair - a swirl upwards into a chignon - she rummaged in her bag-of-tricks, produced a square piece of darkest green velvet, and popped it on top of the auburn swirl, quickly pinned it on with hairclips, and then stood back, head tilted to one side.

A quick critical look and a "hmmm," then a swift rummage again in the tapestry bag."

She produced some Woolworth's best hook-on pearl earrings, clipped one on to the corner of the square above Caroline's forehead and one at each side above her ears.

Again, a totally authentic look to this Tudor bonnet.

"That'll do for now - I'll sew it up later."

"Splendid!"

Professor Peterson was admiring. "Come along, dear friends? Let us haste away, e'en now to some as yet unknown viticultural delight of St. James' fabled cellar. Thither we must resort! I wonder what it will be? Batard Montrachet? Nuits St. Georges?" (It was, in fact, to be a straightforward young Piesporter, well chilled and quite delicious).

The Elizabethan consort clattered down the great oak staircase, the steps of which Queen Elizabeth I herself had trod when visiting the college in 1575. (She left a pair of gloves behind - a gift from the City Fathers - perhaps they did not fit, for they now reposed in a glass case at the top of the stairs outside the Great Drawing Room along with other touching artifacts associated with King Charles I and the siege of Oxford).

Brenda, last out, looked down over the balustrade and remarked on how much they resembled a group of souls caught in some time-capsule of the sixteenth century.

"Perhaps ghosties will walk, roused by this vision of us living mortals in their garb."

Professor Peterson swished his scarlet robes and uttered an eerie moan.

"Let us sing some mournful madrigals in the garden - that'll rouse 'em!"

At this, Lady Westhoe issued a solemn warning to beware of jesting on such matters. The grey monk might take offence and, horrors! perhaps even more college matches might be unaccountably lost, or worse things - if indeed there be anything worse than this woeful eventuality - might result.

Prophetic words indeed, for no one in college was to get a wink of sleep that very night.

They made their way outside through the hall and via Lady Westhoe's kitchen, microwaves and all, in sharp contrast to the ancient spit in the fireplace and great meat-hooks in the ceiling. They crossed the President's lawn to the place where Lord Westhoe stood, bowing a gracious greeting, presiding, corkscrew at the ready, over a delectable collection of wine bottles and crystal glasses, set upon a silver tray on a long wooden table.

The ancient mulberry tree leaned overhead, casting a welcome shadow over this corner of the sunny garden. Behind, a blaze of electric blue delphiniums against the college wall lent an air of coolness to the scene.

Professor Peterson led the procession somewhat smartly to the table, the others following at a more sedate pace.

"Tut-tut, Peterson, my dear chap, such undignified haste!" John Spry murmured this aside to Caroline out of the corner of his mouth.

"Can't wait, can he? Silly old toper!" Caroline went pink.

"You should talk, John. I hear that you are always first at the port after dinner in the hall!"

"And probably last away, I suspect." Joy smiled a tolerant smile.

John reddened slightly. He was defensive.

"Well, you know, it's all very well for these old boys who've held high office for years. They're utterly ruined. Only the best of everything and never known anything different in half a century. It all simply tumbles out of the sky for them, from that great cornucopia of all good things, the University of Oxford. I wonder how they'd like it, scratching about at the bottom of the ant-heap as we have to."

He was quite bitter, an untypical display of emotion. Caroline put her arm through his, and was consoling.

"Never mind, sweet boy. He is an old man -- you are young, and one day a chair will fall out of the heavens for you - that is, if you work at it - 'As the pen doth fall from the trembling fingers of the aged academic', as Proverbs might have said."

"That is to say, if you don't drink too much port and invite a coronary before that great day dawns," Brenda murmured from behind.

They arrived at the table and exchanged greetings with Lord Westhoe. Professor Peterson tried his best to hide his disappointment over the Piesporter.

"Yes, indeed, these contemporary German wines are really quite captivating."

"Whatever that means!" John whispered to Caroline.

"Almost a hint of Muscatel," the Professor continued, holding his glass up critically to the light. He swirled it round, sniffed it and took a delicate sip, swallowing slowly, as all connoisseurs do.

"A fine, youthful little wine, most palatable."

"Langsam mit Ausdruck - pompous ass! Ouch!"

John winced as Caroline kicked him in the ankle. She smiled demurely at him.

"'Malice cometh before a swift kick in the ankle,' as Confucius did not say." John stood on one foot.

"But he did say; 'do not take off your boots in a melon field'- do you think he meant minefield? Honestly, I feel rather as though I'm in the middle of one now - vulnerable, you know, after that nasty encounter with the knife. Quite traumatic."

"Oh, the man at your door, you mean?"

"Precisely."

"Sorry, sweetie!"

Caroline gave him a quick hug in a sudden fit of remorse.

"Poor lamb."

John was consoled and twinkled nicely.

Vertue appeared at the open window of the Great Drawing-Room and settled down on the sill for a grandstand view of the proceedings down in the garden. She arranged herself à la sphinx fashion for a long session.

By this time, three or four other graduate choir-members, gowns over their shoulders, had joined the group. Yes, they would all be available to sing at the great event.

"They smelt the wine - like bloodhounds," said John sourly.

Joy was delighted, for that made ten voices in all. Lady Westhoe promptly disappeared into the library and came back with an armful of music.

"Since we are so many, we can sing something a little more ambitious as well, I think." They warmed up on simple madrigals from the Oxford Book.

"Very pretty indeed." Lord Westhoe was approving: "Ah, would that I were not tone-deaf, for I am filled with a desperate longing to sing!"

Lady Westhoe shook her head.

"No, dear, not this time round.Next life, perhaps."

The balance of vocal parts was good and they sang some lovely things, including Orlando Gibbons' 'Hosanna to the Son of David', as he had been at the college at some stage in his career. A popular theory widely held was that he had composed 'The Silver Swan' for St. James' as a tribute after a particularly fine banquet in the hall, when roast swan was consumed.

Next, in contrast, they sang Thomas Weelkes' setting of the 'Hosanna', fiery and exciting and totally different from the smooth and mellifluous Gibbons. (However, one must bear in mind, of course, that Weelkes was after all a New College man.) The next piece they sang was a lovely 'Ave Verum' by Peter Phillips, with long, high, suspended harmonies echoing sonorously round the college precinct. Swallows and swifts screamed overhead as if in competition.

Two college groundsmen appeared round the corner of the east wing, grinning at the display. They listened for a while, said something to one another and then disappeared.

"One dreads to think what they were saying," said John. "Good thing we can't lip-read" returned Brenda. "Better left to the imagination, I should say."

The singers became more adventurous and decided to try the Weelkes. 'O Lord, arise into thy resting-place'.

This was indubitably Joy's favourite anthem, ranking above all others. Having first heard it in her student days, sung by King's College Chapel Choir in Cambridge, directed by the matchless Boris Ord, she had, as she herself put it, been "ruined for life," for nothing could ever compare with Ord's breathtaking skill with early choral music. It sent that singular chill up one's spine, which is the hallmark of only the most inspired music-making. What a pity that recording techniques in those days were not so good and a great deal of his musical wizardry was lost to the world, except for a few marvellous '78's and the hearsay of those who had been privileged to hear his performances.

"Indeed, he made King's choir what it has become - a legend," nodded Professor Peterson. "I remember him well. A great man!"

They began to sing the work - but not before a slight skirmish had ensued among the basses about who should sing the delectable counter-tenor parts in the difficult great-anthem.

It seemed unfair, somehow, as Caroline observed, that deepest bass voices should be able to exchange high and low parts with such consummate ease. It made one quite jealous. Natural male superiority had been, however, their own assessment of this enviable faculty, and so, as they observed, it was after all quite logical.

Nevertheless, by the time they had arrived at page three of this reading, grave problems arose, resulting in the complete collapse of the counter-tenor line, and the choir disintegrated in loud laughter.

"Mind you, it is very difficult for them, isn't it? It's a fiend of a thing to get right. If they collapse, we all do. Their line holds the whole work together," said Brenda kindly, with a sweet smile.

The gentlemen were not to be consoled, however, and took themselves off, abashed, for further libations of Piesporter.

"Good thing the groundsmen didn't stay," Joy remarked. "They would have simply loved it."

The shadows lengthened across the lawn as the sun went down. Another marvellous sunset, made all the more beautiful by the sudden appearance of menacing deepest grey-purple storm-clouds moving in quickly on the horizon, driven by the warm west wind. The most remarkable kaleidoscopic colour effects resulted - Turneresque and changing moment by moment.

Better get off home before the storm, they all decided.

Joy and Brenda pedaled off together up St. Giles', but they abandoned the idea of a quiet drink at the Royal Oak as the sky blackened and increased in menace. It would be more sensible to get home quickly and avoid a soaking.

Immensely relieved to see Petronella's lights on upstairs, Joy arrived home to be greeted, as usual, by all the cats sitting in a row on the drive.

"Cupboard love," she said to them, "Come on, foodies!" Erica's house next door was in total darkness. Most eerie. One sensed a presence but saw no one.

Vague strains of pop music floated down the stairs from Petronella's flat, and the accompaniment of a mercurial laugh or so comforted Joy greatly.

So wonderful to be young and carefree. It was such a tonic to have young people about the place - in spite of their musical tastes!

Blind Fred decided that he had had enough of his airing-cupboard for the moment and demanded, with a commanding miaow, an evening peripheration round the garden. He was most skilled at climbing trees and demonstrated this by flying up the Bramley apple tree at the speed of light, straight to the top. He flatly refused to come down again when called, and settled himself down on a topmost bough of the tree, switching his tail wildly at the sound of swifts and swallows, darting and screaming overhead on a last foray in the gathering dusk after midges brought out by the impending storm.

The wind dropped in an instant and as Joy walked peacefully round the garden, breaking off a dead rose-head here, pulling up a weed there, darkness descended and a sultry, stuffy atmosphere pervaded the gathering night. The swifts and swallows went quickly to bed and there was an odd skirling chuckle from the blackbird population as they settled down in the bushes.

By this time, all the cats had joined Fred up the apple tree and Joy could just dimly discern that they were all concentrating on something at the bottom of the garden. All was now unearthly still.

Then there was a slight movement. A young fox was sitting by the potting-shed, his white shirt-front clearly visible, watching Joy most carefully. She spoke to him and he promptly disappeared silently over the garden wall.

This was definitely worth following up. She went quickly indoors and mixed some brown bread with a little cat food and put it down near the potting-shed, then retired to the top of the garden and watched.

Sure enough, a minute or two later, the fox reappeared over the wall and after assessing Joy carefully with a long look, settled down to supper.

A dull rumble in the western sky and a dim flash indicated that the promised storm was on its way. It would not be long now and that was just as well, for the garden needed a good night's rain, provided it wasn't too heavy.

The fox disappeared like a ghost, one moment there, the next he was gone. Joy looked across the back-gardens at the windows opposite. She started as suddenly a dark sash window somewhere high up over yonder shut with a loud crash. Once again, a strange bolt of fear shot through her, but why? It was only someone closing a window. So silly, but she shivered involuntarily and went back into the house, leaving the cats in possession of the apple tree. Being sensible animals, they would come in before the storm began, and Fred knew his way back through the cat-flap, so all would be well. A quick look at the late news on the box, and then to bed. It had become unbearably sticky and hot in the past hour, so she threw the bedroom window wide open before drawing the curtains.

The flashes in the sky became brighter and more frequent, and the ominous rumbles louder.

However, she fell gratefully into bed and was quickly asleep, lulled by the sound of the mellow musical tones of Dave Brubeck (or whoever) drifting downstairs from Petronella's flat.

CHAPTER X

'Draw on, sweet night, best friend unto those cares..'

First Set of English Madrigals

John Wilbye 1598

At, precisely half-past midnight (everyone was agreed on this) an almighty crash of thunder rent the night air; it was accompanied by full orchestral tympani, like echoing drum-rolls, reverberating round the night sky.

Valhalla!

Joy woke standing upright by the bed, the shock was so great.

As she recalled later, it was quite the worst thing she had ever heard since the wartime bombing when she was a child.

She stood for several moments, neither awake nor asleep, swaying slightly, as her senses tried to achieve total wakefulness. Then, instantly, she came to herself, jerked fully awake by a cataclysmic explosion in the heavens. Krakatoa must have sounded like that when it blew, as John Spry observed later.

Simultaneously, a blinding pink flash illuminated the bedroom, in spite of the thickness of the drawn curtains. It was awe-inspiring

"O'lord! Fred!"

She stumbled to the window, still stupefied, and dragging back the curtains, leaned perilously out. All was blackness outside.

"Fred! Fred! Where are you?" A violent hot wind blew the curtains outwards through the window. Again there was a blinding flash of pink lightning, this time lasting for a second or two, lighting up the whole scene in microscopic detail, in all its daytime colours, except that they were lit by this extraordinary light, and she was reminded fleetingly of the paintings of Samuel Palmer, or was it Gauguin, perhaps? The weird juxtaposition of complementary colours, pink and lime green, was electric and unearthly. The only colour which retained its original tone was the mellow red brick of the house walls.

A third blinding flash, almost blue this time, lit the gardens like floodlight and at that moment Joy saw in relief an empty apple tree. But - horrors! there was Erica Trondheim, clad only in a long white nightgown, her hair lashed round her face by the wind, standing in her garden, staring fixedly up at her mother's bedroom window, motionless, like a piece of sculpture.

At that instant the rain lashed down in fury, the heavens literally opened and the deluge commenced.

"Erica! For God's sake, get inside quickly! What are you doing out there?" Once more, there was instant pitch darkness, and a tempestuous downpour set in with a vengeance. The sheer noise of the rain drumming a tattoo on every roof was deafening. Immediately, guttering and drainpipes were flooded beyond capacity and instant waterfalls cascaded down all around. Within seconds, there was another brilliant flash of lightning. Erica had vanished and the garden was empty.

Joy doubted the evidence of her own eyes. Perhaps she had imagined it? Maybe Erica had not been there at all.

However, there were more important considerations at the moment. She went quickly downstairs, anxious for her beloved animals, Fred in particular.

She need not have exercised herself in the matter; for there was Fred, curled up, fast-asleep on a fur rug in the hall, and the others were all comfortably arranged on various chairs in the drawing-room. Except, that is, for Iffley, who in time of stress, would mountaineer up into the most unexpected places. Once it had been to the top of the grandfather clock in the hall. This time she was on top of Great-grandmother's cupboard, which stood nearly as high as the ceiling; goodness only knows how she had got up there. A vertical twelve-foot jump? Two grey ears alone betrayed her presence, just visible over the top.

The great storm had even wakened Petronella, which was an astonishment in itself! She normally slept on through anything - even dustbin day at 6.30 on

Monday mornings - which was a miracle by any standards! The noise was always horrendous.

Her lights came on and a great deal of clattering around ensued as she made herself a hot drink or some such thing.

Joy tottered feebly back to bed about 1.30 a.m. but as for sleep, there was none. The guttering and down-pipe, which was shared with Erica's house, came away with the weight of the water and crashed down into the back-garden at about 2 am. and Niagara Falls had nothing on St. Julie's Road until about seven o'clock, when the storm abated almost as quickly as it had begun.

Meanwhile, at St. James' College certain things had also been happening although in the first instance events were less dramatic. They made up for it later on.

Lady Westhoe, a light sleeper, had noted the rumblings in the western sky and had prepared herself for a bad night. She had taken to bed a good Barbara Pym novel, which was due for a re-read. She had herself been a contemporary of the writer at Oxford so the book was of double interest.

Lord Westhoe, a sound sleeper, had retired early in order to be up at five o'clock for a prompt start next day, as was his wont.

Lady Westhoe did not stir as the overture to the storm began at 12.30. She read on quietly, knowing that it was going to be a long night. However, after something like the fourth heavenly cataclysm, she sighed and put her book down. All was not well.

A strange gurgling sound came from outside the bedroom window. It sounded like the glugging of a blocked bath waste-pipe.

"Oh dear, oh dear!" she said, reaching for her dressing-gown, and got out of bed to investigate.

She put on the hall light. It went out immediately, as did every other light in the college. The blackness was all-enveloping.

The storm raged on relentlessly outside.

Lady Westhoe felt her way blindly back into the bedroom, found her torch and picked up the telephone. Of course, it did not work. It was completely dead.

She woke Lord Westhoe. He was up and ready for action in a trice. One moment fast asleep, the next he was fully awake. This was his own especial gift.

In a moment, he had assessed the situation and no words were needed. He dressed swiftly, putting on a golf jacket and tucking his pyjamas into his Wellingtons, then donning his tweed cap. He got his large black brolly, went into the drawing-room and lit the silver candelabrum, taking it with him down the stairs.

Before he was even halfway down the great staircase there was an almighty "crump" from below.

"The dining-room!" called Sylvia Westhoe. "Oh lord! The Van Dyck! And the Memling!" He was in there immediately and she joined him, breathless, a moment later, as he was already at work on the rescue operation, for that is what it was to become.

The flickering candelabrum dimly lit a fearful sight. Nearly a quarter of the magnificent decorated plaster ceiling had come down over the fireplace, leaving a huge gaping hole through which poured a deluge of rain-water mixed with debris of various kinds.

The Van Dyck hung askew on the wall over the fireplace, but still intact. The pale face of King Charles I gazed down mournfully at them, his head tilted acutely to one side in the dislodged and damaged frame. Mud of some kind slid down his face like tears. "Quick," said Lord Westhoe, and together, by a superhuman effort, they got him off the wall, to the guttering and sputtering of the candles.

"The Memling!" He indicated it with a nod, where it hung by the door and she snatched it from the wall, down which the water had begun to trickle in fast rivulets, about to engulf the tiny, precious picture. Its very smallness saved it from damage for she could shelter it under her dressing-gown as she ran out into the hall, to the safety and dry warmth of oak panelling and solid wooden flooring.

How cool its liquid and luminous tones looked, even in her torchlight, as she examined it for possible damage - the pale face and even paler lemon dress of the "Unknown Woman," as its label ambiguously proclaimed.

She was recalled to attention by an urgent hammering on the hall window.

"Your ladyship!" A torch shone on her face from outside and the urgent knocking continued.

"Madame, open the door!"

She did so and a distraught night porter fell through into the hall.

"Please, Madame, tell 'is lordship to come to the library at once! All the electronics is out, an' Oi can't open the door. The lock's jammed solid an' Oi can't move it. An' there's someone in there. Oi saw 'im at the winder!"

By this time there was general movement around the college, with slamming of doors, thumping of feet and voices raised in urgent enquiry. It was going to be a long, hard night and Heaven only knew what other catastrophes were happening elsewhere in the building. These two alone were more than enough to cope with.

It was something to be thankful for that at last term was over, so the college was not teeming with undergraduates, and there were not many people in residence to contribute to the confusion.

Lord Westhoe went speedily to the library, leaving instructions for the dining room rescue with John Spry and two other resident graduates who had come down from their rooms, candles already lit. Indeed, it was interesting to note how many people actually did have candles to hand, although some of these were in strange shapes. John's for instance, was in the form of a Christmas tree, decked with baubles and evidently a left-over from a party.

They went to work at once and quickly moved out all the dining-room furniture and any other portable artifacts into the main hall, with the exception of the dining table, which, as a vast Elizabethan black, oak refectory table, was quite impossible to move.

"Not that it will suffer much damage. It's probably been through a lot worse in the past five hundred years," John grunted, as he struggled to roll up the saturated eighteenth century carpet, heavy with water and plaster debris.

Nothing could have been done, in any case, about the table. It was wider than the doors and was thought to have been made in situ in the sixteenth century by college joiners, whose initials were carved into the decoration. College inventories and records of the time indicated this. It was, in fact, the original built-in unit furniture so to speak.

Sylvia Westhoe, candelabrum in hand, for by this time her torch battery had run out, checked the college treasures on the staircase. The needlework of the ladies of the Court, done here during the Siege of Oxford, was intact in the glass case, and so were Queen Elizabeth I's gloves.

The mediaeval college banner - fifteenth century red silk with angels 'Or' rampant and rejoicing, painted thereon, was also still safe under glass on the staircase wall, where it had hung since it fell into disuse at the dissolution of the monasteries, as the emblem of the college carried in the monastic collegiate processions, and instead of being destroyed, it was suspended, forgotten and never taken down again.

Vertue miaowed and rubbed herself against Lady Westhoe's legs. The commotion had wakened her too, and she was a cat who loved her bed. Unfortunately, however, that bed was the window-seat in the Great Drawing-room. Her eyes glowed fluorescent green in the flickering light and she was saying that the situation was not to her liking. Failing to attract sufficient notice, she went off into the kitchen in search of food. Cats, reflected Lady Westhoe, always seemed to get their priorities right somehow, even in times of stress. Cat food would be there in plenty, of course, so somebody at least was happy.

Lord Westhoe meanwhile had crossed the quad in the tempestuous downpour, umbrella whipping in all directions in the continuing gale, and joined the porter at the library door.

He wrestled again with the lock, but without success.

·

"Oi can't budge it, your lordship, and there's definitely someone in there. Oi just saw "im again at the winder!"

Lord Westhoe addressed himself to the problem. By the light of the porter's powerful torch he fitted the ancient key into lock. There was a firm *click* and the sixteenth-century door opened slowly, creaking with age. Lord Westhoe went forward into the pitch darkness.

Then the powerful beam of the torch illuminated a strange sight.

"There 'e is, sir - look yonder!" The porter pointed a finger fearfully towards the end of the library and they saw, for an instant only, a figure standing there.

It was the merest impression of a tall man in a dark robe, a cowl over his head, just a glimpse of the lower half of a pale face ... and then it was gone. "The grey monk!" The porter was aghast. "Oi've 'eard tell of 'im, sir, but this is moy first soightin'.

Lord Westhoe did not comment, but moved forward into the blackness, shining the torch around in a speedy inspection.

"Dear, oh dear, what a mess!" he said, with a click of the tongue. "Jim, get anyone you can and get them here as quickly as possible, please!"

His torch beam lit up a most extraordinary scene. Manuscripts and books lay scattered around in wild disarray, on the floor, on the reading desks, all over the room. It was as though a naughty child had got into the library and had run a hand along the shelves, sending books and papers cascading down. Original manuscripts of John Donne and Edmund Spenser and even a Shakespeare folio were strewn about everywhere.

Lord Westhoe shone his torch ahead and so did not step on a snowfall of papers, the topmost of which was a manuscript in the hand of Andrew Marvell.

The electronic alarm system, which would have given warning of all this, was as the porter had said indeed "out," and that was a very serious matter. With some of the rarest and most valuable books and manuscripts in the world in its collection, St. James' library was protected like Fort Knox by the most sophisticated alarm system ever designed. It should have been "fail-safe" and yet it was now completely dead, and the whole college in total darkness, to boot.

It was to be first light before power was restored. However, an efficient vigil had been kept by John Spry and his colleagues throughout the confusion of the night.

"A kind of pyjama-clad Securicor, we were," as he observed later: "A most efficient set of security guards." And, joking apart, they did a wonderful job.

It was only at such a time as this, when they were threatened by such danger, that the value of the college's treasures could be appreciated, for there were so many lovely things and so many of them intimately connected with the college's history.

Leaving aside the King's night-attire and the Queen's gloves, the Court ladies' needlework, and so on, there were other lesser, but nevertheless touching mementos of the college's past, such as the magnificent stuffed trout in a glass case in the bottom corridor by the dining-room. 'Caught in 1941 by a Fellow of the College by Parson's Pleasure', read the label, and it was possibly the biggest trout ever stuffed by a taxidermist during wartime, but it should be remembered that with most men away in more martial pursuits, fish and indeed other wild life escaped the usual culling and increased and multiplied uninhibited by man. This one, however, was held to be geriatric in piscine terms and as such probably tough and inedible.

So here hath been dawning Another blue Day:

Think wilt thou let it Slip useless away.

Out of Eternity This new Day is born;

Into Eternity, At night, will return.

Thomas Carlyle's words and the English Traditional Melody hymn tune of Vaughan Williams were what Lady Westhoe was humming to herself as she made yet another pot of tea, and still more mugs of coffee for the diligent night-watchmen. It had been a long night but daybreak was breathtaking in its beauty as a compensation, azure blue with a wonderful sweetness in the air, almost as though there had never been a storm at all. Mystic indeed are the vagaries of the English climate! Only the myriad rainbow dewdrops and the mirror-like puddles of water lying here and there in the college grounds told the tale of the ferocity of the nocturnal tempest.

That is, if one accepts the sorry tale of the dining-room ceiling. A dawn inspection of the seventeenth century lead roof immediately above showed where the fault lay. A dead wood-pigeon lodged in the head of the down-pipe and no doubt drowned in the storm had blocked the guttering and the water had poured through somehow under the lead.

"Blown off 'is perch, looks loike, an' drownded," Bert, the college maintenance man now diagnosed.

"Ar; bad do - chance in a million. 'Oo'd 'a thought a pigeon would a' done all o' that. Can't 'ave 'appened afore in three 'undred years!"

"And without even really trying," yawned John Spry wearily, sitting on the stairs with his coffee mug in his hand.

The mopping-up operation recommenced.

Astonishly enough, a first assessment showed no damage in the library: no damage, it would appear, to any of the library collection and, as far as could be seen as yet, no theft. As for the electronic alarm system, the whole thing would have to be renewed as a matter of urgency - at vast expense, regrettably, but it was a 'must' of the highest priority. The unidentified person in the library was not referred to subsequently. A curious business altogether, but sometimes the inexplicable is best ignored.

The cow dung (for that is what it proved to be after analysis) which slid down the dining-room wall and passed over the King's countenance, was found on investigation to have been part of the lath and plaster structure of the ancient ceiling. An interesting component of old building works with a most pungent and definitely vaccine smell when wet.

After a fitful dose towards dawn, Joy was jerked to instant wakefulness by a banging and thumping from next door. It would seem that Erica was expressing herself in some way. Intermittent screams followed the bangings and thumpings, and after about half an hour of this self-expression Joy tumbled wearily out of bed.

Little tabby was not pleased, as she was firmly entrenched in position on Joy's feet at the bottom of the bed, and grabbed a passing toe with a half-sheathed claw and a firm clench of the teeth.

"Aoouw!"

Tabby let go after a space, and curled up tight in an attitude of sleep, but with one green eye half open to watch for further developments.

Opening the bedroom window, Joy peered down at Erica's quarters in the basement next door.

"Erica?" she called.

Instant silence. The manifestations ceased at once. She leaned out of the window. The rain had stopped as first light shyly revealed itself in the eastern sky. It revealed something else, too. Guttering and drainpipes lay all over Erica's neglected rockery.

"Oh dear, Oh dear!"

Looking up at her own roof and guttering, Joy was relieved to see that hers had simply come away from the wall slightly where it connected with Erica's at the shared down-pipe. It looked as though this might be all the damage the house had suffered.

"Thank the Lord for that!"

At least it would not mean all the complex rigmarole of big insurance claims and the like. She had a horror of such things; and as for the clattering around of builders and their scaffolding, that was sheer agony - especially their transistor radios! And the cats hated it. But Erica' problems were another and sorrier tale. All her guttering had come away in toto, as well as some of the roof tiles, a chimney pot and part of the stack. Alas, such was the legacy of neglect of the general maintenance of the fabric of the house. The old lady had simply let it go over the last few years. This present catastrophe would surely entail much trouble and strife when Erica saw the full extent of the damage. Joy felt in her bones that she herself would be found to be blameworthy in some mysterious way, improbable though it might seem.

And so indeed it proved to be. However, what was to trigger off Erica's violent eruption was not the damage to the house, but something else, which Joy had not noticed in the dimness of the early dawn.

"You have murdered my tree! My tree!"

Joy had collapsed back into bed for that last blissful hour, when all men sleep so deeply - the one that comes just before getting-up time. That wonderful hour of luxurious warmth and comfort, no matter how poor a sleeper one is in the general way.

A missile of some kind hit the bedroom window with a loud rap. Then came the outburst about the tree.

Struggling out of the bliss of a lovely healing sleep, Joy stumbled to the window. It was now quite light and a glorious sun lit the still, dewy morning.

In Erica's garden, a horrifying sight was to be seen.

In a long nightgown, hair streaming down her back, and looking utterly demented, Erica stood defensively in front of what was left of her greengage tree.

"Oh no!" whispered Joy under her breath, "Not the dreaded greengage tree! I just don't believe it. Madre de Dios!"

This tree, the love of Erica's barren life, lay split very neatly in two down the middle across the lawn behind her, where she stood and raged. The lightning had evidently struck it well and truly during the storm. What an irony! The only thing for which Erica had cared in her life.

Its history was fascinating. It had been brought as a seedling from Germany when the old lady and Erica got away at the outbreak of war, and it was the only thing they had been able to preserve from their lovely house in the Kaiserstrasse in Berlin.

The seedling had been growing by the side of its parent in their beautiful formal garden. The parent tree was called "Binchen" after Sabine Trondheim, Erica's grandmother, the adored wife of Herbert Trondheim, an eminent man and most distinguished lawyer in the Berlin of his day. Somehow the seedling had survived in its tiny pot, and after much adventure, had been ceremonially planted by the Rabbi in the garden of their Oxford house, in memory of Dr. Werner Trondheim, who had died in Auschwitz. It was, as it were, his monument and had flourished like the Psalmist's tree planted by the waterside, from the very beginning and in the face of all the odds against its survival. It had brought forth its fruit in due season, the very best greengages in abundance. It was a supremely happy tree and seemed to love Erica as she loved it, in a kind of symbiotic relationship.

She spent most of her time at home sitting under it on fine days, reading or writing or listening to her language course beneath its protective shade. Its fruit was her manna: she adored rather sour greengages and always ate them before they were ripe, at a stage when they would of course be indigestible to anyone else. But, she never gave any to anyone else. For herself, she could be observed selecting with the greatest care a really unripe fruit and bringing it down with a long pole with a hook on the end. Then she would re-arrange herself on her deck-chair and slowly devour it with a relish approaching the cannibalistic.

And now the early light showed the death of the tree. For a brief moment Joy was struck by the resemblance between the vision, of Erica down there in the garden and the demented woman in the paintings of Edvard Munch, so weirdly alike were the ghastly pale face and ash-blond-hair. Erica's passion mounted and she shouted abuse, mostly in German and mostly unintelligible. Joy caught the word "Hexe" several times, apparently directed at herself. The outburst ended with a kind of tribal war-dance and Erica promptly disappeared.

Petronella came downstairs at about eight o'clock, clad in a delightful green Chinese silk dressing-gown embroidered with golden dragons. She looked charming, her hair ruffled from restless sleep. She really was the sweetest girl and it crossed Joy's mind that she would have been proud to have her for a daughter. How much she was going to miss the child when she finished her degree course.

These idyllic thoughts were quickly banished as Petronella retailed her woeful tidings. Water had come in through her bedroom ceiling and soaked the bed. This she had moved and had put a bucket under the leak. Evidently the house had not escaped unscathed after all. They took their coffee out on to the terrace and surveyed the damage through Petronella's binoculars.

Erica's guttering seemed, as far as they could see, to have caused the worst of the damage. It had come down as though some giant hand had wrenched it away from the wall, bringing with it cement, bricks and other debris. Also one of the chimney-pots and part of a stack had toppled sideways on to Joy's roof in descending and brought off a few roof tiles over Petronella's bedroom, where apparently the water had come through.

The diagnosis made, they talked of other matters to take their minds off the whole dreary business for the moment.

How was Bruce? What about a boiled egg and toast for breakfast? They decided on a poached egg on toast as an Epicurean treat for such a morning and then returned to the matter of Bruce.

Yes, Petronella had to admit that she was very fond of the man. He had become part of the furniture and fittings in her life over the past two or three years, without her actually realizing it. Strong, intelligent, reliable - to a degree, which was sometimes infuriating - roguish, but sensitive and kind. A lovely man.

What could Joy say? It was all very difficult. Why not marry him? Well, that was a hard one. Perhaps one might think about it sometime.

That was the end of that conversation.

They couldn't find the egg-poacher, so Petronella did "camper's poached eggs" - a pan of slowly boiling salted water, just simmering, with the raw egg slowly slid into it from a saucer, taken off the gas for a moment, then returned to the heat and slowly simmered again until ' gelled'. Then it was fished out gently with a slice and popped quickly on to hot buttered toast, adding black pepper and a dash of salt, et voila,'camper's delight,' a delectable dish made all the more so by the freshness of the morning and attendant hunger after a sleepless night.

Ruminating over its deliciousness, they were startled in mid-digestion by the telephone. It rang insistently and an inner voice commanded Joy to leave it unanswered, but it would not stop.

Of course, it was Madge Spragnell, it could be no one else.

Petronella beat a hasty retreat upstairs, with a quick "thank you" in sign language to Joy, who was attempting to cope, with difficulty at this early hour, with the verbal waterfall which engulfed her.

It was all absolutely dreadful. My dear, what was one to do? One simply couldn't cope. One couldn't remember a thing - not a thing! The whole situation was completely chaotic, and the Event was so near! When was the fair? Two Weeks hence? My dear, quite, quite awful - such a rush! Since the loss of one's diary, everything had - become altogether impossible. Why did life depend on the written word? So fraught, my dear! Oh well, couldn't be helped; one would survive, one supposed. One simply could not remember phone numbers, and addresses and appointments and things without one's diary, could one? Now, dear, was everything ready? All prepared? Oh good! Just be there!

The message was clear. If one didn't comply, there would be hell to pay. Then an immediate change of gear: Madge in tender mode. Had one suffered from the tempestuous night? Oh, dear me, one had? How very sad. But never mind, make a quick insurance claim - that was the thing to do. Yes, at once, this very minute.

No, no, Madge herself had had no problems, Deo Gratias! The house was sound as a bell, yes indeed, and so was the General's sleep! He had slept through the whole thing, such a mercy, the poor darling; he really was getting a teeny, weeny bit crotchety, you know, hard of hearing, cantankerous, lame and arthritic. Still, bless him, he had (like all good dogs) had his day, and such a fine, handsome dog in his uniform! It quite turned one's head to remember those splendid days! The military balls, my dear, and the Trooping! Such ball dresses one had had - a dream, dear, an absolute dream! One really must root out those marvellous photographs and bring them round one day. Perhaps a nice glass of sherry and a canape. Reminiscing was such fun, wasn't it? And yet so sad! 'The snows of yesteryear,' was that the expression? (Joy thought donnishly that it was a little out of context).

Now dear, about the fair. It's tin-rattlers one wants, you know, good hearty souls, with big, big hearts and lovely big, big smiles to bring in the money, dear. Yes, the money! That's what it's all about, my dear!

What about Erica? No? Oh dear, not really! So sorry. Well, she always was a bit funny, wasn't she?

Well then, we leave it with you, dear. Tin-rattlers, don't forget, tin-rattlers with big, big hearts. I am relying on you, dear. Bye-ee.

Click!

That was the end of that. Madge's homily was terminated.

Joy spied the milkman passing in his float and dashed out to catch him.

The phone rang again. Running back to answer it, she missed him and the intended purchase of a pot of fresh cream.

It was, of course, Madge, who else? - with an afterthought.

"Now, dear, I want you and your darling little choir to sing from 9 p.m. prompt, and tin-rattlers from 7 p.m. Don't forget. I am relying on you utterly, dear!" Click!

The emphatic tone of voice was in some curious way menacing and made Joy oddly uneasy for a moment.

"Petronella!" Joy called up the stairs, but there was no reply. Petronella had 'done a dormouse' and adroitly slipped off to bed for a further cat-nap. How very sensible. Perhaps she should do likewise for a while.

It would have been fine if she had had the chance.

However, the phone rang yet again. This time it was Miss Dacre with an instant salvo - a full broadside from the old man o' war.

"Miss Hetherington, do you realize what your drains are doing? It simply ought not to be allowed. It's a perfect scandal, I tell you! Do something instantly, or I shall be compelled to make a complaint!" Click!

Drains? Quick - take a swift look round the house at the drains! She looked out of the back windows. Nothing at all was amiss. The main drain from the bathrooms and kitchen was quite in order. What a relief!

The only other one was the down-pipe from the guttering at the front of the house, which was intact, so Miss Dacre appeared to have been hallucinating - or perhaps she had made a mistake and Erica's drain-pipes were responsible?

She went to the drawing-room window and looked down. Nothing at all wrong there. Miss Dacre was definitely wandering in her mind, or just trying to be tiresome?

Then she looked down the drive towards the gateway beyond her car. Ah yes! There it was, Noye's Fludde, indeed! Oxford's unique drains had once more 'done their thing'. The car appeared to be some kind of aquatic vehicle, up to its 'Knees' (or tyre-rims) in floodwater. The iron grid in the gutter outside the gate had rebelled. It was, of course, part of Oxford's rich heritage of antiquities, sharing this honour with many pillar-boxes, street signs and letter boxes, dating from the penny-black era; and far too small for modern postal needs, but the ingenuity of Oxford postmen is such that they cope somehow.

Stamped on the delicately wrought-iron grid was the legendary name of the makers,E. Druce & Co., Oxford, which was still a thriving business in the original factory. These excellent grids had withstood over a hundred years of heavy use, but plastic cartons, coke tins, cans, beer plastic cans, plastic bags and the like had proved too much and Joy's grid outside the gate had choked on a surfeit of modern litter and leafy debris.

The flood was extensive. Indeed it came halfway up the drive and there was a veritable torrent rushing down the road. Joy went down the drive as far as the car and looked out cautiously over the floodwaters. She espied something red and plastic-covered floating on top - a small booklet of some kind.

Fishing for it with a branch of forsythia which was floating nearby she brought it to shore and perceived it to be a waterlogged diary, still intact, owing to the plastic cover and a press stud clip-flap.

Diary! Of course, Madge's diary, late-lamented, lost down the drain when her bicycle jettisoned her shopping everywhere that day some time ago! It had come up again. She fished it up gingerly out of the water and took it down to the potting shed, propping it high on a shelf to dry. She really must remember to give it to Madge. She promptly forgot all about it, of course.

CHAPTER XI

'Yet, sweet, take heed!'

The Second Set of Madrigals to 3, 4, 5 & 6 parts

John Wilbye 1609

A few blissfully uneventful days passed, during which much academic work was done. Such heaven to bury oneself in one's books and forget about people for a while! This luxury was, however, soon to be denied her, brought about by the incessant and irritating ring of the telephone.

Joy was, of course, at the bottom of the garden when the phone began to ring, hanging out the washing. At first she ignored it, hoping it might stop, but inevitably it rang on, insistently demanding to be answered.

"Madge," she thought grimly, wiping her damp hands on her pinafore, "Oh damn!" Petronella's duvet cover slid gently from the washing line on to the path below for it was not pegged on yet. No time to rescue it, and too late; it would be ruined anyway from falling on to the rather muddy pebbles beneath. She would simply have to wash it all over again. Damn, damn!

Madge it was, of course. The homily went much as before, but a curious edge to Madge's tone of voice was just a little intimidating.

Now, Joy must not, but simply must not forget! Remember, it was only next week! Yes, yes, it was as near as that, dear! No, no, not the first night of the fair - the second night, when of course it all tended to happen, didn't it, dear? When there would be lots of lovely generous people to give lots and lots of lovely money for the charity, dear! And be sure not to forget the most important thing of all - to sing up to, and during the draw of the great raffle at 10 p.m. Now, Joy was to remember (a little extra edge on the voice here) - up to and during the actual draw: this was of paramount importance. Oh good! As long as it was clearly understood, then that would be simply marvellous!

Then the tender passage in honeyed tones, the voice dropping an octave. Of course, dear, one simply had to put oneself out, and do as much charitable work as was humanly possible in Oxford, didn't one? After all, it was one's duty and definitely the done thing, wasn't it, dear? Of course, it wasn't that one was actually seeking for honour or anything like that, was it? But quite honestly, dear, the General would simply adore it if one were by chance to pick up an M.B.E. or something, and after all, one had done absolutely so much, but so much over the years, hadn't one? It was just a tiny thought, and strictly off the cuff as it were, and merely a sort of aspiration, but when one did think about it, it wouldn't be absolutely unmerited, would it? So Joy was to do her very, very best with her darling little choir in those simply divine little Elizabethan costumes, wasn't she, dear?

And that had been the end of the conversation.

"Silly old trout!" Mark had exclaimed, when Joy told him about it later. "Poor old Rupert Spragnell, she must have led him the hell of a life, nagging him to death all the time. It's a wonder he's survived so long, with Madge to drive him up the pole. I would have strangled her years ago!"

"He's well anaesthetized with Glenfiddich, I would think," Joy had retorted with a rueful smile. "And he really is such a darling old thing. Such a pity!"

"Perhaps the poor old lad had had a skinful when he proposed to her - the miserable old battleaxe; that would account for it, I suppose."

"Mark, dear, don't be such a cynic. I expect she was quite stunning when she was a young gal."

Mark had smiled quietly to himself at this, for even the very thought of Madge Spragnell ever having been a 'young gal' was something just a little improbable.

"Much more likely she was a scheming little minx, on the look-out for a rich young sucker, ay dear Aunt!"

He had then lit a pipe, and after thoughtfully watching the traditional smoke rise for a while, had said: "I wouldn't trust Madge an inch, and that's for sure!"

Joy, truly scandalized, had rebuked him for this uncharitable comment. She agreed that Madge was a great nuisance, but she certainly wasn't dishonest, was she?

But Mark was not to be moved on the subject, so that was an end of the matter. He simply would not credit her with any good qualities. Surprising, really, for Mark was one of the most affable of men, generally uncritical of people, and he could be kindness itself, especially to the elderly.

Evidently Madge did not qualify for any of this.

Bruce's departure for Australia passed almost unnoticed, which was very curious. There was no great skirling of bagpipes or farewell party in the garden. He just took Petronella out for a quiet candlelit dinner one evening at a select bistro on Little Clarendon Street and was gone the next morning. He made a quick call from the airport to say goodbye to her, and that was that; love and thanks to Joy for being so kind, etcetera, and "Fare thee weel, lassie." He did, however, promise to write.

Petronella became rather quiet and seemed to lose a lot of her natural sparkle overnight, but she was intensely busy with her work, so that was a mercy. Joy tried to think of things to cheer her up, but nothing came immediately to mind - except, of course, for the fearful fund-raiser at the fair, "so soon to be upon us! Horrors!" she thought. The nearer the day drew, the less she liked the thought of it.

There was something new now in Madge's manner which grated on one's nerves. She became more and more tense at every encounter and all her fey charm seemed to diminish as the fair drew nearer. Maybe she was desperate for the M.B.E.: that could be an explanation; or perhaps the General was getting difficult. He was, after all, extremely frail nowadays and must be quite hard work to look after, for he could hardly walk and his memory was failing him rapidly. Better to be charitable and think positively, for it would in the final analysis all be over in a matter of two hours, at least as far as their singing episode was concerned.

She asked Petronella if she would come to help at the event.

"You could rattle a tin, or something - in costume, of course."

Petronella agreed gracefully, more from a sense of duty than anything else, for the very last thing on earth she really wanted to do was something of this nature. However - must try to keep Prof. H. happy; she was that great rarity - a really good landlady, so it was worth the effort.

Brenda Page-Phillips fitted her up with a most effective costume, made as usual from an ingenious combination of bits and pieces, consisting of a faded green velvet curtain for a skirt and a tight black velvet waistcoat over a long-sleeved silky blouse, with a ruff at the throat, while a string of pearls placed on her head formed a coronet, with one single earring clipped on to the pearls, centre forehead, looking most fetching. The whole ensemble was finished off with much junk jewellery - festoons of long necklaces and many finger-rings, in hopefully authentic imitation of Elizabethan splendour.

Petronella tried hard to make a show of enthusiasm but it was a vain attempt. Brenda commiserated gently over the matter of Bruce, having suffered a broken heart herself once or twice over the years. Petronella, however, was not to be consoled. She said that no understanding whatsoever had been arrived at with him, and that it would all seem to be completely open-ended; most unsatisfactory altogether.

"Never mind, he'll write. Just you wait and see!"

Brenda had smiled a beaming smile of encouragement and thereafter Petronella had begun to feel a little better about things.

Peter Rumbold, Michael Walters and Joy talked about the strange goings-on and the apparent lack of any explanation so far of Cledwyn's strange death and the other disturbing occurrences.

Joy's comment that possibly the police had lost interest, for nothing at all seemed to be happening, was met by Michael's quote: "The mills of God grind slow," etc. Peter laughed and remarked that he thought the mills of God were very apt. He had always found that the Oxford police had in the end been singularly efficient, although sometimes that end seemed very long in coming and there was a prolonged and seemingly eventless lull in between, when presumably investigations were under way.

Peter also observed that he had himself unhappily experienced some unwelcome excitement recently with one of the characters in this drama - Erica Trondheim. Joy was interested, as she hadn't seen much of her in the last four days but had heard her banging around in the basement during the night at odd times in an inexplicable way which was most unnerving, and she was thankful that Petronella was in the house; it could be frightening to be alone.

Peter's encounter had not only been unpleasant, but also rather costly, he related. Erica had made a lengthy order by telephone, namely five boxes of quite expensive bedding plants and had, after much delay, arrived to collect then; she had then picked a fight with an unsuspecting customer, had thrown the whole lot on the floor in a fit of terrible rage, and then exited, mouthing threats.

"Can't have done the plants a lot of good," said Michael.

"Quite so; they were completely ruined and, what's more, she didn't pay for them."

Peter was not pleased. He frowned a dark frown.

"She's not setting foot in here again and that's for sure! Twenty-five pounds worth of fine plants completely destroyed. Quite, quite mad."

Joy expressed unease about Erica. She certainly did seem to be getting worse. As long as she didn't 'do a Mrs Danvers' and set fire to the house, that was all one could pray for.

"If that awful old diesel boiler of hers went up, it would probably take my poor old house with it as well! The party-wall is not very substantial, even though it is quite good old Victorian solid stuff."

Unhappy thought indeed, and these were once again prophetic words.

The dull rumble of heavy lorries passing down Woodstock Road in the direction of town about midnight the following Saturday heralded the setting up of St. Giles' Fair.

Joy awoke with a start. Heavens, the fair - oh no!

Iffley, again taking up most of the bed, graciously allowed her to turn over with a quizzical "Rrrrr?" followed by a yawn and a luxurious stretch.

It is now traditional in Oxford that the fair is set up during the night, as soon as St. Giles is closed to traffic on Saturday evening. The fair is always held on the first Monday and Tuesday in September each year.

In spite of the constant bustle of traffic and many bicycles, St. Giles somehow always manages to retain its atmosphere of discreet grandeur; the wide boulevard lined on both sides with trees, the colleges nestling sedately behind, with a sprinkling of shops and pubs interspersed with the college facades. Martyr's Memorial stands at the south end in front of St. Mary Magdalen Church with its ancient graveyard, and the Randolph Hotel alongside on the corner of Beaumont Street.

To the uninitiated, the transformation when the fair is set up is truly astonishing - a complete eye-opener.

It has often been said that Oxford is the city of contrasts, and nothing demonstrates this more graphically than the annual event of St. Giles' Fair. At one moment, it seems, there is the sober academic setting, and the next, all the vulgarity, noise, fun, screams and extremes of the mammoth fair.

Mark declared that a quiet stroll through the fair on Sunday evening would be the order of the day. It had been years since he sang, as a choirboy with the City church choir at the traditional Sunday Evensong, held on the carousel - commonly known as the Gallopin' 'Orses - which is always set up near Martyr's Memorial at this event.

And so it was that he, Michael and Joy walked down together to inspect the fair, now set up and ready for off on Monday morning.

All was peace as they walked down Woodstock Road; no traffic at all, of course, because of the road closures ahead, and no sound except of people walking along and talking among themselves. The motor-car had been temporarily banished.

The scene was otherwise quite normal as far as the Radcliffe Infirmary and the Royal Oak, but beyond this point the road was blocked off and a truly amazing sight was to be seen.

"A far cry from the mediaeval fair as it was, isn't it?" Mark was pensive.

"Just imagine it; jugglers, acrobats, fire-eaters - dancing bears, even, mystery plays - sale of livestock, probably. That was a different world."

"No doubt," Michael shrugged his shoulders; "But it sure isn't like that now - 'oh, Sirrah Jack, no!"

This was true. Everything that was big, brash and improbable confronted them. Huge generators mounted on enormous trucks formed the rearguard, and beyond these rose up great hoardings proclaiming 'The Ghost Train' and "The Wall of Death," and so on. Suitably horrible pictures adorned the hoardings above the entrances to these amusements, with charges of course writ large on each.

They picked their way gingerly between booths and trucks, stepping over heaps of writhing pipes, laid out like so many dormant python; but no doubt pulsating with the life-blood of the fair. Once through this veritable obstacle-race, an extraordinary vista lay before them. As far as the eye could see, amusement arcades, stalls and merry-go-rounds stretched away into the distance. The skyline was punctuated by gigantic constructions, haphazardly towering above the college facades. The nearest was by St. Giles' graveyard, a fairy castle affair with a helter-skelter wound round the outside of its structure of fine imitation Gothic stonework. "The Mat," it proclaimed over its entrance. 50p adults, 25p children.

"Goodness me," said Joy; "that looks dangerous!"

"Only if you slip off your mat and get your posterior polished!" Mark laughed.

"Tremendous fun! Just look at that!"

He indicated the Big Wheel, looming still and silent over St. James' College tower, like some enormous metal spider's web.

"Good Lord, if it falls over, it could crush St. James's flat!" said Joy.

The Octopus stood close by, arms extended to the sky, with twirling seats stuck precariously on the end of its tentacles. "Terrifying!" Joy shuddered, "So realistic!" They inspected the bumper-cars by the Gallopin' 'Orses.

"Must have a go on those!" Michael was intrigued. "You and me, Joy. Shall we?"

Joy was not at all sure about this proposed adventure, but she had the uneasy feeling that Michael would have his way in the matter, come the day!

Such peace in St. Giles. It was almost tangible.

As they approached the Gallopin' 'Orses, the clergy and choir, fully robed, came towards them from the City church to sing Evensong. It was an incongruous but touching sight to watch them file quietly past Martyr's Memorial and mount the steps of the carousel, which is a vast and beautiful original antique, lovingly kept in immaculate order by the owners, painted and gilded exactly as it originally was, and still with its fine mechanical organ. The proud horses, nostrils flared, necks arched, rise and fall majestically to the sound of the marvellous music when this unique merry-go-round is in operation, a wonderful spectacle beloved of generations of Oxonians.

A silent assembly of people now stood reverently in front of the still carousel to take part in the service. Joy saw Percy Chad and Tina, who sat as good as gold by his feet. And there - of all people - was Miss Dacre (without Pongo, happily) standing sedately in a silk suit - with black accessories, Joy noted, very proper; nice hat with veil, of course, white lace jabot at the throat, with a fine cameo pinned neatly thereon, dead centre below the chin.

She studiedly ignored Joy, the corners of her mouth firmly drawn down in an expression of severe disapproval. Joy ventured a nod and a discreet wave, but Miss Dacre of course wasn't having any, and produced a fine lace handkerchief, with which she elegantly dabbed the end of her long, aristocratic nose, and looked steadfastly at the clergy and choir, who were by now standing in front of the horses on the podium. The service began with a hymn, 'Sun of my soul, thou Saviour dear', a good old Keeble hymn, as Michael commented later, and most suitable for the occasion. Miss Dacre's reedy soprano held its own against the choir, which of course sang beautifully. Michael had an irreverent thought and muttered out of the side of his mouth: "What if someone were to start the machinery?"

Mark struggled to stifle a laugh.

"We could have lift-off - ," Michael continued in a whisper. Joy - sobersides normally - nearly suffered a seizure with the physical effort of stopping herself giggling.

Percy and Tina, close by, noticed the subdued convulsions. Tina tilted her head to one side, anxious to understand the meaning of all this.

They managed, with superhuman effort, to save themselves from utter disgrace by not openly laughing, and thereafter concentrated hard on the service.

Walking back afterwards towards St. Giles' Church, they stopped a while by the Wall of Death and inspected the site near the War Memorial by St. Giles' graveyard wall where Madge's famous stall was to be set up. The ancient fig-tree leaned comfortably over them as the Salvation Army Band (section) played suitably rousing hymns by the Wall of Death entrance. The brass, few in number but invincible in spirit, played triumphantly as though to encourage such brave souls as would dare to enter there. They finished, appropriately enough, with "Abide with Me,"

"Always moves me to tears!" Michael blew his nose.

Mark said nothing, but Joy noted the far-away look in his eyes.

"Not quite the Royal Marines band, Mark, but very fine, don't you think?"

He didn't seem to have heard her, so she quickly changed the subject and spoke instead of Madge's stall and the arrangements for the proposed singing.

It really did look like a lost cause, she observed, a complete waste of time and effort.

"Oxford, the home of lost causes.." Michael quoted absently.

This one, however, looked utterly hopeless. Feeling dwarfed by the Wall of Death towering over them, she cringed again at the idea of attempting to sing against the deafening roar of the motor-bikes, the screams of the populace, the constant rumble of diesel engines and generators, the general din of the fair.

Better not to do it at all!

Mark did not agree, however. "No, no, go ahead with it.

It'll still look good and the object, after all, is to make money for the charity, when all is said and done. You can't let Madge down, even if she is a silly old..."

"Mrs Feather?" Joy cut him off quickly. "Madame Arcati?," Mark ventured.

"No, old battle-axe, of course," said Michael, stamping out his cigarette-butt and scowling at the thought of Madge Spragnell. "It's the only way to describe her - a female bulldozer, she is!"

Michael returned to the subject of bumper-cars and was quite determined to get Joy to ride in one, so after much persuasion as they walked back home up Woodstock Road, she reluctantly agreed to this dreadful idea.

Mark announced that he would bring a girl-friend along and they would have their own little stock-car event. The one who scored the least hits, he decided, was to buy the drinks at the Royal Oak afterwards.

Joy trembled, but said nothing.

Before separating, they arranged to meet at 7.30 p.m. the following evening and walk down together to the fair.

Joy told Mrs Badger this the next morning and the latter, sniffing in profound deprecation, spoke her mind on the matter.

"Daftness, Oi calls it, Miss Hetherington. A lady of your years should ought to know better. Could quite upset your inside, it could. Don't want to be a' startin' somethin' a bit nasty orf, do yer, naow? A woman's inside be very delicate at the best o' toims, but when yer gets to your age, you got to watch it, an' that's for sure. All that jerkin' abaout! Just look at wot 'appened to moi dear old Auntie Aggie when 'er was 'elpin' that there thatcher get them reeds up to 'er roof!"

She fixed Joy with a significant look.

"Never the same again after, she wa'nt: Terrible 'twas!"

Nothing more was said on the subject, and indeed Joy dared not ask what it was that happened to Aunt Aggie after helping the thatcher, but clearly "all that jerkin' about" had brought about a terrible disaster judging by the look on Mrs Badger's face.

As usual, Mrs Badger then made a stately departure on her bicycle with her basket, also as usual, full to overflowing with a veritable cornucopia of delights including, of course, Mr. Badger's bottle of Whiskey carefully wedged in the middle of a selection of finest fruit and vegetables - nothing was too good for Mr. Badger.

"Just remember wot Oi says now. Best not to eat nothin' at all afore you goes" - she called over her shoulder as she pedaled off up the road. "Don't want to be sick and disgrace yourself, now, do you, moi duck?"

Words of cold comfort, indeed! Petronella, when told, was quite overcome with mirth at the delicious thought of it all, and only wished she could go too, but she was desperately behind with her work and simply couldn't spare the time. However, Joy suspected that if Bruce had still been in Oxford, Petronella would have somehow contrived to make time to go to the fair. It was a sad little story, but then that was Oxford, after all, here to-day, gone tomorrow.

The following day, surely like some portent of doom, Erica Trondheim set up the most terrible commotion imaginable in St. Julie's Road. There was a loud tooting of car horns, much aggravated revving of engines, screechings of brakes and voices raised in anger.

This happened at about ten o'clock in the morning.

Joy, fearing the worst, peeped out through the drawing-room curtains. Miss Dacre, she noted, was already in position at her window, with a grandstand view of the proceedings.

The road was jammed solid with stationary traffic, in both directions, and behold, there stood Erica in the middle of the road, waving her arms above her head and shouting in a kind of demented wail at the top of her voice.

Harriet Spinster's head appeared over the garden wall next door. "I think Erica's making a protest," she said with a mischievous grin. "Something to do with St. Giles' Fair, one would think."

She pointed out Erica's ancient VW beetle, which she had parked neatly across the middle of the road, effectively blocking all traffic in both directions; Overnight, the police had put up "no waiting" signs all along St. Julie's Road, and in consequence it had become a kind of race track for the duration of the fair, as all through traffic was directed along it to avoid the city centre. Evidently Erica had taken exception to this arrangement and had most effectively stopped it in her own inimitable fashion!

The substance of her screams and shouts seemed to be that she was not going to have it at any price; they had no right to do this thing at all, and their noise and fumes was a serious health hazard, etc.

Joy and Harriet watched, amazed, as something approaching a riot ensued.

Mercifully, somebody - probably Miss Dacre, they surmised - had called the police, who came swiftly, moved Erica's car back into her drive, calmed her down and took her into her house in a kindly, conciliatory fashion; and the traffic thankfully moved on.

"Just let you or I do something like that, Harriet, and see what would happen to us!"

"The divine right of the mad," said Harriet, shrugging her shoulders. "She really does get away with murder, doesn't she?" And who knows, possibly she had.

Thereafter, the distant noise of the fair was a constant background to the day's activities; a kind of thunderous rumble overlaid with a cacophonous mixture of deafening pop music, the silvery tinkling of fairground organs and booming amplified jovial voices, inviting the world to "come along now, ladies and gentlemen - all the fun of the fair!" The maniacal laughter and horrifying screams from the Ghost Train could be heard quite clearly, coupled with the muffled roar of the Wall of Death motor-bikes, alternating in crescendo and diminuendo as the brave troupe rode the wall in death-defying horizontal circuits.

How dearly Joy hoped the boys would forget all about the fair that evening! No such luck, however. Michael telephoned at five o'clock to ensure that she would be ready and waiting at the appointed time. Petronella tried hard to hide her amusement, failing miserably of course and spluttering with a mercurial burst of laughter instead. Joy was not altogether comforted by this overt show of glee, but thought to herself that at least something had cheered up the poor girl in her hour of sadness over the loss of Bruce.

"Never mind, you'll have a wonderful time, just wait and see," said Petronella. "Nothing like a traditional fair to blow away the cob-webs!"

Promptly at 7.30 p.m. Michael appeared on the doorstep, closely followed by Mark and the lovely Scandinavian girl he had taken a fancy to at the "Jolly Sailors." They were in happy mood and Joy soon captured the spirit of the occasion, and even began to feel quite uplifted as they all walked down together. Marit, the girl-friend, was most excited about it all. What stunning good looks the Scandinavians have, thought Joy. Platinum-blond hair - but real, as nature ordained - sea-green eyes, a lovely fine-boned face and a truly wonderful figure. She was the sweetest girl, and so full of fun and vivacity. Mark had such good taste!

As they drew near to the fair, the noise got louder, the flaring lights got brighter and Marit became more and more excited.

They picked their way across the writhing pipes and between the great throbbing engines and entered the fair.

All the senses were assaulted at once!

The evil stench of fried onions and hamburger hung on the air, combined with the sickening smell of diesel oil. (Thank God, thought Joy, that she had taken Mrs Badger's advice and had eaten nothing since lunch). The visual impact was kaleidoscopic; flashing laser lights shot blinding beams in all directions, a myriad multi-coloured electric light bulbs created an illuminated tiara overall, and the big wheel turned slowly on powerful majesty, elegantly adorned with a necklet of lights.

The colleges, inches away, were dramatically offset by the illumination, like some improbable stage back-drop, standing silently, all hatches firmly battened down against any invasion from the fair. For an invasion this most certainly was. The big wheel seemed almost to touch the facade of St. James' College, as it rotated head onto it. The seats, as they swung perilously over the bop of the wheel, gave the optical illusion of actually touching the stonework.

As they drew nearer, Joy pointed out one poor desperate little gargoyle on the facade about twenty feet up, sticking out its tongue, eyes popping out in what might fairly be construed to be abject terror, judging from its facial expression, as the wheel spun inches from its weather-worn nose It appeared, from the way it had been sculpted, to be drawing backwards, pushing away hard with its front claws and frantically attempting to take off with its poor little stunted bat- wings. It was quite uncanny.

"When you think it's been up there frightening off the evil spirits for about five hundred years or so, and now it looks as though it's given up at last and wants out, with this lot for the opposition."

Mark pointed out another one a little further along the facade. "For instance, just take a look at him, poor old lad! He looks just about ready to expire at the sight of the dreadful goings-on."

He indicated the mitred head of a bishop; the lean and patient face bore the expression of one suffering great pain and sorrow, the cheeks lined, the mouth drawn down at the corners in silent anguish, presumably at the awful spectacle before him.

The next one was a kind of cross-breed between a lizard and a dragon. It gave the impression of being most anxious to escape up the stonework, for it had been carved writhing and twisting upwards. It also had that terribly urgent look on its face which enhanced the overall sense of desperation.

They passed through the 'madding throng', as Mark described it, with difficulty, for it was like some kind of large-scale obstacle race. All sorts and conditions of humanity were there, utterly absorbed in the frenzied activity and ranging from the highly respectable to the frankly disreputable: dons and their families, hippies, old Oxonians, country folk, drop-outs and tramps and a veritable multitude of foreign students, forming fascinating and ever-changing patterns.

The party arrived, after a struggle, at the bumper-cars, close by the gallopin' 'orses. The cars whizzed round at an alarming rate, merrily smashing into one another at every opportunity.

Michael beamed a great smile of pure joy.

"Can't wait," he said, rubbing his hands together in anticipation of great things.Joy flinched at the horrendous bangs and crashes. This was going to be dreadful, it really was.

"Perhaps I could just watch and cheer you on?"

No such luck, however;Michael was adamant. She would thoroughly enjoy it once she had actually got in the car, it was all immense fun!

As the current session came to an end, Michael leapt into the nearest car and Joy, resigned, climbed gingerly into the passenger seat. Mark and Marit secured another one and then they were off, the electric engines starting up slowly. As they speeded up, the bumping began in earnest and poor Joy felt quite sick at the first impact.The arena was packed and cars seemed to be whizzing around at an incredible speed.

After a while, weaving round and avoiding things, Michael espied Mark and Marit. The Scandinavian beauty threw back her head, golden hair streaming out behind and waved enthusiastically, letting out a wild Nordic whoop of delight as they sped past, missing Michael and Joy by a whisker.

"Let's get 'em!" Michael, the scent of the chase in his nostrils, whirled the car round at speed, planning to meet them head-on when they came round again on their next circuit.Unhappily, he hit several other cars instead, and after throwing his own car into a nauseating spin, saw them approaching through the thick of the traffic and set his course to meet them head-on once more.He had set himself up perfectly for this manoeuvre.

"Hell's teeth!"

Another car shot across Michael's bows, effectively blocking his direct hit on Mark's approaching nose.

A familiar face smiled serenely at him in passing; Lord Westhoe accompanied by his young grandson, who was riding shotgun, so to speak. He weaved his way through the chaos with amazing skill, somehow managing not to get hit at all, which was no mean feat in the throng and press around him.

Instantly, Mark's car appeared, and with a fiendish grin he hit Michael and Joy firmly amidships, spun round, and to add insult to injury, Mark's car appeared to hit him again! Marit screamed with delight.

The cars then ground slowly to a halt, for it was the end of the session, and Michael muttered dark words of resentful resignation about buying the forfeited drinks of defeat at the Royal Oak.

Lord Westhoe and his grandson stayed put in their bumper-car, opting for another ride and clearly thoroughly enjoying themselves.

Joy was only too glad to escape without being sick and tottered feebly down the steps to wait for the others. The crush of humanity was now a solid mass and everyone in the vast crowd, she noted, seemed to be eating either a bag of soggy chips or a weaver's spindle of candy-floss. What curious ways people had of enjoying themselves, but how Cledwyn would have loved all this manic scene, she thought sadly, as the gallopin' 'orses rose and fell in dignified formation on their magnificent whirligig.

"Like a go on those?" Michael joined her at the foot of the

steps. "We shall have to wait for a while."

"Mark and Marit are having another go on the bumper-cars, so

Joy agreed somewhat wearily and they climbed aboard for the next ride, Joy anticipating further nausea - but instead it was an unforgettably lovely experience.

She rode, side-saddle, of course, on the outside line of horses and found it not only comfortable, but soothing. It was also rather like taking a ride back through history and had a curious mesmeric charm.

The ride began. The magnificent organ started its musical accompaniment and the carousel began to move slowly round, the horses rising and falling in stately formation, hypnotic and lovely.

Michael rode behind, completely absorbed. He loved it.

They started off facing inwards towards St. John's, moving round slowly to pass St. Mary Magdalene Church and Martyrs Memorial. Perhaps ghosts were watching this strange spectacle from the quiet darkness of the adjacent graveyard behind all this garish scene, but who could tell?

Next, the Randolph Hotel passed by, brightly lit and still somehow imbued with Victorian dignity. Worcester College lay quiet at the bottom of Beaumont Street, then further round, the Ashmolean Museum and the Taylorian Institute, steel-shuttered against vandalistic invasion.

The broad avenue of St. Giles had completely disappeared under an all-enveloping sugar icing of stalls and side-shows and Blackfriars stood quietly back, away from it all, down on the left in low profile behind the trees. To the north, St. Giles' Church tower had completely vanished behind the Mat and the Wall of Death and Banbury Road had also got lost under yet another encrustation of fairground delights. There was a high population density of burger-bars and fish-and-chip vans at that end, hence the smell.

Poor old St. James', tucked away, down on the right beyond St. John's, looked distinctly threatened by the close proximity of the big wheel, looming over it in gigantic silhouette.

On the second time round Joy began to note faces in the crowd as the carousel gathered speed. There, sitting on the steps of Martyrs Memorial was that fellow Dick with his dog. He sat with an altogether insalubrious group of down-and-outs. They passed a bottle round the group and each took a swig - it seemed to be a cider flagon, Joy noted. Well Cledwyn would have been with them, she supposed, if he had been still alive, and to this sad thought succeeded another: better out of it than to end up like that, drinking some evil mixture out of a shared flagon.

The gallopin' 'orses began to move faster and faces flashed past. She caught a glimpse, for an instant, of that quiet man who did his crosswords at the Jolly

Sailors, standing alone and looking up towards St. Giles' Church. He seemed to be deep in thought, despite all the distractions around him, looking somehow isolated, even in the crowd. Then, in a trice, he had disappeared, lost in the sea of faces out there.

The carousel swept round even faster. Michael shouted "Yippee!" from behind, and then, for a fleeting moment, Joy spotted one-legged Willie playing his mouth-organ to Dick and the others on the steps of the memorial. They were having a great time without actually spending any money. Or were they? Her scale of values seemed to be tilting like the 'orses. Then everything became a blur as they achieved their maximum speed. It was such a marvelous experience - everyone should try it! The Victorians certainly knew how to do things right - the whole ride was pure enjoyment.

As they slowed down and came to a halt, Mark and Marit waved to them from below.

"And again'" challenged Michael, with an inviting wave.

No further bidding was necessary and Marit was first to jump smartly on to her chosen steed, eager for the ride. Mark laughed with sheer delight as the ride commenced. Marit looked lovely, golden hail streaming like a Valkyrie, waving to the crowd, caught up in the fun of the fair.

They all walked happily back together, threading their way through the crush, and achieved the relative peace and sanctuary of the Royal Oak a few minutes later.

Joy's comment was that she couldn't remember having enjoyed herself so much for years. They agreed about this and Marit was so delighted that she completely forgot her English for a while and bubbled away in her own tongue with sheer excitement.

Michael, officially conceding defeat in the matter of the bumper-cars contest, bought the drinks, for the opposition had indeed won hands down with no trouble at all. Pity, but never mind, there would be another time.

Petronella joined them later for coffee and liqueurs on the terrace when they returned to Joy's house. Marit's natural gaiety was infectious and they spent a delightful hour together laughing over what had, against all odds, in Joy's expectation at least, turned out to be quite a champagne event and a memorable evening.

Of Erica, thank goodness, there was no sign, although laughter, to quote Mark, was more or less calculated to flush her out. Mercifully, this time it did not.

They said goodnight and departed about eleven o'clock. Petronella opted to stay up and read, for she had so much lost time to make up. Joy went to bed, after making sure that everyone, that is, all the cats plus the local tame fox, had been fed and watered.

She drifted off into a peaceful sleep and only half-woke at about two o'clock to the sound of a kind of rumbling, rather like a distant, semi-active volcano. She was also vaguely aware of the sound of powerful throbbing engines and a sensation of general unrest and people moving around next door. Action on her part, however, seemed uncalled for and sleep irresistible, so she slept on until morning, pinned down perforce, since Iffley, firmly in position on her feet, never moved all night

CHAPTER XII

'Fyer, Fyer!'

The First Book of Ballets to Five Voices

Thomas Morley 1595

A gentle tap at her door woke her at half-past seven. It was Petronella, weary and rather bleary-eyed, for she had had very little sleep during the night, as she explained, and a good deal of excitement which she could well have done without.

Joy listened in astonishment to a tale of disaster. Erica, it seemed, had not quite done a Mrs Danvers, but had come pretty close to it.

At about one in the morning Petronella, who was quietly reading, had smelt a horrid smell - a hot, burning, filthy, oily smell, and since her windows were wide open, soon black smoke began to drift in.

Swiftly, she had gone downstairs to investigate, right down to the basement. She could see no sign of fire, but she quickly located the heat source to the party-wall with the next-door house. It was baking hot down there and the wall was actually roasting to the touch!

Terrified, she wasted no time and rang the fire brigade and they, efficient as always, were promptly on the spot and in action.

As there was no sign of life in Erica's house, they went straight in - just in the nick of time, so it seemed, to avert catastrophe.

The famous boiler was just on the verge of exploding, in a kind of "melt down" as one of the firemen put it. In making a quick search of the house they found Erica comatose but not dead, in a smoke-filled bedroom. It appeared that she had knocked herself out with Valium, after setting the boiler so high that it had at last given up the ghost in its attempt to satisfy her whim for tropical temperatures throughout the house.

She was now in hospital and it looked very much as though Petronella through her vigilance had saved her life - and the house from an explosion into the bargain.

A substantial breakfast for Petronella was clearly next on the day's agenda, especially as this was the day of Madge's Great Event! So bacon and eggs, delicious hot buttered toast and a pot of good strong filter coffee was consumed by both with considerable relish, as Joy's appetite had been stimulated by a feeling of relief that her awful premonition had at least been fulfilled without her dear old house actually being burnt down in the process, and Petronella's by the fact that she was so utterly exhausted, that food, and plenty of it, must be the fuel source to keep her going on what promised to be a most exacting day, culminating in a wearisome couple of hours or so at that charity thing in the evening, as he privately phrased it.

Joy waved her goodbye at the garden gate and watched her pedal off up the road to college with what was intended to be a tactful reminder to be at St. James' at seven-thirty to get ready for the great event; howbeit, in actual fact this reminder emerged as a somewhat peremptory didactic instruction.

Petronella, however, was philosophical and smiled, bracing herself for the day's academic skirmishings and hoping somehow to keep up enough of a head of steam to sustain her through the fair in the evening.

Meanwhile, St. Julie's Road was enduring the irritation of continuous banging and hammering from Erica's house as people came and went and presumably did things to the boiler to make things safe. Thank God, at least there had not been a major fire, or worse, an explosion to wreck the house!

Miss Dacre kept close surveillance of all the happenings from her drawing-room window, Pongo in close attendance, barking his agitated little yap, for most of the day, under the impression that he was performing a most necessary service.

Joy had been hoping to do a little work on a lovely manuscript of Samuel Scheidt during the day, but the noise from next door and Pongo's incessant commentary on the workmen's activities put paid to her powers of concentration. In desperation she retired to the potting-shed for a little peace and quiet; tidying-up might be a good way of clearing the mind and, incidentally, the cobwebs. It was, however, rather eerie down there alone, or almost so, except for silent feline friends now in attitudes of repose in, on and around the shed. They all loved the quietness, especially little tabby, who sat discreetly, with her Sphinx-like smile, on an old chair in the corner.

Clearing out some rubbish from the top shelf, and remembering momentarily with a quick shiver the business of the mask and the cloak and the stolen washing, Joy worked quickly, putting away unpleasant thoughts. As she wiped the shelf over with a damp sponge, she knocked something down on to the floor beneath - a booklet of some kind. Ah yes, Madge's diary, of course. Well, if she remembered, she would return it to Madge that evening at the fair.

Taking it into the house, she put it on the hall table by the telephone.

Mrs Badger did not comment, apart from a loud sniff, on the excursion to the fair, when she came later to do a few chores. She polished the front door brass with unaccustomed spirit, however, expressing her disapproval, Joy surmised, in a positive manner, so she kept out of the way. She made Mrs Badger an extra-delicious cup of filter coffee with a handsome flotation of cream on top, and gave her a slice of Elizabeth David chocolate cake to go with it. At that, Mrs Badger mellowed somewhat.

Fixing Joy with a steely eye, she planted her handbag firmly on the table in front of her and delivered the day's homily.

"Now, Miss 'Etherington, Oi was't goin' to say nothin', but seem' as 'ow you're a set on doin' this 'ere thing tonight, Oi shall 'ave to say a word!"

She leaned forward.

"Now, moy duck, first thing - you' 'aven't twisted nothin', 'ave you?"

Joy assured her she hadn't, although, to be quite honest, she wasn't sure, as she felt aches and pains all over after the bumper-cars episode.

"Very good!" Mrs Badger nodded approvingly. "Now then, Oi 'ave to say my piece now, so as Oi don't 'ave to say 'Oi told you so' later, but as Oi sees it, wot you're a-goin' to do tonight is downright foolhardiness it is, an' Oi don't 'old with it!"

She looked intently at Joy, who felt very uncomfortable indeed. "There's a terrible lot o' riff-raff goes to that there fair, an' no mistake, an' Oi don't want to 'ear after as you've been in trouble down yonder."

She wagged a finger. "Oi wants you all in one piece tomorrow when Oi comes."

Bleak words of cold comfort again from the lips of the oracle. Joy saw Mrs Badger off at the gate. Riding away up the road on her faithful steed (no basket of shopping this morning, Joy noted), Mrs Badger gave a cheery wave, both to Joy and an invisible Miss Dacre - invisible, that is, except for one hand holding back the corner of the lace curtain at the drawing-room window. At the wave the curtain was of course instantly dropped.

"Now just you remember wot Oi says, moi duck. All in one piece tomorrow mornin'!" Cupboard love? thought Joy, for she hadn't yet paid Mrs Badger for last week's work - must leave her a cheque on the hall table.

"Cheerio, then!" she carolled, gathering speed as the Corporation dust-cart snorted up behind her. She won the race to the cross-roads and disappeared up Woodstock Road, hotly pursued by the gargantuan vehicle, looking for all the world as though it were about to gobble her up!

In the afternoon Joy managed to get down to some work on Samuel Scheidt, which pleased her greatly. Such a marvelous composer! She was particularly fond of his 'In Dulci Jubilo' for brass and voices. They really must put it on in the college chapel at Christmas - now there was a lovely idea!

The phone rang, totally breaking her concentration.

Who else could it be but Madge, of course. She seemed to be particularly exercised about the raffle and who should draw the tickets for the prizes. Joy had no thoughts on the problem at all and said so.

After rambling on at length and going over, yet again, all the final instructions (Really, how could she be so tiresome?) Madge terminated the conversation abruptly with the tidings that Oh dear, the General had done it again and that she must see to him at once! She rang off before Joy had even time to mention the recovery of the diary, which she had intended to do.Oh, well, no doubt it would be re-united with its owner in due course. At the back of her mind she wondered vaguely what the poor General had done to cause the distraction. Nothing serious, one hoped, bless him! At least Madge seemed to care for him, in spite of being such a self-centered woman, and that was rather touching. He really was such a love and still so handsome in venerable old age.If only he were still able to write his memoirs, what tales he would have had to tell of the legendary life of the Raj. Joy recalled one particular yellowed photograph of him and his fellow-officers, which stood on his desk in his study. There they posed solemnly in youthful authority, immaculately attired in splendid uniform riding boots polished to perfection, taking drinks on the verandah, surrounded by white-coated and turbaned servants holding silver salvers on which were massed the finest crystal decanters and glasses full to the brim with delicious cordials. It was a tiny vignette of pure history in one faded photograph.

Later that day, after struggling through the scrum of the fair, Joy arrived, somewhat breathless, at St. James' gatehouse. There she met John Spry and Caroline Grieve, both in happy mood. They evidently thought the whole thing was going to be tremendous fun, so this must surely be a good omen.

They went through the gate and the transition from the deafening din, restlessness and brilliant lights of the fair to the silence and near-darkness of the quad was quite numbing to the senses. The ancient stone walls of the college effectively cut out all the noise and there was only a vague rumbling in the background, presumably from the generators.

The wall lamps cast a mellow glow across the emerald lawn. The fountain in the middle (a modest copy of the Fontani di Trevi) splashed gently, water droplets distilling in the lights as they fell into the pool below.

The strains of an elegant Bach fugue came from the chapel. St. James' had a particularly fine organ, a rare Father Smith, possibly unique in Oxford, and almost in its original state, without officious restoration and re-furbishing, its baroque pipework lending itself perfectly to the playing of Bach.

They paused outside the chapel door to listen for a short while. The clock overhead wheezed and clanked, preparing to strike the half-hour.

"The G minor, I think," said John Spry. "Splendid rendition. I wonder who's playing?"

A faint light from within filtered through the stained glass window lending a mystical touch to the scene. The glass in the chapel was a unique treasure for much of it had by good providence escaped destruction during the Reformation and the Victorians had made a fine job of putting in glass which matched the original lights very well; these were predominantly toned in blues, reds and purples, reminiscent of Chartres, though on a much smaller scale.

Lights coming on in the President's residence across the quad indicated it was time to go in. The music stopped, then the chapel door opened and Lord Westhoe emerged, carrying a volume of Bach's organ works. Compliments were paid, for it was indeed he who had played so beautifully. He received their appreciative comments with a modest smile, and gentle disclaimer natural to him, for he was that rare combination of incomparable brilliance and a completely unassuming charm.

He told them what a great luxury it was to play the instrument at all, for there was simply no opportunity normally during term, since undergraduates naturally had priority, so he was dreadfully out of practice. His only hope was that it had not been too painful for the listeners.

Caroline prodded John firmly in the floating rib as he was about to embark upon an elaborate exposition involving, no doubt, learned comparisons between Lord Westhoe's interpretation and that of Marcel Dupre, Jeanne de Messieux and anyone else he thought of. He got no further than the French school, though Albert Schweitzer might have been a more appropriate name to drop - for his discourse was cut short by a further prod in the ribs and the echo of footsteps on stone cobbles and a murmur of voices heralding the approach of the rest of the choir.

Exactly on cue, the porch light of the President's residence came on as they drew near. The great black oak door opened slowly and a variety of delicious scents stole out, chicken stew predominating and followed more hesitantly by - could it be? - sultana pudding. A mellow, welcoming light came from within and a smiling face appeared round the door. Livia - so it was - said: "'Allo, ladies and gentlemen, 'Er ladyship is expecting you - please do come in."

Lord Westhoe, enigmatic as ever, had quietly disappeared in the meantime, probably by some secret route to the backstairs to the refuge of his study.

They went in and Lady Westhoe was there to greet them at the top of the great staircase, leaning over the balustrade. She waved a cheery welcome.

"Come on up, everybody, let's launch this noble effort with a Buck's Fizz or two - that should elevate our spirits somewhat."

Professor Peterson was first up the stairs, inevitably.

"Tutt, tutt, such unseemly haste, old man," murmured John Spry.

"You old soak." Brenda Page-Phillips, coming up behind him, laughed but added reproachfully: "John - you fraud! I'll just count exactly how many glasses you drink! The poor old Prof will never be able to keep up with you, I'll be bound!"

"Pot calls kettle black again!" said Caroline with a demure smile.

Buck's Fizz was exactly the order of the day - a happy drink, and most uplifting. Their spirits rose indeed, exactly as predicted by Lady Westhoe and they laughed and joked a good deal as the Fizz did its good work. Even the prospect of the daunting task which lay before them seemed to become simply more like an amusing little escapade. It was all going to be fun, and what did it matter anyway if they looked just a little ridiculous. After all, the fair was pretty ghastly in any event, so no matter. Thus reassured, the company relaxed.

As they laughed and talked encouragingly together, Joy noticed out of the corner of her eye a figure in the passageway through the open door of the Great Drawing-room. To her surprise she perceived it to be the robed figure of an Arab Sheikh, walking slowly away towards the stairs! No one else appeared to notice it, so she did not comment. Perhaps she had imagined it, for she looked again and the figure had vanished.

Lady Westhoe consulted the long-case clock; it was one of Thomas Tompion's finest masterpieces, which he had specially made for the college, and which still kept perfect time, ticking away quietly in the same position it had always occupied, standing guard by the drawing-room door, for well over two hundred years.

"Time to robe, I think, ladies and gentlemen."

Drinks were downed swiftly, for her ladyship was a most punctual person, and so it was that the gentlemen departed to Lord Westhoe's dressing-room to change, while the ladies repaired to the master-bedroom.

As they walked down the corridor, Brenda touched Joy's elbow.

"Now, what did I say? Just take a look behind you."

Joy turned round quickly and there, caught in the act and totally unaware, was John Spry. He had slipped back into the drawing-room and was quietly quaffing the remaining Buck's Fizz at a fair speed, head thrown back.

"A tiny cameo of human nature," said Brenda.

"Cameo - that's a good word!" Joy smiled to herself. The long corridor, the open door and the figure of John at the far end of the drawing-room gave the illusion of a cameo; a tiny figure framed in a series of diminishing rectangles. Joy was also reminded of a painting, probably a Della Francesca, where the figure in the distance was framed in a similar series of rectangles and arched architectural features, creating that cameo effect. But no - there was something else that sprang to mind.

The portrait of Lord Westhoe, recently finished and now hanging in the long gallery (The rogues gallery, so called by members of staff) along with all the other portraits of Past Presidents of the College. Having observed the painter working on the portrait in the President's Lodgings, such a charming young woman from London she was, and rapidly making a name for herself in portraiture of the finest quality.

Joy had talked to her as she worked at her easel, putting the finishing touches to the exquisite painting in the long gallery which was itself the setting for the portrait, with Lord Westhoe, sitting, fully robed, in the foreground, slightly right of centre, at his desk with an open book in his hands.

Behind him the long gallery stretched away into the distance, sunlit by the medieval mullion windows on the left, portraits of former presidents of the college to the right: and there, half way down the gallery, stood a figure walking back towards Lord Westhoe - Lady Sylvia: most apt, with Vertue sitting alongside her on the windowsill - and all so well seen by the painter, a perfect vignette of life.

Lady Sylvia Westhoe, the benign and efficient power-behind-the-throne: discreet and modest, but always 'there'.

Had the artist thought of the Dutch School as she painted this lovely work? Joy had enquired. Vermeer? De Hoogh?

Well, no: not consciously, but, yes indeed - she could now see it, the subconscious influence was evidently there.

There were indeed echoes of Pieter de Hoogh about it. How extraordinary! Oh dear - how she did hope and pray that the critics would not accuse her of conscious imitation! Curious how unconscious influences came through in ones work! It was rather like that particular interior painting where the hostess stands with her back to the painter, in the left foreground, talking to the male guests, sitting at a table by the window.

Her elegant stance and quiet demeanor was indeed, exactly like that of Lady Westhoe; except for the fact that she stands the other way round, looking back to Lord Westhoe in the Presidential portrait.

However with regard to the present matter of John Spry, quietly quaffing away there as rapidly as possible in the middle distance - what fun de Hoogh would have had with him. Pieter Bruegel - even more so, one would imagine, a veritable painter's delight!

"Just look at John; he leaves the poor old Prof standing in the drinks race, doesn't he?" Brenda laughed, a tinkling laugh which dissolved the picture, and they watched him as he scuttled through the door at speed, and then, with a complete change of tempo, assumed a stately pace as he caught up the others in the long gallery, hands clasped behind his back, in an attitude of deep thought.

"Really, whoever would have thought it?" Joy was scandalized.

Dressing up was a revelation, an exciting experience which they simply loved, admitting that it was just like being back at school and getting ready for the Shakespeare play at the end of the summer term.

There was much giggling as Brenda attempted to cover up Joy's ample midriff bulge, which she managed to do with difficulty, by fitting a large padded roll and hanging a piece of tapestry curtain over the front of the skirt like a Tudor pinafore - an ingenious, if inelegant contrivance.

Lady Westhoe had meanwhile disappeared; presumably she had gone elsewhere to change.

Petronella came in looking very weary, but a few minutes of uninhibited levity with the others soon dispersed the cobwebs of fatigue. She giggled at length over poor Caroline's struggle to get into her rather tight Tudor bodice, for Caroline was a fairly full-bosomed wench. After a good deal of pulling and pushing and much laughter, they succeeded in easing her into full costume, and Caroline emerged, resplendent, as an exceedingly lovely Elizabethan lady. Brenda had achieved a miracle with her talent for clothes, her unerring eye for colour, and her expertise with fabrics and their capabilities.

"Sheer genius, my dear." Joy was full of admiration.

Brenda inclined her head gratefully.

"That's the name of the game, my dear. As I have said before, we are only a cottage industry at Botticelli's, but we do get it right, and that's the secret of success. Things don't have to be expensively made to be the best - not that we use old curtains like this, you understand - we just use materials which look like old curtains!"

Joy cast a despairing glance at herself in the long mirror.

"Oh Lord! I look just like my idea of Good Queen Bess's nanny - perfectly ghastly! I must go on the Cambridge diet immediately!"

"Do you think we should riposte with the Oxford diet?" asked Petronella thoughtfully; "I'm sure we could invent one."

This interesting proposal was lost on the air as the door opened and a tall, stately figure in Elizabethan dress appeared. It was of course Lady Westhoe, but artfully disguised and utterly unrecognizable.

"Gosh," breathed Petronella, "Straight out of the Holbein drawings."

"Well," said Lady Westhoe, "I decided against the stuffed sofa image - I thought I'd better go for Hamlet's mother instead."

She had powdered her face to look ghastly pale and with the sombre costume the effect was quite chilling.

"You look absolutely marvelous!"

Brenda inspected her closely, examining the stitching of the dress through her half-glasses.

"Perfect in every detail!"

"Either do it right, or don't do it at all; my dear grandmother's words."

Lady Westhoe eyed herself critically in the long mirror.

"Yes, not bad at all. I'll do. All thanks to Livia, of course she's absolutely wonderful with a needle. I simply couldn't manage without her!"

She glanced at the clock.

"Come along, ladies, it's time to go downstairs. Don't forget to hitch up your skirts on the staircase; we don't want any twisted Elizabethan ankles, do we?"

They went down to the main hall laughing happily together.

The gentlemen had foregathered there and watched admiringly as they came down.

"What a remarkable sight," said Professor Peterson. "They seem to be almost gliding along, don't they?"

The others agreed, for the ladies' full skirts billowed gently as they descended and did indeed give that illusion.

"Perhaps they're on roller-skates," said John Spry with a grin. "Skate-boards, even."

The assembled gentlemen spluttered quietly in concealed mirth, but managed to compose themselves by the time the ladies joined them in the hall.

Professor Peterson polished his misted glasses and replaced them carefully on his nose.

"Ladies, shall we proceed?"

He bowed low, with a flourish of his velvet hat.

Livia opened the front door, smiling broadly.

"Ladies and gentlemen, you look-a-lovelee! Good luck! Buon fortuna!"

"We surely need it, amici!" An unknown voice uttered this comment from the back.

They went forth through the semi-darkness of the quad. Livia watched them depart with a benign smile. They would be all right. She crossed herself and said a little prayer for them as they walked to the gatehouse in solemn procession, talking quietly as they went. She petitioned St. Jude. As he was the man for lost causes, she felt he was just the person to help in this rather curious case. Everything seemed to be against them in this enterprise - an impossible situation; yes, St. Jude was definitely the man to ask. She prayed for their safety and success in the task afoot - in spite of all the odds. She then finished off with a quick Hail, Mary, just to make sure. As an afterthought she threw in a swift petition to St. Benedict - for no particular reason - just that he was so reliable and had such strong connections with Oxford, via his Order.

She then went to do the washing-up, waving goodbye to the Arab Sheikh as he passed the kitchen window and left the college by the side gate. He waved back and gave thumbs-up. Yes, all would now be well, for the one who was strong, kind and sure would be there to help. Satisfied that her prayers had been answered, she switched out the lights locked up and went home by the back entrance of the college to avoid the fair.

CHAPTER XIII

'Sing we and chant it'

The First Book of Ballets, Five Voices

Thomas Morley 1595

Meanwhile, the choir passed through the inner gate and collected themselves for a moment. A quick check on music and a swift look over costumes by Brenda and they were ready.

They halted briefly in the ancient gatehouse precinct and for an instant became part of history.

The porter, sitting in his office, watched them standing there quietly in the dim lamplight's glow. Just like something out of an old film, was his thought. He lit his pipe and puffed reflectively. Took some courage to do what they were going to do, and good luck to 'em. He hoped they'd do well for Cancer Research, and he gave them thumbs up to cheer them as they went through the gate.

The noise hit them like a bomb-blast as they stepped through the little door out on to the pavement. "Oh, Jehovah! Shall we go back? I don't think I can face it!"

Caroline looked to John for direction. "No, no," he replied with a bland smile. "It'll be quite all right, just you see, Courage, my child!"

He took her gently by the arm and she felt comforted.

"Follow me, dear friends!"

Professor Peterson gave yet another grand flourish with his hat and placed it carefully back on his head, perfectly horizontally. Then, instead of threading his way through the back of the amusement arcades and generators so as not to be noticed, he led them straight out between a coconut shy and a shooting range into the central thoroughfare of St. Giles', packed solid with teeming humanity.

"Lord save us!" breathed Joy to Brenda.

Brenda laughed her special little laugh with its rising cadence.

"We're going to enjoy it thoroughly! You wait and see, it'll be marvelous!"

"Quite so," said one of the graduates behind her. "It will be fun, don't worry!"

And so the solemn procession made its way slowly up the middle of St. Giles' towards the Wall of Death looming large and menacing outside the graveyard.

Oddly enough, nobody got in their way as they proceeded two by two round them, but no one hindered their progress or, which was still more surprising, even seemed to notice that they were there. It was the strangest experience.

"Gosh, I feel like a ghost!" Petronella shivered, holding firmly on to Joy's arm.

"Yes, isn't it odd?" said Brenda from behind her. "Perhaps we are."

"I think there is possibly a perfectly logical explanation," said John. "Just look around you and see what people are wearing. We are really nothing at all out of the ordinary."

And this was manifestly true. In addition to the inevitable "Kiss-me-quick" hats, papier maché Union Jack painted bowlers, grotesque and funny faces and so on, there was an abundance of eccentric dress of every description. Or was it in fact eccentric? Possibly not, for there were people from every walk of life in the motley assembly, including hippies in their usual ghastly garb - torn leotards, dirty leather jerkins, lank hair hanging in grease, punks with weird clothes and hairstyles in pink, green, purple and orange, and war-painted faces and lots of people in assorted fancy dress, so Tudor costume was really nothing very extraordinary.

The smell of fried onions became quite overwhelming as they passed the Mat because of the high concentration of burger-bars close by.

"I think I'm going to be sick," said Petronella.

"No, you're not, darling girl. Courage, ma vieille!" John gave her a beaming smile over his shoulder.

The roar of the motor-bikes on the Wall of Death arena rose to a horrifying crescendo as they prepared to do their circuit. This in conjunction with the screams from the Ghost Train and the vision of the animated skeletons jerkily performing their Dance of Death over the entrance added to the utter incongruity of the whole scene.

They walked on. Madge's charity stall came into view a little way up Banbury Road, sandwiched between a candy-floss stall and an ice cream van.

Joy was comforted by a feeling of warm dependence from Petronella as the girl held on tightly to her arm. Bless her, she really was a nice little thing.

Suddenly, through the kaleidoscopic blur of blinding lights and people's faces, Joy saw to her horror, just for an instant, a hideous, unforgettably awful face - the mask she had found on the dumps. It appeared momentarily in the crowd, then vanished in the restless movement.

She started violently with shock.

"Are you all right?" Petronella gripped her arm.

"Yes, it's nothing. Just a party mask. Don't worry!"

"My goodness gracious me, business is brisk!" said John, stopping and glancing round. And indeed it was! Madge's stall, simply groaning with every conceivable bargain-hunter's delight, was doing a roaring trade. It was stuffed with simply everything: bric-a-brac from high-class boxrooms, handsome cast-offs from elegant wardrobes, and the products of the city's cottage industries - pots, stuffed toys and jellies, jams and preserves, home-grown plants and a mouth-watering display of home-made fudge and superb cakes.

The centre-piece was a large selection of all the very finest wares, with a big notice proclaiming: "Grand Raffle - tickets 25p." Only the Best Prizes." This indeed was self-evident. There were four best-quality Dundee cakes in tins, several bottles and half-bottles of the best brands of Scotch whisky, various wines, a bottle of brandy and a bottle of gin.

There was also a fine selection of boxes of chocolates, ranging from Terry's All Gold to - could it be? Yes, it was! Thornton's own epicurean selection in a beautiful box with a red rose in the middle tied on with a golden cord.

The prizes also included the traditional enormous stuffed toys; a panda, a heffalump, Paddington bear, a ginger cat with a purple bow tie, and the finest of all, a huge and extremely beautiful teddy-bear, wearing a bowler hat jauntily cocked over one ear and looking exceedingly doleful. Another martyr to Madge's Good Cause, perhaps. He was labelled "First Prize."

"I wonder how many people our Madge terrorized to get hold of that little load of booty?" A familiar voice spoke behind Joy and Petronella.

"Oh, Mark dear, there you are - how nice!"

Mark and Marit, arm in arm, stood close by, smiling encouragingly.

"Moral support, my dear aunt," Mark winked roguishly.

Marit was absolutely loving the whole thing, throwing back her head and laughing with delight.

Behind the mountain of goodies Madge was darting back and forth like a wraith. She appeared to be working entirely single-handed, which was surprising, with no army of subservient minions to bully. Notwithstanding, however, she was everywhere, with nothing and nobody escaping her vigilant attention.

"Do you know, it's almost as though she's got telescopic tentacles" said another familiar voice from behind.

It was Michael Walters, wearing a sardonic grin, shared by Peter Rumbold, who stood beside him, looking like Tweedledum with Tweedledee.

"She really is quite extraordinary, isn't she? Like some heat-seeking missile where there's money, she's there!"

They watched, spellbound; as Madge "did her thing."

It was a performance of the very highest quality, and Joy was reminded of her student days in London, when she had seen Ruth Draper in her remarkable solo appearance on stage in Drury Lane in the 'fifties. A completely empty stage peopled with invisible characters called up by the powerful imagination of the artiste.

Madge stood alone in the middle of her stage, that is, behind her stall, seemingly acting out her own personal drama. Like a ballerina she flitted gracefully from one end of her stall to the other, selling her wares at top speed with a vivacious smile alternating at times, perhaps by some effect of the light, with a gratified leer, the shark's teeth undisguised. She wore the most extraordinary shimmering diaphanous drapes, a-glitter with a dusting of sequins.

"I see we're into the blue period tonight," said Mark, offering a comment about Madge's current hair colour. "Where on earth did she get those ghastly earrings?"

Petronella looked more closely.

"I'm sure I saw those very ones in the Oxfam shop in Summertown the other day; sort of like mobiles with a half-moon stuck on the end - perfectly hideous, but isn't it odd, they look absolutely right on her"

Peter Rumbold's voice came from behind. "I know who she reminds me of - Cruella de Ville in One Thousand and One Dalmatians!"

A subdued giggle rippled through the whole group at this.

"Except that Madge is rather better upholstered than Cruella, of course," observed Michael thoughtfully.

Suddenly Madge spotted them in the crowd.

"Ah, there you are at last! (there was heavy stress on "at last") Come along, dears! Now, come on, you tin-rattlers!" She pointed a commanding finger at Mark and Marit. "And you too, darlings!" indicating Peter and Michael. "Come along, chop-chop! Time is money!"

"What did I tell you?" said Michael, "The missile is on course!"

Obediently they took their tins, stationed themselves two at each end of Madge's pitch, and began the rattling good work.

It was Marit, of course, who stole the show completely. Her natural warmth and gaiety, coupled with her wonderful good looks quickly attracted attention and money began to pour in. She did a little Norwegian dance every now and then, banging her tin like a tambourine and this of course brought the house down.

The others soon caught the spirit of the occasion. Mark affected the swagger of a Regency man-about-town and this worked wonders with the elderly ladies, who fed his tin with money at an amazing rate. His stylish deep bows and charming smile opened hearts and purses.

Not to be out-done, Tweedledum and Tweed1edee devised their own ploy and did a kind of Egyptian sand-dance together in spontaneous unison and once again, money poured in. The crowd cheered.

"This really is most encouraging," said Michael, puffing hard with exertion:"What else can we do?"

Peter Rumbold immediately came up with an inspiration.He snatched a sari from the stall's hanging rail, wrapped it quickly round himself, draping the end of it round his head, covering his face, and embarked upon a most convincing belly-dance!

Instant success! The crowd loved it.

The choir watched, fascinated; however it was now their turn, as Madge focused her laser beam on them and promptly had them under marching orders.

"Now, choir!" she carolled in a piercing soprano over the deafening roar of the motor-bikes. "Come along, dears, here's your place," pointing to a gap at the front 1eft-hand side of her stall.

"Now, get singing, dears, chop-chop! Don't waste time! Remember time and tide..."

They filed, resigned, into position, just by the stuffed toys. The giant first prize teddy-bear looked more and more miserable by the minute. He had lolled sideways slightly and his eyes were bleak. Such a sad, sad bear, thought Joy. His dark button eyes seemed to be pleading for something - rescue, perhaps, or oblivion? But she was being fanciful.

As they sorted out their music and arranged themselves in a semi-circle; their curious audience assembled to watch the proceedings. There were broad grins all round and ill-concealed mirth at the spectacle of the solemn Elizabethan consort preparing to sing. John Spry produced a tuning-fork and struck it on his heel to get "A."

"Well?" said Joy, waiting for the note, "Can we have 'A'?" With that, there was a tremendous crescendo from the motor-bikes.

John shrugged his shoulders, "Can't hear a thing against that little lot - absolutely hopeless!

"They'll stop in a minute," carolled Madge. "It's the end of the session - just sing in between while they're collecting their audience together!"

As they stood patiently for what seemed like hours, waiting for the end of that session, there was time again to look around, and see who might have come to listen to them. And a motley assembly it was! There were amiable country-folk eating candy-floss and toffee-apples and grinning at them in a friendly fashion; also suspicious-looking idlers in the shapeless uniform of the drop-out brigade, and some rather surly-looking hippies in a variety of tattered and dirty apparel, smoking peculiar and malodorous hand-rolled cigarettes. Some of the burly specimens looked primitive and menacing, with long hair and straggling beards.

Meanwhile, the horrendous roar subsided to a loud tiger-purr as the motor-bikes finished their epic ride and revved their engines more gently while waiting for the next spectacular.

"Come along, choir - sing!"

Madge's head appeared momentarily round the side of the giant

teddy-bear. She stuck a large notice in between his front paws. It read: "Grand Draw - 10 p.m." The bear drooped still more miserably as though the prospect depressed him, and she jerked him upright rather unkindly, so that his hat fell off. She picked it up and jammed it unceremoniously back on again.

"Oh dear!" said Petronella, "I really must buy lots of raffle tickets and try to win him. He's desperate for a good home!"

"Come on, now, choir, sing!" commanded Madge again in the imperative.

So directed, the choir began, with a zestful, appropriate madrigal: "All creatures now are merry, merry-minded!"

To their surprise they seemed to be fully audible in spite of the din of the fair. They were standing under a canopy with the wooden-sided stall next to them, so the sound was contained, instead of being lost on the air.

Enthusiastic cheers and clapping followed their first effort,

The tins were energetically rattled and money again poured in. "Good, good!" called Madge, "And again, choir! Now, something really jolly this time! What about that divine little thing about the china dishes and the flying fishes - and the volcano? ...Yes, 50p, dear! Thank you so much! All for charity!"

With that, she vanished behind the crowd of eager purchasers of her wares.

"She means 'Thule, the Period of Cosmography', you know, the Thomas Weelkes," said John Spry, finding it in the Oxford Book of Madrigals. "What a good idea!"

They sang this extraordinary madrigal with immense spirit and brought it off most beautifully. They even had time to sing two or three more before the motor-bikes roared into life again for their next circuit and drowned them completely.

Madge's head appeared again round the back of the giant teddy-bear at this juncture.

"Why don't you go to the Royal Oak for a shandy or something? Come back in half an hour - don't forget, now, half an hour! No, not you!" She waved an imperious hand at Mark and Marit, who had put down their tins, assuming that they too were released from bondage for a short while.

"I need you to get the money! Keep rattling!" She fixed Tweedledum and Tweedledee with an icy stare just to ensure that they stayed at their posts.

"Nobody moves until after the Grand Draw! Is that clear?" At the end of this salvo she smiled the sweetest smile and vanished again behind the bargain hunters.

As they walked through St. Giles' graveyard to the Royal Oak, Joy fancied she saw the tall Arab she had seen earlier, but then, of course there were many foreigners at the fair, and a large number of local families in eastern dress of various kinds, saris, and so on, so it need not have been the same person, but somehow he looked familiar.

They put their feet up in the relative peace and quiet of the ancient paneled bar and settled for a gin and tonic to give them verve for the grand finale. Petronella decided on a Pimms and sat in her corner looking perfectly sweet in costume, imbibing her delicious drink with quiet enjoyment.

The landlord smiled genially at them over the bar and bethought himself how right they looked against the background of the oak panelling and old prints of Oxford, just like something out of olden times.

There was a ripple of laughter as they talked of Madge's aspirations for an M.B.E. John Spry announced with solemn authority that he in fact saw her rising effortlessly to the heights of damehood, wafted there by the breezes generated by myriads of shaking tins. Dame Madge Spragne11 would sound very well, he thought.

This produced a great deal of mirth and Caroline reflected. "Heaven help all the other unsuspecting Dames when she joins

their ranks! I wonder if they have get togethers or hen parties on great occasions? Madge'll be bossing them all around like a charity fête. May they be spared!"

With this unkind wish, echoed by the others, the last of the drinks were downed and they collected themselves for the final session much restored by this therapeutic interlude.

"Ready, chaps?"

John Spry shook his robes and led the way back with Professor Peterson.

"Up, guards, and at 'em!" exclaimed the Professor. Once again, these were prophetic words!

The fair was now full to capacity and building up to its climax, with the noise rising to frenzy. High-pitched screams came from the Octopus as it achieved its terrifying maximum speed. Surely any moment it must jettison its catch of tiny humans, packed like so many sardines in the twirling seats held so tenuously on the end of its tentacles. Blood-curdling screams and demonic laughter rose in dramatic crescendo from the Ghost Train.

They cut through the graveyard once more, approaching Madge's stall from the rear, and talking quietly as they walked along the path in the semi-darkness, with the silent graves to their right.

Petronella touched Joy's arm.

"Look," she whispered.

Barely visible in the half-light, they saw the figure of a man, partly hidden by the gravestones, standing completely still, with his back to them, watching something intently in the vicinity of Madge's stall. He seemed to be wearing a black jerkin and cap, but the impression was too vague to be sure.

As he heard them approach, he vanished silently behind the tombs. Joy shivered involuntarily and held on to Petronella tightly.

"I feel cold suddenly," she said, though it was a warm night. "Come away, come away, death,

And in sad cypress let me be laid"

A deep voice soliloquized from the front of the procession

sharply.

"Professor! Please, don't!" Brenda Page-Phillips rebuked him "You might raise the spirits!"

Professor Peterson, oblivious of the request, continued to the end of the sonnet.

"Good Lord preserve us, it's like being in some mediaeval funeral cortege!" Caroline Grieve was aghast.

The Professor finished his oration with a solemn declamation, "Requiem aeternam dona eis, Domine: et lux perpetua luceat eis." By this time they had reached the gate, and mercifully he stopped.

"Gosh! I've really got the willies - it's just as though we're going to some really tragic event or something!"

Petronella held on to Joy even more tightly. It had been an eerie experience and Joy too had forebodings. They emerged from the darkness into the brilliant lights, noise and excitement of the fair, where the clamour seemed to have reached its peak, and the stench of hamburgers and fried onions hung on the air in a nauseating pall. A visible layer of blue smoke from this culinary enterprise covered the end of Banbury Road by St. Giles' churchyard. Madge's stall was in the very centre of this miasma.

"Frying tonight, I"see!" said John Spry. "Anyone for a fatty bag o' chips? Or a delicious epicurean hot dog with soggy onions? Brown sauce or tomato ketchup? Sweet-sour glue?"

"Ugh!" said Caroline, "Stop it, John, or I swear I'll be sick!"

They threaded their way through the back alleys behind the stalls and went through the gap to the front of Madge's thriving emporium. She was selling at feverish speed, or so it seemed, but if one looked more closely, she didn't appear to have a great deal left to dispose of except for the Grand Raffle items, looking like some visionary Christmas hamper display for the enjoyment of the array of stuffed beasts presided over by the bear in the bowler.

Mark and Marit were now definitely wilting but Tweedledum and Tweedledee were carrying on heroically and the money was still rolling in. It must surely have been a good night for Cancer Research, Joy reflected with satisfaction. She noted one curious addition to the band of collectors: the Arab Sheikh was now standing beside Marit and rattling a tin! He wore dark glasses and his burnous was arranged so that the bottom half of his face was completely concealed. He salaamed solemnly and deeply as people put their donations into his tin and was doing a roaring trade. She found it most intriguing.

But that was not the only curious circumstance. An odd change had come over Madge, who was giving off vibrations of intense agitation, quite perceptible in spite of all the surrounding distractions. She kept dropping things and giving the wrong change, which was not like Madge at all, at least not when she was in "business overdrive," so to speak. (Although at other times, when her vital interests were not at stake, she would scatter everything around her with abandon). Now the fixed smile had disappeared entirely and her face was a mask, unmoving except when she cast nervous glances at the Sheikh from time to time, almost as though he represented some kind of threat. Who was he? But now it was time to sing again before the Grand Draw took place.

They turned to face the thronging crowd and opened their music, preparing to sing. Once again, it was some time before the roar of the motor-bikes subsided and so there was time to examine the assembled audience. Again a mixed bag, with the unsavoury element now just a little too close for comfort. The shambling hippies were there, in the front row, but spaced out now and interspersed with a number of dirty down-and-outs. The general effect was menacing and Joy looked at Mark for reassurance. He winked kindly at her.

"It's O.K., Auntie Joy, don't worry, they're harmless!"

Auntie Joy, however, did not feel any too sure about this. Tweedledum and Tweedledee gave a 'thumbs up' to the choir as they amused the crowd with a further demonstration of the Egyptian sand-dance followed by a quick burst of Flamenco, with invisible castanets, rhythmically convincing, even in sports jackets and flannels!

At this point, however, Madge completely stole the show by knocking the cash box off the stall with a loud crash. This caused a total diversion for a while as coins rolled everywhere, and then it was all hands to the pumps, for there was a considerable amount of money to be retrieved, and most of it was restored, for the crowd joined in enthusiastically and not much was pocketed.

The cash box was returned to its position and the choir collected itself and sang 'Sing we enchanted, when love is granted', a spicy little madrigal with a snappy rhythm, followed by Thomas Morley's 'fyer, fyer!' This went down very well and there was again enthusiastic clapping and cheering and, oddly enough, no jeers at all. They got in three or four more madrigals before the Wall of Death riders began to rev up thunderously for yet another hair-raising spectacular.

Raffle tickets were selling at an amazing rate and Petronella bought a large number, for she dearly wished to get the first prize, the mournful bear. She had a beautiful old wing-back chair in her room which she had decided would be exactly right for him. He would be such a happy bear with her - please, please, she murmured to herself, let me win!

CHAPTER XIV

'Farewell all joys: O death come close mine eyes --'

from 'The Silver Swan.'

The First Set of Madrigals and Motets of 5 Parts

Orlando Gibbons 1612

The time for the draw was at hand and the choir was now feeling the strain. They decided to go and sit in the graveyard for their last break, just to breathe some fresh air, but of course Madge would not have it at any price. She commanded them to stay at their post till the bitter end, and no, it didn't matter at all that they wouldn't be heard over the motor-bikes. "Just keep singing! Finish only when St. Giles' clock strikes ten! Remember, we must keep up appearances," She barked, now without a vestige of a smile.

"Now, what's that supposed to mean? Whose appearance? Hers, presumably, the silly old trout!" John was fed up.

"My dear John, really!" said Caroline, "That was hardly gentlemanly of you, was it?"

He flushed slightly and, feeling a little remorseful, she gave him a comforting hug, realizing that his sharpness hid sensitive feelings exacerbated by fatigue and noise.

They sang on determinedly and in spite of the losing battle with the motor-bikes, nobody laughed. It had all become a very serious business. There was a feeling of intense concentration, as though attention was centering on some unseen objective; but perhaps it was just heightened expectation before the draw took place. Joy looked at Mark and Marit, dutifully tin-rattling. They smiled and joked manfully, though clearly tired, while Tweedledum and Tweedledee kept up their act beautifully to the last. The unknown Arab continued to collect and salaam, impeccable and imperturbable.

St. Giles' clock struck ten, sounding quite distinctly through the barbaric din of the fair with a strong reverberating chime, and the choir finished adroitly on the dying cadence of the "Silver Swan." A sombre note to end with and not as planned, for they had intended to close with something jolly, but their timing was wrong, and so it was:

'The silver swan, who living hath no note:

When death approached, unlocked her silent throat.

Leaning her breast against the reedy shore,

Thus sang her first and last, and sang no more.

Farewell all joys; O death, come, close mine eyes;

More geese than swans now live,

More fools than wise.'

Which terminated their performance with solemn finality.

Madge's head appeared suddenly above that of the mournful bear, from behind the stall, and she announced in a stentorian voice:

"The Grand Raffle will now be drawn!"

The crowd edged nearer - although this already seemed to be humanly impossible in view of the crush.

There was a short interlude when nothing at all happened. Madge was invisible.

"What on earth is she doing?" Joy looked at Mark with raised eyebrows.

"Ssh!" he said. "Quiet, Aunt - just wait!"

Joy's eyebrows rose even further. Mark stood very still and was looking intently into the crowd.

"Mark, what is it? What's going on?" She asked quietly.

"Don't worry, just wait," he replied, out of the corner of his mouth. Petronella shivered and held tightly on to Joy once more.

There was a curious tension in the atmosphere round the stall. She was frightened and whispered: "I'm scared! What's going on, Joy?"

The choir stood silently in the gap between the stalls and all the others seemed to have gone strangely still, too. Tweedledum and Tweedledee, Mark and Marit and the tall Arab, who stood on the far side of the stall, completely enveloped in his robes, were silently awaiting developments.

Round them the hubbub of the fair rose to a higher pitch, till it sounded like the wailing of Banshees, but it did not affect those round the stall. They were waiting in expectation for the draw to be called but not for that only - for there was something else, something more sinister, even catastrophic, of which some were aware, but most were not.

Suddenly, looking more like Cruella de Ville than ever, Madge appeared at the front of the stall carrying a large, antique, rotating wooden cylinder affair with a handle, resembling some ancient artifact from a mediaeval kitchen - a butter churn, or a mincing machine, perhaps. She was wearing her most striking bejewelled blue spectacles attached to a decorated gold chain, and she smiled the most brilliant smile, which embraced the choir, the tin rattlers and the audience.

"The Grand Draw will now take place," she announced once more at the top of her voice, putting the cylinder down on the front of the stall with a loud thump.

"Now," she said, the shark's teeth leering, as she looked round the assembly. "Whom shall I choose to draw these wonderful prizes?" She acted it out quite beautifully, looking meaningfully at Lady Westhoe who instantly slipped behind a large male member of the choir to keep out of the firing-line.

Madge put a delicate hand to her temple. (Who was she now? Madam Arcati?)

"Whom shall I choose?" (Strong emphasis on shall.)

She turned dramatically, scanning the assembly with her mental laser beam.

"Ah, yes - you, sir!" pointing a finger at the silent Sheikh. He said nothing, but bowed a deep salaam.

"Come - to the draw!" she announced, swirling round in her diaphanous drapery in a manner reminiscent of Isadora Duncan, "come!"

The Sheikh came, as bidden, and stood, arms folded, awaiting further instructions. She began to rotate the drum, with difficulty, it seemed, for the mechanical action seemed stiff and clanked loudly in complaint.

"Bicycle oil?" said John to Petronella.

"Oh dear, it's rather stiff!" Madge cast a helpless look round her.

"Sir - would you oblige?" She addressed the Sheikh, whose knowledge of English was evidently good. He bowed again and began to rotate the drum vigorously. Clackety, clackety, clank, clank, clank, it complained unhappily but performed its requisite duties, masticating the raffle tickets prior to disgorging the winning numbers.

"Stop!" commanded Madge, raising her hand in an imperative sign, in case her alien helper should not have understood.

However, he stopped at once, and she opened a flap on the side of the drum with a flamboyant gesture rather like a conjuror at the end of a triumphant routine.

"Dear Madge, such panache," murmured John to Caroline.

"I myself will draw the first three prize tickets," she announced imperiously, with a winning smile addressed to no one in particular.

"It's got to be a fix!" Petronella was aghast. "What about my teddy-bear?" She clutched her sheaf of raffle tickets to her bosom in despair.

"This is most certainly not on! It should be an independent person who draws the raffle." Joy was indignant.

"Typical Madge," said John. "Everyone a winner - so long as it's Madge! Probably got it rigged for her grandson to win."

"Rubbish, John!" Caroline was scornful. "How can you possibly rig a raffle?"

Meanwhile Mark, as before, stood silent, looking intently into the crowd and, curiously enough, not even glancing in Madge's direction. Tweedledum and Tweedledee were smiling blandly in unison at nothing in particular.

"Get on with it, missus!" A voice directed from the crowd, "Mine's a bottle O'whisky!"

Madge smiled again, regally, in the direction of the importunate yokel, and with a further imperious wave of her hand dipped her arm up to the elbow into the open cylinder, swirling her hand around inside for fully half a minute in the search for the winning ticket for the poor sorrowful bear.

"Ah, yes - Voila! Here we are! Now, people, who will be the lucky, lucky winner?" She was positively skittish in her manner as she produced a folded ticket and held it high above her head with a triumphant gesture. Adjusting the bejewelled spectacles carefully, she unfolded the ticket and announced:"Blue ticket number one hundred and one, one-O-one, blue ticket."

Poor Petronella! noh, no, it can't be true! I just simply know he's my bear! Please, please let it be wrong!" She moaned in genuine anguish and Joy patted her arm. "Never mind, dear, it's simply the luck of the draw, as they say, and we can't help it."

There was in fact no immediate response from the crowd, no claimant came forward, and again Madge called:

"Ladies and gentlemen, the winning ticket for the first prize is one-o-one, blue ticket - please come to claim your prize!"

Again there was a pause, then a sudden movement in the crowd. A young man darted quickly forward, tall, well-built, handsome and dark-haired, wearing a sports jacket and cavalry twills - a rather noticeable figure. He looked pale and strained, in fact rather ill. Indeed, there was to Joy an air of silent desperation about him. She seemed to know his face from somewhere, probably North Oxford. He quickly thrust his raffle ticket into Madge's hand.

"One-o-one - blue ticket. The lucky winner!"

Madge swirled round in the diaphanous drapes to pick up the bear. In the process his bowler hat fell off, and she also knocked over the handsome ginger cat with the purple bow-tie.

"Oops!" she said, righting him again. "There we are, dear! Now off you go," thrusting the unhappy bear unceremoniously into the arms of the lucky winner, who took him rather in the style of a rugger blue taking the ball, preparatory to making a really good try, clutching the bear tightly under his arm.

Mark suddenly came to life. "Antonov!" he said incisively - and improbably - to one of the degenerate hippies standing idly at the front of the crowd. He did not even spare a glance for the young man so desperately clutching the teddy bear, but pointed to someone in the crowd, a little way back to the left.

Those nearest, that is, Joy and Petronella, John and Caroline, followed the line of his pointing finger. The hippy vanished immediately in the direction of Mark's pointer.

Joy knew the man indicated at once. He was the one in the black leather jerkin who sometimes did crosswords at the 'Jolly Sailors." His face could be seen clearly in the crowd for a fleeting moment, then it disappeared abruptly in the sea of restless movement.

Instantly all hell was let loose, as though some emotional catapult had been released, while the howling of the Banshees, rising to a climax, was echoed in the turmoil which broke out around them.

"Jasper - it's you!" exclaimed Petronella, recognizing the young man all at once as, petrified, he clasped the bear to his chest.

Hearing her, Jasper turned away in a trice, looking for a gap in the crowd to make a quick getaway. There was none. He turned again, now a frightened animal, and perceived the choir standing in the gap between the stalls and the dark gangway beyond. He literally ran at them.

"Excuse me!" he gasped, frantically attempting to push past John Spry. Howbeit John, a slow mover at the best of times and, incidentally a rugger blue full back, twice capped, did not oblige quickly enough, and poor Jasper bounced off, staggering back a pace or two upon impact. At this, he disintegrated completely.

"Get out of my way!" he screamed hysterically, "Let me through!" Like lightning, one of the burly tramps, and a particularly unsavoury one to boot, stepped forward and took hold of the bear firmly by the midriff. He said something to Jasper that no one else heard, and Jasper let out the most blood-curdling scream of anguish (later, John referred to it as the cry of the tormented soul in hell, as in "Gerontius"!) and then shouted "He's my bear! Get off him, he's mine, damn you!"

An athletic-looking punk with crimson hair then stepped alongside and took hold of Jasper by the arm and the scruff of the neck in a distinctly professional manner.

The crowd, hitherto mesmerized by these inexplicable proceedings, now became animated and a voice exclaimed: "Get off the lad! Wot's goin' on? It's 'is bear, mate - get off 'im!" Another voice called out: "Yeah - come on, lads, let's get them there layabouts - put the boot in boys!"

The boys needed no further bidding and a complete free-for-all ensued, an almighty barney in which Queensberry Rules were disregarded and no punches were pulled. In the middle of all the commotion Jasper fought to hold on to his bear, with the tramp now hanging grimly on to the bear's head, as he was attacked by Jasper's defenders, all vigorously trying to drag him off. Nevertheless, he kept his hold, even though the boot was now being put in most effectively as directed by the voice. Jasper pulled hard one way, the tramp the other, and the result was inevitable. Suddenly there was an audible ripping sound and the bear's head came off - a clean decapitation.

"A really fine execution," as John Spry neatly summed it up later. "No blood!"

As the bear lost its head, the action seemed to stop, for what happened next, though it took only seconds, appeared to last an immeasurable time. That was everyone's impression when reviewing events subsequently.

The tramp fell backwards, the bear's head firmly clasped to his breast, into the arms of John Spry, while Jasper staggered back with the torso into the burnous of the Arab Sheikh, and the unhappy bear's stuffing cascaded everywhere. There was a corporate gasp of horror from everyone who witnessed the strange drama. Small, clinically packed polythene sachets of a powdery substance slid all over the area in front of Madge's stall. There were dozens of them.

John Spry righted his captive tramp and let him go. The Arab Sheikh, however, held on to his struggling prisoner by the back of his collar and the belt of his trousers. "Drop it!" he shouted, loud and clear, treating Jasper like a dog with an illicit bone.

Jasper screamed again, as if in agony, "No, no! He's my bear, do you hear?" "Drop it!" commanded the Sheikh once more. Jasper fought like a dervish to escape from the iron grip, evidently resolved not to let go of what was left of his bear (possibly because the arms and legs still had their stuffing intact). In his desperation he seemed to gain superhuman strength and almost wrenched himself free, tearing his jacket down the back seam as he fought to escape. Then, finally, he swung round and thrust the limp torso of the bear into the arms of his captor, who momentarily let go, as the burnous fell away from his face, revealing the features of Lord Westhoe!

Seizing his opportunity, Jasper vanished instantly through a gap in the crowd and was gone, leaving Lord Westhoe with the bear in his arms.

While all this extraordinary commotion was taking place Mark had stood perfectly still, looking into the crowd, and evidently quite unmoved by the fracas. Suddenly he pointed upwards to the giant Ferris wheel. "There he goes," he said, apparently to no one in particular.

Immediately, the crimson-haired punk, accompanied by a girl-friend with spiky pink and yellow hair and yet another shambling hippie loitering nearby, made off into the crowd at speed in the direction Mark had indicated.

The tramp had meanwhile assumed control of the bear and its stuffing and had co-opted the assistance of Tweedledum and Tweedledee to ensure the safety of the stall and its contents. But where was Madge?

She had vanished completely; leaving behind, however, a token, rather larger than the Scarlet Pimpernel's, in the shape of her handbag, upside down on the ground behind the stall, the contents spilled around it in confusion.

The tramp addressed Joy and the choir. "Police, Madame," he said, producing his warrant card from within his shabby mackintosh. "Will you kindly assume control of the stall and the collecting tins, please? We shall impound all the raffle prizes, but would be grateful if we could leave everything else in your safe-keeping for the charity. The foot patrol will be here shortly to assist you and we will be in touch with you tomorrow."

Even as he spoke, Mark said in a low tense voice: "Look, he's going for it!"

Everyone looked up, following the direction of his gaze. The giant Ferris wheel slowly began its first rotation, seats swinging sickeningly backwards and forwards as it gathered impetus. It was almost full to capacity and to the untrained eye all that could be seen was a colourful but anonymous group of people sitting tight in their seats, holding on for dear life as the great wheel swung upwards and over, high above the college roofs. However, the second time round, what it was that Mark's keen eye had spotted could now be clearly seen. There was a gasp of horror as the full implications of what was happening became alarmingly plain.

The big wheel began to move faster, rapidly gathering speed. The figure of a man in black then stood up quickly and climbed on to the seat he occupied, with quite remarkable agility, as the wheel went up, for the gravitational pull must have created severe drag. He stood with his back to the crowd, poised like an acrobat ready to fly the trapeze, holding on to the strut which secured the seat to the frame. It was a quite unbelievable sight - worthy of a really good stunt from a James Bond film - John Spry's very words in his subsequent summing-up.

"Don't do it, Antonov, I need you!" breathed Mark, almost to himself. Joy overheard him, but prudently did not comment.

Utterly defying Mark's telepathic instruction, Antonov did it - and in such breath-taking style, too! As the wheel took him over the top and began to descend towards the college facade, Antonov literally took off and flew, like the afore-mentioned acrobat. It was a most elegant and astonishing leap, when at roof level, across and down, perfectly timed, neatly making allowance for the gravitational pull, into the gully between St. James's steeply-angled roofs. Thereafter, he disappeared from view.

"Damn!" said Mark quietly. "Round the back, lads!" He himself then vanished into the crowd, accompanied by two men in T-shirts and blue jeans. The choir, silently witnessing all this, looked at one another in complete incredulity. For a moment no one spoke.

"Well, well, who'd 'a thought it?" Professor Peterson straightened his velvet hat and addressed the group. "Action stations, good people. All hands to the pump!"

It was the most laconic of briefings, but automatically the group knew exactly what to do in this singular situation. The crowd hemmed them in on all sides with voluble queries about the raffle and quite a scrum ensued.

Professor Peterson and John Spry took command of this particular area of confusion, posting a notice to say that the raffle would be properly drawn at St. Giles' Church Hall the following Tuesday at 7.30 p.m. This was done after a quick conference with the Rector, who by good fortune was standing nearby, observing the extraordinary events.

Tweedledum and Tweedledee took charge of the collecting tins, and Caroline and Marit assumed control of the cash box and general stage-management at the back of the stall.

The tramp, now assisted by uniformed police, collected the raffle prizes together to be taken away for examination. He said that any "clean" prizes would be quickly returned for the draw.

The poor decapitated bear was carefully put into a large plastic bag, along with the ginger cat, but the third prize, Paddington Bear, was missing. Brenda Page-Phillips had the answer to this, for she had seen Madge out of the corner of her eye snatch the smaller bear from the display as the furore began and then disappear quickly round the back of the stall. How very interesting that the bear had evidently been much more important to her than her handbag!

But where was she? No one knew.

The tramp personally supervised the collection of the contents of Madge's handbag with considerable care. Joy and Petronella assisted him, crawling into obscure dark places under the stall to retrieve things which had rolled away. It was a devastatingly sad experience, for it told the complete truth about Madge Spragnell to the last dot and comma.

Apart from the usual selection of lipsticks, mascara, powder compact and scent sprays, earrings, etc., there were touching mementos of her husband and herself when young. A photograph taken on their wedding day and particularly fine one of him in full ceremonial uniform.

Next, oddly; a pair of dice and, rather unexpectedly, a mini-chess set with her own name printed on it. It was a touching thought that she and the general must have played chess together with it.

The next find, however, was something even odder. It consisted of two wigs, one blond, one black, tightly rolled up in a plastic bag with a pair of tinted glasses, and a black plastic mac in a small transparent plastic case - just the sort of thing Madge would never normally have worn, even in an emergency. Her rainwear was extremely elegant - Burberry or Aquascutum or something of equally high quality. However, these finds were perhaps not more unlikely than some of the scraps of paper lurking in various corners of the capacious bag and which turned out to be betting slips. Something which one would hardly have expected to find and a hitherto undiscovered propensity of this pillar of Oxford society and acme of respectability.

This series of discoveries built up to a somewhat sinister climax. Under the rear of the stall Petronella found a black, rather bulky plastic case with a press-stud fastening which had popped open. The case was fairly small, measuring about eight by ten inches, and out of it protruded two passports, one British, one French. Inquisitively, Petronella took them out and peered inside the case at the heavy object at the bottom. Before the tramp could stop her, she had taken out something wrapped in a khaki handkerchief, which fell open in her hand, to reveal, astonishingly, a handsome pistol, which glittered silver in the light.

"Give it to me, madam," instructed the tramp firmly. "Careful!"

"Gosh?" said Petronella, stupefied at the find.

"Hmmm - fully loaded," said the tramp, inspecting the weapon carefully, holding it in the handkerchief so as not to touch the gun itself and obscure any prints.

"What a beauty! A collector's piece, to be sure!" He looked at one corner of the handkerchief, whereon was stitched a small white name-tag with the lettering sewn in red.

"P. Simoneau," he read out loud. He flipped open the French passport. "Helene Simoneau." He addressed Joy. "Madame, do you know a Helene Simoneau?" He showed her the photograph. It portrayed a woman in glasses with shoulder-length black hair.

Joy shook her head. "No, sorry!"

He opened the other passport; it was Madge's own. Putting the two pages containing the photographs side by side, he said: "Quite a family likeness, wouldn't you say?" showing them to Joy.

"Yes, there seems to be a slight similarity about the shape of the face. Perhaps it's a relation or something - a cousin, maybe?" She looked questioningly at the tramp. He examined the French passport more closely, flipping over the pages quickly.

Opening the back page, he exclaimed "Well, well, now!" There, neatly clipped inside the back cover were five high denomination French banknotes. He then opened the British passport at the back page, and there, clipped inside the back cover, were half a dozen high-value Swiss banknotes and two 500 dollar bills.

"Good gracious," said Joy, perplexed, "It looks as though Madge is preparing to go away, doesn't it? What about the poor General? Who would look after him if she went away?"

The tramp did not reply, but looked once more inside the seemingly bottomless abyss of Madge's handbag.

"That's about it, I think," he said, "But no keys."

"Oh, that's easily answered," ventured Joy. "She keeps them on a cord round her neck; her car keys too - my idea entirely, because she was always losing them."

Looking inside the bag again, the tramp found a side pocket with a zip. He undid it and fished around inside. He withdrew, first, a diary, then a hypodermic syringe in a clinical pack, and finally, six sachets of a powdery substance and some swabs in a sterile pack.

Joy and Petronella gasped in unison with sheer horror.

"Oh,no! I don't believe it!" Joy was wholly aghast. "Not Madge!"

Again, the tramp did not reply, but put the bag and its contents into another black plastic bag, which he sealed carefully. "Thank you, ladies and gentlemen, we will be in touch." He then had a word with the uniformed police patrol and disappeared into St. Giles' churchyard.

Petronella sat down wearily on the kerb by the stall, exhausted. "I am absolutely shattered! Whatever is going to happen next?" She looked up at the church clock. "Good grief - it's only half-past ten! I thought it was midnight! How can so much happen in half an hour?"

Everyone was, however, far too busy packing up the stall to answer this profound enquiry. St. Giles' rector had very kindly offered to store the stall and the few left-overs from the sale, so it was all quite quickly taken down and stowed away.

"What shall we do with all the money?" queried Michael Walters, "There seems to be an awful lot of it - it weighs a ton!"

They decided to take it all back to Joy's house, where it could be counted and signed and sealed for the charity to pick up on the morrow. Roast beef sandwiches and coffee would be provided. Thank goodness she had roasted that superb round of best Scotch beef in the morning. There was lots of it and with salad and horseradish sauce it would make a good supper for everyone.In case anyone fancied something sweet, there was the trifle she had made yesterday; it would be simply lovely with cream and perhaps a sprinkling of chocolate chips on the top?

They went speedily to St. James' College to change, bade Lord and Lady Westhoe goodnight and walked, in subdued mood, away from the noise of the fair, up Woodstock Road to the peace of St. Julie's Road.

As they went, they talked of the cataclysmic events of the evening.

What concerned Joy most, however, was Mark's role in all this. It was quite clear now, of course, that he was working with the police. As yet there was no sign of him at all and she just prayed that he was all right wherever he was and would come back safely. The whole business seemed to be so fraught with danger and the discovery of the gun and the drugs had been an appalling shock.

"That damned elusive Pimpernel" - this quote came into her mind as she walked along thoughtfully with the others. That fitted Mark - to a 't' - gallant and charming and utterly lovable, but also utterly infuriating!

"Well, dear friends, at least Madge showed the flag - she left the money behind!" John Spry smiled a cynical smile. "But I rather suppose it was just a little too heavy to carry!"

This time he suffered no rebuke for his cynicism, and they arrived at Joy's front gate in a quiet mood.

The cats were all outside to greet them with a rapturous warmth and peculiarly feline solicitousness, with much rubbing against legs and sonorous purring and standing up on back legs in sheer ecstasy, stretching up for strokes.

Miss Dacre's curtains parted wider than usual as she peered at them closely through the drawing room window and Pongo barked furiously in the background.

Joy turned at the gate and in a last-ditch effort at good-neighbourliness, waved a hand at Miss Dacre. To her absolute astonishment, Miss Dacre waved back! Admittedly, it was only a sketchy attempt at a wave but nevertheless the gesture had been made.

"Well, I never! What do I see? The hand of friendship extended at last, albeit a little querulously? I thought, Joy, that Miss Dacre was your deadliest enemy?" Professor Peterson looked enquiringly over his glasses, eyebrows raised.

"Indeed, I'm quite mystified, for as far as I know, she is still going "round telling everyone I killed the old lady!" Joy frowned. "It really has all been most unpleasant, to say the least. Let's hope that somehow this evening's events herald the end of all things horrid" She really had no idea why she said this; it simply came out without any conscious thought, rather as though someone else had said it. No one however, seemed to have heard it and it did not seem worth repeating. She walked on ahead quickly and opened the front door. The delicious aroma of roast beef still hung on the air.

"Ah, yes, indeed! The roast beef of Olde England!"

Professor Peterson, first to follow Joy through the front door, sniffed the air expectantly like a bloodhound and was quick to identify the main course of the forthcoming supper.

"Greedy old hog! Always first at the pig-trough!"

"John, do shut up!" Brenda tweaked his ear. "Pax!."

Joy stopped suddenly at the hall table. "Look!" she said, "Madge's diary!"

The others were puzzled, not quite appreciating the significance of this exclamation.

"There was a diary in her handbag wasn't there?" She turned to Petronella, who nodded an assent. "Well, it must surely be the replacement for this one."

She picked it up and showed the others, explaining how she had found it some time ago during the episode of the flooded drain.

"Well," said Michael, "In view of what has happened this evening, I must surely make red-hot reading! Probably bursting with important clues!"

"Much more likely everything has been obliterated completely by it lengthy immersion - or perhaps not, if she used a ball-point pen? Shall we have a look and see?"

"Joy handed it to him with a shudder. "Ugh!" she said. "There is something quite odious about the whole affair - please, Lord, let this be the end of it!"

Peter and Michael went off into the study with the diary - to do a little private sleuthing, as Michael described it, whilst the others sank gratefully into comfortable armchairs in the drawing-room in the pleasing expectation of delicious provender - and liquid delights too - with any luck! Happily, the liquid delights came first, borne by Marit on a large tray with clinking glasses providing a pleasant obbligato.

"Ah, yes, indeed - another intriguing little wine!"

Professor Peterson cast the professional eye over the bottles. It was, in fact, an entirely obscure and rather cheap Riesling Joy had bought from the winemart in a bin ends sale some days previously and it had an extremely garish label depicting drunken peasants from about the time of Pieter Breughel, all in glorious technicolour.

"Hmmm!" John snorted in deprecation of Peterson's comments. "Corkscrew? Ah, yes - here we are - Voila!"

The professor quite shamelessly produced his own corkscrew from his inside pocket and deftly opened the bottles with a flourish borne of long years of practice.

"Another one for the record books - it must have taken him at least 30 seconds to open all 4 bottles - good fellow!" John murmured to Brenda.

So saying, he advanced upon the drinks tray.

"Nectar, sheer nectar!" he said, downing half a glass in one.

Suddenly remembering himself, he picked up two glasses and began to serve the ladies of the assembly.

"Thank you, dearest boy!" Brenda twinkled at him. "Such good manners!"

A ripple of laughter went round the room and soon all present had peacefully settled down with a welcome glass of what proved to be a most palatable wine.

Marit reappeared with a veritable mountain of excellent beef sandwiches with a mouth-watering salad garnish. Everyone tucked in with a will.

"Quite, quite delicious, my dear Joy!"

The professor addressed her as she entered the room carrying a large percolator of steaming coffee. The aroma was superb.

"Oh good - glad you're enjoying it! Now, my dears, a really strong continental roast to steady the nerves! Where are the boys?" She looked round the room. As she spoke, Michael and Peter came in behind her, looking for all the world like Tweedledum and Tweedledee. Peter wore the broadest grin imaginable and Michael, in sharp contrast looked exceedingly solemn, holding the diary open in his hand.

"Well, lads, what's the verdict?"

"Not a lot," said Michael. Peter grinned a half-melon smile. "Our Madge really is a dark horse! It's all appointments and initials, plus some phone numbers, but not a lot else. It was a very good thing she mostly used a ball-point pen, so it survived the inundation quite well. And what we have concluded at the end of our investigation is that she had some kind of an assignation with an ant!"

Michael rebuked Peter with a frown.

"An ant?" Petronella giggled. "What on earth do you mean, Peter?"

"He means," said Michael with quiet deliberation, "that Madge met someone occasionally - possibly an Anthony or someone with a similar name - which she abbreviated as 'Ant.' However, another name mentioned in the diary is one 'Cled', so _"

"Cledwyn! poor, poor Cledwyn! Dear God, how truly awful!" The full horror of what this meant became brutally clear to Joy.

"Drugs! Cledwyn was indeed murdered because of drugs - and because he was trying to protect me in some way. But why?"

"Well," Petronella put her glass down on the table with an air of finality. "There is nothing surer than this. It's got not just a little to do with the allotments. For instance, that business of me being shot at in mistake for you, Joy."

Michael looked into the distance over the top of his glasses. "You are quite right, my dear. One or two of the meetings took place quite close by - at Medley Bridge. So perhaps, Joy, you may have had the unfortunate knack of being in the wrong place at the wrong time?"

"The allotments after dusk, do you mean?"

"Precisely so, my dear! You simply got in the way, as we surmised and indeed, as poor Cledwyn so clearly told you. Courageous boy! He paid a high price to protect you, it seems! At least, you're not fighting the proverbial feather-pillow anymore. This is without doubt positive material evidence at last. We'd better get down to the cop-shop quickly! I am sure Inspector Vardon will find this little chap most illuminating!"

He held up the diary to show the silent assembly, which sat, intrigued, around him. "This little book probably holds the key to the whole sorrowful mystery."

The telephone rang. It was Mrs Badger. Joy pulled a face silently to the choir as Mrs Badger let fly. She had heard all about it on the Radio Oxford News - and what had she said all along? Perhaps one day people would learn to take notice of what they were told and keep out of trouble's way! When she could get a word in, Joy enquired about what had been mentioned on the news. The tirade recommenced. Joy's expression changed from one of sheepish embarrassment to one of utter shock. "No!" she gasped, "Oh, no!" Eventually, she put down the telephone, clearly stunned by what she had heard, and stood for a moment in silence. With a deep sigh, she turned to Petronella. "I am afraid it's rather bad news, my dear" Your friend, Jasper is dead, I fear. I am so sorry

At this bald statement Petronella looked at her uncomprehendingly for a moment.

"Jasper? Jasper Philberd? My God, you can't be serious, Joy!" Joy nodded wearily.

"I'm afraid it's quite true. He's been killed on the railway line at Trap gate. Mrs Badger has just heard about it in a news flash. A serious disturbance at St. Giles' Fair, followed by a police chase of certain suspects, and then Jasper's death, apparently connected, it is thought. Unhappily for us, but fortuitously for the police, the press were present at our little event, as they had proposed to run an article on us, I hear, so they recorded everything as it took place hence, presumably, the speedy statement on the radio.

The assembly greeted this news in total silence, as though wrapped in some shroud of solemn meditation. It seemed minutes before anyone spoke.

Professor Peterson eventually broke the spell. "'Requiem aeternam dona eis, Domine, et lux perpetua luceat eis' - a Requiem for Jasper it was then, which I said in St. Giles' graveyard this evening. I knew it was indeed for someone, howbeit unknown, but now it is manifest. How awesome and how sad!"

Petronella looked sorrowfully down at the cats, so comfortably settled on the hearthrug, purring away gently, blissfully unaware of the stark tragedy on the human plane.

"Poor old Jasper! You know, the only thing he lived for was this thesis he was writing on birds of some sort. He'll never finish it now, alas! He was always away over the meadow watching for herons and that sort of thing - all times of the day and night. So boring, I always thought, but he loved it, splashing about in the mud with his binoculars!"

Joy was suddenly smitten by a singular thought. "Did he ever use a telescope?"

"Mmmm - well, now, I don't think so. I never saw him with one - but he was really into all this technical equipment: special cameras and things, so who knows? Why?"

She looked quizzically at Joy, who shrugged her shoulders in response. "I don't know, really - just a thought."

After a quick sandwich and a glass of wine, Michael and Peter made off to the police station at St. Aldate's with the documentary evidence and the others were

left to sit quietly in peaceful contemplation of the crackling log fire, the sweet scent of apple wood pervading the room as Joy threw on a log from the old Bramley prunings.

"Dona nobis pacem," said the professor, absently helping himself to a further libation of the humble Riesling with a sign of pure contentment.

The phone rang yet again.

"Methinks you spoke too soon, credo, old boy!" said John, doing the honours round the room with the new bottle.

This time, to Joy's evident relief, it was Mark. She listened intently as he spoke to her at some length.

"Yes, yes, of course, my dear, I'll tell them, most certainly I will - and please, please, take care - see you tomorrow!"

Putting the phone down, she stood thoughtfully gazing into the white-hot heart of the fire. Sparks, hissing and sputterings came from it, the only sound at all in the room, apart from the soothing feline purring from the hearth-rug.

"Well," Caroline broke the spell. "What news?"

Brenda, half asleep in an armchair, feet up on the piano-stool, opened one eye enquiringly, like an endearing Beatrix Potter dormouse.

"What's happened to our Madge?" said she, rubbing her nose quickly, exactly like the dormouse.

"Don't know," said Joy with a shrug. "It's all a complete mystery at the moment, it seems, from what Mark has just said. It would appear that the principal characters in this extraordinary drama have vanished completely - except, of course, for poor old Jasper! Mark's only positive words on this evening's events were to thank you all for being so co-operative and so bombproof - those were his very words! Perhaps, dear friends, tomorrow we shall hear something more concrete to explain the whole sorry affair."

"I'll drink to that!" Professor Peterson raised his empty glass, which was

promptly filled by John Spry en passant, with a concealed wink at the others.

"Waouw!" pronounced Iffley from the hearth-rug in apparent approbation. Blind Fred gave tongue with a quizzical "Rrrr?" stretched himself and then settled down to a luxurious sleep, curled up nose in tail. John looked down at the pussies reflectively.

"And so to bed, dear friends! As my dear great-grandmother used to say, 'Good-night and sweet repose - half the bed and all the clothes'"

He sighed, leaned back in his chair and also languidly stretched himself, emulating Fred, then promptly dozed off with a gentle snore.

"Doesn't he look angelic?" Brenda looked at him fondly. "Like some fresh-faced choirboy!"

John opened one eye and smiled a seraphic smile and Brenda threatened to swat him with a copy of the Times which lay conveniently to hand on the coffee table.

Professor Peterson reproved them with a look; "Now, now, dear children, let us address ourselves to more adult matters! Did I perchance scent Benedictine on the wind, dear lady?" He sent an inquiring glance towards the grand Victorian sideboard which held Joy's drink reserves. "It would go so perfectly with your most delectable coffee, Joy."

At these words, John awoke in a trice, bright-eyed and bushy-tailed at the mere mention of the famous name.

"Benedictine? Quite so, my dear professor," said he with a winning smile, rubbing his hands vigorously together in anticipation of this singular delight; "Absolument, n'est-ce pas?"

Joy, ever the perfect hostess, produced from the archives not only Benedictine, but a fine cognac as well, so hearts were well and truly warmed and by the time she bade them goodnight at the door, all were really 'very nicely; thank you', as Petronella described it aptly on her way to bed.

"Now, how does it go?" called Joy as she waved to them. Goodnight and sweet repose - all the bed and half the clothes?"

They walked off down the road with their peals of laughter echoing around the silent street.

CHAPTER XV

'O Lord, in thy wrath rebuke me not…'

from the Burial Service,

Henry Purcell 1658-95

Next morning, bright and early - that is, about half-past eight - Joy heard Mrs Badger's key in the door. Oh dear, this was definitely an ominous portent, for she was always punctual but never particularly early, so it was reasonable to guess that there was a storm brewing.

"Morning," said Joy brightly from behind her Times, affecting as carefree an attitude as she could assume. "How are you, my dear? Coffee?" She waved the coffee-pot temptingly, newspaper still upright in a defensive position.

"Terrible - and yes, please - strong and dark brown, one sugar, as usual," came the stern rejoinder.

The handbag descended on the table with a firm thump and Mrs Badger's ample frame descended equally heavily on to the chair opposite Joy.

Peeping cautiously round her newspaper, Joy perceived that her worst fears had been realized, for Mrs Badger's face was like a thundercloud and distinctly incarnadined in hue.

There was silence for a moment or two and some heavy breathing from the other side of the table as Mrs Badger collected herself for the fray. After a delicate sip of her coffee, followed by a quick snort, she was ready for combat.

It crossed Joy's mind that it was unlikely that a great deal of work would be done in the house that morning. Pity, for the old brass coal-scuttle needed a really good polish. Ah, well, perhaps Mrs Badger might settle for a quick hoover of the main staircase? Nothing too taxing, she decided, just something simple and soothing.

"Now, see 'ere, Miss 'Hetherington, Oi 'ave to speak!" Joy laid down her newspaper, resigned to the inevitable. She smiled placatingly at her irate employee.

"What is it, my dear? Is there something wrong?"

Mrs Badger snorted again, like an angry bull.

"Wrong? Wrong? Oi should say there is just about something wrong." She looked fiercely over the top of her glasses.

"Moi 'ubby told me Oi 'ad to come an' tell you straight as you be lucky to be aloive this mornin' wi' all they wicked villains gettin' up to all that terrible mischief last noight at the fair. You could 'a been laid out on a marble slab down the mortuary wi' your toes turned up this mornin' if things 'ad 'a got out of 'and any more than wot they did!"

Joy said nothing, but listened meekly to the admonishing lecture which inevitably continued at length.

"Oi 'ad the bad vibrations from the very beginnin' an' straight all the way down the loine. Oi never did trust that Mrs Spragnell, Oi tell you - wi' 'er toight corsets an' 'er dingle-dangles an' 'er blue 'air! An' that's that an' all about it!"

She sniffed again and glared fiercely at the Bramley apple tree down the garden with a look enough to kill it, as was her wont when affronted.

"Oi do not know wot the world's a'comin' to - an that's for sure. T'was never loik it in may day, an' that's it for sure an' all; as Oi maya' said afore," she added as an afterthought. Taking a further deliberating sip of her coffee, and placing the cup carefully on its saucer, she adjusted her glasses on her nose, folded her arms across her bosom and proceeded to speak in an entirely different tone, her voice dropping a minor third, she smiled, the gentlest smile of friendship.

Joy felt distinctly warmed, and listened intently.

"Now, moy dear, Oi observed as 'ow things was gettin' a bit out of 'and some toime ago, wot with all them quare 'appenings, an' Miss Erika gain' steadily off 'er 'ead as she 'as been a'doin' for a long toime now, since the old lady popped it, so ..."

She paused for a moment or two and looked out across the back gardens at the house opposite. "So Oi did moy own bito' detective work on the quiet."

She smiled a bland smile of self-satisfaction.

"Oi moignt as well say to you 'ere an' now as Oi 'ave 'ad a personal word of thanks for all may invaluable 'elp over this affair - from the Police Inspector 'imself in charge of this case. 'owever, at the toime Oi just knew as Oi 'ad to put moyself out 'n get things sorted, 'cos Oi knew as you was in mortal danger, no less an' you 'ad to be protected some'ow or another, bein' a single lady all alone."

"Protected?" Joy raised a quizzical eyebrow.

Mrs Badger nodded sagely and looked out again across the back gardens towards one particular house almost opposite. "Yes, moy duck, Oi got that worried about it all as Oi got on me boike an' did moy own investigations, Oi did."

She waved a cautionary finger. "'Twern't easy, Oi can tell you, but after a bit of a look-about, Oi 'appened on a sort of a clue down the Post Office..."

"Clue? Post Office?"

"Yes, moy duck. Oi saw an ad. on a postcard - you know, if you got summat to sell or buy;' or you're lookin' for a room, or some such thing - there was an ad. for a cat as 'ad gone a' mission' - old Mrs Graystone's, 'twas, over yonder."

She inclined her head in the direction of Mrs Graystone's house beyond the back garden opposite.

"Yes, indeed, dear Mrs Graystone, terribly good about doing things for the animal welfare charities." Joy nodded in approbation.

"Well, now," Mrs Badger leaned forward and looked intently at Joy. "Mrs Graystone said on 'er card as 'ow she'd lawst 'er good cat on such a date, an' as 'ow there was a good reward for information leadin' to its return, et cetera. 'An as Oi read the card Oi 'ad that Quare creepy feelin' - not that Oi knew of the cat's whereabouts nor nothin' loike that, moind; but Oi 'ad that funny koind of an 'unch as Oi knew wot moight 'ave 'appened to it. So wot did Oi do?"

She sat upright, squaring her shoulders and thrusting forth her bosom.

"Oi went straight round an' saw Mrs Graystone, just on the off-chance, sort of a thing."

"And?"

"An' Oi told 'er wot Oi 'ad seen."

She paused for effect, polishing her glasses carefully Oh, how she loved being centre-stage! But there was an element of grim meaning in the proceeding, so she was to be forgiven, thought Joy.

"Oi 'ad seen Miss Erica a couple of tomes a'doin' somethin' she wouldn't normally be seen dead a'doin', namely, feedin' a cat on the back garden wall. Sardines, 'twas, Oi remember, but wot Oi couldn't actually work out was - She simply hated cats! Wouldn't tolerate 'em at any price, she wouldn't. It just didn't make any sense at all. Well, now, may duck, judgin' by the description, twas Mrs Graystone's cat!' So, when it went a'missin, Oi put two and two together, sort O'thing."

She looked inquiringly at Joy.

"You know - she mioght a' made away with it, or summat 0' that sort, seein' as 'ow she 'ated cats."

Joy again raised an eyebrow.

"So - me an' Mrs Graystone put our 'heads together, an' then Oi did a search."

Mrs Badger was now in her element. She blew her nose at length and continued with an air of even greater self-satisfaction.

"Didn't take me long noither, moy duck. When Miss Erica was out, Oi went down the garden to that awful old derelict shed in the bushes, you know - the one as looks as 'ow it's got dead bodies in it - an' as Oi got near, Oi 'eard this feeble miaowlin', Oi did. Old Iffley Come along O' me an' started a'scratchin' at the door, she did, an' yowlin' blue murder, so Oi pushed the door 'ard, 'cos 'twas jammed up with all sorts O' rubbish - an' out shot Mrs Graystone's cat! Thin as a rake, it was. Gawd only knows 'ow long 'e 'a been a' shut in there, but 'e went loike a rocket back 'ome over the wall, soon as Oi got the door open a crack!"

She paused for breath.

"So?"

She blew her nose again. Oh dear! The suspense was killing, it really was.

"Oi flew round to Mrs Graystone's on me boike, an' we 'ad a quick parley, sort O' thing. We 'ad noice coffee an' a suggestive biscuit, an' discussed the 'ole matter at length, we did - wi' the poor old cat alongside of us, fair stuffin' isself with all the grub 'e could eat, to make up for bein' starved nearly to death. We reckon 'e weren't dead only 'cos 'e'd managed to catch a few mice to keep 'itself aloive, poor old moggy!

Well, moy duck, you should 'ave 'eard wot she told Oi - enough to make your 'air curl, 'twas! She said as 'ow Jasper - 'er lodger - was goin' spare' cos 'er cat 'ad vanished without trace. 'E worshipped that old moggy, 'e did. But, on the quiet, she told me as she was a bit worried about Jasper, 'cos 'e was startin' to be'ave most peculiar, 'e was."

Mrs Badger gave Joy a significant look over the top of her glasses and said: "'E used to dress the cat up in funny clothes!"

"Really?"

Mrs Badger nodded and tapped the tip of her nose with her forefinger.

"'Tis true, may duck, 'tis true as Oi sits 'ere. Cap and muffler an' that kind o'thing, you know, kids' stuff, kinda-sorta. Poor old moggy - 'e 'ated it, O' course! An' do you know wot? 'E went all funny about 'is room, 'e did. 'E went an' changed the lock on 'is door - an' 'e wouldn't even let the cleaner in there to do for 'im, 'e wouldn't. 'E said as 'ow 'e must 'ave complete privacy at all toimes, or some such thing. Poor old Mrs Graystone! She didn't loike to interfere, but she did say as 'ow she was a little bit frightened, but she did 'ave two other very nice undergraduates as was very reliable lodgers so that made it a bit easier. An' Jasper was always very regular with 'is rent, so she couldn't say any thin' really, without causin' offense, but 'e was definitely goin' a bit quare in 'is 'ead. A very solitary boy, she said 'e was."

Mrs Badger paused for a short time of rest and recollection, finishing her coffee with relish and proffering the cup for a refill.

"Ta, moy duck, Just wot the doctor ordered. Now, Miss 'Etherington, 'ere's the juicy bit!"

She leaned across the table and spoke in hushed tones.

"One evenin' at dusk Mrs Graystone went down the back garden to check the green'ouse or somethin' o' the sort, an' as she was makin' her way down the path through the shrubbery she 'eard voices at the bottom o' the garden by the boundary wall."

"Good gracious, Mrs Badger, who was it?"

"Well, moy duck," Mrs Badger paused impressively, inflating her lungs deeply for the grand denouement.

"'Twas Miss Erica an' Jasper, talkin' over the wall in wot should 'a bin whispers, but it 'ad turned into a row so they was talkin' a bit loud loike, the more aggravated they got. Well, now, poor Mrs Graystone just didn't know wot to do, so she stood back in the bushes an' listened in for a bit, an' then crept back indoors."

"And what did she hear?" asked Joy, enthralled. "It really is a quite extraordinary tale, isn't it? The whole business is like some awful nightmare."

Mrs Badger fixed her with a look, but it was a kindly one.

"Oi suppose as 'ow you moight say that if you was that way mounded, but my 'ubby always says, be practical, just get on your boike, an' go an' sort it out, so Oi did. Moy 'ubby always knows best, 'e do. 'E don't say a lot normally, but when 'E do speak, e's always roight, an' that's that, an' all about it.

Pausing to finish off her coffee with a flourish and an "Ahh!" of satisfaction, Mrs Badger continued to relate her engrossing saga.

"Mrs Graystone was absolutely torrified at wot Miss Erica said, she was. 'Not the words of a lady', is wot she said about Miss Erica's ragin' at the lad. Ragin' loik a mad bull, she was.

She kep' on a'sayin' as 'e 'ad to do it (wotever it was) as 'e kep' on a'sayin' no, no, 'e couldn't do it, not at any price - e'd sooner doie than do it, 'e would. Well, the more 'e pleaded with 'er to let 'im off the 'ook, the more she raged on at the poor lad, threatenin' 'im with all sorts - loike she would ruin 'im, an' 'e would never lift 'is 'ead up ever again in Oxford when she'd done with 'im - an' all that koind o' thing. Well, moy duck, by the toime as Mrs Graystone crept back to the 'ouse, the poor lad was in tears. She could 'ear 'im sobbin' 'is poor little 'eart out, sayin' 'No, no' all the toime. Fair put the wind up the poor old gal, it did. She told me as 'ow she went indoors an' locked 'errself in quick, she was that alarmed."

"Well, well, now. I wonder just what chicanery our dear Erica was up to?" Joy was pensive and frowned into the depths of her coffee cup.

"I wonder, too, just exactly what kind of a hold she had over Jasper? Must have been something pretty dire to provoke such a response from him!"

"Blackmail 'twas, for certain, anyhow," declared Mrs Badger with an air of finality. "Nothin' surer than that!"

"Quite so, it certainly looks like it, in the cold light of day." Joy nodded in agreement. "However, I feel it will be hard to extract the truth from Erica now since, as I understand via the grapevine, she is now completely unhinged and does not talk a lot of sense nowadays - nothing official, of course - this is simply what I have gleaned from certain acquaintances of mine recently."

"They keepin' 'er up yonder, are they? Mrs Badger inclined her head in the general direction of Littlemore, up on the hill.

"I think they probably will, by the sound of things."

Mrs Badger sniffed, then remarked: "Best thing for 'er, too, I should say, seein' as wot 'appened, an' 'er bein' bang in the middle of it all the toime. At least they'll keep 'er out a' mischief up there. Oi wouldn't be at all surprised if 'twasn't 'er as tried to set fire to your 'ouse, an' that's the truth, an' no word of a loie, as well."

Joy thoughtfully put on her half-specs and folded her 'Times', crossword uppermost. She read a clue, pen poised.

"Or Jasper, perhaps - under her direction - do you think?" When, filling in the answer to the clue, she exclaimed: "There's a coincidence! I've just got it - chicane - how very interesting!"

Mrs Badger looked blank. Joy explained: "Chicane, yes indeed, we've kept the French word for it, you see, Mrs Badger. The chicane is a twisting bend in the Grand Prix circuit, did you know? And we use the word ourselves, keeping almost the original meaning - twisting, artifice, trickery, double-dealing, trying to deceive, etc. The application of the word here, of course, would seem to indicate that the fire was an accident and all my fault, of course, for having left the pan on the stove to burn the house down as I slept. Ultimate chicanery, and all very cleverly thought out."

Mrs Badger nodded hopefully, completely out of her depth, and Joy continued, somewhat ineptly, to try to explain the meaning of the word and its origin: "You know, French - like cul-de-sac, or depot?"

Mrs Badger was looking uncomfortable.

"Anyway," announced Joy cheerfully, "It was the answer to the clue about the Grand Prix."

A lost cause, she thought. Better change the subject speedily. "So the police were very pleased with your detective work?"

Brightening at once, Mrs Badger sat up straight, squaring her shoulders and thrusting forward her bosom in a manner characteristic of her when desirous to impress. Holding her handbag firmly in front of her on the table, she began:

"Not 'alf, Miss 'Etherington, but of course," her voice dropping down a tone and becoming almost a whisper, "you must realise as 'ow the 'ole matter is entirely sub-juicy so I can't say too much at the minute, sort O' thing."

She winked and smiled the broadest of smiles.

"An' of course' moy hubby is most pleased as Oi 'ave protected you from mortal danger,'e is. 'E says as 'ow we 'ave to look after you good an' proper - after all, Oi 'ave been a'workin' for you for some years now, an' we'd 'ate to lose you, koind o' thing, for no good reason, loike."

"Most touching," said Joy, thinking privately that perhaps Mrs Badger might just possibly be fishing for a wage increase. And, come to think of it, might this not be a bad idea? Mrs Badger was, after all, irreplaceable, was she not? There was simply no question about it, a pay-rise was indeed indicated, but best leave it for a day or two, and then suggest it. Nothing excessive, though - a couple of pounds a day, perhaps - just to keep her happy. And it was also time, thought Joy,to tell Mrs Badger what a treasure she was and how very fortunate one was to have such a good and reliable person in one's employ. So this she did, briefly and sincerely.

Mrs Badger's reaction was most gratifying. She went pink and took off her glasses, polishing them vigorously and claiming that they were a little steamy. Blowing her nose loudly, she wiped a tear from a 'watery eye', as she asserted, and announced that she really must get on with her work, declaring that the brass all needed a proper good polish, so it did.

"Very good," thought Joy. A little praise was certainly not out of order now and then, as the occasion demanded, of course.

Mrs Badger departed, mollified, to give the brass an extra shine, and later, when it shone to perfection, she left, calling "Cheerio, moggies'" and "See you in the mornin', Miss Etherington," followed by a firm slam of the front door.

"Ah, peace, perfect peace," thought Joy, making her way to her study to do some urgent reading.

However, within minutes the doorbell rang.

"No peace for the wicked," lamented Joy to Iffley, who was curled up on the hall table. Iffley opened a golden eye in disapproval and shut it again, expressing indifference to any disturbance.

Joy opened the front door and was confronted by two large gentlemen, one wearing casual country clothes and an ancient cloth cap, while the other wore a ski-cap pulled well down over the ears, a track suit and running shoes.

"Good morning, Madam," said the countryman, doffing his cap, "Detective-constable Bimworth, Drugs Squad."

"And Sergeant Meade," said the sporty type, quickly whipping off his ski-cap and revealing, astonishingly, the punk hairdo of the young man involved in the skirmish at the fair the previous night.

With a shy smile he pulled it back on again to conceal the outrageous hairstyle.

"Heavens above! Well, now, please do come in, gentlemen." Joy settled them in the drawing-room in cosy armchairs and made them coffee.

"Strong and black, please, madam. It's been a long night," said the detective constable, stifling a yawn as he spoke.

Joy had thoughtfully provided a quantity of milk chocolate digestive biscuits as well, and they tucked in with relish.

"Would it be rude to ask, madam," said Bimworth, with a straight look, "if perchance you might have a drop of whisky in the house - to lace the coffee?"

Joy smiled kindly at them; she could see that they were utterly exhausted.

She brought out a bottle of her best whisky and put it on the table, saying: "Help yourselves, please, gentlemen."

This they did, sitting back gratefully with a deep sigh of satisfaction and slowly absorbing the soothing effect of the beverage.

"It will be a long time before we get any sleep, so here's to you, madam, with many thanks."

They toasted their hostess with the steaming mugs of laced coffee.

"It's a pleasure, gentlemen. Here's to the Drugs Squad! And have you succeeded in your arduous mission?" she asked, observing them closely.

"Yes, madam, and I was indeed the tramp you saw at the fair last night - sorry about that!"

Joy was impressed. The disguise had been so good, and the dirty and ragged appearance so convincing that she could not conceive that this young man was the same person as the shambling being she had seen at the turbulent event the previous night.

After a second mug of coffee, laced with a generous libation of whisky, the policemen, now revived, got down to business. Detective Constable Bimworth did most of the talking, with an occasional interjection from Sergeant Meade.

Most of the questioning related to the Madge Spragnell. They wanted to know how long Joy had known her, and asked searching questions about her background and origins.

Unhappily, Joy found that she could not furnish them with much information, and had to confess that she knew surprisingly little about Madge. It was curious to find that although one thought one had known someone quite well over a long period of time, yet the opposite had proved to be the case, and Madge ultimately remained an enigma.

Albeit, Joy did dimly recall that Madge had once mentioned her mother, who was apparently French - from Marseilles? - and had something to do with the theatre, since she had met and married an Englishman when on tour over here. A whirlwind romance, Madge had claimed, and their marriage had lasted many years. And - yes, that was it - Madge's father was a musician. It was all coming back now. She was very proud of the fact that he had played the trombone in the regimental band, and had established his own brass band on coming out of the army. Some famous composer of the period had, it seems, written a prodigious amount of music for him, as he much admired his work with the band.

Was it Elgar? or Stanford? She couldn't be sure, but she did know that Madge had all this wonderful unpublished music tucked away in a trunk somewhere up in the attic. This information Joy had gleaned from Mrs Badger, of course, who had found out about it from Madge's daily help, from whom, apparently, no secrets were hid, or at least, that appears to be what she had mistakenly assumed.

And the cache must now be worth a fortune!

Later, Mrs Badger, on hearing the saga, had commented that Annie, the daily help, always claimed to know it all, but in the end Mrs Spragnell had run rings around her, hadn't she just? She'd only let Annie know what she wanted her to know!

But how stupid it was not to have done something with it. Perhaps the General was against it for some reason - who could know? Joy herself would dearly love to get her hands on those manuscripts - purely for academic research, of course. However, this was a digression, and one really must stick to the point!

Now Madge had always been a do-gooder of the most ardent kind; she was on every committee, into every conceivable charity organization, and always up-front, being seen by all to be doing the right thing. People did find her a bit much, as a matter of fact - overwhelming in her enthusiasm, but no real harm in her - just a respectable North Oxford type. The General, bless him, had no surviving relatives, and he depended utterly on Madge for absolutely everything. She was his lifeline, she really was, and he simply adored her. It was most touching.

At this point the two policemen looked decidedly bleak, and Joy paused, raising an eyebrow enquiringly.

Bimworth, sitting up straight in his chair, cleared his throat and looked most unhappy.

"What is it, gentlemen? Is there something wrong?"

Bimworth nodded unhappily, going quite red in the face with emotion and blowing his nose loudly.

"Yes, I'm afraid so," he said, "I am very sorry to have to tell you that General Spragnell is dead."

"Dead?" On hearing this pronouncement Joy was incredulous. "How on earth ...?" Her voice tailed away in disbelief. "Well ...?"

Bimworth paused for a moment to collect himself, then went on: "It's all very unfortunate, but when we realized that Mrs Spragnell had disappeared, our men went round to her home at about 11.30 p.m. They could see him through the window, sitting in front of the fire, fast asleep with his old cat on his knee. Waiting evidently for Mrs Spragnell to come home.

"It took them a while to rouse the old man, but of course in the circumstances it had to be done. Eventually he came to the door and they explained the situation to him as briefly as they could, without saying too much about the details of the case, or stressing the serious nature of it. However, when the General realized that Mrs Spragnell had actually gone missing, he collapsed on the spot with a heart attack and died instantly. There was nothing our men could do to revive him before the ambulance came, but though they have to be tough because of the nature of the work, they were really upset to see the poor old man go down like that ..."

"My God - how absolutely awful!"

Joy felt overwhelmed with sorrow at this cruel blow her old friend had suffered, and could not hold back her tears. The two policemen sat completely silent as she struggled to compose herself.

So, quickly wiping away her tears, she galvanized herself into a practical mode for thinking about ways of dealing with the problems this sudden catastrophe might present. Madge gone and the General dead, what was to become of the animals? There was Wellington, the cat, and of course Napoleon, and what about Papillon, the chihuahua? This diminutive mini-dog had always been Madge's pride and joy. It was quite impossible to believe that she had vanished, leaving it behind without a thought for its welfare. She raised these points and Bimworth brightened and responded with reassuring news of the temporary provision which had been made.

"Ah, yes," he said, "Mrs Alder next door has taken charge of the chihuahua and is quite happy to keep it if necessary, but says she can't cope with the old cat and the Mynah-bird as well - she's agreed to look after them for a day or two, until some arrangement is made for them to be taken away."

"Oh dear me!" exclaimed Joy in dismay: "Well, I suppose I'd better take Wellington. After all, he is a very old boy - about seventeen, I think, which is quite a venerable age for a cat. And if it comes to that, what's one more cat?" - looking round the room at her cats comfortably draped over the back of the sofa, and occupying various easy chairs, with blind Fred on the hearth-rug. "But - I simply can't be doing with another bird!" She paused a moment, then - with resignation: "Oh, very well, I'll take Napoleon too. I'll go straight round and get them when you've gone. I really can't bear to think of poor old Wellington with no home. He's such a nice cat, and he's always been used to such a comfortable life. He'll miss the General dreadfully."

"Well, that's that, then, madam. Very good. We'll be in touch."

Bimworth stopped at the front door as they left; he stood and looked down at Joy from what seemed to be a great height: "I can tell you this much, madam. Mrs Spragnell's car was found in the river, just beyond Clifton Hampden, early this morning. It appeared to have gone off the road on a sharp bend, but there was no sign of Mrs Spragnell whatsoever. They are dragging the river now and the divers are making a search."

"Dear God - what an unspeakable catastrophe! It gets worse and worse!" Joy was horror-struck. The two policemen departed with a cheery wave, doffing their caps politely, and remarking: "Thank you, madam, you've been a great help."

Across the road, Miss Dacre stood on her front doorstep in full view of all the world; she was watching their departure with evident approbation, and to Joy's astonishment she waved a discreet hand at the two policemen and they waved back! Whatever next? Meanwhile Pongo barked a staccato obligato as he stood alongside Miss Dacre on the doorstep, wagging his minuscule plumed tail enthusiastically as he did so.

Joy looked down at Iffley, who had emerged to see the action.

"Just what is going on, Iffley," she asked. Iffley replied with a questioning "Rrrr?" then returned to resume her snooze on the hall table, displaying her indifference to the outside world.

Joy picked up her jacket and her car keys, muttering to herself: "The better the day, the better the deed," and went on her way resignedly to Plantation Road to sort out the matter of the cat and the bird.

Mrs Alder was most upset; she confided that she and Mrs Badger had been life-long cronies (and, of course, 'know-alls' - and entirely au fait with all the gossip relating to the affair) but in the end "this 'ole crool business," as she put it, wringing her hands, had come as a terrible shock to them both. "'Oo'd a' thought it could all end loike this? Mrs Spragnell bein' such a respectable lady - an' as for the poor old General, well, now - it just didn't bear a'thinkin' about, did it?."

They went into Madge's house together, rather fearfully, both feeling that it was an eerie experience. The house was silent and empty, but it seemed as though there was someone still there, a strong presence, and not at all welcoming.

They went into the sitting-room and there, on the General's chair, sat poor old Wellington, forlornly waiting for his person, who would not be coming back. He miaowed piteously at them, as though bewildered. The mynah-bird sat quietly in its cage, apparently similarly bereft.

Come on, Wellington," said Joy, "Let's take you home." He miaowed again, putting his paws round Joy's neck as she picked him up gently. He was a huge ginger persian cat with a white shirt-front and what appeared to be a permanent smile; this illusion was created by two white patches, one on each cheek, just above his mouth.

Mrs Alder brought the bird out to the car, and with some difficulty, for its cage was enormous, they got it into the back of the vehicle.

Wellington, apparently unconcerned that he was being taken away from his home, had settled down quietly next to the birdcage on the back seat. He even began to purr loudly.

The two women stood outside Madge's house for a short while, utterly numbed by the sequence of awful events. The house was a charming Georgian cottage with roses and clematis round the door and white shutters, geraniums in the window-boxes, in fact all the trapping of a home of total respectability and well ordered lives. It was an incongruous setting for such a disastrous conclusion.

"May the good Lord rest their souls'" Mrs Alder sniffed, as she wiped away tears of real grief. Then she bent down and picked up the milk bottle still standing on the doorstep. "'Tis all beyond 'uman understand, it be. Well, then, they won't be needing this, for sure, will they?" She took up the wire milk-bottle container, which read 'Two pints today, one orange juice, one double cream' on its rotating label, and turned it round to read 'No milk today'. "I'll take the milk an' stuff, an' see the milkman tomorrow and cancel the papers as well, while I'm at it"·

Thus, the business of the day now done, Joy and Mrs Alder bade one another a subdued farewell at the garden gate.

"Papillon'll be all roight. She's no trouble," assured Mrs Alder, adding: "Good luck with your two. That mynah-bird's a menace, moind!"

Not immensely reassured by this warning, Joy departed with the two orphaned pets to St. Julie's Road. She drew up outside her house a few minutes later and breathed a sigh of relief. It was going to be a bit of a struggle with the bird-cage, but dear old Wellington was no trouble at all, thank goodness!

The bush-telegraph had apparently been busy in her absence, for all the house cats had gathered in the front garden to await developments; even blind Fred was there, sitting next to Iffley, who always acted as his personal guide-cat, and would sit shoulder-to-shoulder with him to make sure that he did not wander away.

When all the feline greetings had been exchanged and strokes shared out impartially, Joy settled Wellington in the kitchen with a tasty snack and went out to collect Napoleon from the car. Getting the cage out was an awful business: the poor bird clung to its perch as though glued to it by fright, as it see-sawed to and fro, and fixed Joy with a wild hypnotic stare. (Joy was reminded of Melody). What was more unnerving it did not even emit a single squawk! She really must remember to make sure that the cage was anchored securely to some heavy table, so as to avoid a drama such as befell Melody when his cage toppled over and Tabby made her attempt on his life!

Joy could feel Miss Dacre's gaze riveted on her as she wrestled with the bird-cage, while the cats sat, saucer-eyed, catching the progress of the operation and drooling at the prospect of this delectable future blackbird dinner - a gastronomic delight still to come! Oh dear! There were obviously going to be problems with ensuring the bird's security.

Joy managed to negotiate the perilous journey to the drawing-room without dropping the cage on the way, and she put it down on the table by the window. After checking its food and water, she left it to settle down, with a nice view of the garden for its entertainment.

The grandfather clock struck twelve, reminding her that time was passing. However, Mrs Badger had gone, thank goodness - and all was peace, so she thought she'd better make a quick lunch; Wellington could be bedded down in the cat-basket in the kitchen for the present; he seemed quite happy and later, but not just yet, she would take him out in the back garden for a walk-about. Thereafter, when all this was achieved, she would settle down to do some work. She must make a start on those fascinating Clemens non Papa manuscripts which had just turned up in an old chest in Norwich Cathedral - an odd place, surely, for them to have come to light?

She had noted a particularly attractive onomatopoeic effect in places, which was unusual and touching, like hearing angelic voices rejoicing in heaven, accompanied by the pulsating rhythm of a myriad ethereal wings beating, which came through vividly in the musical text and reminded her of some other music, but she could not remember what it was.

Pensively, she sat at her desk, luxuriating in the knowledge that she had a little space and time in which she could consider and pursue these themes without fear of interruption. There was, in fact, total peace and quiet; all was silent except for the gentle cooing of a pair of collared-doves courting in the pear tree down the garden. What could be lovelier? And she could do a nice little piece on this theme, with angelic voices, fluttering wings and bird song all intertwined, reminding her of something she already knew - of course, Henry Purcell's charming song, 'Hark, the Ech'ing Air', all about enthusiastic Cupids clapping their wings; and there was Schubert's song, 'Die Vogel', with the flowing accompaniment suggesting swallows and swifts swirling around overhead. And what about Schumann's delightful song, 'Die Taube', with the excited fluttering of the birds demonstrated in the rapid staccato rhythm. And finally, there was the magnificent aria from Haydn's 'Creation': 'On mighty pens uplifted soars the eagle aloft ...', surely the most perfect example of nature interpreted in music.

Joy was getting quite carried away, and she began to jot down notes about making a case for comparison between Clemens and Purcell, finding this an interesting avenue for exploration. They were both able to express intense emotion and passion in their music, far apart though they were in time, and hence in style; instances occurred to her, such as Purcell's 'My beloved spake..." and Clemens' 'Adjuro vos', and 'Adoro Te'.

She decided that this was where lateral thinking was needed, and indeed was very important in lecturing to young undergraduates, producing some paradoxical juxtapositions to add spice and variety to what otherwise might seem tedious and boring to the listener. And she didn't care a jot about academic critics claiming that her ideas were rather too far-fetched and abstruse. Let them snigger behind their hands - she knew that her personal style and delivery could work wonders and inspire her students. She thanked the Lord for her Irish grandmother, who had taught her everything about the Irish sense of humour, i.e, never mind being laughed at, just laugh with them about yourself; this always confuses the enemy.

But it was time to return to Purcell, and she must not forget to mention that supreme example of wild passion, the mysterious song 'Mad Bess of Bedlam', or indeed the desperation given voice in that amazing piece, 'The Blessed Virgin's Expostulation'. All fire and sparkle; she would tell her students, and this suggested a captivating title for her lecture:'Clemens non Papa and Henry Purcell, all fire and sparkle: A comparison of style and content'. Looking out of the study window, she gave a little sigh of satisfaction and smiled in appreciation of the rare luxury of peace and tranquillity after the morning's turmoil. She contemplated a sinful smoked salmon sandwich for luncheon, and perhaps braised steak and onions for dinner? And it occurred to her that she ought to make enough for two or three, just in case Petronella or Mark came in, or Even Michael Walters, for it was likely that he would show up sometime later in the day to talk things over. So she must put two or three large potatoes in the oven to bake, as a precaution. She could always use them up tomorrow if no one...

"Hello, darling! How simply divine to see you - simply divine, simply divine!," screamed Madge's voice from behind her. Joy froze with shock and horror; then she turned slowly to face the open door to the hall and saw - no one! She got up and walked slowly and hesitantly towards the drawing-room, whence the voice seemed to have come: she peered cautiously round the door, and as she did so the Mynah-bird instantly came to life. Shaking his feathers and putting his head on one Side, he fixed her with a beady eye, announcing imperiously: "Rupert, Rupert, shut that door!," followed by "Hello, darling, hello, darling!" and a piercing whistle.

"Napoleon! Oh, no - I don't believe it!" Joy was aghast.

"Napoleon - Napoleon Bonaparte!" screamed the bird, bobbing its head up and down and jumping 'from perch to perch in great excitement. "Siege of Moscow, Elba, St. Helena!" it proclaimed, and that was only the beginning!

The bird had worked itself up into a veritable frenzy in no time at all. It evidently liked its new home, and its vocabulary was amazing - it even spoke French, once again in Madge's unmistakable tones, including a number of Gallic swearwords with which Joy was not familiar, although she caught an occasional 'Merde'. Otherwise it was quite difficult to interpret the quickfire argot emitted by the bird, and varied by snatches of the Marseillaise, sung with enthusiastic untuneful vigour, and punctuated by piercing whistles.

So finally Joy packed up her papers and retired to the kitchen, closing the door firmly in a vain attempt to exclude the noise. However, the smoked salmon sandwich and strong coffee she made went some way towards restoring her equanimity, although there appeared to be no escape from the bird. The cats, too, seemed to be in a state of acute nervous stress within an hour of its arrival. They sat, jaws working with extreme frustration, in a silent row outside the drawing-room door. Once again she was reminded of Melody's fate.

Within the hour also, all the other birds in the neighbourhood had got the message, and every starling, magpie, rook, etc. within calling distance had arrived and were sitting around in the trees and on the shed roof to observe this new phenomenon which had come to hold court in their territory and dared to scream at them at the top of its voice.

Napoleon, it seemed, had assumed the role of Melody, and was as indefatigable and as penetrating as the little green budgerigar had ever been, and Joy, exasperated, felt she must escape. She decided upon a walk down to the Jolly Sailors, though she was not normally a lunchtime drinker, just to get away from the tyrannical bird. Pausing at the crucifix outside St. Julie's Church, she put up an earnest prayer to St. Frideswide, finishing with: "O Lord, show us an end to all this sorrowful matter soon!" As she gazed at the painted carving, just a little less than life-size, she was struck again by its ghastly ugliness: the rose-pink body, the chocolate-brown hair, the crudely painted eyes and crown of thorns.

It was also dirty and weather-stained, with muddy streaks down the arms and body, and deserved to be regarded as the absolute nadir of good taste and artistic presentation. Who on earth could have designed such a monstrous thing, and whoever had allowed such a preposterous artifact to be erected there? One might not perhaps have been surprised to see such an image by the roadside or outside a village church in France, but even so, the French equivalent would have traditional relevance and look right, whereas this particular object just looked all wrong.Nevertheless its message was there, plain and stark: 'Attende, populi qui transivit: Attende me!" "Well," she thought, "It was just typical Oxford – everything back to front, but its message was still clear. No wonder Lewis Carroll wrote 'Alice'. One would never fully understand this mystical whimsical city with its strange mix of beauty and vulgarity, but still she loved it, for there was no other place like it in all the world.

As she walked down the road to the pub she seemed to hear a voice from many years ago, of Horace, a grand old man of Jericho, and a faithful college servant all his life. He had died well into his nineties, and he had many amazing stories to tell of happenings long years ago in Oxford. Joy had heard these tales as a young undergraduate at St. James' College and they had left an indelible impression on her memory. Horace had spoken of his childhood recollections when his father had been head porter at Christ Church, way back in the mid-nineteenth century. He recalled with absolute clarity the day when he had stood, hand in hand with his father, at the entrance to Christ Church, under Tom Tower, and had watched the arrival of Queen Victoria's son Prince Leopold as his carriage drew up to deliver him for his tutorial at the college, one day in a now far distant spring. He recalled that, young and overawed, though he was, he had noticed that the prince looked pale and unwell, and he retained a distinct impression of a frail, and rather sickly young man; perhaps he had not even been fit enough to walk the short distance from his grand lodgings, or did Princes always ride downtown for their tutorials? Who knows?

Horace had also spoken with great affection of Oscar Wilde, who had been at Magdalen, and who had always walked everywhere, waving his Derby bowler and greeting everyone in that universally cordial way which is peculiar to the Irish. What a lovely, caring, flamboyant character he was, generous to a fault, never to be forgotten!

Walking on, lost in reverie, towards the Jolly Sailors, Joy experienced a sudden revelation - the crucifix! She stopped in her tracks and looked back at the crude image hanging there, forever impaled, head dropping, under the swaying branches of the overhanging trees which seemed in some strange way to be trying to embrace and protect it from the scoffing gaze of man and the rude blast of the elements.

And then suddenly it all came back to her and she knew the real reason why the ghastly crucifix had been placed where it was; and, extraordinary as it might seem, this had nothing to do with the church. Horace's grandfather had told him that his (Horace's) great-grandfather remembered the building of St. Julie's Church and the development of North Oxford as a residential suburb in the mid-nineteenth century, and had told his son that the crucifix had been placed there because that was the spot where the ancient gibbet had stood, and the corpses of felons had been hung on it in chains after their execution on the Mound in central Oxford. Horace also related how his great-grandfather had actually been taken as a boy to witness the last execution on the Mound, presumably, as was customary at that time, in company with a large crowd of persons curious to see that grisly event.The executed man, so it was said, appeared to jerk about and dance on the end of the rope as his neck broke in his death throes.

Chilled by this recollection, Joy walked on quickly towards the welcoming warmth of the Jolly Sailors and the enticing vision of a sparkling glass or so enjoyed in cheerful company.

However, as she turned to look back once more at the crucifix she heard Horace's voice again: "Course, the reason whoy they put the gibbet so far out o' town was as 'ow they 'ad to hang 'em to rot outside the city walls, an' the outer wall was just a little way down wot is now Kingston Road.There's still bits of it left in the cellars of the 'ouses just down the road a bit.My Auntie Annie 'ad an 'ole piece of it in 'er cellar.The 'ole o' one wall was all old stone. They do say as 'twas the boundary wall o' the old monastery wot was where Leckford Road is now till 'Enery the Eighth knocked it all flyin', whenever 'twas. So you see, that's the reason whoy - no word of a loie."

Arriving at the Jolly Sailors, Joy found the saloon bar deserted. "Hey, Missus!" Tony's head appeared round the corner from the other bar. "Your lad's in t'other bar - public. 'E looks fair knocked out, 'e do."

Joy's spirits rose instantly. Mark was back - such a relief! As she made her' way to the public bar, she realized how deeply attached she was to her nephew, such was the intense relief she felt on hearing that he had returned, safe and - she hoped - sound. God only knew what kind of night he had had, and presumably with no sleep at all; this surmise proved to be correct.

Mark was sitting on a stool, ashen-faced, elbows on the bar, with a pint of beer alongside and the Oxford Times laid out before him, but he was not reading, indeed he seemed to be just staring, unseeing, at the text. However, he turned and saw her, managed to smile and, stifling a yawn, said: "Hello, Aunt! It's been a long night - the hell of a long night!"

Joy gave him a fond hug and kiss, noting that, tired though he was, he had still found time to shave and put on a clean shirt. Good army training.

She forbore to tax him with any questions, and left him to his beer and newspaper, after getting his assurance that after a few hours sleep he would indeed be round for an early meal: yes, braised steak and onions would be just right. Six-thirty, then? Fine! Something to look forward to - he could eat a horse now, even! But never mind, a cheese roll would fill the aching void in the meantime. Two baked potatoes? Yes - just the ticket. Big ones with lashings of butter and black pepper. Broccoli? Fabulous! Roll on, dinnertime!

He produced a rather wan smile as she left, and she returned home warmed within and at peace with the world, giving some serious thought to the matter of what kind of delicious pudding she could concoct for the evening meal. Cooking was for her a wonderful therapy, and enjoyment was doubled when you had someone else to cook for. She must think of something to suit the occasion, and now she had it! Plum duff was the solution, with Bird's custard, of course - 'summat to stick to yer ribs', as Percy Chadlow would say. There were plenty of plums this year from the venerable Victoria plum tree in the back garden, so that would be quite simple. And probably Mark would have to be at work again later on, so he would need something really substantial to keep him going. Petronella would like that, too; she was an enthusiast for good wholesome food.

She decided to give Michael Walters a ring at his office, to see if he was free, and luckily she got him straight away. Yes, he would be delighted to come along (Joy's cooking was legendary and even the most pressing engagement would be cancelled at the prospect of a meal at St. Julie's Road.)"How about a bottle of Chateau Neuf to do honour to the beef? Yes? Excellent. Six-thirty, then."

Well, there might be some interesting news about the events at the fair. It was such a strange business and there must be much more to be told. In pleasant anticipation, she returned to the kitchen and settled down happily to prepare the meal, watched at first by all the cats with silent intensity; this was subsequently to be replaced by a concerted programme of civil disobedience.

CHAPTER XVI

'Leave, alas, this tormenting!'

The First Book of Ballets to Five Voices

Thomas Morley 1595

It rained all afternoon, a driving rain borne in on the west wind from over the Cotswolds: only in Oxford can it rain like that. It was as though the heavens opened and a total deluge descended.

Glancing out of the drawing-room window for a moment, Joy noticed that the drain outside the front gate was flooding right across the road yet again, and reflected as so many times before that the council really should - but probably would not - do something about the drains. It occurred to her, however, that strangely enough it was the flooded drain which gave up its secrets (if there were any) in regurgitating Madge's diary! Was she dead? And was she really a criminal, as might be supposed, judging from the evidence revealed so far? Or was she just a well-meaning sincere soul seeking to do her best for her fellow-beings, who had fallen into an unforeseen snare of unlucky circumstances and become the victim of evil scheming? Perhaps Mark would provide some clue this evening about the real state of things? But on second thoughts, perhaps not, since of course the whole matter would be sub judice for the present.

For the whole of that afternoon the cats behaved like perfect pests; they hated the rain and were obviously bored so they set about playing with everything she was using in the kitchen; every time she picked up a knife to chop an onion or a carrot, a paw would flash out from below decks and deftly snaffle a piece. Not much notice was taken even of threats that they might lose a claw or two if they persisted, and Tabby ran up the curtain in defiance; she was a little wild cat from Wytham Wood and no one was going to tell her what to do! It crossed Joy's mind that she must make sure that the drawing-room door was shut, in case the mischievous animal might decide to have a go at the William Morris tapestry sofa, which was original and highly clawable, already with loose threads here and there. And there was also Napoleon - he must be protected!

When Fred began to chew the cable of her electric mixer, she realized that action must be taken so she banished them all from the kitchen, shutting them out in the hall, with the drawing-room door firmly closed. Their tactics in revenge for this treatment took the form of flying up and down the stairs and playing mad games with every detachable object until at last they were exhausted and peace ensued, and they returned to their chosen resting-places, Iffley on the hall table and Fred in the airing cupboard as usual.

Joy finished her preparations for the evening meal and sank gratefully into her wing-back chair in the study; she did not want to disturb Napoleon in the drawing-room. What on earth was she going to do with him? Should she look for an ornithologist with an aviary where the poor bird could at least fly around and stretch his wings and perhaps even find a mate? She dare not let him out of his cage, for she had no idea how he might behave, and some birds could be aggressive. Unable to resolve this problem, she dozed off for half an hour, waking just in time to watch the television news.

To her great surprise the events of the previous night in Oxford were actually shown on the national news network; there was a comprehensive report about the St. Giles Fair, with excellent film footage. The commentator said that this film had been shot on the first night of the fair for a forthcoming documentary, but an extraordinary event had occurred on the last night, so some footage had been released to give a general background to the story.

First, there was a fine shot of the view down St. Giles, looking toward the Martyrs' Memorial, with the fair in full swing in all its brash vulgarity, and lights and lasers twinkling and flashing against the night sky. All that was missing was the noise, with the stench of fried onions and sizzling hamburgers in the background to complete the impression. Crowds milled around, Enjoying the fun of the fair.

Then the camera focused on the big wheel outside St. James's College, rotating menacingly close up to the facade, and the commentary proceeded to relate the dramatic events of the night. There had been a massive haul of drugs at the fair and the police were now investigating the matter. In addition, the tragic death had taken place of a young member of the University who had been involved in the affair, and a prominent member of Oxford society had disappeared during the disturbance, and in view of her involvement in what had led up to the drugs seizure, the police were now searching for her as a matter of urgency.

The camera moved on down the fair after this startling disclosure coming to rest on the Gallopin' 'Orses, zooming in on a close-up in which Joy, to her astonishment, saw herself and Michael sail serenely past, followed by Mark and Marit gracefully gliding up and down on their noble steeds as they went round in eternal rotation, trapped forever in a magical orbit of everlasting delight from which there was no escape. And Marit in close-up was looking for none, her blond hair streaming in the wind, and Mark beside her, delighting in her pleasure. Joy was almost awestruck at this juxtaposition of ecstasy and tragedy in pictures on a television screen.

Suddenly, Joy felt depressed; she was experiencing, rather late in life, her personal moment of truth revealed to her by that glimpse of herself caught on television in the report on St. Giles' Fair, and it came as an awful shock to see herself through the unmercifully clinical eye of the camera. There she was: a tubby, red-faced, prosperous-looking elderly party with a self-satisfied air of successful achievement making a fool or herself, going round on a gallopin' 'orse - what a silly old frump!

This orgy of self-punishment was, however, cut short by the arrival of Petronella, who swept in with a flourish, then collapsed on the sofa declaring herself to be utterly done and in a state of terminal exhaustion; this required an immediate remedy, and a dramatic improvement was produced after Joy had administered a glass of Harvey's Bristol Cream, a well-known corpse reviver, which always worked wonders, Joy reflected, as she saw resuscitation take place before her eyes. With a deep sigh, Petronella leaned back and closed her eyes for a while; then, after a discreet interval she opened an eye and, raising one eyebrow, gently waved her glass in the direction of the sherry bottle. She winked in gratitude as it was graciously replenished, drank it down rather quickly and declared herself completely restored to life, adding a suitable Latin quotation in her usual style.

Joy laughed and went off to the kitchen to see to the meal, thinking that the girl was really a tonic, effectually banishing her own gloomy mood. She opened the oven and was met by a waft of delicious-smelling beef stew. What a good thing she had added those old bottles of Guinness - the Irish answer to a perfect stew and providing the most delectable gravy! But her reflections were interrupted by a prolonged peal from the doorbell and a loud rat-tat-tat with the door-knocker. The boys had arrived, Mark, Michael - and here was Marit, too, which was a nice surprise, but she was very apologetic, declaring that she had been having "the twisted arm to come along - if this was the expression correctly? But she was most pleased and honoured and had brought a small gift." She produced a plastic bag written allover in Norwegian, that when opened yielded one large Jarlsberg cheese and a bottle of Schnapps, with some rather strange looking cake - "Fresh from Norway," said Marit,"And brought by dear aunt Aase since three days ago. Very good." And so it was, as the company found out at the end of the dinner party. Very good indeed.

Joy settled the company down with sherry and nutty nibbles and left the girls to keep them entertained while she went off to the kitchen to make sure that there was enough to eat. She knew that the men were starving hungry so that would be goodbye to the baked potatoes, since they would wolf the lot, so she must think up something suitable to supplement the menu. Luckily, thank goodness, she had a quantity of boiled rice in the 'fridge, left over from a previous meal, so she quickly tossed it in the wok, throwing in a can of Mexican sweetcorn, and another of French petits pois. The result was an excellent bed of risotto-like consistency for the braised beef to repose upon, and now she was ready to feed her guests.

Mark was still evidently very tired and seemed disinclined to talk, but Marit's bubbling effervescence revived him and he began to twinkle nicely as the evening progressed. Michael's Chateauneuf was a particularly fine vintage but alas! It did not go very far, so Mark was sent down to the cellar to rummage around for more cheer. He returned with a reasonable claret, of no great marque but a pleasant enough wine to follow its aristocratic predecessor.

And now it was time for the contents of Marit's bag, and the meal ended with Jarlsberg and biscuits, black coffee and Schnapps, with a piece of Aunt Aase's 'special Norwegian cake', which was rather like a German 'Torte', but with some unidentifiable scrunchy bits - "Could they be pine cones?" Michael wondered, on tasting it. Surely not, and anyhow it was really delicious, as everyone agreed. However, Marit remarked that knowing Aunt Aase as she did, it could be anything, since she was a great one for foraging in the forest, as was traditional in their family, going back hundreds of years, and this particular cake was an ancient secret family recipe, not written down but passed on by word of mouth from mother to daughter for generations.

"Could the scrunchy bits be beetles?" asked Michael, irrepressibly. Marit, earnest as ever, said: "Could maybe be beetles. Please to ask Aunt Aase. You can eat such things in the forest - it is quite possible"!

At this piece of information the hitherto enthusiastic mastication of the remarkable cake was brought to an abrupt halt, but at that stage of the evening it did not really signify much since everyone was by now replete. It was a very happy party and the girls were a great asset, laughing and chattering together over trivialities, affecting the company like a glass of good champagne. Fatigue was forgotten and a convivial spirit pervaded, providing a perfect aid to digestion - "Much better than Rennies" was Michael's comment, and Mark agreed, remarking quietly aside to Michael that the cake had evidently done no damage as yet, and a good laugh with the female of the species worked wonders - there was nothing like it and he felt much better.

After dinner the men retired to the study for a quiet cigar and coffee with Marit's Schnapps, which was all well and good, apart from one thing: the bird cage and its occupant, which had been put in there, so as not to drive everyone mad with incessant chatter. They were soon forced out, however, by the fiendish bird, which suddenly came to life and let rip with a broadside of oaths, interspersed with the refrain 'Shut that door, Rupert!' and followed by the inevitable piercing whistles. Deafened by the din, they retreated to the drawing-room and took refuge in armchairs by the fireplace.

Petronella and Marit decided to leave them to their peaceful reverie and went upstairs to look through Petronella's wardrobe and discuss important matters such as the current fashions at Botticelli's and the new knitting patterns. When they came downstairs again, Marit announced that she was just about to embark upon a great work, to wit, the knitting of a traditional Norwegian oiled-wool sweater for

Mark. She explained this at length, but not before Michael had put in a bid to be next in line for one for himself, please, when Marit had time and energy to knit it - size forty-four, and it would be greatly appreciated if it could be ready for his birthday but there was no rush as that was not until the end of January, so not to worry. Marit responded with a little smile, saying she would "think about it, please," and went on to describe in detail the ancient tradition of sweater knitting.

It had always been the task of the women of Norway, from far back in history, to sit through the long dark nights of the Scandinavian winter and knit the famous oiled-wool sweaters for the whole family. "it was a happy task - a labour of love - and practical, too, for after all the sweater is like - how do you call it? A hot water-bottle, so warm - everyone should wear one." Listening to her, Mark was captivated by her delightful way with the English language. She had a charming manner of pronouncing certain vowels; for instance, the word 'so' came out as a cross between 'sew' and 'sue'. Similarly, 'do' became something between 'doe' and 'due'. And Mark observed that Marit was quite aware that she was being amusing, but she didn't really know why, so she pursued the saga of the Norwegian sweater, holding her audience spellbound.

Each family, Marit said, had its own special design based on ancient patterns. So, one of these designs could still be seen today, she believed, carved on the standing stones dotted around Scandinavia. This intrigued Michael Walters and he saw the opportunity to slip in a jocular interjection, which earned him a sharp kick on the ankle (author unknown) under the table. Undeterred, though slightly deflated, he asked: "how was this special oiled wool obtained? Was it from the coat of the reindeer, or elk, or goat, or sheep, perhaps? Were there flocks of sheep, for instance, in Norway?"

Marit's cool green eyes rested on him thoughtfully as she considered the question, taking delicate sips from her glass of white wine. After a few moments she said that this was a most interesting question, indeed it was, and that she had never given it any thought before this question was asked. She spoke very slowly, giving each word due weight, and Michael began to feel that his attempt at light-hearted wit was falling rather flat. Was she serious? Looking at her, it was impossible to tell.

She was absolutely po-faced and earnest in manner, and quite disarming as she warmed to her subject. Later, however, Michael was to discover that Marit had simply run rings round him. He had unwittingly become the victim of a clever Norwegian plot whereby the jester who is bold enough to poke fun at the apparently humourless nature of the Norwegian temperament soon finds that the opposite is the case: neatly, almost imperceptibly, the tables are turned and in the end the jester himself is made to look a perfect fool.

All this was achieved very neatly and nicely. Shaking her head solemnly as she thought the matter over, Marit said slowly that perhaps the source of the oiled wool would not be reindeer or elk; they were excellent in so many ways, for meat and for their beautiful skins with such fine fur. They were also good for other things - their wonderful horns - antlers, wasn't it? They could be used in lots of ways, but not for knitting needles, perhaps? She would ask Aunt Aase about this, just to be certain, and of course there was the matter of Santa Claus and his sledge; yes, a very good and useful animal, the reindeer!

As for goats and sheep, this was most interesting, Marit continued, completely straight-faced. She was not at all sure about the goat as a source of oiled wool, but yes, maybe, and again she would ask Aunt Aase, as she did keep a goat for milk and cheese. And sheep? Yes, of course Norway did have sheep in certain areas, so this was most probably the source of the wool. And yes, she had a little story to tell them about the knitting of these oiled-wool sweaters, and it was a most touching tale, so she was sure they would like to hear it, yes?

Her mother had always been a great admirer of the much-fabled Wagnerian soprano Kirsten Flagstad, and Flagstad was a dedicated knitter of the oiled-wool sweater; for her it was totally relaxing just to sit and knit after some great performance, which would be followed by a party backstage. Marit's mother had been present at such events and had observed Flagstad sitting quietly in a corner, a glass of brandy at her elbow, industriously knitting away, with a beaming smile at the adoring assembly, but saying nothing; if spoken to, she would simply nod amiably and murmur "Ahaha," slowly sipping her brandy and getting on with the knitting of endless oiled-wool sweaters. It was an excellent therapy and the perfect antidote to stress.

Joy was much moved at the thought of the incomparable diva composedly knitting after giving the performance of a lifetime on the stage at Covent Garden. Perhaps it supplied a sense of continuity and normality amid the euphoria and razzmatazz of the world of stardom.

At this point Marit and Petronella announced that they would like to do the washing-up, and departed to the kitchen, the former thus showing a delicate sensitiveness to Michael's discomfiture over his total demolition as far as oiled wool was concerned, and wishing to give him time to lick his wounds fortified by a dose of Schnapps. Meanwhile, Joy took the opportunity to tell them that she had seen the television report about the goings-on at the fair. At once Mark came to life and was most interested, asking in detail about what was portrayed. But he would not be drawn at all when questions were put to him, albeit tentatively, about the events of the previous night, remarking that there was very little he could tell them at present, but it would all be made manifest in due course, no doubt. And it was evident from the way he spoke that 'due course' was still some way off in the future.

This was tantalizing for his frustrated listeners, but he did volunteer the information that they had all been very good and had been of considerable help to the police by reacting so well in the emergency. He was sorry, he added, but this was all he could say for the moment. Then he lent back in his chair and dozed off. Michael yawned in sympathy, stretched luxuriously and followed suit. Two delightful dormice, thought Joy, looking at them fondly; then she retired to the kitchen to shoo off the girls and finish off the washing-up herself.

Perceiving that both the men were asleep and dead to the world, Marit and Petronella went upstairs to have a quiet talk, and this gave Petronella the chance to delve into the mysteries of knitting oiled wool sweaters, in which she was really interested being determined to learn how to knit one (not a lot of good, perhaps, for Bruce in the Australian outback, but she might knit one for herself as a practice run for future reference. The patterns were so lovely but too complex to be sure of success at first try.)

Meanwhile Joy was happily up to her elbows in washing-up water, finding this a welcome change from academic matters just to stand at the kitchen sink and contemplate the outside world, looking out over the garden in the afterglow. How she did love to feel she was captain of her own ship (or in this case galley) where kitchen matters and culinary arts were concerned. It was a pleasant interval, of peace and time for recollection, and sometimes even inspiration. She enjoyed the soothing, dream-like feeling of no rush and no deadlines to meet, and just the mechanical action of washing the dishes as she turned over in her mind her present pet project on Clemens non Papa and Henry Purcell. She really must get down to some detailed research on a possible affinity between the two composers. It would be quite amusing to present this somewhat improbable thesis, even if no actual evidence of imitation was to be found.

Then, as she looked rather absently out of the window, she observed in a pool of light on the lawn the white shirt-front and luminous green eyes of a handsome dog-fox. There he sat, patiently waiting for his tit-bits from the kitchen, and opening the window, she called: "Just a minute, foxy, I shan't be long!" Instantly he vanished into the bushes to await developments, While she collected left-overs from the meal for him and the vixen should she be about.

As she did so, however, the telephone rang; it was for Mark and it sounded very official indeed, so she went to fetch him and found them both asleep, looking so peaceful that it seemed a great pity to wake them. But it must be done, and Mark sprang to life like a coiled spring as she gently roused him, while Michael slept on soundly, quite undisturbed by the commotion.

Mark took the call and promptly vanished, after giving Joy a fond hug and kiss and saying he was so sorry, he had to go, love to the girls and apologies for his sudden departure but it had to be - things were happening. He gave Joy thumbs-up and drove off, watched covertly and attentively by Miss Dacre, twitching her curtains delicately and noting every detail of the proceedings.

Marit was very disappointed to find that Mark had gone, but rallied quickly and was soon her bubbly self again, laughing and joking with Michael, who loved it and was delighted with her Nordic charm and lovely sense of humour and readiness to laugh at herself over her eccentric use of English. Petronella joined in the amusement and the guests eventually departed in good spirits, although Petronella's were slightly dampened by a question from Marit about Bruce. Visibly quietened, she replied that she had received & postcard from Australia portraying an ostrich in the bush. Bruce wrote to say that the work was hard and the environment was a challenge, and certainly no place for a woman, but he sent his love, and said he was missing Oxford and all the good times they had had together. So at least that was some kind of reassurance. Commiseration was offered but Petronella was quite philosophical and merely remarked that no doubt time would tell. Meanwhile there was always work to be done, and that would give her plenty to occupy her mind.

Marit, apparently meaning to comfort Petronella, here quoted some especially revered Norwegian sage as they said goodbye. When translated it ran thus: 'Things may come, things may go, but the mountains and the fjords will remain'. There was an extra bit to follow, but Marit said it was "quite problematic to translate, as it concerned the emotions"; the Norwegians are, it seems, a very matter-of-fact people, rather like the Scots, who find the expression of emotion rather difficult, so the meaning remained obscure, with a mysterious reference to hobgoblins which was never explained. Petronella however thanked Marit very much and said she would remember it when she felt depressed.

After everyone had departed and Joy had sorted out the cats and locked up for the night, the 'phone rang, so, clutching her hot water bottle to her bosom, she went downstairs again to answer it and was surprised to hear Mark's voice, and still more surprised at the request he made: would she mind very much if he sent a man round with a recording machine to make a tape of the Mynah-bird? Sorry, but yes, first thing in the morning, please, it was most important. Many, many thanks, and lots of love and sleep well. Have a good night.

And Joy did just that. Though slightly perplexed by Mark's strange request, she slept very soundly and was up bright and early at six o'clock, in eager anticipation - something was happening at last! Thank the Lord!

She fed and watered the mynah-bird and talked to it, which was fatal, for it launched immediately into its repertoire of profanity, preluded of course by an infernal barrage of wolf whistles.She was strongly tempted to open the cage and let the pest fly out of the window, but that of course she could not do yet anyway. Nevertheless she must look for some nice ornithologist to take the wretched thing off her hands before it drove her dotty and she put her murderous thoughts into action. It had developed a technique to drive her to distraction with its bawdy wolf whistles, rattling its cage and then firing off a fusillade of indecent oaths in several languages - five at least, and possibly more, as yet unidentified.

One Arab visitor had interpreted one or two of the bird's remarks as "Come to the kasbah," and "Son of a camel." The rest, however, he would not translate, suppressing a smile as he listened to the tirade and spoke quietly to the bird in Arabic by way of encouragement. Its favourite German expletive was "Kartoffelnkopf - Kartoffelnkopf!" repeated incessantly for several minutes at a time. An ornithologist who heard it thought that it bore some resemblance to a bird call and the bird had adopted it as such, and he unfortunately demonstrated this aloud, which of course set the wretched bird off, and it simply would not stop. Joy was at the end of her tether, calling out in desperation "To hell with Kartoffelnkopf," which was promptly included in the repertoire, as the bird bounced up and down in ecstatic gratification.

Its accomplishments included some Hindi and Gujarati words and an Indian student had said that it knew a series of military commands of the kind which would have been used on the parade ground. These must have been taught it by the General in memory of his time in India, together with some of the orders he gave to his household servants. Joy was touched as she realised how much he must have missed India after he had to leave.

The most surprising element of the birdie vocabulary was, however, something which was identified by cousin Jayne one evening over dinner, when it was prattling away with enthusiasm - how it did love visitors! Jayne listened, then declared suddenly! "I'd swear that's Mandarin."

"What - Chinese?" Joy queried, incredulous.

Jayne went over to the cage and said something to the bird. Its reaction was immediate and its response, however unintelligible to Joy, was not so to Jayne, who returned to the dinner-table and reflectively sipped her wine.

"Well?" asked Joy.

"You'll never believe this, said Jayne solemnly, "but it's saying 'Peking duck with sweet-sour sauce', and its other order is 'Chicken chow-mein, chicken chow-mein'."

"What an extraordinary thing," commented Joy, "I wonder who taught it that?"

However, its most uncanny utterance would always be, to Joy at least, Madge's distinctive "Hello ...," perfectly mimicking her rather nasal voice, with the curious down and up stress on the final "o." It was even more poignantly evocative, mimicking the General's plaintive tones, calling "Madge, Madge! Where are you? Where are you?" A more prosaic and less identifiable occasional remark in the bird's repertoire, uttered in what sounded like a bass-baritone voice, was "Diamonds are trumps, diamonds are trumps"; this must have been picked up by the bird at Madge's bridge parties which took place in her sitting-room, where his cage was kept.

And now a permanent record was about to be made of all this strange rigmarole. At precisely nine o'clock the front doorbell rang and on the doorstep stood the man with the tape-recorder, as Mark had instructed.

Petronella, who was off to college on her bike, raised an eyebrow as she departed, but said nothing. Joy made the visitor welcome with a mug of coffee and a selection of biscuits and left him to it. She did, however, listen for a while outside the study door while the man spoke to the bird, encouraging it to talk and whistling to it - in mynah-bird language, she supposed. Not that it needed much encouragement for almost immediately it began to exclaim at the top of its voice: "Rupert, Rupert, shut that door!" Then, egged on by the policeman, it screamed: "Shut up, shut up, you silly old fool!" Joy was unable to repress a shiver at the eerie sound.

The bird went on to repeat snatches of actual conversation between Madge and the General; then there were interjections such as "Hello, darling, is that Boris? Is that Boris?," followed by repetitions of: "Shut up, Rupert! Shut up, Rupert! Silly old fool! Silly old fool!" It also became clear that the Mynah-bird had lived within earshot of the telephone, and some of its talk was in French, punctuated by exclamations of Merde! Merde!"

Feeling rather shocked and distressed, Joy walked away, wondering what kind of secrets the bird could give away that would be of interest to the police. It was becoming clear that the bird had incriminating things to say and that Madge was deeply implicated in criminal activity. As for the poor old General, his life must have been sheer hell, for he would inevitably have suspected that Madge was involved in some kind of conspiratorial dealings and for an upright and law-abiding man with a high sense of honour, who was also a loving husband, the conflict of loyalties must have been almost intolerable. He was indeed better off dead, for he could never have stood up to the terrible scandal which must follow. Let him rest in peace.

Over an hour and several cups of coffee later, the policeman emerged from the study, smiled discreetly and thanked Joy gratefully for her kindness and co-operation. The results of the investigation were of considerable value and would prove to be very useful indeed.

At this point Mrs Badger came pedaling up the drive and cast an approving look at the departing policeman.

"Nice lad, that," she observed. "Distant relation o' moy 'ubby's, 'e is. 'Is second cousin's son, if you get moy drift." Joy reflected that Oxford was really a very small pond. Everybody was either related to, or knew or was known to everybody else.

Meanwhile Mrs Badger, with an unexpected burst of inspiration declared her intention to "'Ave a go at the attic."

Surprise, surprise! thought Joy. This was really good news. To her certain knowledge it hadn't been "'ad a go at" for a lifetime, and heaven only knew what was up there - possibly even a dead body!

After the obligatory cup of coffee and chat about current bargains to be found in the covered market, Mrs Badger took herself off upstairs, followed by a warning cry from Joy: "Mind your head on that beam up there!" and "Does the light work?"

There was no reply to this, except a good deal of banging about and movement of heavy objects, sounding like grand pianos, but eventually the noise ceased and Mrs Badger was heard to say:

"Well, Oi'll be jiggered! Miss 'Etherington, could you come up 'ere for a minute?"

Joy puffed her way upstairs to the top landing, thinking what a long haul it was up those steep Victorian stairs to the top of the house, and how hard it must have been for the poor housemaids of former times, toiling up to their quarters in the attic after a long day's work.

The attic itself was rather spacious, with an unexpectedly high vaulted ceiling resembling a small chapel. Mrs Badger's head appeared above Joy as she lent over the banisters. "Come up quick an' 'ave a dekko," she urged, with a hint of triumph in her voice, or so Joy surmised, as she arrived at last, breathless, at the top of the stairs, determined that she would not be doing this too often, it was much too taxing and as far as she was concerned the attic could remain uncharted territory, only to be visited when absolutely necessary, and preferably not at all.

Mrs Badger led the way to a small window, so narrow that it reminded Joy of a leper's squint, which overlooked the back garden. Opening the window, she pointed a finger in the direction of Mrs Graystone's top floor back windows and asked: "Do you see wot Oi see?"

Joy peered out across the back gardens.

"No, I can't see anything. It's all a blur. I haven't got my glasses. I'm as blind as a bat without them."

"Never moind, moy duck. 'Ere's some opera-glasses from out o' yon trunk as Oi got them old pots out of," indicating some curious pieces of dusty pottery of various shapes and sizes. Joy instantly recognized one piece, a vase of Persian origin, brought back from Iran many years ago by Great-aunt Annie, following her Grand Tour of Europe and the Middle East, performed after the manner of Victorian ladies of means, who brought back strange trophies from their travels. This vase was of a most extraordinary shape and certainly did not qualify as a beautiful artefact. It looked rather like an Edwardian lady with a very tight corset - bulbous at the top and bottom, but with a very narrow waist it was covered with curious wiggly designs in blue and white and had handles on either side resembling a pair of enlarged jug-ears. It was impossible to divine its purpose or use. However, when later, in a fit of guilt over never having had it on display, Joy had put it in an alcove in the drawing-room, it was instantly identified by a ceramics expert as extremely rare and worth a considerable sum of money. What a surprise! Joy had a photograph of her great-aunt in the family album, standing, tall and stately in long voluminous skirts, with a high-necked, long-sleeved blouse, and a topee perched elegantly on top of her upswept hair after the fashion of the day. She stood beside a haughty-looking camel and in the background, obviously chosen for effect, loomed the Sphinx! Great-aunt Annie was an intrepid traveller, taking herself across the world, even as far as South America, and encountering dangers and discomforts from which the modern imagination shrinks and turns away - there would be no water-closets in the Kalahari desert, but there might be any kind of monster ready to spring at you from behind a cactus!

But Joy's confused reflections, called up by contemplation of the vase, were sharply interrupted at this point by: "'Ere, Miss 'Etherington, now just you come an' 'ave a look at this!," Mrs Badger was quite excited, and such urgency was unusual for her. She handed Joy the opera-glasses and after some twiddling to get a proper focus, Joy observed the following: the sash windows in the other house were wide open so she could see quite clearly two men moving around in Jasper's room, apparently carrying out a very thorough inspection of everything in it.

"An 'just you look at that!" Mrs Badger indicated that there was movement below in Mrs Graystone's garden.

"They be searchin' for somethin', Oi reckon."

Two men, working side by Side, were methodically examining every inch of the garden, from the house right down to Joy's boundary wall. These proceedings were being observed by the cats from various vantage points, Tabby having the best view from her perch in the apple-tree. Did they perhaps think the man might flush out a mouse or two on which they could pounce?

"An' just 'ave a peep at that there, now," Mrs Badger pointed to a third man coming from the house with a black Labrador at his side, evidently a working dog, moving quietly forward on the end of its lead, nose to the ground in deep concentration. It didn't take long to seek out what it was sniffing for, as Mrs Badger remarked. It had a thorough sniff round the greenhouse but after a close inspection of the interior, came out and towed the handler on down the garden, pausing for a short while to have a "good smell at the compost heap" (to quote Mrs

Badger) before resuming its steady progress down the garden towards the shed at the bottom end.

And there the excitement began. There was a quick "Woof, woof!" and an urgent demand to be let in, tail wagging and furious scratching at the door, so in they went. A few minutes later the dog handler came out and called sharply to the other two men in the garden. They ran quickly to the shed, went inside and closed the door behind them.

Joy and Mrs Badger watched as though spellbound, but for a while nothing seemed to be happening. There was complete silence and no activity could be discerned in or around the shed. Eventually, however, the door opened and one of the men came out and made his way to the house, reappearing shortly carrying a crowbar and a small spade.

"Christ Church bells!" exclaimed Mrs Badger, "Wot is 'e about?"

"Goodness only knows," Joy breathed. The possibilities were alarming. "They're digging for something inside the shed. That's rather odd, isn't it?"

"Well, moy duck, Oi just 'ope as 'ow it ain't a dead body!" declared Mrs Badger with a hint of relish in her voice.

Joy shivered & little at this comment, remembering recent events, but she said simply: "Oh dear, Mrs Badger, I do sincerely hope not!"

At last the shed door opened and out came the dog and its handler. They went away up the path to the house, and Joy thought that the dog seemed distinctly pleased with itself, looking up at its handler for approval, with the satisfied smile of a dog who knows it has done a good job; and it was rewarded with a kindly pat as they disappeared round the side of the house.

It was some considerable time before the other men left the shed, and for the watchers the suspense was killing; they were rooted to the spot. Joy thought with resignation that not much housework would be done that day.

"'Ere they come.," announced Mrs Badger triumphantly. She picked up the opera glasses and peered intently at the scene below. "There we are then - quick, take a look!"

Focusing the glasses again with difficulty, Joy was able to see that the men were leaving the shed, carefully carrying two bulky black industrial-type plastic bags filled with something heavy and rather lumpy looking, resembling bags of sugar or some similar substance. Joy was puzzled: could the bags contain stolen goods? Had Jason been a cat burglar? Oxford would have afforded rich pickings if that were so.

"Well, then, there goes the booty," said Mrs Badger, with a smile of satisfaction. "Who'd 'a'thought it? Dirty work's been gain' on an' no mistake!"

"Quite so, Mrs Badger, quite so!"

"That's gotta be they new-fangled drugs that's bein' flogged round the place, that 'as! Can't be no other explanation for it, moy duck."

Turning away from the window, she peered keenly at Joy over her gold-rimmed glasses.

"Now, Miss 'Etherington, Oi will tell you 'ere an' now about wot's been a' goin' on roundabout 'ere for the last little while.

"Oi ,'ave 'eard from down yonder," pointing in the general direction of the town centre and the university, "As 'ow there 'as been a 'uge lot a' these 'ere new-fangled drugs an' the loike comin' into Oxford, an' all the youngsters 'ave got 'old of it some 'ow. Nobody seems to know where it's a'comin' from or even 'ow they gets the money to pay for it, but it's 'appenin'." She looked out of the window agin, and continued: "Well, at least it seems as 'ow it ain't a dead body after all, so that's good" with a sniff "Bags ain't big enough."

"Ugh!" Joy shuddered involuntarily; it occurred to her that there was just a hint of disappointment in Mrs Badger's voice; and then, in a flash she saw vividly presented to her mind's eye the dead face of Elise Trondheim, with its strange expression of intense surprise, the eyes wide open behind the gold-rimmed spectacles.

"Mrs Badger, don't, please! I really can't bear it!" They watched the two men walking purposefully away up the garden, carrying the bags with the unknown but possibly sinister contents and Joy was reminded, perhaps not altogether inappropriately, of Dido's Lament, from Purcell's "Dido and Aeneas":

"When I am laid, am laid in earth

May my wrongs create no trouble, no trouble in thy breast!

Remember me, remember me,

But ah! Forget my fate..."

It rang like a kind of Requiem for Erica and Cledwin, and Jasper, too, all dead, and their deaths somehow mysteriously connected as a hitherto unrecognised pattern of events was gradually becoming plain. But how could all the pieces be fitted together? At the moment all she could see appeared as a kaleidoscope of images and their relationship to one another was tenuous and obscure. A Chinese puzzle without a doubt!

Nevertheless, in spite of the lack of evidence as yet to prove it, Joy was absolutely convinced that the deaths of these three people were connected and in some way an essential part of the pattern of events gradually being revealed: there was Erica Trondheim, for instance, and Madge Spragnell's disappearance; was she dead? And the General's sad death, alone and bereft of love and care; then there was Petronella - she could so easily have been killed in that dreadful encounter with the unknown gunman by the Trap grounds; and, Joy reflected, she herself might have died in the fire at her house, if it had taken hold, and dear Iffley, that most efficient guard-cat, had not saved her life by rousing her in time. Such a clever cat! There she sat, a sphinx as usual, on the shed roof; the silent grey watch-cat, observing all.

She had reached this point in her conjectures when her train of thought was disrupted by Mrs Badger exclaiming: "Come on, moy duck, this won't buy babby a new frock. Best get on wi' some work, aye?" So saying, she picked up her mop and shaking it like a halberd, said to it:

"Up, guards, an' at 'em!" and: "Onward, Christian soldiers!"

CHAPTER XVII

"Music divine, proceeding from above,

Whose sacred subject often-times is love..."

Songs of three, four, five and six parts

Thomas Tomkins 1622

Leaving Mrs Badger to get on with the good work, Joy went downstairs to put some more thoughts on paper about the parallels between Clemens non Papa and Henry Purcell. It might be a far-fetched notion, but she had struck lucky so many times before simply by guessing at some improbable connection between diverse and apparently incompatible composers, but, sure enough, some obscure manuscript would turn up, retrieved from a dusty archive, to prove that her idea had in the end been correct. It was all about echoes in the mind - and what a splendid title that would be for a book! She must make a note of it for future reference.

Now, if only a link would come to light between Clemens and Purcell, what a triumph that would be - what a delightful boost for her reputation as a musicologist! But she must not get too smug and self-confident over her achievement before it became fact. And she seemed to hear an echo of the words of Billy Beale, her old Berkshire gardener, when he had cause to disbelieve some extravagant boast: "Oh, ar," he used to say, with a cheeky wink, "We 'ad one an' all, only the wheel come off." So she must sing small about her ambitious theory until she could prove it was correct, or she would merit the belittling Lancashire put-down: "Oh, aye, we 'ad one an' all, only ours 'ad a brass fender."

Howbeit, by now Joy was more or less indifferent to derisive comment on her ideas. She worked on inspiration and if her thesis turned out to be just a spoof, it would at least give some stuffy academics something to scoff at. To have the enviable reputation of being the most whimsical eccentric in the academic community was, she thought, a distinct advantage and, after all, she had the chair, so she felt relatively invulnerable. One could indeed do the most extraordinary things and get away with it simply by being regarded as quite dotty.

As a way of living up to her reputation, and because she had been feeling rather bored with the humdrum performances of Early Music, and the lack of interesting events in Oxford during the summer, with everyone away, she had played with the notion of a splendid venture which would wake up Oxford with a truly great Musical Event, something spectacular for the summer visitors to enjoy. If it were successful it might set a precedent for the future. Some years ago she had been to the Royal Festival Hall in London, and had been overwhelmed by the first performance in a modern edition of the Monteverdi Vespers, 1610. She had vowed that one day she would stage that magnificent work in Oxford, perhaps at the University Church of St. Mary the Virgin. It would be a splendid setting, with perfect acoustics, and a lovely organ as well. It seemed to her that now was the time, with a wealth of musical experience behind her, and an excellent band of enthusiastic Oxonians from all walks of life around her. It would be a mammoth task, but she would do it! And, difficult though it might prove to be, she would prepare her own edition of the work, with lots of early instruments, and perhaps a few little embellishments of her own (of which she hoped the composer would have approved). It would be expensive to stage, but she would raise the money somehow, with jumble sales and book sales and such like: Oxford had ingenious ways of fund-raising; (what about Oxfam?)

Thumps and bangs from upstairs disturbed her vaulting aspirations. Mrs Badger was evidently preparing to descend from the attic, and presently she came thumping downstairs in quest of a nice cup of coffee and the inevitable post-mortem on the events of the day.

"Fair gaspin', Oi be," she puffed, taking off her steamed-up glasses and giving them a vigorous polish.

"Well, now," she said, "They be 'avin' a roight party over yonder, an' no mistake. Such comin' an' goin' as wot you never did see in your 'ole born days!"

After a brief interval of silence, refreshed by a cup of delicious Melitta coffee, Mrs Badger continued:

"They're still searching' Jasper's room - turnin' it upsoide down they be! Poor old Mrs Graystone, Oi reckon she's goin' to 'ave to do a fair amount O' re-decoratin' when those lads be done over yonder. Fair tearin' the place apart, they be - accordin' to wot oi see through these ere glasses!"

"Oh dear! Well, I'm sure it's got to be done, Mrs Badger, otherwise they wouldn't be doing it, would they?" said Joy, with blinding logic.

"Oh, aar, Oi don't question that, may duck. It's gotta be done all roight," she said, nibbling a digestive biscuit, her brows puckered in deep thought.

"Now, then, Miss Etherington, Oi bin a'thinkin' about all this terrible affair - an' do you know wot? About that Mrs Spragnell, Oi bin a'ponderin', an' Oi 'ave come up with the followin': Oi do now believe as 'ow she ain't dead at all, moy duck. Oi think as that old gal be a crafty old cove, an' Oi rackon as 'ow she engineered 'er own disappearance, Oi do!"

"Really, Mrs Badger, whatever makes you think that?"

Even as she spoke, Joy recollected that all Madge's effects had been left behind at the fair - that would fit in with this theory, and there was the wig, and the false passports and so on, and the gun! It looked extremely likely that Madge had arranged a neat escape route for herself, should matters go amiss at the fair.

"Aye," said Mrs Badger, speaking as one whose word is beyond all question, "Oi do 'appen to 'ave moy own personal contacts in the grapevine, namin' no names, sort a' thing."

She gave Joy a meaningful wink and tapped the tip of her nose with a forefinger.

"It is thought that our Mrs Spragnell got clean away an' is quoite probably out O' the country an' she be somewhere in foreign parts. "Ow about that then for a game O' soldiers?"

"Oh, I say, how exciting! Where do you think she is?"

"Well now, Miss 'Etherington, as to that, Oi can't quoite roightly say. This 'ere is the extent of moy proivate information, d'you see?"

She sniffed and looked out across the back garden towards Mrs Graystone's house.

"But just you mark moy words: that there jumped-up madam certainly 'as summat to answer for when they catches up wi' 'er, an' no mistake!"

With this pronouncement, she rose majestically from her seat, bade Joy farewell and departed with a regal wave of the hand, calling to Joy from the front hall: "Tabby-bye, moy duck. See you tomorrow, should Oi be spared! Oh, an' boi-the-way, Oi brought them old pots down for you. They be 'ere in the 'all. Cheerio!"

Oh dear, thought Joy, Great-aunt Annie's antique pottery - utterly hideous stuff, all of it, if her Memory of it was correct. The collection had been acquired on that fearsome world tour, round about 1912. But she must do something with it, to keep Mrs Badger happy, after the trouble she had taken over it. She might hide these objects of unparalleled hideousness in dark alcoves, where they would be technically on display, but would not offend the sensitive eye by obtruding themselves on anyone's notice.

She went out into the hall and inspected them unhappily. There were about ten pieces in all, of varying degrees of ugliness. The first object to catch her eye was a large drinking vessel, Portuguese, nineteenth century, perhaps? It had twirly lurid red, yellow and green designs painted all over it on a pale ivory ground, and even as a flower vase it would be absolutely useless, for the spout was very small and there was no aperture at the top of the vessel to put flowers in. It looked rather like an over filled hot water-bottle with a pig's snout stuck on the side.

Next to it was an odd-looking tall thin white vase with a bulbous base; it looked like some kind of phial, or perhaps the base of a lamp, with a suggestion of the Arabian Nights - suppose she had a lamp made out of it, would a genie pop out if she rubbed it?In addition to its strange shape, it was patterned all over with wriggly designs in relief and gilded on all the high points of the design.But it was an uncanny object and she did not want it on display alongside her own lovely examples of all that was best in antique porcelain, such as her little Bow sheperdess, a rare and delightful specimen, with her low-cut bodice and paniered skirt, her straw hat perched coquettishly on her head, and her lamb held close to her bosom, her pretty lips wearing their unchanging charming smile.She was a piece of English history exquisitely recorded in the finest ware.

And then there was her captivating Staffordshire blue-glaze china figure of Robert Burns! He was the love of her life, and sometimes as she sat at the desk, at a loss for inspiration, she would take him down from the drawing-room mantelpiece and place him on the desk in front of her. He was so handsome, standing there, all of eighteen inches tall, looking at her so gravely, his fine features caught with magical skill on the painted porcelain. Joy imagined some Staffordshire wifie, sitting at her bench in the old Stoke-on-Trent factory and lovingly painting this masterpiece all those years ago; and this one finished, she would go on to the next, and the one after, unaware of course that her hands were creating an image of such beauty for the future inspiration of some Oxford don.

The poet was leaning against a tree stump with Scotch thistles growing round it. In his right hand he held a Tam o'Shanter and in his left an open book - presumably his own poems. He wore an elegant dark blue frock-coat, pink knee-breeches and black ankle boots; at his throat he had a neat white cravat. A long multi-coloured scarf hung round his neck. He was a delight to Joy, who found that after gazing at him for a little while she would go off into a kind of dream and suddenly, without fail, inspiration would come.

But, to return to the strange objects from the attic, it occurred to Joy, as she looked more closely at the white vase with the wriggly decorations, that it might be more interesting than it first appeared.She turned it upside down to examine the base and found stamped on it in relief the legend "Copeland, Crystal Palace Art Union." So this ugly specimen was probably rather valuable. Here was something not picked up on the world tour! Could it be associated with the Great Exhibition of 1851? Well, hideous it might be, but henceforth it must occupy a discreet place of honour somewhere, perhaps filled with chrysanthemums? Tthat would certainly enhance it, and maybe was what it was intended for, with that long slender neck. Now, where should she put it? Ah, yes, on that small table by the grandfather clock, in a suitably unobtrusive position.

She passed on to the next piece, which was a large white glazed water jug with a charming decoration of ropes in relief and coloured dark pink;possibly a copy of an ancient water pitcher, but it would make a lovely receptacle for a dried flower arrangement. She thought it was probably Staffordshire, and certainly Georgian. It would, she decided, be most useful.

The next two or three objects were not as note-worthy; one, an aspidistra pot with sombre decorations of dull brown leaves, all round it, was by any standard definitely ugly, but it would certainly come in useful for the next church bazaar, and being Victorian, would no doubt fetch a good price.

The last piece was the strangest of all and she did not know what to make of it, but it made her shudder slightly even to look at it. She took it into the kitchen for closer inspection of this mysterious object, and decided that anything which looked so aged ought to be in a museum. It stood about fourteen inches high, and judging from its shape, it could have been some kind of primitive drinking vessel, for its form was bulbous, thinner at the top and fatter at the bottom, with a funnel-shaped aperture at the top. There was something eerie about it, suggested perhaps by a sinister-looking burn mark down one side, as though it had been in a fire. It had a dull brown zig-zag pattern all over it, and on the front at the top was modelled an animal's head resembling a cat of some kind, possibly a panther - or a leopard? After some consideration, she decided that it was indeed a cat, but with rather small ears, and that the object might be a ritual drinking vessel from an ancient Peruvian civilisation; she resolved that in due course she would take it down to the Ashmoleon to find out. When, some time later, she did take it there for an expert opinion, she found to her horror that it was identified as a rare example of a Peruvian funerary urn dating from an ancient epoch when ritual human sacrifice was practised. The experts were wildly enthusiastic about it, and since they had no specimen in their collection, she promptly donated it in memory of Great-aunt Annie, and was extremely glad to get rid of it, notwithstanding the fact that it was a collector's piece of considerable value! She was not going to have it in her house at any price!

That, however, was still in the future, and as she continued to contemplate the object, the cat's head, broad, with its small ears, uncannily resembling Mrs Graystone's unfortunate animal, she recalled with a gasp of horror an incident she would have been glad to forget. In an instant she saw, crystal clear, the fearful vision of the mask and cape lying in the undergrowth on the dumps, with the cheeky squirrel playing round them, and the rare fungus close to the rotting sofa nearby and as she watched, fascinated, the picture came to life, like a grisly cartoon film, with the mask grinning mockingly at her, insects running all over it and in and out of the eye sockets; and in a vivid flash of total recall she saw again a glint of metal and a strip of green velvet, with a bell and disc attached - a cat's collar, she was certain - lying beside the mask and the tweed cape! It sparked a connecting link in her mind: Mrs Graystone's cat always wore a green velvet collar with a disc and a bell attached. "Christ Church Bells!" This was Mrs Badger's favourite exclamation in response to surprise or dismay.

But at this moment the mynah-bird began to scream hysterically "Rupert, Rupert! Shut up, you silly old fool!," followed by a snatch of the Marseillaise, and she felt that this was not to be borne, it was like some terrible haunting; and she knew that she must go back to the dumps at once and search for that collar. It was the one thing she most dreaded but it had to be done, eerie though it might be to return to that nightmarish spot.Nor was it a place to visit alone.

Nevertheless, she was resolute, putting on her old slacks and wellingtons and her scruffiest anorak, and making her way quickly to Aristotle Lane and the bottom gate.As she passed through the gate she paused, for it was so quiet, there was simply no one about, and she hoped desperately that someone friendly would appear, coming along the path from the allotments, but this was not to be, and she advanced alone, telling herself firmly "Courage, ma vieille!" and wishing she had a dog, a good big one like a Rottweiler, or something equally hefty. But dogs were such dependent creatures, rather like children, needing constant attention, and lots of love - and "walkies," of course. Not at all like cats, who, being quite the opposite in every way, could look after themselves very well, thank you, provided that reasonable comforts were available, which comprised a constant supply of tasty eats and a quiet refuge to which to retire from the world to have a good long undisturbed sleep, for cats are the most private of beasts.

So Joy tried to sustain her courage and divert her attention with such comforting thoughts as she walked towards the dumps, but was struck by the abrupt transition from the peaceful view down the canal from Aristotle Bridge to the noise and frenzied activity on the nearby playing field where the Arab students were fighting it out, literally, at a football match, playing as though their lives were at stake.

As she passed on her way she noticed one of the company who was not playing, a tall, quiet young man of aristocratic bearing, standing alone, gravely watching the players; he was, so Joy had been told, a billionaire at the age of seventeen. However at this moment he was wrapped in deep concentration on the game, and she wondered what his thoughts were and whether he felt the contrast between the burning sands of the desert and this cold, windy playing field on the edge of Port Meadow, and what memories he would take back from this strange arcane yet cosy fortress of learning, to the Middle East whence he came. Would he have pleasant memories of Oxford? Who would ever know? Maybe history would tell in due course.

She left the playing field behind, and the sounds died away, fading into silence as she went through the Trap gate and walked along the enclosed pathway, thinking that she must not dwell too much on the events which had recently happened here. The dank, sweetish smell of decay was all-pervading, and the dense green foliage of the surrounding thicket with its over-arching canopy of brambles deepened the sense of mystery brooding over the scene. It even seemed as though nature itself were trying to hide some shameful secret; and she also had a distinct feeling that she was being watched, which certainly increased her discomfort.

Joy shook herself, telling herself that such fancies would not do at all. A hymn from her schooldays rang in her memory:"He who would valiant be, 'gainst all disaster."

How she had hated her boarding school and dreaded going back after the holidays, but it had provided a marvellous education which got her to Oxford and some of its discipline had remained with her through life. She hummed the hymn tune as she walked alone to the gap in the wire fence; she needed encouragement for the possibly fruitless search to find a cat's collar among all that rubbish and the tangled growth which nature spreads, when unchecked, over man's mementos and also the traces of his crimes. But she must try at all costs to discover it, so she climbed cautiously through the gap in the fence and surveyed the scene, rather perplexed. The only possible landmark would be the old sofa, if she could find it, but where was it? "God alone knows, an' 'e's not tellin', as Billy Beale would have said.

However, she must start somewhere, and she remembered her Girl Guide training: tracking was the answer, but where were the tracks? She studied the scene intently. At her feet was a large heap of sand, with coltsfoot growing riotously allover it, but not concealing the print of a large boot, which looked quite fresh, and an empty Olde English Cider flagon alongside it. Joy bent down to examine it and got up quickly, for the stench from it was quite nauseating; it was definitely not just cider - it was definitely methylated spirit. She peered into the undergrowth beyond and soon discerned a track which looked like the well-trodden path of many seasoned meths-drinkers, judging by the trail of empty bottles and cans strewn along it.

Well, she must follow it, so she proceeded carefully along the track fighting off clawing brambles and skirting defunct refrigerators, old bed-springs, soiled mattresses and other discards, and trying to ignore the all-pervading smell which was fighting with the sweetish odour of decay. She was reminded of latrines around Florence in the height of summer, remembered from her youth, when as a young undergraduate she had explored the glories of that magical city. She would never forget her astonishment when first confronted by the statue of David by Michelangelo in the Bargello, and the awe she had felt at the singular, naked beauty of this young man with his sling over his shoulder.

As she advanced, looking at the track, she suddenly started violently with a gasp of horror - she had nearly trodden on the decomposing corpse of a rat lying at her feet. Bluebottles were flying in and out of a large cavity in its abdomen. It was nauseating and gave her very bad vibes!

She stood still, staring into the dense undergrowth and wondering which way to go, and at that moment she heard something rustling in the branches overhead. It was a squirrel leaping from one tree to another, and to Joy's amazement it landed adroitly at her feet a moment or two later and sat, juggling with a nut and looking expectantly up at her with a bright and quizzical eye.

"Hello, squirrel" she exclaimed, surprised, and it vanished instantly, evidently unused to being accosted by a human being out there in the wild. However, after a short while it suddenly reappeared on the bough of a tree, at eye level, to the left of the path. Joy stood quite still and watched, while, observing her with its gimlet eye, the squirrel ran down the trunk of the tree and scampered across the path, stopping momentarily to sit on its haunches and look back at her. The intention was quite clear; the clever little animal expected her to follow it!

Intrigued, she moved forward a step or two into the tangled undergrowth, and there was the sofa! The squirrel sat on top of it, watching Joy intently. Well, she thought, since this must be the same sofa, could it be the same squirrel as before? But all grey squirrels looked the same, didn't they? So it was hard to tell; however, this particular squirrel had made it very clear that it knew her, and she felt it had to be the same one, for it began to perform exactly the same routine as on the last occasion, juggling with its nut, running up and down the tree, pausing every so often to see that she was still watching, than recommencing its delightful acrobatics, ending up with its peek-a-boo antics around the sofa, popping in and out from underneath it, still clutching its precious nut.

Joy was now sure that this was the same sofa, as she recognised the battered William Morris brocade, mouldering, but with pieces still showing intact between the springs pushing through here and there and revealing the ancient horsehair stuffing.

Its cameo act performed, the squirrel made off down its private little pathway round the side of the sofa, exactly at the spot where Joy had found the cape and the horrible mask. She moved forward cautiously to avoid falling into the dense mass of brambles, as happened before, and bent down to look for the cat's collar. It was not there, and she stood up, thinking she must leave this awful place, when suddenly she saw the squirrel again, peeping out at her from under the bushes. Once more, it vanished abruptly, and as it did so, she caught a glimpse of glinting metal on something green lying beside the path the squirrel had taken, to the left of the sofa.

With a chilly sense of foreboding and nerves tense with anticipation, she reached out and managed to extract the object from the brambles - and it was the cat's collar! It was soggy and mildewed, but with the disc and bell, though tarnished, still attached to it. She tried to read what was engraved on the disc but it was such tiny print that without her reading glasses it was just a blur. This was extremely frustrating but there was no course open except to take the thing home with her, so she put it carefully into the pocket of her jacket and turned to make her way back to the Trap gate.

And then she almost died of fright: for there, only a few feet away from her, she saw two faces of silent watchers looking out over the top of an old spring mattress. At first all she had was a vague impression of the faces of two men who were somehow familiar to her, but as in an instant they disappeared without a sound or trace of movement, she realized all at once who they were: one-legged Willie and Dick Ballard! They must have been watching her every move as she searched the dumps for the collar. She could not imagine what they were up to, but she judged that it would be more prudent to make a hasty retreat, than to stop and try to find out.

However, when she reached home and hunted for her reading- glasses, she simply could not find them anywhere. At last, in desperation, she went out into the street to see if perchance some kindly soul might appear and help her to decipher the engraving on the disc, but of course there was no one. Then she looked across the road and detected a movement - Miss Dacre's curtain twitched ever so slightly. Joy decided she must venture to ask the good lady if she would be kind enough to look at the disc, but she must do it at once or her courage would fail. So she crossed the road quickly and went through Miss Dacre's garden gate, but before she could close it behind her the front door opened and Miss Dacre's face appeared round it.

"Yes?" she asked, with an edge to her voice, "What is it?"

"I was wondering..."

Joy's voice trailed away as Miss Dacre's steely eye caught sight of the cat's collar in her hand, and she took a swift step forward, seized it and examined it closely.

"Where did you get this?" she demanded sharply.

"On the dumps," replied Joy, feeling herself go pale. "Could you possibly...?"

"Greystone, 16 Belstead Road, Oxford," said Miss Dacre, handing the collar back and retreating at once, closing her door firmly behind her. Evidently there was to be no further communication on the matter, except from Pongo, who fired off a staccato salvo from within to dismiss the visitor.

Joy returned home and on opening the front door she was comforted by the sight of Iffley curled up, fast asleep, on thehall table. The cat opened one golden eye and, presumably supposing that now there was a prospect of food, stretched luxuriously and plopped down at Joy's feet; preventing further progress down the hall until the ritual of fussing and chin-scratchings had been observed. This performed, Joy stood up - and saw her spectacle case on the hall table! Iffley had been sleeping on it, following the feline custom of reposing on some essential possession of the owner: even a spectacle case will do!

Joy followed the culprit into the kitchen and was pleased to see that the other cats were peacefully asleep in their usual nooks and not interested in snacks; only Wellington twitched an ear as she passed. So, remembering Iffley's past service in saving her from being burned to death, she did not mind spoiling her a little, and forgave her for hiding the reading-glasses.

After feeding her, Joy set the glasses on the end of her nose and examined the identification disc on the collar and read, as she expected: "Graystone, 16 Belstead Road, Oxford." Though the disc was badly tarnished, the writing was quite clear.

She realized now that this could only mean one thing; it was quite conclusive that Jasper Philberd had locked up the cat, but why had he gone to such lengths as to deposit the cat's collar and other incriminating articles in the dumps? Perhaps it was just to get rid of them, but it seemed a mad thing to do. The poor boy must have been completely demented.

Of course the first thing she must do was to let Mark know what she had found, and she must ring him at once. She tried and there was no reply, which was exasperating, but she thought that he was probably fast asleep after a long night. She did wish that her dear nephew would communicate with her more often and confide in her rather more. After all, she might even be of use to him in some ways, since she knew so many people in the international sphere, who came and went, in and out of Oxford. Nevertheless, she knew in her heart that this was not going to happen; Mark was a loner in his professional life.

It took her an hour or more before she got hold of him on the telephone, but he was intrigued by the story of the collar and thanked her very much for the information, saying that he would pass it on immediately; indeed, it might shed some light on the case. Sometimes even the smallest details could be important, no matter how trivial they might appear to be at the time. He admitted that there had been some developments, but he couldn't say anything further at the moment except that Madge Spragnell's body had not yet been found in the river, though it could easily be several days before a corpse came to the surface, so time would tell; and yes, she might conceivably have got out of the car before it sank, but he couldn't say anything positive about that, of course, so that was how things stood at present.

This was unenlightening but could be pursued no further for the moment, and as she perceived that the day was fast wearing away Joy cycled off to the Bodleian to follow up her research into her theory about Clemens and Purcell.

She got home at seven o'clock, accompanied by Petronella, who caught up with her on her bike with a shrill "Yoo-hoo!," half-way up Woodstock Road, by the churchyard. They pedaled together, laughing and talking, and decided to have supper, 'à deux' in the garden, as it was a warm evening. The meal they produced jointly was simple but choice: smoked salmon on toast(provided by Petronella), and cold roast beef with potato mayonnaise (provided by Joy). The cats were of course in attendance, Wellington making himself at home on Petronella's lap, and Iffley keeping watch over proceedings from the shed roof and making sure that she did not miss any titbit on offer.

Joy recounted the sequence of events so far, ending with therecovery of the cat's collar and its possible significance.

Petronella was pensive, gazing into her glass and twirling the water round at the bottom as though some message might be readthere. After a while, she sighed deeply and remarked that, dotty as poor Jasper had undoubtedly become, she did not believe that he would ever have locked up Mrs Graystone's cat. He simply adored animals, and she could not imagine that he would do such a thing. However, he did not seem to like people very much, as she herself had observed, and he might conceivably have been prevailed upon to do something not very kind to a human being, but certainly not to an animal, and especially not to Mrs Graystone's cat, which by all accounts he absolutely worshipped. No; her woman's intuition told her it must be a 'plant'.

Joy was mystified and asked what had led Petronella to this rather surprising conclusion.

Petronella replied confidently that it was all so simple - even a baby could see it. Someone knew he had killed the old lady and wished to incriminate him, and this person had also known where he had thrown away the cape and mask. The person might have followed, or even accompanied him to the dumps? Possibly it was someone involved in the drugs business? And it was certainly someone with a nasty twisted mind, a cruel and calculating character intent on an evil deed. Wasn't that a fair guess?

Having given Joy this imaginative food for thought, Petronella departed upstairs, remarking on how tired she was, and leaving Joy to clear away and wash up, and saying she must do some work on her thesis, which had reached a difficult stage, and she wasn't sure which way it should go; she had arrived at a crossroads and did not know which direction to take. Inspired guesswork was needed where the archaeological evidence was lacking, and of course a spot of good luck.

She went on to confess that she was somewhat confused and doubtful as to her feelings about Bruce. He had left such a gap in her life that she felt rather shaken up. They had always done so much together, and for such a long time, ever since coming up to Oxford, about five years in all; so now she was totally thrown by her sense of loss, almost as though she had been bereaved - it was really overwhelming.

Poor Petronella looked so sad and depressed that Joy gave her a warm hug and assured her that all would yet be well.She gave the assurance, however, more in faith than on the basis of any factual evidence. But it served to cheer Petronella, who mounted the stairs with what seemed a light and optimistic tread. She even sang a little song to herself as she reached the top landing, her spirits apparently restored.

"All well and good," thought Joy, as she stood listening at the foot of the stairs. It was the Skye Boat Song:

'Speed, bonny boat, like a bird on the wing,

"Onward'!" the sailors cry...'

That must be for Bruce, far away overseas, and what a charming light soprano voice - perhaps she might persuade Petronella to sing in the projected Monteverdi Vespers? It would be a nice idea, and she must get on with the score as quickly as possible; optimism and positive thinking must provide the essential impetus to enable her to cope with the demands of present turbulent events. With this in mind she buckled down to the washing-up, and then decided to walk down to the "Jolly Sailors," looking forward to some cheerful company and possibly a game of darts, should a suitable opponent appear in the public bar.

Here she was lucky, for Michael Walters was in the pub, and as they played, Joy gave him a detailed account of recent developments.

This was hardly fair, for he was so distracted by the extraordinary tale of the cat's collar that he missed his final double one and Joy, tactfully concealing her glee, pipped him at the post with a neat double twenty.

Then Peter Rumbold arrived and had to hear about the latest events, at which he remarked that "the thick had well and truly plottened, forsooth." But neither he nor Michael could come up with any possible explanation for the business of the collar, although they were agreed that it was a dotty thing to do, and only a mind verging on the criminally insane could have perpetrated it. Peter went on to remark that it was particularly sad that Jasper's brilliant thesis on bird life remained unfinished when he died; apparently it had a guarantee of immediate publication on completion. Peter had gleaned this information from a customer who had at one time been Jasper's tutor.

So one would have thought that he had every incentive to go on living, and certainly not to take his own life, if that turned out to be the result of the investigation. But the whole affair was so mysterious that it was impossible to guess how it would end, or when they would hear the whole story, and that indeed would not be for a long while yet, as the police sifted through the evidence and followed up clues. At this point Tony, the barman, joined them for a darts foursome and they had a highly competitive match from which Michael and Tony emerged victorious after an exciting set of best of eight games, a cliff-hanger all the way. The vanquished bought the victors drinks, and they toasted the winning side.

After a little while, as they sat talking, the bar door flew open and in came a somewhat flustered and excited Petronella, full of glad tidings. She had heard from Bruce - he had phoned just after Joy went out, and she was over the moon and downed a lager shandy almost in one. Bruce was to be transferred to Sydney for a minimum period of three years, and would be living in a large top-floor flat in an old house (by Australian standards - i.e. a hundred years old), with a breath-taking view over the city, a lovely garden and Victorian 'lace' wrought iron verandas. Bruce said it was just the place for a woman like her and would she consider coming out to join him when she had finished her thesis and got her doctorate?

Eyebrows were raised slightly at this, and she rushed on: Yes, as his wife, he had actually proposed to her there and then over the phone! This had caught her completely off-guard and on impulse she had said "Yes'. She was bemused by the suddenness of all this and could not think how Bruce was going to organize it, but he seemed supremely confident about everything, so she would simply "go with the flow" - a kind of behaviour most untypical for her, to be swept along like this by her emotions, but anyhow she would keep her word, having committed herself to marry Bruce.

This was a pretext for instant celebrations, with packets of crisps and cashew nuts all round (courtesy of Michael Walters) and a round of drinks (on Joy). The party did not break up till closing time, and as they walked home together to St. Julie's Road, Joy and Petronella agreed that it had been a marvelous, if somewhat traumatic day. When they got in, Petronella was far too excited to go straight to bed so they sat up and drank coffee until after midnight, finding so much to talk about: there was Sydney, surely the most beautiful city in the world, set in its lovely harbour; and then, with a leap of Joy's grasshopper mind to practical - and urgent - considerations, what about clothes? After some discussion, they decided upon a selection of Liberty summer skirt lengths as Joy's contribution to the bride's trousseau. And perhaps, later on, if there were a sale at Botticelli's, she might find some exotic garment for evening wear in the tropics, but this would be nearer the date of departure (giving Joy time to save up she hoped).

As it was about one o'clock in the morning when they retired, they both slept late and well, meeting in the hall in the morning, rather bleary~eyed, round about nine, to look through their post. Mrs Badger, arriving shortly after, found them still there and was greeted with the news of Petronella's betrothal, at which she expressed her pleasure, but frowned darkly over the traces of extreme fatigue, ascribing it to careless self-indulgence. Waving an admonitory finger, she declared that:

"'Twas all very well, this 'oigh livin' an' such-loike, but they must surely 'ave 'eard the old saying 'Early to bed, early to roise...' an' they 'ad better remember it next toime they was tempted to sit up till all hours!"

With a slightly contemptuous sniff and an aggressive flourish of her feather duster to attack her foe, the dust, which she claimed, "poiled up considerable, wot with all them comin's an' goin's in an' out the front door these days!"

Joy did not attempt to counter this implied reproach.

CHAPTER XVIII

'Flora gave me fairest flowers,

Non so fair, in Flora's treasure'

The First Set of English Madrigals John Wilbye 1598

The days passed, fairly quiet and uneventful, and on Friday morning Joy loaded up her car with flowers for Christ Church Cathedral, it being her turn to do the arrangement for St. Frideswide's tomb; she had selected some of her finest fresh chrysanthemums, which would open up nicely and look perfect on Sunday, and she added some of the little white dahlias with flowers like pom-poms, the petals just tipped with red, almost as though they had been dipped in blood! They would provide a vibrant splash of colour to offset the deeply resonant gold and crimson of the larger flowers, with a backing of trailing dark green foliage, perhaps variegated ivy and a few sprigs of myrtle from her back-garden wall, and some rosemary, to give the display a sort of cottage-garden effect, a touch of the unexpected, which in her estimation was the essence of a good floral arrangement.

She drove through the gateway under Tom Tower into Christ Church, parked the car in the quad and carried her richly glowing burden of flowers into the cool darkness of the cathedral. She paused for a moment by the tomb, then went to the door leading to the flower room.

She stopped for a moment and looked at an ancient oak cupboard set in a stone recess by the door, almost hidden away, as though it concealed some secret in its dark corner.

It was not the first time that her curiosity had been awakened as to what might be inside it, and she determined that she would this very day get the key and have a look.

However, that was not to be, for the flowers took a great deal of time; one of the ladies had not turned up and the other helpers were hard pressed, but laboured on and were not unrewarded, for the final result was triumphant, and Joy was sure that Christ Church flowers were unique, unmatched by any other cathedral, though others might contest the claim.

She went on to speculate that St. Frideswide might in some mysterious way be a benign influence; perhaps she had been a botanist, for like all those living under monastic rule she would have had an intimate knowledge of herbs and flowers grown for medicinal purposes. These thoughts reminded her of her recent visit to Stanbrook Abbey to see a dear friend from her old college who had become a Benedictine nun. Joy had gone with another old friend, Dame Priscilla Blackmore, and they had shared a strange experience.

They had been given afternoon tea in the parlour with their friend Sister Anne, and they talked of their college days and shared their reminiscences, and it was very pleasant and reassuring after the sombre and rather forbidding aspect of the Abbey as they approached up the long drive to the imposing pile built in the style of the Gothic Revival. Sister Anne, however, though dressed in the severe black habit of the Order with its suggestion of mediaeval austerity, had retained the sense of fun they remembered from her student days, and that they had a happy reunion together.

Their talk was interrupted by the insistent ringing of the chapel bell and the door to the cloister opened slowly, revealing the tall stately figure of the nun who had come to take away the tea trolley. She stood framed in the Gothic doorway, exhorting Sister Anne to make all haste to go into chapel, and the sun streamed in through the open door behind her, silhouetting her against a blaze of glory. It was a visionary scene, full of some strange meaning she felt she must discover. It reminded her of a painting she had seen somewhere, but she could not remember where; it might have been a Van Dyke, or a Pieter de Hough, but she could not be sure and must leave the question unanswered for the present.

Subsequently she was to recall that the work she had in mind was an unlisted painting by Samuel Palmer that was in the possession of a friend of Joy's in North Oxford, and had been painted by Palmer as a special commission for her great-grandfather, who had been in charge of the Botanic Gardens in Oxford. It depicted a figure standing in a doorway with the most extraordinary blaze of colour in the background. Presumably the figure was that of her friend's great-grandfather, with a sunlit garden behind him, but what a garden!

There he stood, a tall, imposing figure of a man, wearing a long black frock-coat and stove pipe hat of the period; mutton-chop sideburns and a severe expression conveying a sombre, almost sepulchral impression. This contrasted sharply with the glowing magnificence of his garden as shown behind him in the painting; the breathtaking beauty of floral patterns and colours was a testimonial recorded in paint to his horticultural genius, so skilfully and vividly captured by the artist. It was Samuel Palmer at his best, flowing eloquently in liquid green and gold, violet and orange tones.

It was, however, some time later that Joy connected that painting with what she saw when the tall nun opened the door wide as the chapel bell rang; the view disclosed was of a cloister of Gothic arches leading left to the chapel, while straight ahead lay the convent garden, a vision of exquisite beauty, order and grace, and a startling contrast to the grim, stern aspect of the Abbey itself. Velvet green lawns stretched away into the middle distance, edged by herbaceous borders forming a glorious patch-work of colours. Dame Priscilla observed that St. Frideswide would surely have loved it - it was her kind of place!

On Sunday morning Joy went to early communion at Christ Church with motives which were not purely pious - she was keenly anxious to see how her flowers were looking, and to her immense satisfaction they were absolutely lovely, glowing in the early morning sun's rays through the East Window. So she went home to her breakfast well pleased.

To her surprise, Petronella was already up, and met her in the hall, fully awake but still in her dressing gown, with tousled hair, after a rather short and restless night. However, before she could give her full attention to what was wanted, the cats which were making perfect nuisances of themselves, purring round her legs and tripping her up, must be staved off with some kind of treat, and cat biscuits, which they adored, must be the answer to keep them quiet till breakfast was over.

She returned to Petronella, who explained that there was a sale of Liberty materials in Summertown, starting the next day, and might they possibly...? (Good thinking, Petronella, and crafty with it - for the answer was of course a "Yes," and consequently the following morning they pedaled off together to Summertown, Joy armed with her credit card, and Petronella buoyed up with the anticipation of matchless exquisite bargains to be had for as little outlay as possible.)

Her ambition, however, was ranging too high and she could not be dissuaded from gazing rapturously at curtain materials, and might they just possibly...? So Joy had to bring her down to earth and practical considerations such as measurements of the windows and the cost of transportation to Sydney, none of which had entered her mind. Reason prevailed and it was agreed that Joy would pay for the cost of the curtains retrospectively, i.e., when the measurements had been provided and the order given. This was satisfactory to both parties, and Petronella departed, well content; her apathy had vanished and she was full of good resolutions to finish her thesis with all speed, leaving Joy, lighter in pocket, but also in spirit, to get on with her day.

She spent the afternoon at Christ Church, having obtained the key to the mysterious cupboard, which proved to be larger and deeper than she had thought, and seemed to be a repository for unused ecclesiastical trappings: altar frontals, tallow candles, processional banners, one of which looked rather like the magnificent specimen hanging on the staircase of the President's lodgings in St. James' College. There were also several boxes of Victorian choral music, but nothing to do with Purcell, except for a number of yellowed copies of the Bell Anthem. Ah, well! But her expectations had not been high, so she was resigned to the prospect of continuing her quest, and an opportunity to do so immediately presented itself.

On her way back across Tom Quad she chanced to meet the librarian and tried out on him her theory about Clemens and Purcell. He smiled, made no commitment to this, but then, as though an idea occurred to him, remarked that he recalled a box of documents, mostly relating to College domestic matters, but dating from that period; they comprised letters to the Dean and miscellaneous bills, etc. and some were concerned with musical matters. No one appeared to have found much of interest in them, but perhaps she would care to look through them some time? It would be a long job, for there was a lot of material, much of it on faded parchment, almost indecipherable. Joy jumped at the offer eagerly, and later in the week she settled down happily in the library with the large box of documents, and spent hours poring over them, finding them fascinating and diverting; she came across a bill, for instance, for 'mending ye organ bellowes and removing vermin from ye pypes!'Would that be mice? And how on earth did they do it? Did they bring in ye catte?

She knew from personal experience that cats will get into church organs, for she had once enticed one out of the organ in St. Julie's by tempting it with sardines in tomato sauce, after she had heard pitiful miaouwing, while doing a flower arrangement for the sconce. When the cat was returned to its owner, she said it had been missing for over a month, and they concluded that it had survived on a strict diet of mice, for it emerged from the organ casing a noticeably slim, but remarkably fit tabby cat, in comparison with its former pampered and lethargic self. The most curious feature of this occurrence was that the church had been in constant use and no one had noticed any sign of the cat's presence until Joy heard its miaouwing. The organist, however, produced a possible, indeed obvious, explanation: that the supply of mice had run out and the cat was hungry, having consumed the entire population of the organ! And how was it that the cat had endured being subjected to a barrage of powerful organ works with all the stops pulled out, by the likes of Bach, Vierne or Widor, these being favourites of the organist, without a single protest? Indeed, it even seemed quite reluctant to leave its ecclesiastical hideaway!

Joy continued her examination of the musty contents of the box, but found little of any interest to her and thought she had drawn a blank, until she reached the very bottom, and there, in the left-hand corner, was a roll of ancient documents which she greeted as a treasure trove and smoothed out with the greatest care. She found, however, that there was no need to worry about their fragility, for they were quite tough vellum documents, all of them relating to musical activities at the cathedral, and for the most part dating from the seventeenth century. There were receipts for payments to gentlemen of the choir, and some letters to the organist and Master of the Choristers about musical events, some indeed involving Royal Personages.

And then she came upon something of real interest to her. It was a faded letter, written in a fine and elegant hand which took Joy some time to decipher, but she got the gist of it, and to her astonishment and delight it contained something which might possibly lend support for her theory. First, she examined the signature, which read: "F. Purcell." So this must be Francesca Purcell, Henry Purcell's wife - what a find! The letter was an apology for the cancellation of Purcell's visit to Oxford, since he had taken a fever and was confined to bed, to which he had retired in a state of great weakness, this latter much aggravated by his disappointment at being unable to make the arduous journey to Oxford, for he was greatly excited by an idea for a work he had thought to compose and was most anxious to confer with the organist of Christ Church about the matter.

The letter referred to a visit which Purcell had recently paid to Antwerp, where he had been much affected by the traditional church music he had been privileged to hear, some of which seemed alight with a spirit of zestfulness unusual in works of that period. This was particularly noticeable in the music of one Clemens, delightfully light-hearted, permeated throughout with the laughter and jubilation of the angelic host.

So here was her conclusive evidence, and what a flutter in the dovecotes it would cause!

But feeling that her glee might be tinged with malice and she could be accused of the sin of pride, she was driven to make an act of contrition, and later in the day she cycled back to Christ Church to do penance by refreshing St. Frideswide's flowers with her water-spray; then she knelt at the tomb and thanked the Saint for the marvellous discovery, feeling sure that it was indeed she who had led her to the find.

She returned home, her conscience appeased, and waited for Petronella to come in, so that she could tell her the good news. She came back late after dining with friends to celebrate the joyful prospect now before her, but she and Joy had half an hour together over a tall glass of Pimms No I before retiring. Petronella was much amused at the amazing discovery and hugged herself with delight, imagining the reactions of peppery old academics when Joy delivered her paper and wishing she could be a fly on the wall to watch the fun.

Next morning Mrs Badger appeared early, wearing a smug expression like a cat with a pot of cream. However, she said nothing, and got on with her work with unusual gusto, while singing herself a little song. Joy waited patiently for the expected revelations over coffee, for which she prepared by grinding her best Kenya Peaberry very fine and filtering it very well, in the hope that this would encourage disclosure. Then she opened the kitchen door so that the aroma would drift upstairs to Mrs Badger, as she changed the beds; and sure enough, very shortly afterwards an appreciative "Ooh" was heard from above, and a voice carolled down the stairs: "Is that moy coffee on the boil, moy duck?"

"Indeed it is, Mrs Badger."

"Oi'll be down in 'alf a mo', then," came the reply. So now Joy's curiosity, so well restrained so far, must surely be satisfied.

"Dear, oh deary me - wot a performance!" said Mrs Badger, clumping down the stairs, her arms full of sheets and duvet covers.

"Moy hubby won't 'ear of 'avin' one o'these 'ere new-fangled 'duvvets'" as she pronounced the word, "but Oi'd love one - saves all that there bed-makin', but e's that old fashioned,'e won't 'ave any o' this 'ere new-fangled tackle, as 'e calls it. 'Good old Witney blankets an' nowt else', 'e says. 'Wot was good enough for moy grandma be good enough for me'. You'll never change 'im, moy duck, stubborn as they comes, 'e be."

So saying, she popped the bedding into the washing machine and started up the hot-wash programme.

"Now then, where's that there cup o' coffee, moy duck? Smells a treat, it do, an' Oi be fair gaspin."

Collapsing into an elbow chair with a deep sigh, she sipped her coffee with relish, licking her lips.

"Just what the doctor ordered," she pronounced with deep satisfaction. Then she sat back and fixed Joy with a straight look.

"Now - wot's all the scandal, then?"

"Scandal, Mrs Badger?"

"Yes, you know - news o' the day, moy duck."

Joy smiled demurely, "Well, now, I was hoping that you might just have a little something to tell me, perhaps?"

"About the business, you mean, moy duck?"

Joy nodded, "Precisely, Mrs Badger."

Mrs Badger appeared to ponder for a moment; she leaned forward, elbows on the table, then carefully adjusted her glasses on the bridge of her nose, her usual preparation for some weighty pronouncement. Then she cleared her throat with a genteel "Ahem!" She proceeded:

"Now then, 'tis quare as you should ask that, as a matter o' fact,'cos a little bird told me as 'ow," she paused in that tantalizing way she had, shirting her glasses and rubbing her nose as she collected her ideas. "Well, now, Oi shouldn't be a-tellin' you this, but Oi 'ave 'eard..."

But the remainder of the sentence was drowned by screams from Napoleon, who suddenly erupted with a burst of hysterical French, followed by his own version of the Marseillaise. "Oh, that damned bird! Some day I'll kill it, I swear I will!" Joy went out into the hall and shut the study door with a bang, provoking still louder screams from the importunate bird. Wellington, who was sleeping peacefully on the kitchen window-sill, yawned, stretched, and then, as though to show his indifference to his comrade's performance, went back to sleep, a happy cat, thoroughly contented with his new home.

"Well, Mrs Badger?" Joy felt she must not appear too eager for information. "More coffee?"

"Oi don't moind if Oi do, moy duck, 'tis goin' down a treat!" Restraining herself from showing too much interest, Joy sat back, trying to look as casual as possible, though itching to find out what the Badger family bush telegraph had to communicate this time. It seemed, however, as though Napoleon's disruptive intervention had succeeded in unsettling Mrs Badger (if that were his intention!), for she clammed up, then said rather hesitantly:

"Well, now, Oi shouldn't really be a'tellin' you this, Miss 'Etherington, but matters 'ave in fact escalatored - or so Oi 'ave bin informed."

Joy kept her countenance with difficulty.

"Yes, moy duck, and escalatored in a big way, they 'ave.'Tis all 'appenin'!"

She squared her shoulders, thrusting out her bosom as Boadicea might well have done, charging in her scythe-wheeled chariot against her foes, to mow them down. Mrs Badger, however, had decided to leave the field; quickly downing her coffee, she snapped her handbag shut and stood up.

"Oi must go," said she, casting a glance over the back garden then remarking: "They Bramleys be very good this year."

"You must have some, Mrs Badger, when they're ready."

"No, no, moy duck, just a thought. Any'ow, back to business - you'll be 'earin' somethin' very soon, moy love, so not to worry. O.K.?" She winked and tapped her nose after that inimitable old Oxonian fashion, with the obscure comment:"'Ere - Oi nose 'e, an' 'e nose' Oi -"

Joy looked questioningly at her.

"Yes, moy duck, it goes: 'Ere'" touching her ear, "Oi," pointing to her eye, "knows 'e," touching the tip of her nose, and then pointing a forefinger at Joy to indicate 'E' (Oxonian abbreviation of 'thee'). "An' 'E knows Oi," pointing at Joy and then at her own eye, "An' Oi knows 'E,'" (with heavy stress on the words 'Oi' and 'E').

Leaving Joy to puzzle over this conundrum, Mrs Badger made a stately exit, but turned at the door to give a meaningful wink and a "Tatty-bye." Joy followed her down to the gate, hoping to get some further elucidation of those cryptic allusions, but she was disappointed, for Mrs Badger mounted her steed and rode off without further remark, her basket overflowing as always with all kinds of goodies for Mr. Badger; she lifted an arm in a grandiose wave as she sailed down the road, which was no mean feat, considering the weight of the ancient bike and the mountain of shopping in front; an achievement borne of years of practice.

Joy turned to the silent grey plush observer sitting on the garden wall.

"Well, Iffley, what do you think of that?," she asked.

Iffley evidently unable to cast light on the mater, answered 'Rrr?' and responded by jumping down from the wall and walking away, tail vertical, in the direction of the kitchen, apparently construing the question as an invitation to eat. Joy shrugged resignedly and resolved to be patient and await developments, and happily the wait was not to be too long.

Realizing that she needed some exercise after a prolonged session at her desk, she went over to the allotments to look for late summer beans and a picking of Swiss chard for supper, as a nice accompaniment to grilled lamb chops. On the way she met Percy Chadlow with Tina, who bounded along ahead of him, carrying a large beetroot in her mouth and wagging her stumpy tail as she ran. She tossed the beetroot in the air and caught it again with practised expertise, and then dropped it neatly at Joy's feet with an endearing grin.

"There we are then," said Percy, "present. Go on, then, Tina, fetch us another one, then!"

In the end Joy was the lucky and grateful recipient of three very nice beetroot, adroitly retrieved by Tina. Joy was duly appreciative, remarking that one would be lovely as a hot vegetable with the meal that evening, and the other two would be marinated in vinegar overnight for salad tomorrow. Many thanks, Tina!

Tina was evidently delighted to be admired and showed it by running around in elaborate figures-of-eight, while Percy turned to Joy, asking:

"Now, then, Miss 'Etherington, 'ave you'eard about the doin's?"

"The doings, Percy? What then?"

"Oh aar, the goin's on, moy dear. It's all bin 'appenin' over 'ere the last couple a' days. Big toime!"

He leaned on the allotment gate and looked down to one side, indicating a piece of ground where nettles and thistles had been cut back and well trodden.

"The police bin 'ere wi' they sniffer dogs, an' 'tis said as 'ow they found summat small, accordin' to Old Bill, an' they found it just 'ereabouts.Bill was 'ere doin' a bit o'diggin' an' 'e watched 'em pick up this 'ere thing an' put it in a plastic bag an' seal it up.'E said as they 'ad one o' they tramps along of 'em - that there one-legged Willie, is it?"

Joy nodded.

Percy shrugged his shoulders and pulled a wry face.

"Well, now, moy duck, not a lot to wroite 'ome about, but Oi reckon as it all 'as a lot to do wi' that poor young lad as Oi found drownded in the well not long back. An' Oi tell you wot else, moy duck, it didn't take that old dog too long to sniff out wot it was they was after neither. Just a couple o' shakes of a lamb's tail an' e'd got it, straight under 'is nose, 'e 'ad. But - it was that old boy Willie it was, as fetched 'em to this 'ere spot, so 'e must 'a known all about it, wot ever it was. Any road, old Bill says as 'e went off in the police car wi' 'em when they went away, an' the dog went straight away an' all with 'is 'andler in a van, so that must 'a' bin the job done. Quite excitin' it was, by all accounts. Well, now, must go, moy duck. 'Ere, now then, just go an' pick yourself a nice couple o' lettuces when you goes up along o' moy plot. Oi got Cos an' Little Gem, so take your pick. Cheerio, then. Mind 'ow you goes, an' don't do anythin' as Oi wouldn't!"

With a cheerful wave of his walking-stick Percy limped away over the level crossing with Tina trotting obediently beside him.

Dear Percy, Joy reflected, the salt of the earth - one of the best, as the old boys would say.

She looked down at the patch of trodden ground by the gate which Percy had pointed out, and thought how very sad this whole wretched business was. She wondered what on earth it could have been which the police had found - something so small, yet obviously of great importance to them. There was nothing to be seen at the site except the flattened patch of ground about eight feet square, and the trampled grass by the gate. She noticed a small transparent plastic bag lying in the grass behind the gatepost. It was tattered and had split open, and would soon be overgrown by the herbage. She looked again, more closely, and a little chill ran up her spine: for, growing up through the remains of the bag were some small fungi - the magic mushroom!

She recognised it, but could not remember the name; she must look it up some time. But surely it was very odd that Cledwyn's precious magic mushroom should be growing by the gate. Evening meal? Someone, but surely not Cledwyn, must have dropped the bag there?

However, she dismissed it from her mind, determined to get on with the immediate task of getting her fresh vegetables home to come home to something wholesome and nourishing. To consider what kind of pudding should follow this substantial first course - perhaps ice cream with hot chocolate sauce would provide a tasty finish, with a sprinkling of chopped hazelnuts to add zest and a touch of sophistication? Yes, that would be excellen

CHAPTER XIX

'All creatures now are merry minded..'

Madrigals. The Triumphs of Oriana to 5 and 6 Voices.

Composed by Divers Authors

John Bennett 1601

In the event, Petronella came home early, and declared herself delighted to be spoilt yet again by such a delicious and unexpected supper. So saying, she pedaled quickly down to the Jolly Sailors and brought back a very nice Beaujolais - it would go with the beetroot, she remarked - same colour!Joy shuddered inwardly at the recollection of some foul-tasting home-made beetroot wine which she had once been forced, out of politeness, to drink and praise. However, she suppressed the thought and duly thanked Petronella.

Over the ice cream and chocolate sauce they speculated about the meaning of the police activity on the allotments, and deplored the slow progress and the way that the case was dragging on. Petronella observed that it was like some terrible nightmare, such as fighting one's way out of an inflated plastic bag, or running at top speed and yet not moving forward at all.

For a change of scene and subject, they took their coffee into the drawing-room and watched the nine o'clock news, lying back luxuriously in deep armchairs, feet up on footstools, gently dozing - and then the 'phone rang.

It was Mark: could they both possibly come at once down to the Jolly Sailors for a quick drink, please? Yes, now, this very minute. A small celebration was on the programme for the evening.

"Oh, very well," Joy conceded. "In about a quarter of an hour, then?"

They set off, yawning, for the pub, more ready for bed than for revelry, but cheered by the idea that there might possibly be some news of developments in the mysterious "doin's."

This was not to be so, but the occasion was much more uplifting and heart-warming than they could have anticipated. They looked in through the window of the saloon bar, but there was not a soul to be seen except for old Charlie Mars and his labrador, comfortably ensconced in a corner with a pint of bitter and the Oxford Mail spread out on the table. So they walked round to the public bar and opened the door, to be met by peals of laughter and the concerted clamour of a mass of people enjoying themselves. It was like encountering a dense wall of sound.

"Ah, there you are!" Michael Walters appeared through the scrum and took them both by the arm, deftly steering them through the crowd to the bar.

"Tonight, dear ladies," he said, "we have something to celebrate."

There was no time, nor indeed any opportunity for explanations. Glasses of champagne were thrust into their hands by Peter Rumbold, who said something to Joy, but it was of course completely inaudible in the general hubbub.

"What on earth is going on?" Petronella mouthed to Joy.

"No idea," she mouthed back, shrugging her shoulders and holding her champagne glass aloft to protect it from the jostling throng.

"Veuve Cliquot," She mouthed, pointing to the bottle in Michael's custody, "So it must certainly be something well worth celebrating forsooth!"

Then a gap opened up in the crowd, and she spied Mark at the bar.

"Auntie Joy!" He hugged her most affectionately and gave her a tender kiss on the cheek, and to Joy's surprise, Marit, standing next to him and looking absolutely radiant, did the same.

"Auntie Joy," Mark spoke into her ear to make sure that she could hear above the general din, "We've taken the plunge, Marit and I are engaged."

"Gracious me! How utterly marvelous!"

Both Joy and Petronella were quite thrilled at this welcome news. Marit shyly showed her left hand, revealing a most beautiful engagement ring set with fine diamonds, which glittered in the lights of the bar.

"Ooh!" Petronella was rapturous. "What a gorgeous ring! Many congratulations!"

Marit gave her a kindly hug and kissed her tenderly on both cheeks.

"Thank you, darlink, but soon, also, I think, you'll be having one similar, yes?"

Then she tossed back her golden hair as though trying to shake off anxiety and remarked with a resigned expression: "But I am not knowing quite yet what Aunt Aäse will be thinking of all this when I telephone to her to tell I am marrying an Englishman! Although she does like very much Shakespeare so maybe she will accept."

"How about a dress-circle season ticket for Stratford?" interjected Michael Walters. "That should keep the old girl happy. We'll arrange it!"

"Would you really do this thing?" asked Marit, taking the offer perfectly seriously, in her earnest Norwegian way. "What a marvellous idea! I am thinking that Aunt Aäse is always too serious in her enjoyments, so it is quite suitable."

"There, old man - now you're really lumbered," murmured Mark aside to Michael, who promptly vanished with the champagne bottle to do the topping up process which, conveniently for him, appeared to be the pressing need of the moment.

"Yes, it is so," continued Marit, "Aunt Aäse is always most serious in these matters. Do you know, she is still, in the age of sixty, skiing on Sundays, as all Norwegians do? Did you know also, we Norwegians consider this skiing almost as an act of - how do you say? – penance for Sundays?' All must go from Oslo to the forest to ski. It is tradition, we must all do this thing. From the city it is two or three kilometers maybe to the woodlands, and all must go - it is rather like your old English tradition of going to church on Sundays, yes?"

But the rest of Marit's description of the austere, almost Ibsenesque nature of Norwegian leisure and amusements was drowned by a raucous chorus of "For he's a jolly good fellow," and "Why was he born so beautiful, why was he born at all?"

Mark tolerated it all with gracious good humour and in response made a little speech beginning inevitably: "Unaccustomed as I am to public speaking..." Nothing much more was audible for then the rugger ballads took over.

At this point the ladies retired tactfully to the saloon bar to discuss more important matters, such as wedding preparations. Mark's wedding would certainly take place at St. Julie's Church, and later on there would be a ceremony in Norway. But when? The sooner, the better, as far as Marit was concerned, and Petronella, delighted and enthusiastic, was insisting on helping to organize the occasion. Joy was pleased to see that her recent low-spirited despondency had been completely dispersed by her own happy prospects and Mark and Marit's exciting news, and she had recovered her bubbling zest for life. It was easy to see that she had in mind possible arrangements for a like event in Australia, to take place at some time in the future, and she saw Marit's wedding as a useful practice run and was full of imaginative ideas. She hugged herself with sheer delight when Marit said she intended to wear a traditional Norwegian wedding dress, and if her young nephews and nieces could be brought over, they too would wear traditional costume as pages and bridesmaids.

Marit went on to explain that her mother had died some years ago, (so accounting for the dominant role played by her twin Sister, Aunt Aäse), but her father would most certainly be there to give her away. He was such a darling man, so easy-going, hence he was, of course, completely dominated by Aunt Aäse! No, no, there was no emotional connection at all. Aunt Aäse had had a husband, from whom she was estranged, and he had tucked himself away on a small island at the far end of some lesser-known fjord, and had subsequently committed suicide, possibly in order to effect a final escape from his wife.

It was a strange, even mysterious business. In the beginning no one knew whether it was suicide or not. He had been found one afternoon lying dead in his rowing-boat in the middle of the fjord, quite peaceful, with an empty Schnapps bottle beside him, having, it was supposed, simply drunk himself to death. No suicide note was found in his house, and the only small indication that he might have killed himself was a bottle of sleeping tablets in his pocket, but there was not much trace of barbiturates in his blood, just a huge amount of alcohol. It was not until some time later that, quite by accident, the truth was discovered. Some young boys were fishing along the shore some way up the fjord and came upon a sealed up Schnapps bottle with a note inside it, which proved to be the suicide note, and very good news it was for Aunt Aäse, since it meant that she could now inherit his estate with no legal complications.

When he abandoned her for his hideaway on the island, he had left her with very little to live on, but she was hard-working and had survived by using her great skills in traditional handicrafts and her renowned knitting of Norwegian oiled-wool jerseys. Her husband had been a writer, specializing in sombre dramas loaded with deep meaning about life in Norway in the late nineteenth century, in which most of the characters died a miserable death or committed suicide, and yes, he was respected as one who portrayed most accurately everyday life in his country at that period.

"Like Strindberg?" asked Joy.

"Ah, yes," said Marit,"Maybe a little similar." However, Marit herself was not over-familiar with the works of these so serious writers. She was better acquainted with books by Grahame Greene and Somerset Maugham and Aldous Huxley which, she said were "So much more fun to read in this beautiful language of English! Yes, it was so, she must confess she was a complete Anglophile and was sure she would have no trouble at all in settling down in Oxford. It was such a mad place, was it not? One could be simply outrageous and it didn't seem to matter somehow, did it? Nobody took any notice, whatever you did. Now this could never happen in Norway. No, indeed, but perhaps Norwegians were a little old-fashioned in their outlook and traditions? Well, maybe, but surely that was not a bad thing. After all, there was nothing wrong with a little discipline in life, was there? What was the expression in English? Tedious but necessary, perhaps? Like the skiing on Sundays in Oslo, a discipline and not, as it might be regarded by other people, a pleasure or a luxury or even a sport. How would you say in English? One man's swings, another man's roundabouts?"

Petronella collapsed in silent hysterics at this unconsciously and irresistibly ludicrous misquote.

Joy suggested that Marit might be thinking of the expression "One man's rubbish is another man's treasure?"

Marit agreed that this more nearly conveyed her meaning and went on: "Yes, indeed, maybe so, but to explain, please, she meant in fact that skiing was the great luxury sport for the British, but to the Norwegians it was simply a rather boring essential exercise, so...

But here the door opened quickly and in sidled Mark, a finger to his lips.

"Shh! I've managed to escape for a moment. Now listen, Auntie Joy, can you lay on a supper party next Saturday night? An engagement party - I'll stand the racket. Slay the fatted calf, crate of champagne - the lot. Could you?"

Joy acquiesced, wondering where the fatted calf was to come from, or what in Heaven's name she was to substitute for it.

"Good girl!" he said, beaming from ear to ear. "Please invite everyone who has been involved in the case, will you?"

Joy opened her mouth to ask a question.

"No - not now. Must get back to the rabble next door. Everybody you know who was involved on your side, O.K.?"

She nodded, mouth still open, hoping to ask about possible numbers, but there was no chance. "I've got something to tell you," said Mark, blowing Marit a kiss, then vanishing with a saucy wink at the group. As he went through the door he winced slightly as a great roar of voices greeted him, raised in bawdy song. Squaring his shoulder he resigned himself to the inevitable: far too many drinks to be pressed on him, and a terrible hangover on the morrow, but the ordeal must be faced and he was ready for it.

When he had gone, Marit sat still, looking pensive, her extraordinary green eyes gazing into the far distance; she said: "You know, really, I am thinking...," she paused.

"Yes, Marit?" Queried Petronella, all agog with anticipation of further gems from Marit's vocabulary.

"I was thinking I would like very much some quite beautiful music for this wedding. You know this thing?" She hummed a tune.

"Yes, that's it - 'Here is coming the bride' - I simply must have this for my arriving. Now, please, what else can we have?" Joy needed no further prompting and jumped in eagerly: "Well, now, my dear, if you've got no one else in mind for it, I'd love to play the organ for the wedding. The church has a really fine instrument, a Willis, actually, and as I do play it occasionally, I would regard it as a privilege..."

"Oh, please, please, yes - do this. So wonderful it will be most certainly!" Marit was gratifyingly enthusiastic, and Joy, warming to the subject, waxed eloquent.

"I know - I'll play some Grieg! Now, what could we do?" She played an imaginary keyboard on the table as she considered the matter.

"I've got it - the Holberg Suite! That's it, I'll play that before the service. It's lovely, and such a happy piece. And something from Peer Gynt for the signing of the register, perhaps?"

Petronella giggled. "And what about 'In the hall of the Mountain Kings', Joy?"

Joy reproved her with a frown.

"No, Petronella, there are some delightful tender passages in

'Peer Gynt', and I shall seek out something suitable. Morning, possibly. Really, you know, Grieg is such a wonderful composer, his music is so varied, but nowadays he does not seem to enjoy the popularity he truly deserves. Musical fashions come and go, I suppose. He has in fact all the colour and fire of Ravel and Debussy, and the deep passionate emotion of Tchaikovsky, and yet he speaks so refreshingly and unmistakably in the accents of his native land. Wonderful music..." Joy was carried away, but then Tony put his head round the door.

"'Ere" Missus, better rescue that lad o' yours. E's goin' to have a roight 'ead-banger in the mornin', judgin' by the way they're goin' on in 'ere!"

"I shall now go to rescue him at once!," said Marit, departing promptly to the public bar, but she popped her head round the bar door to say:"By the way, please don't be forgetting some beautiful hymns for the wedding. I wish for something very serious about marriage and children, and a happy strong home. Most necessary, isn't it? Thank you."

Closing the door behind her, she set about the awkward task of extracting her future husband from the clutches of his good friends and true, who were quite clearly determined to get him as drunk as possible.

"What a hoot!" exclaimed Petronella. "Now, what hymns should there be? How about 'O God, our help in ages past', or 'Fight the good fight', perhaps?"

Joy frowned again in reproof.

"Well, it does mention 'home', Joy."

"Don't be flippant, Petronella dear, there's a good girl. I feel we ought to go for something with cherubs in it, you know, to suggest the blessing of children in the marriage - something tasteful ..."

"Good-night, Auntie Joy."

With a bang of the door, Mark came into the saloon bar, walking rather unsteadily and being gently steered by Marit.

"I think we must be going home now, carefully and quickly," Marit said, po-faced but twinkling away, with a flash of her sea-green eyes. "I think we have had enough of today and it is time to be going to our beds."

"Quite so, good-night, Mark darling. See you tomorrow, perhaps, and many congratulations, my dearest boy."

No sooner had they gone, that the bar door flew open again with a crash and an inebriated group of people came into the bar in Indian file, singing:: "Aye-aye conga..." and weaving their way' round the bar tables, much to the astonishment of St. Julie's Church Parochial Church Council, who were concluding a peaceful meeting over a glass of wine and Perrier water in a corner of the bar.

"Michael, you ought to be ashamed of yourself!"

Joy was scandalized, for the procession was led by Michael Walters followed by Peter Rumbold, with the Jolly Sailors darts team tagging along behind.

"Really, Madam?" - Michael was somewhat glazed and swayed a little unsteadily on his feet. "How so? Do we not have some cause for much jollification, then? After all, it is not an everyday event when one of North Oxford's notoriously confirmed bachelors meets his Waterloo, now is it, good lady? So celebrations are most definitely in order, to be sure!"

With that, the conga procession wound itself through the far door to do a serpentine circuit of the pub forecourt, then wend an unsteady way back to the public bar.

Peace was re-established in the saloon bar, and after the rude interruption St. Julie's P.C.C. continued its quiet discussion and finished its business without further disturbance.

"Well, what a night to remember!" commented Joy as she walked home with Petronella, who was crowing with delight.

"It's going to be a riot! I'm simply dying to meet Aunt Aäse, she must be an absolute dragon - probably looks like Brunhilde. Do you think she's got a spear and a Viking horned helmet?"

"No, not at all, Petronella, my dear. I visualize a tall, buxom, moon-faced personage with a long golden plait wound round her head, and of course a meticulous centre parting, and wearing a voluminous folk-weave skirt with traditional embroidered Scandinavian blouse - long sleeves and a high neck. Oh, and possibly sensible hand-made reindeer leather sandals on the bottom end, with heavy-duty knitted stockings, of course."

Thus musing they walked up the still and silent road, and were met at the front gate by all their furry feline friends, fawning around and almost under their feet. A hearty welcome, but with an ulterior motive, for Iffley was already leading the procession purposefully in the direction of the kitchen in the hope of a quick snack of cat-biscuits and a saucer of milk (this was a rare treat, for Joy considered that plain clean water was much better for cats' health).

The importunate felines satisfied, Joy and Petronella at last retired to their beds, overcome by sleep, and were visited with pleasant dreams: Bruce of course figured large in Petronella's, while Joy had dreams of vanquishing the enemy and emerging triumphant from the battle to justify her contention regarding Purcell and Clemens non Papa. All most satisfactory.

Next morning, over coffee, Joy discussed the preparations for the engagement dinner-party, including the guest list and the menu.

"Best way to do it is to wroite one each, an' then read 'em out to one another, moy duck. Oi'll do one of 'oo Oi think oughter come, an' you do one of 'oo you think oughter come."

This they did in complete silence. It took some time and several cups of coffee, but they both found it rather fun to do. They sat, wholly absorbed and not even noticing Iffley, who had quietly climbed up on to the table, which was normally forbidden, and was sitting watching them, purring loudly, her great golden eyes half closed.

Joy's list of names got longer and longer, certainly far too many for a dinner-party. It would have to be a buffet supper, for there was no other way that the catering could be properly organized. Looking across over her half-specs, she noted that Mrs Badger's list was quite short. It would be most interesting to see whom she might wish to summon to the feast. Presumably it would indicate how far Mrs B. felt she was personally involved in this whole tiresome business. She totted up her own list and found that it contained about twenty-five names. Heavens above!

Now, what about the menu? There were so many men on the list, all presumably with hearty appetites, and obviously it would have to include good, wholesome and filling dishes, but also some light and delicious epicurean items to please the girls, some of whom might possibly be a little sensitive about diet!

She looked across at Mrs Badger and thought again that not much work was destined to he done about the house that morning. However, Mrs B. was after all nugget gold, and the party was the most important consideration at the moment, so what would she suggest?

"Bangers, beans and mash," breathed Mrs Badger as she jotted down her proposed menu. Joy bent over her note pad and pretended not to hear.

"With pickled onions - Master Mark's favourite, 'twas, when 'e was a lad."

Joy shuddered.

Mercifully, at that point the door bell rang. It was Harriet Spinster.

"Hello, my dear, would you like these? They're absolutely delicious!"

She presented a bowl of the most fearful-looking toadstool-like fungi, as one offering a dish of caviar.

"Such a rare find, and we've got dozens of them. They make the most wonderful omelette, but they must be eaten today, the little darlings. They don't keep, you know. By-ee!"

When Harriet had gone, Joy inspected them cautiously. Ugh! They looked quite poisonous and certainly unlike anything she had ever seen before. They were very small and their colour was a hideous pale greenish mauve. The thought of eating them made her feel sick.

However, when Mrs Badger espied the precious gift, she let out a great "Ooh! wot 'ave you got there, moy duck? Ooh, Oi say!" She took a closer look.

"Wherever did you get they little green dodgers from, then? Funny little things, they be! Moy 'ubby used to go out over the meadow about this toime 'o the year an' look for 'em. Very 'ard to come by, they be. Yes, moy 'ubby, 'e's a great one on the mushrooms, 'e be. Knows 'em all backwards 'e do, loike most o' the old boys 'ereabouts, o' course. Brought up as lads out on Port Meadow, they was, with all its woildloife, flowers, 'erbs, an' mushrooms, an' all the fish an' such other tackle. But all that's bin an' gawn an' vanished, nearly. The young lads these days don't seem to know a lot about it, do they?"

She gave Joy a Sideways look, very old fashioned.

"'Cept o'course for such loike as that lad Cledwyn. Oi don't think as 'ow Oi mentioned as 'ow moy 'ubby knew him, did Oi? From collectin' mushrooms over yonder in the early mornin'. Now then, that lad knew more nor moy 'ubby knew about they mushrooms. Showed 'im them magic mushrooms, un' all, 'e did, Said as 'ow they gave you fantastic visions, loike bein' in Fairyland. Moy 'ubby wouldn't touch 'em, o' course. The lad told 'im the name, somethin' Latin - loike 'Movoculate' some such word, Oi do forget. Very 'ard to understand. Moy 'ubby looked it up in the book, but the book's all wrote in French, anyway it's got lovely pictures, an' this book goes by the name of 'Cham-pie-nons', it do."

Joy restrained herself with difficulty from betraying any sign of her enjoyment at Mrs Badger's rendering of the book's title. Mrs Badger continued: "By some old boy... ," she paused, searching for a name. "Marcel wot's is name..."

"Marceau?" suggested Joy flippantly.

This was instantly dismissed with contempt.

"No! Ruboish, moyduck. 'E's an old French filum star!

Mrs Badger's tone was crushing, and rightly so.

"Don't you ever watch BBC 2 then, moy dear? You're missin' a treat if you don't. Oi loves they old French filums they puts on sometimes. You know Yves Montand and Simone Signoret."

She got the pronunciation perfectly right - learning by ear was obviously simpler than any application of same to the written word - viz. "cham-pie-nons."

Mrs Badger went, on "Moy 'ubby, 'e loves 'em an all, so romantic, they be"!

The idea of Mr. Badger as a dedicated romantic struck Joy as extremely improbable. In build and appearance, for instance, he resembled Dr. Johnson, and indeed he was also a Staffordshire man by origin, some way back. He was a large man, with a quiet manner, ruddy-faced, with a heavy jowl, and chary of speech. Romance, however, may lurk in the most unexpected haunts.

"Yes," continued Mrs Badger, "'E loves they old films. 'Is very favourite actor was always Fernandel. Wonderful, 'e thought 'e was. Alawys reminded 'im of 'is grandfather,'e says. Deadpan expression on 'is face, an' up to all sorts o' mischief, an' yet you'd never think as butter wouldn't never melt in 'is mouth!"

Harriet Spinster, sitting out on her terrace next door, overheard the whole of this conversation, which was clearly audible through Joy's open window, and was simply convulsed with mirth.

Joy and Mrs Badger, however, had to get back to business, and each read out her guest list. Joy's was quite straight-forward and included all her choir members plus a few others who had been involved in recent untoward events, such as Michael Walters, Peter Rumbold and Percy Chadlow. She had toyed with the idea of inviting the policemen who were concerned with the case, putting a question-mark by their names, although she thought it unlikely that they would come. She wondered whether Lord and Lady Westhoe would be free, but thought it was doubtful, since term was soon to begin and they would certainly be hard-pressed for time; nevertheless she decided to invite them. She went through her list again and reached a total of approximately twenty names, so she would allow for twenty-five, in case anyone had been forgotten.

Mrs Badger nodded in approval as the list was read out.

"Very good, moy duck. Now Oi'll read you mine." She cleared her throat and proceeded:

"Now then, 'ere we goes: Mr. Badger, Mrs Badger, Mrs Graystone." She paused momentarily, looking at Joy over the top of her glasses, coughing delicately as she did so.

"Miss Dacre," she continued, disregarding Joy's raised eyebrows. "Plus four or five other persons 'oo must remain anonymous for the present toime."

"Anonymous, Mrs Badger?"

Nodding her head sagely, Mrs Badger then said, with a solemn look: "Oi fear so, moy dear, professional reasons as you moight say - an' beggin' your pardon o'course."

"Well, then, Mrs badger, that looks to be about thirty in all?"

Mrs badger nodded once more in agreement.

"Yes, that seems to be about it, then. Let's 'ave a look at this 'ere menu, shall we?"

She frowned, pondering deeply.

"Now, moy duck, regardin' this 'ere sausages an' mash.

Oi knows as 'ow a lady loike yourself would think it a bit outrageous for a party an'such loike, but Oi think you'll foind as it'll go down a 'treat with about a dozen of 'em 'oos a'comin'. An' - if you don't moind, Oi'll make it meself an' give it to the "do" as Master Mark's present, koind O' thing. So Oi'll make it at 'ome an' pop it in the oven 'ere on the noight for an hour or so, an' that'll be perfect - just you see if it ain't!"

"Thank you so much, Mrs Badger. Most kind of you."

Joy had grave doubts about Mrs B's claims regarding the popularity of this dish, but she forced what she hoped was an encouraging smile and said:

"Personally speaking, I rather thought that a salmon mousse would go 'down well, and perhaps a cheese dip, potato salad, cold meats, pate, cheese board with hot French bread, etc. You know, a kind of buffet for them to help themselves, with a fresh fruit salad and cream to follow. Elegant but substantial. What do you think?"

Mrs Badger considered this seriously.

"Yes, that'll do foine, moy dear, go down a treat, that will."

As she departed, she gave Joy a beaming smile and a mischievous wink.

"We'll 'ave a whale of a toime, moy duck, just you wait an' see if us don't!"

Joy, however, whilst agreeing in principle, was not in the slightest bit convinced about the merits of sausages, beans and mash, with pickled onions, as appropriate festive fare.

It took quite a while to round everybody up for the party, but most people responded quickly with an enthusiastic "yes" to the invitation. There were a few "Don't knows," but a gratifying number of acceptances, so she would certainly have to cater for thirty. Good - but where was she going to put them all? Should she pray for a fine evening, so that the overspill could go out on to the terrace? Well, maybe.

But now she must get on with the preparation of the salmon mousse. As she had most of the world's best cookery books on her kitchen shelf, she was somewhat spoilt for choice when selecting a recipe, but after a conscientious read through all the best, from the formidable Mrs Beeton, and Alice B. Toklass, Elizabeth David, and so on, she was finally faced with a difficult choice to make between the recipe in the Dairy Cookbook and the one in the Woman's Weekly Recipe Book. In the end she chose the latter, which read: "Money-wise mousse, cheap to make" (at least as cheap as one could manage, with fresh salmon as the chief ingredient!), but effective and easy to make.

She was still shuddering at the thought of Mrs Badger's bangers and mash. Pickled onions - ugh! but doubtless Mr. Badger would thoroughly enjoy it, even if no one else did, and the foxes could consume what was left over; they would be coming round much more at night, now that autumn was approaching, and the young cubs would be needing solid food, minus, of course, the pickled onions!)

Now then, what about a huge potato salad with dill? She really must get hold of Hildie, her dear old friend from Walton Well Road, to get her special recipe for Kartoffelnsalat, which was delicious and, naturally, a closely guarded secret, but Joy knew that the arcane ingredients of the oil dressing would be divulged for this important occasion. She vaguely recalled that there was ground elder in it, imparting a slightly spinachy flavour and a hint of a bitter taste. Also she must remember to invite Hildie to the party. She might even be persuaded to contribute one or two of her Epicurean specialities, such as sweet-sour gherkins. Joy thought of a possible bribe of a Lancôme special offer gift pack - she had recently got one as an extra when she bought a quantity of Niosôme - wonderful regenerative cream foraging facial tissues!

And what next? Well, yet another salad, but a very different kind - plum tomato salad with finely chopped Spanish onions, garlic and just a dash of paprika; and Mark must have what was his chief delight - cheesy dip with hot French bread. That, she thought, was a promising menu, but she would add some of Argyll's marinated anchovies from Summertown, and of course some olives and the mixed cold meats. All this would be followed by fruit salad and she might even find time to make a luscious sherry trifle, which would go down well with the celebratory champagne - though she herself never willingly drank the fizzy stuff, for it made her giggle ~ not a good idea!

So that was her menu sorted out, but what about the impending threat of bangers and mash? Could it become a reality? With the pickled onions, washed down with champagne? Oh Lord!

But then an idea occurred to her. She would match the onions with some of her own green tomato chutney, and the tasty pickled walnuts which Mrs Graystone had given her from the left-overs after the Grand Christmas Bazaar for St. Julie's Church Roof Fund. The walnuts were from the tree in Mrs Graystone's garden and should provide a delicate refined contrast to offset the odorous and unwelcome accessory.

She went on to consider drinks and remembered a vat of strong home-made scrumpy cider which Percy Chadlow had given her not long ago. Her less discriminating male guests might conceivably find that it pleased their palates, and at least she would be getting rid of it!

Then she was struck by a sudden and irresistible idea - no, not a sherry trifle, a Bombe Alaska! She knew that Mark adored it, remembering special event dinners at St. James' College, when it figured on the menu. It would provide a wonderful finish to what promised to be a splendid party (notwithstanding the dreaded bangers and mash, etcetera).

She could not begin too soon to get it together and began immediately to check through the ingredients, and then the 'phone rang.

"Oh, damn and hell's bells! Was there never any peace?" Evidently there was not. It was Mrs Badger in her most emphatic mood.

"Now then, Miss 'Etherington...!"

"Yes, Mrs Badger, what is it?" Joy feared the worst, and she was right.

"Now, see 'ere, moy dear. Moy 'ubby 'as just said as 'ow you can't possibly 'ave bangers an' mash without wot goes alongside of it, namely ..." She paused for dramatic effect.

"Oodles of baked beans - an' Spotted Dick an' custard to follow."

Joy could not believe her ears. She was struck dumb with sheer horror at the mere thought.

"Miss 'Etherington - are you there?"

"Oh, yes, of course, Mrs Badger," came the faint reply.

Mrs Badger continued, a note of triumph in her voice:

"An' Oi'll chuck in some lovely fried onions as well, not forgettin' the H.P. sauce, o' course."

"Yes, of course, as you say," gasped Joy, wilting under the shock. "Quite so, Mrs Badger."

"Well, then, Oi think that's agreed. Oi'll do fifty pork bangers an' loads O' mash. That should feed the troops."

She put down the 'phone smartly, and Joy tottered away, aghast. She went to prepare her Bombe Alaska in a mood of utter despair, seeing her lovely party ruined. What would the Westhoes think? That was something she dared not even contemplate.

She finished preparing the basic bombe and put it into the deep-freeze to await the day of her ordeal, as she now saw it. She would trust Mrs Badger to do the final honours by popping the bombe under the grill briefly on the night and bringing it to the table to be given its baptism of fire with brandy. Surely she could be trusted to get that right and any act of industrial sabotage could be ruled out - or so Joy hoped, with what justification remained to be seen.

CHAPTER XX

Come, Sirrah Jack, ho! Fill

Some tobacco!

Ayeres or Phantasticke Spirites for three voices

Thomas Weelkes 1608

The fateful day came in due course, and Mrs Badger arrived, bright and early, her coming announced by a loud toot on the family saloon's motor horn. Jack Badger, a jovial pipe-smoking Oxonian, waved cheerily from the driving seat of the venerable Morris Oxford.

"Wot 'oh, Miss 'Etherington, moy duck. Ow be then?"

"Oh, very well, Mr Badger, lovely to see you, keeping well?"

"Oh aar, moy duck, an' you?"

"Fine, thank you."

Ritual greetings exchanged, Mr. Badger heaved his bulky frame out of the car and opened the boot with a flourish, to reveal trays of glistening brown bangers, ready-cooked for a re-heat in the oven.

"'Ow about that, then?" said Mr. Badger, beaming from ear to ear. There were four large trays of mashed potato, creamed to perfection lying alongside, together with the inevitable and highly odoriferous tray of fried onions. The smell was quite sickening and suggested to Joy some awful transport cafe meal on a bypass in the middle of nowhere. And there was more to come: next to appear was a large tray of spotted dick, with a container full of custard, and, looming over all this richly unrefined feast was a half-gallon tin of baked beans in tomato sauce. Joy's immediate reaction at the sight of this last was an impulse to hide the tin-opener, but this was neatly frustrated by Mrs Badger, triumphantly producing her instrument of torture.

"An' Oi've brought over moy big tin-opener, just in case!"

"How very thoughtful of you, most provident," murmured Joy, conceding victory to the enemy who had produced the secret weapon. All was now well and truly lost. It was a total defeat and her own exquisite masterpieces of culinary art were to be thrust into the shadows, banished to her grandmother's old sideboard along the far wall of the dining-room; and there was simply nothing she dared do or say about it. She could only grin meekly and try to put a brave face on it.

Mrs Badger worked all morning with a will, humming a happy little tune as she prepared the feast. The mynah-bird, apparently inspired to sound off in its turn, suddenly gave vent to its piercing wolf-whistle, followed by snatches of the Marseillaise, and every now and then there was the chilling echo of Madge Spragnell's voice petulantly commanding: "Rupert, shut that door!" The cats sat watching, in a row on the floor in front of the cage, chattering their teeth now and then in frustration and obviously trying to hypnotize the wretched bird out of its cage. After all, it had almost worked with Melody!

But not with the Mynah-bird, however. It jumped up and down triumphantly, hypnotizing them in its turn, its head cocked to one side, fixing the cats defiantly with a brilliant beady eye.

By one o'clock all was ready, with the tables laid for the great event, and Mrs Badger departed for the afternoon "to put 'er feet up in front of the telly," as she expressed it, while Joy collapsed gratefully on to the library sofa for a quiet read and a quick nap. She knew nothing thereafter until just before six o'clock, when Petronella woke her with a loud "Hello!" and a bang of the front door.

"All ready for the party?" she carolled down the hall.

"Oh, Petronella! Thank God you woke me, I was dead to the world!"

"Jolly good thing too, you'll be fresh for the party. I just can't wait. It's going to be a super go, I know it is. The vibes are terrific, it's so exciting, with all the police and everything!"

Off she dashed upstairs to change and get ready for the jollifications, and Joy realized it was time for her to do likewise. She decided on black velvet and pearls, in mourning for the wreck of her party menu; routed by a superior force.

Mrs Badger arrived punctually at six o'clock with a loud "Yoo-hoo! Battle stations!" And got on with preparations in the kitchen, and ere long the scent of fried onions wafted forth through the open kitchen door, accompanied by the fragrance of the pork sausages heating up in the oven. Joy was in despair. How dreadful for the guests to be greeted by such odours!

"Ooh!" Petronella called down the stairs, "What's that fantastic smell?"

"Bangers and fried onions," announced Mrs Badger, popping her head round the kitchen door. "Luverly?"

"Smells yummy," said Petronella, "Can I try one?"

"Course you can. Come down 'ere to the kitchen."

Petronella appeared, looking absolutely lovely in a pale turquoise silk dress which swirled gracefully round her slim figure as she danced down the stairs.

"Oh boy! They are just too yummy for words," she declared, enthusiastically munching a juicy pork sausage drenched in H.P. sauce.

"Can I have another one?"

"No, you can't. No more now! Just you 'old your fire. 'Tis for the party - an' there's spotted dick an' custard to follow. 'Ow's that, then?"

"Wowee," said Petronella, "I'll be first in the queue!"

Then she ran upstairs again to put the finishing touches to her toilette.

Depressed and anxious, Joy went to the kitchen to give her instructions about the presentation of the Bombe Alaska.

"And you won't forget to toast the top of it under a very hot grill, will you, Mrs Badger? It must go brown and crinkly."

"Don, worry, moy duck, it'll be perfect. Just you leave it to me!"

Ominous words, and Joy's heart sank. Oh please, dear Lord, let her get it right, and not make a complete dog's breakfast of it!"

The doorbell rang. The first of the guests had arrived, and they were Mark and Marit.

"Oh, what a wonderful smell! What is it?" asked Marit. "It is rather like the smell of my grandmother's reindeer sausages."

She took herself off promptly to the kitchen to investigate, and discuss with Mrs Badger the virtues of her grandmother's sausages, while Mark set about his task of acting as mine host, opening bottles and setting up the drinks.

Thereafter more guests began to arrive, and soon it was a steady stream, and the party was in full swing. Joy noted that noses seemed to be twitching expectantly at the pungent odour of pork sausages and fried onions!

Inspector Vardon and his colleagues appeared, and his very first comment was to declare how thoughtful it was of Professor Hetherington to provide a hearty meal for his troops, as most of them had just come off duty, and were much in need of it, and to judge from the appetizing smell coming from the kitchen it was just what the doctor ordered!

What a mercy that the Westhoes had not yet arrived, thought Joy, as the kitchen door flew open and Mrs Badger and her serving wenches appeared, bearing first the glistening sausages and mashed potatoes, then the fried onions and baked beans, steaming hot. With the air of a priestess bearing a ceremonial offering, Mrs Badger advanced to set down her huge tray of sizzling sausages on the big table with a triumphant thump.

"There we are now," she announced, "That'll stick to your ribs an' no mistake!"

Marit followed her with the vast dish of mashed potato, and Petronella came after with the baked beans, while Caroline Grieve brought up the rear carrying a large dish of crispy fried onions, with their all-pervading pungent smell, albeit not as nauseating, Joy reflected, as the vile odour given off by their equivalent at St. Giles' Fair on that fateful night.

The pickled onions, an enormous jar, were already in their place on the table, with a Neptune's fork alongside for spearing them, a feat requiring considerable skill, for pickled onions are extremely elusive, even when chased by the most militant of pickle forks.

This unsophisticated fare was being consumed with enormous enthusiasm, and Joy was dismayed to see that the cold buffet was still totally ignored. At this point, however, the arrival of the Westhoes aroused her from her despondency, and then filled her with amazement, for they addressed themselves immediately to the sausages and mash.

"Capital," Lord Westhoe announced, crunching a pickled onion with appreciation. "Lord, it's ages since I had such a tuck-in, baked beans, too. Wonderful!"

Lady Westhoe tactfully approached the cold buffet and selected a black olive; after surveying the festive spread, she remarked to Joy: "How lovely! I simply adore black olives and Pate d'Ardennes." She had evidently perceived Joy's embarrassment and, smiling sympathetically, she explained:

"These cordon bleu dinners we have to live with scarcely give us a chance even to see a sausage, let alone eat one, so it's a rare treat, especially accompanied by baked beans!"

After this, Joy's wilting spirits began to recover, and she was further encouraged to see that people were already making inroads into her elegant display on the sideboard. The salmon mousse was taking a heavy pounding, and Hildie's special potato salad was being attacked with vigour, and thank goodness for that, since she'd made a large quantity and would have hated to see it wasted. Good, so things were going well.

She saw the serving wenches departing to the kitchen and realized that the time had come for the spotted dick to appear. In a few moments they returned, bearing the tray of pudding and a large steaming jug of hot custard.

"Oh boy!" exclaimed Mark, "Lead me to it! Auntie Joy, you're a genius!"

Joy smiled discreetly, saying nothing, then watched with amazement as the locusts descended and the pudding seemed to be all gone in a flash. So now must be the time for the Bombe Alaska. She popped her head round the kitchen door.

"Is the bombe ready, Mrs Badger? The spotted dick's nearly gone."

"Just a mo', Miss 'Etherington. Oi'll be with you in two shakes of a lamb's tail!"

However, there was a long interlude between this assurance and the appearance of Mrs Badger with the Bombe Alaska. No matter, thought Joy, for things were going well - even splendidly it might be said - and even an unexpected disaster could be successfully survived. This confident assumption was shortly to be put to the test, as subsequent events were to demonstrate.

Eventually, and theatrically, Mrs Badger made her entrance bearing a large salver.

"'Stately Spanish galleon, coming from the Isthmus ...'" quoted Professor Peterson in sheer admiration. "My goodness me!'

For Mrs Badger had changed into her party attire and was a sight to behold. She appeared to float, like a wartime barrage balloon, clad in a most extraordinary dress resembling exotic camouflage, with viridian green as the background colour. On this was printed a mixture of pink and crimson flowers crisscrossed with palms and bunches of bananas flung here and there over the general design. And on anyone else it would have looked perfectly awful and the height of vulgarity, but draped round the statuesque figure of Mrs Badger it fell in classic and majestic folds and swirled around her seductively as she advanced. As if to enhance this impression, the dressmaker had cut the material so that a hand of bananas was carefully sited over each ample breast. "Most remarkable," Peterson was heard to observe later on. "Was it done by accident - or wicked design?"

Mrs Badger's thick mop of snow-white hair was turned back and upward into a chignon kept in place by a Spanish tortoiseshell comb set with mother-of-pearl and she wore round her neck a choker with five rows of pearls which gave her a look of the late Queen Mary in her stately and breathtakingly dignified progress bearing the salver before her.

But what of the bombe?

As Mrs Badger approached it became clear that something untoward had happened to it. It seemed to have suffered a volcanic catastrophe.

"Good Lord!' exclaimed Peterson, "What is this I see before me? The Paps of Jura under snow after a mighty blizzard?"

"Don't be crude," admonished Brenda with a frown, poking him sharply in the ribs.

"Ouch!" he exclaimed, as he belched and hiccupped.

"Drunken sot!" said Brenda, "Shut up and behave yourself."

Mrs Badger placed the Bombe Alaska on the table for all to see, and it presented a most remarkable sight. As Peterson had observed, it did indeed resemble the Paps of Jura under snow. Two mounds of appreciable mass were visible rising from the surface of the contents of the salver, but what were those curious little black lumps sticking out all over it? Rocks? Moreover, with closer inspection, whatever were those minute multi-coloured bits of something scattered over the snows of Jura's paps?

Joy was speechless, thinking: "Oh, dear God! My bombe! What on earth has she done to it?"

Lord Westhoe was the first to examine it at close range. "My dear Mrs Badger, what a triumph! What is it?" he asked. "What a simply splendid creation!"

"Well, my lord," she declared, looking him straight in the eye, with a winning smile:"This is my famous Prunes Bombe, my very own secret recipe." "May you be forgiven!" whispered Joy, sotto voce.

Sensing that a crisis had arisen, Mark gallantly intervened. "Mrs B., kindly pass me the brandy and I shall perform the pyrotechnics."

Mrs Badger tried to say something, but he already had the brandy bottle, passed along the table to him by Peter Rumbold, who had already guessed that there was to be a touch of the unexpected in all this.

Mark took a light from the candelabrum and poured brandy over the snowy Paps of Jura, setting it alight with a theatrical gesture, holding the taper high above his head. Instantly there was a flash of flame and a "whoosh," accompanied by a loud sizzling sound as the whole mass appeared to swell up like heaving breasts (according to Peterson's comment after the event).

"Good Lord! What on earth's going on, Mrs B.?" asked Mark, amazed at the spectacle.

"Well, now, Master Mark," replied Mrs Badger, wagging an admonitory finger. "Oi did try to tell you, but you was altogether too quick on the draw. Oi'd already given it a good dollop o' that French stuff in the kitchen cupboard before Oi brought it in."

"That pure peppermint alcohol you brought back last year," whispered Joy, quite mortified, into Mark's ear.

"Good Lord - rocket fuel," he whispered back. "Amazing it didn't take off and stick itself to the ceiling!"

So that was the history of the Bombe Badger and, nothing deterred, everyone tucked in with a will, spooning up the exploded bombe as it quickly collapsed and pouring it into their spotted dick dishes.

"Superb!" declared Lord Westhoe, "But what are these curious coloured dots floating all over the surface?"

"They be 'undreds an' thousands," said Mrs Badger, "Plus a few little silver balls for Christmas cakes as Oi found in them in the kitchen cupboard."

(Later, Mrs Badger confessed to Joy that she had in fact put the bombe in the oven instead of under the grill, by mistake of course, and it had instantly begun to collapse, so emergency measures had to be taken and she had "thrown a tin o' prunes at it, plus the 'undreds an' thousands, as a cover-up job, an' the little silver balls, in a kind o' panic sort o' thing, an' then dolloped it wi' that French stuff out o' the bottle!")

Result: "Inspired gastronomic perfection – Cordon-bleu chef-d'oeuvre!" was the verdict as delivered by Lord Westhoe, as he spooned up the ice-cream slurry with the boyish enthusiasm of a participant at a dormitory feast.

The following week, at the next meeting of the consort at St. James's, Peterson called for a rendition of Thomas Weelkes' splendid madrigal "Thule, the period of cosmography" to be sung in memory of the Bombe, now destined to pass into legend. It seemed singularly appropriate, as all were agreed, as the high drama of volcanic eruption seen through Elizabethan eyes:

"Thule, the period of cosmography

Doth vaunt of Hecla

Whose sulphureous fire

Doth melt the frozen clime

And thaw the sky

Trinacrian Etna's flames

Ascend not higher

These things seem wondrous..."

They all went great guns as they sang the first part of this exciting madrigal, but in the second part, "The Andalusian Merchant," they came to grief; all went well until the difficult passage about the China dishes and flying fishes, and the performance finally disintegrated in fits of giggles at "These things seem wondrous ...," and the choir gave up entirely, thanking their lucky stars that they had not attempted to perform that piece at Madge's now notorious event! Even Joy managed to smile graciously, pretending to enjoy the joke, and she did not mention the fact that the cause of the total collapse of the madrigal was the glaring false entry so confidently delivered by Peterson himself at "These things seem wondrous..." It was better to be tactful and say nothing.

However, all this lay in the future, when the strange events preceding and following St. Giles' Fair had all been explained and cleared up. The need for this to happen was felt by the guests at the party, and expressed by Peterson, who remarked:

"This is all very fine and of course we are all loving the pleasures of good food, fine wines and jovial company, but we are aware that so many ends remain untied in this curious affair, and it would be gratifying to have some kind of explanation provided about what really happened and, especially, why it happened, so that the mystery surrounding the tragic deaths and the disappearances can be elucidated. Shall we soon know?"

So saying, he gazed thoughtfully into his glass of dark crimson Chateauneuf, twirling the liquid gently against the light of the candelabrum on the table. There were murmurs of assent all round, of "Quite so," and "Absolutely."

However, when one looked round the room it was obvious that certain members of the company knew more about the meaning of things than the rest. The police and their supporting team were smiling broadly and, as Brenda Page-Philips remarked, had "the look of the cat with the cream." Apparently, only the academics and the laity had been left in the dark.

Joy reminded Mark that he had told her an explanation of some kind would be given during the course of the evening, but by whom remained as yet unclear, and as time was passing and it was already after ten o'clock, he'd better be quick about it, as some people actually had work to attend to, come the morrow!

At this point the 'phone rang.

Mark went out into the hall to answer it, then came back into the room looking distinctly relieved, and rather as though he too had a saucer of cream. He announced:

"My Lords, ladies and gentlemen, the explanation is on its way. "D" will be with us in approximately ten minutes' time." "D"? Eyebrows rose simultaneously all round the room and the half-specs slid gently down noses.

The members of the company who were already au fait with the situation grinned broadly and sat back to enjoy the coming revelation. Significant winks were exchanged, and there was a celebratory topping up of glasses in anticipation of the grand denouement. Joy noted that they were enthusiastically downing that dusty old bottle of Laphroaig whiskey which had lain in the cellar for years. Thank goodness, they were getting rid of it! It must taste frightful, since it had been down there for at least twenty years, indeed since her father died, for it had been his favourite tipple, but to her palate it tasted like paint-stripper. There was still some more of it down in the cellar, so if the guests showed no visible signs of having suffered ill effects by the end of the party, she would present them with the remaining bottles. There must be a dozen, at least, probably more, tucked away at the back somewhere. Her dear father had always kept a very well-stocked cellar. Only the very best was good enough for him, bless him!

Mark continued: "Sorry to be mysterious, but that's the "name of the game," so to speak, and it's difficult to be otherwise in our line of business, I fear, but all shall be revealed very shortly."

"Ah, intelligence!" Murmured Peterson to Brenda and friends sitting close by. "Now we're getting a glimmer of light in all this Stygian darkness. The gloom is lifting."

"At long last," said Brenda, "And about time too!"

Lord and Lady Westhoe sat impassive, showing no reaction to the tidings. It was well known that Lord Westhoe had formerly been a senior official at the Foreign Office, much involved in areas of national security. He spoke Russian and Czech fluently, as indeed did Lady Westhoe, for they had spent many years working abroad in Eastern Europe, in the diplomatic service, hence it was not surprising that they appeared unmoved by Mark's rather dramatic and cryptic pronouncement. Lord Westhoe, however, always thoughtful for the enjoyment of the company, quietly topped up the glasses round the table, and then sat back in the carver chair, elbows on the arm-rests, finger-tips together, looking totally relaxed, awaiting the coming of the mysterious "D."

The suspense did not last long. The doorbell rang and Mark went quickly to admit the visitor. A deep bass voice then resounded in the hall:

Many apologies for being so late, but the after-dinner speech had taken some time to deliver, so it was difficult to get away. Would Mark be ready to go in about an hour or so? Yes? Good man.

Then the door opened and in came a man of impressive stature - very tall, burly, with a distinctly aristocratic bearing. He had fair, closely cropped hair and fine features, with a strong chin, and reminded Joy of a full-length portrait of a certain Scottish laird by Sir Joshua Reynolds which hangs in the Tate Gallery. Indeed, the facial resemblance was so close that only the gold-framed spectacles worn by the newcomer distinguished him from the face in the portrait, which regarded the world with the same steel-blue eyes.

"D" was immaculately attired in a perfectly cut dinner jacket and trousers, with a frilly white shirt and a purple cummerbund, and his elegant Italian shoes added the final touch of sartorial correctness.

On entering the room, he paused for a moment, bowed unobtrusively to the Westhoes, and was introduced to Joy, to whom he offered abject apologies for his late appearance - it had been difficult to escape earlier from St. Anthony's! He was at once forgiven and presented with a large cafe cognac; thus fortified, he turned to address the company and began:

"My Lord, ladies and gentlemen, time is short, so I'll try to be brief, difficult though it will be, since this whole business has developed into something vastly labyrinthine and complex, and all because of a mindless, irresponsible student prank."

He looked round the room at his audience - a diverse collection of people from all walks of life in Oxford, smiled rather ruefully, and with a resigned shrug continued:

"Well, this is Oxford and it is a place we all love, I think, but we know, too, that it can turn on us and become an insane and illogical world where everything can go disastrously wrong, as indeed they did in this particular case."

He stopped and looked round the room once more, and at this Lord Westhoe approached, bearing the coffee pot and the Courvoisier bottle, with an offer of further refreshment, which was gratefully accepted, and "D" continued:

"The story begins with the arrival in Oxford of one Colonel Antonov, a brilliant and daring aviator from the Eastern Bloc.

"When one looks at the man and his personal achievements, I think it would be fair to say that if he had known the legendary Baron von Richthofen, they would have been able to swop great yarns about their dare-devil flying exploits.

"The Red Baron has his place in history as the fearless aviator who became a legend in his own lifetime, and perhaps Antonov's name may in due course rank with his in the annals of aviation, who knows? He is an experienced astronaut, much decorated for his bravery in aerial combat, famous for deeds of derring-do and dramatic and highly improbable rescues of souls in tight corners, for he's a veritable wizard with a helicopter; in short, a man always ready to attempt the impossible: the longest free-fall by parachute from the very highest altitude, microlite record attempts, air ballooning - the whole range of aeronautic achievement; so that's Antonov the man, fiercely proud and arrogant and a perfectionist in every way. He must never be seen to do anything wrong or come off second-best; the strongest element in his character is professional pride."

"D" paused and took an appreciative sip of cafe cognac, giving himself time to collect his thoughts, then resumed:

"So when he decided to come to Oxford to do a course in astro-physics and a brush-up course in English at St. Clothilde's there was a good deal of excitement among the spooks. This was a man who must be cultivated - nurtured, if you like - a tender plant, a neophyte landing right in the midst of our welcoming family in Oxford; and we knew we had to treat him with the greatest care, making him feel good and at ease with us. The whole process must run on oiled wheels, for he knew so much and we desperately needed to know about what was going on in the Soviet Bloc: 'Certain things', as the famous quote from 'The Goons' has it, shall we say? We had to gain his confidence and get him to trust us, and bring him over to our side, through the camaraderie of student life in Oxford.

Our plans were well laid, and our man arrived and settled in nicely, thoroughly enjoying Oxford life, throwing himself into it with a will and gradually taking to pub-life in the city. And he worked extremely hard, and played hard, too, joining in any number of sporting activities; even taking up rowing, declaring that his one ambition, had he been younger, would have been to row in the Boat Race.

Excellent, we thought, all is well. He's happy.

However, fate was to take a hand and strike him a devastatingly cruel blow, and this led to his undoing. Alas, an irresponsible and mindless student prank completely wrecked all our carefully laid plans.

In order to understand the man and why he behaved as he did, it is important to consider his background and family history. He belonged to the family of 'The Amazing Antonovs', the legendary acrobats whose exploits won them their fame under the Austro- Hungarian Empire."

"D" paused for a moment to remove and polish his glasses, and carefully replaced them on his nose. He then lit a small cigar, took another sip of cafe cognac, and said:

"Please, as we go along, do feel free to ask any questions if you are unclear on some point in my discourse."

In the ensuing silence, which lasted a short while, the skirl of a fox bark was heard in the back garden and Joy thought "Jennie the vixen!" She went out quickly, collecting some chicken bones from the kitchen on her way. Sure enough, there was the vixen with her tiny cubs, fluorescent green eyes glowing in the reflected light from the house, visible from where they were sitting, down by the garden shed. She threw the bones towards them and they were there instantly, too hungry to waste time on a stealthy approach. The dog-fox was there, too, russet red in the light, with his white shirt-front picked out clear. Returning with all haste to the drawing-room, Joy sat down at the back, eager to hear more of the tale of Antonov as it proceeded. In the background she could hear the Mynah-bird, shut away in the study for the night in his covered cage, beginning to mutter in his sleep and, evidently disturbed by the foxes' barking, he would suddenly let out a great squawk of fear in between his chunterings.

"Antonov," 'D' continued, "was actually born in Kiev, where his parents were on tour with the circus. "His mother was Polish, and his paternal grandparents were Russian and Viennese, and his father was born in Odessa where, presumably, they too were on tour. Many different cultures influenced Antonov's upbringing and were reflected in his life."

His mother was renowned for her daring performances on the trapeze, and this would have sparked his own ambition to learn to be a high flier from an early age.

Hence, regrettably, his breath-taking escape from us that night at St. Giles' Fair. Anyone else attempting that leap from the Ferris wheel would almost certainly have been killed, since by all accounts it was an impossible feat, in view of the speed of the wheel, the angle of descent and the distance of the leap, all the dynamics combining to make it totally improbable.

It should, however, be recorded here that his father, who had likewise attempted an impossible feat, had not been so fortunate, for he died when trying to walk the tight-rope across the Hudson River in New York, by Brooklyn Bridge. The high wire had been suspended between two Skyscrapers, at a great height and, watched by a great crowd, he had got safely halfway across when a sudden gust of wind swept him to his death in the river. His body was never recovered.

Antonov's mother did not marry again, and continued her career as the greatest woman trapeze artiste, with the young Antonov as her partner.

He, however, was resolved to fly yet higher, and when he was old enough he joined the Russian air force, soon qualifying as a jet pilot, and in no time at all achieving great distinction in the service of his country.

And now we come to a really interesting bit in our investigation. Antonov's mother and father, we discovered, had known Oxford quite well, having appeared there in the 'thirties, performing with the circus, when their sensationally daring act on trapeze and high wire without a safety net had been rapturously received. Antonov had himself mentioned this, and spoken of his own determination to come to Oxford to do honour to their memory by achieving academic distinction for the family name, to be recorded for ever in the annals of Oxford. Perhaps, if all went well and he fulfilled his ambition, an Antonov Fellowship might even be set up.

This, however, was destined not to be, for fate intervened with devastating effect and everything went desperately wrong for him. He was not, as I have already remarked, a regular drinker - his vaulting ambition could not have been achieved if he were - but he did develop a taste for the Real Ales of Oxfordshire: the Hook Norton, the Wychwood Ales, and so on; by no means surprising to us who know them, for they are really superb, are they not? But alas! This was a factor which led to his undoing.

He had completed all his preliminary examinations, coming through with flying colours and, rolling stone though he had been hitherto, he had formed an attachment to a young woman, a tutor at St. Clothilde's, who was tutoring him in English, and had indeed become quite besotted with him: possibly this was reciprocated, but of this we are not certain.

However, on the night before Finals he took her out to dinner at the Opium Den, and they finished up for a quiet drink at the King's Arms at about ten. According to our observations of Antonov hitherto, this was an unusual pattern of behaviour for him, since he was definitely an early bird, in bed at ten, up at five, and out on the river rowing to Iffley and back to Folly Bridge before breakfast.

When the couple were in the pub, one of our men tailing him noticed that Antonov's girlfriend was wearing an engagement ring~ which was an interesting new development. At about ten-thirty or so they were seen to drink up and prepare to leave before closing time, but as they got to the door, they were engulfed in a tide of merry undergraduates bursting into the pub before last orders. Unfortunately, one of Antonov's fellow students in the group spotted the engagement ring, and that was fatal. Of course they surrounded him and laid siege, and there was no escape; for him it was catastrophic.

There was absolutely nothing our chaps could do, except watch the action and observe who did what to whom. The fatal incident of the evening's celebration was the spiking of Antonov's drink, and at the time it seemed to us that no one in particular was responsible. Subsequently, however, it became clear that the identity of the perpetrator was crucial and in performing this one mindlessly irresponsible action he made himself both the villain and the victim of the piece, as it was played out.

They toasted the happy couple with champagne, something that Antonov had never drunk before, and then there was a final pint of beer for him, and more champagne for the girl. It was then that our men noticed that, under the cover of the merry junketing! the student who presented Antonov with the beer, quickly laced it with a large vodka before he left the bar - a real Mickey Finn - and that was how the damage was done."

'D' paused a moment for recollection, then resumed:

"The student was, as we found out later, the unfortunate Jasper Philberd. But to continue, the couple made their escape as soon as they decently could, but of course the result was inevitable. Poor Antonov failed to wake up in the morning in time to take his final examination, and that was the ignominious end of his brilliant course at Oxford. He vanished immediately, leaving no trace.

His fiancee, thus abandoned, had a terrible breakdown and ended up in the Warneford, after attempting suicide. According to our information she is still there, desperately ill, and showing very little sign of any improvement. So all this spelt the ruin of her hopes and, incidentally, also the wreck of our ingenious plans."

'D' stopped again and puffed briefly on his cigar; then he remarked: "You know, I am reminded of the famous quote from Robby Burns,'The best laid schemes o' mice an' men gang aft agley'.

Certainly, things went very much agley and very quickly after this event. Our quarry had disappeared, and then a series of undesirable incidents began to occur in Oxford - very disturbing happenings indeed."

With this tantalizing observation, 'D' declared a short interval to give time for his audience to prepare any questions they might wish to put to him. He then moved to sit with Lord and Lady Westhoe, to talk over certain University matters.

CHAPTER XXI

'O, what shall I do,

or whither shall I turn me?'

The Second Set of madrigals to 3, 4, 5, 6 and 6 parts

apt both for Viols and Voices

John Wilbye 1609

Meanwhile, all around an excited buzz of conversation arose, as little groups formed to discuss and prepare their questions. Notable exceptions to this activity were the police and their supporting team; they sat quietly enjoying a further bottle of Laphroaig, which Joy had retrieved from the cellar to replenish supplies, together with a bottle of Glenmorangie of similarly antique appearance. She had also provided a large bottle of Highland Spring water (although of this, she observed, they took no notice whatever).

"Let us go forth and fraternize with the enemy," said Peter Rumbold, taking Caroline Grieve by the hand, and off they went to sit with them and taste the pleasures of the disinterred Glenmorangie and Laphroaig whiskeys. These were being liberally dispensed by a man who, Joy thought, looked vaguely like one of the tramps at the fair on that fatal night. Now, however, he was a short back-and-sides man, wearing a dark suit and a regimental tie. He had a lean, handsome face and silver-grey hair, and looked extremely fit and even youthful, although he was probably in late middle-age.

"What's your regiment?" asked Caroline, observing the crossed rifles on the tie.

"Rifle Brigade, Madam, at your service," he replied, saluting smartly.

Another man, evidently of similar age, was sitting nearby; he was quite small in stature and of athletic build, and Caroline thought he looked like a happy youngish grandfather. She noticed a regimental badge on the pocket of his dark blue blazer, which portrayed a parachute, fully open in descent. Indicating it, she asked:

"What does that mean?"

"It means the Parachute Regiment, madam," he replied, smiling benignly at her incomprehension. "We're the boys of the Old Brigade - what's left of us."

"Aye," said the tramp: "Spent all his time jumping out of low-flying tiger-moths, he did. All this showing-off about open parachutes! Never flew higher than fifty feet off the ground in his life - could have used a rope-ladder instead."

"Oh, my goodness!" said Caroline, utterly mystified by all this banter. The young women of the surveillance team, elegantly attired in Botticelli dresses, gracefully draped, just giggled discreetly, spluttering into their drinks, over this comment.

At the academic table, meanwhile, earnest thought was being given to the matter in hand.

"We must appoint a scribe," said John Spry, "to write down all our questions. And I hereby appoint myself spokesman and shop-steward." He turned to Brenda Page-Philips:

"Brenda!"

"Yes?"

"Pen and paper and away you go."

"Oh dear, must I?" Brenda did not fancy the task, which certainly did not seem to fit in at all with the party mood.

"Yes, dear girl, you must. We're depending on you!" He turned to Joy: "Dominus, stilum et tabellam mihi da!," he commanded.

Obedient to the instruction, Joy went to fetch them and returned quickly with the required items. "Here's your stilus, Domine," she said.

"But we're a bit short on tabellae, so here's a scrap-pad instead. Will a ball-point pen do?"

"Excellent," he said, as Joy handed the articles to the reluctant scribe, and they quickly worked out a strategy for presenting their questions.

"I personally would feel inclined," said John Spry, looking at Peterson, "to adopt an approach like The Thirty-nine Steps here, don't you? After all, John Buchan was an Oxford man - Balliol, or somewhere, wasn't it?"

"Would that be a recommendation or a disadvantage?" Asked Peterson. "I'm a Christ Church man myself, and do most earnestly pray that no man may hold it against me!"

"Hmm: well -" John peered over the top of his glasses at Peterson, and having scrutinized him carefully, said:

"Yes, very well, then, we'll take the Thirty-nine Steps as a rough guide. Quick-fire questions to catch him off-guard, as in the film, should it prove necessary."

"How do we do that?" asked Joy.

"Via your good offices, madam. Give us a list of names of the characters essential to the plot, as you see it, and I'll fire the bullets as required'. Now, Joy, quickly - whom do you see in your crystal ball?"

"Cledwyn," she responded instantly. "I know you may not think him at all important, but I am very grieved at his most shocking death and the waste of a young life, and I am quite sure that it is somehow a significant factor in all this business."

"Very well; Cledwyn - no.1. Fire away, Joy, who next?"

"Elise Trondheim, of course - Erica, too; Jasper Philberd', Madge Spragnell, with her weird vanishing trick. Who else? I can't think - there were so many people involved!"

"That's enough to go on for the moment," said John. "So if the great man should ramble on and we don't feel we're getting anywhere, we'll fire names at him and see what that triggers. Then we'll ask questions about situations and evidence, and so on impromptu."

"Got it," said Brenda, "Any more instructions, O Domine?"

"Not for the moment," replied John. "We'll see how ye cookie crumbleth."

At this point 'D' returned to his position by the fireplace, his replenished glass at his elbow.

"And so, my lord, ladies and gentlemen, we resume. Now, where was I? Ah, yes; the girl, Antonov's tutor. According to the latest reports, it seems she is amnesic and in a catatonic state, and there appears to be no way of bringing her out of it. They have tried everything possible to get her to respond, but there is not even a glimmer of a reaction, as I am reliably informed. But if Antonov himself were to reappear, this might trigger a response from her memory, who knows? However, since he had vanished completely - to somewhere in the Eastern Bloc, we surmised - we found ourselves at an impasse, not knowing which way to turn. We had to get him back, but the question was, how to achieve this. Could we perhaps lure him back by plucking at his heart-strings? If he really loved the girl, he might even swallow his pride and take the risk."

'D' stopped to relight his cigar, and puffed on it meditatively. A perfect smoke-ring rose above his head like a halo, giving him an oddly saintly appearance for a few moments.

"And so," he proceeded, "we drafted a suitable tale, deciding that this was our story and we were sticking to it."

"What on earth does he mean?" Joy whispered into Mark's ear, as he sat next to her.

"Wait and see, Aunt," he murmured. 'D' continued, smiling an innocent little smile:

"In other words we let it be known that we were deeply distressed and penitent that Antonov had been so cavalierly treated, and we were very anxious for him to come back so that some amends could be made. In fact, we grovelled, but unhappily this achieved precisely nothing. We were up against a blank wall.

"Nevertheless, we waited, and some time later there came a breakthrough - of sorts. One of our men, who was off duty, went fishing down the river towards Medley Bridge, and saw a man walking up the towpath in the direction of the Trout at Wolvercote. He had a beard and wore glasses, and was rather shabbily dressed, but there was something about him which seemed familiar. He had a confident stride, with his head held high, and was certainly no tramp. And an hour or so later, the man returned, walking alone, as before, back toward Medley Bridge. Our man was pretty sure it was Antonov, although he was fairly well disguised. So a watch was kept for a day or two, but it yielded nothing. He might have been staying aboard one of the many boats moored along the river, but this was only conjecture. Nevertheless, we were sure that our man had had a sighting of Antonov, for this man is a particularly skilled observer, and rarely wrong in his judgment.

"This being so, we decided to set a special watch, in conjunction with our good friends, the boys-in-blue - not forgetting the girls, of course - an unforgivable omission!"

There was suppressed laughter at this from the police, who were quietly and discriminatingly tasting the pleasures of the fine Scotch whiskeys set out before them on the table.

"There were of course other aspects to the case, and leads to follow up. Strange things had been happening around North Oxford and, curiously enough, a great deal of the action seemed to revolve round you, Professor Hetherington. Could it be that you are a catalyst? After all, it is a known fact that such people exist, and perhaps you are one of them," he said, smiling benignly at Joy over the top of his glasses.

"And it is at this point that I have to thank one of our principal observers, Professor Pyper. He is now back home in Australia, after his sabbatical year here in Oxford, but it is thanks to him, almost exclusively, that we had a pretty clear idea of the pattern of events, and of what was going on in St. Julie's Road. As your near neighbour, Professor, and one who sat up late, he had the opportunity to note certain important events as they occurred, and his usefulness was enhanced by the fact that he was an ex-military man, as well as an eminent naturalist and trained observer. He would sit at his desk, working late into the small hours, and as his window directly overlooked your house and front garden and also the Trondheims', he was in a unique position to observe all comings and goings, so, as you can imagine, nothing much escaped him.

"And thus it was, that on the fateful night of Elise Trondheim's death, he observed something which completely exonerated you, Professor, from any shadow of suspicion of involvement in what happened. First of all, round about nine o'clock, when the party was in full swing at the Jolly Sailors, a figure appeared, walking quickly up St. Julie's Road in the direction of your house. As it drew nearer, Pyper noted that it was attired in your cape and fishing hat and, contrary to Miss Dacre's adamant assertion that the figure was undoubtedly yourself. (For the all-seeing eye, notwithstanding oncoming cataracts, had of course been keeping watch from the drawing-room window), Pyper was able to confirm that the body inside the cape was quite the wrong shape; for with all due respect, Professor, you are small and of rather plump build, whereas the figure observed was definitely a man, tall and slim, a fast mover with a long athletic stride; and in addition, clearly visible below the cape were long legs clad in jeans, and feet wearing trainers."

'D' looked at Joy with a little smile.

"Not exactly you, shall we say?"

When the laughter had subsided, he continued:

"The imposter, shall we call him, walked quickly past your house and turned into Elise Trondheim's gateway. Pyper noticed that no lights came on in the Trondheims' house so presumably, since he did not reappear immediately, the person had somehow gained access and did not wish to advertise his presence; however, about twenty minutes later he emerged and made off in haste up St. Julie's Road, away from the Jolly Sailors. He was now carrying something wrapped in newspaper - something flat and oblong in shape, quite large but apparently not heavy. He disappeared and was not seen to return, and that was all the information we gleaned about him at the time.

"Thereafter all was quiet and still, until you, Professor Hetherington returned home about eleven o'clock - minus cape and fishing hat - and went into the house. You came out again about ten minutes later with your blind cat on his lead, and walked him round the garden for a while, letting him climb up your lilac tree by the gate, then you went back inside, and your lights were off by midnight. Nothing more was observed that night.

"As I mentioned earlier, Inspector Vardon will come in on the case shortly to give you an overall survey of events. Now, where was I?"

John Spry seized the opportunity to ask a question:

"Cledwyn! How does he signify?"

"Who? Cledwyn? Well, very little, really. Unfortunately for him, he just got caught in the cross-fire; he was the dispensable errand-boy. Yes, indeed, very sad. We'll come to him later. Inspector Vardon, I know, will fill you in about Cledwyn's role."

Joy was aghast at this apparently cavalier dismissal of poor Cledwyn, as she saw it, and Peterson, observing her angry flush, murmured aside to Brenda:

"Rhode Island Red, methinks, and I find it rather endearing." Brenda smiled, but said nothing, keeping her thoughts to herself, and he continued:

"Poor Joy, she's always the mother-hen with her chickens. Isn't it touching?"

As he spoke, Brenda reflected on the different ways in which men and women perceive things, and she thought of her mother's hens, at home in Wiltshire.

"Did you know," she said, "that Rhode Island Reds lay white eggs?"

"No, really? What an extraordinary thing! Highly improbable, I would have thought."

Brenda giggled.

"I think I must be getting a bit tipsy," she remarked.

"Have another one," invited Patterson, teasing her with a wave of the wine bottle, and so she did, with somewhat unladylike gusto, downing a glass of Chateauneuf almost in one.

"Coffee?" asked Lord Westhoe, tactfully pouring out a sobering cup of strong black liquid for her.

"Thank you," she said, meekly accepting it as presented, plus a chocolate or two, and it was entirely successful as a remedy for a swimming head.

Meanwhile, John Spry was proceeding with his questions: "Elise and Erica Trondheim: what is their significance in the development of events?"

"Ah, yes," said 'D' slowly, "Two principal figures in the drama, to be sure. Well, to put it quite simply, poor Elise Trondheim had seen far too much with her telescope, so she had to be disposed of. And Erica, her wretched demented daughter, got dragged into the mainstream of events due to her dependence on the Courvoisier bottle and her anti-depressant tablets, a volatile and deadly combination, the fatal effect of which had been proved beyond all possible doubt." He paused, then continued:

"The Courvoisier was obtained for her in regular quantities by the man who killed her mother. It had to be procured secretly because the old lady was strictly tee-total and would not allow alcohol in the house."

He turned to Inspector Vardon, remarking: "The Inspector will shortly give you full details of how it all fits together and who the key figures were."

"Madge Spragnell, maybe?" queried John.

"Yes, indeed. Now, there's a name to conjure with! Madge most certainly co-stars with Antonov in this eerie drama. We took a particular interest in her because of her curious and secretive connection with him, so we kept a close watch on her over a long period of time and, by Heaven, were we not rewarded in the end! Now, here comes the really fascinating bit, for by a fortunate coincidence I myself knew General Spragnell very well. During my time at Oxford, the Horse and Jockey was always my favourite watering hole, and it was there that I met the General, who was indeed a charming old man. We became firm friends and he taught me so much, as we sat together at the bar in the evening. Tuesday and Thursday were our appointed days and it was most instructive and extremely interesting to learn so much about his first-hand experience of army life in the days of the Raj in India, and it was of great use to me, of course, in my study of military history. He gave me all sorts of information of great importance, beyond price, and authentic because he had personally witnessed the events he described - and that have gone unrecorded in history books.

"It was at the Horse and Jockey, too, that I met his wife, Madge, face to face, although when I first came up to Oxford I had seen her at the Freshers' Fair, doing her regal "thing" with us young greenhorns much in awe of this great doyenne of Oxford society. As a personality she was utterly overwhelming, so extremely kind and gracious, but even as a gauche young man, as I was, I sensed an insincerity in her as a person - the crystal did not ring true.

She was larger than life, but it was as though she was playing a theatrical role. Howbeit, she was the soul of hospitality, and I have fond memories of Madge's soirees at the Spragnell home in Plantation Road. She was a fanatical bridge-player - in fact, she taught me to play and to this day I too am a veritable bridge fanatic, so I do owe her a debt of gratitude for that. It is an excellent distraction from one's worries over work when the situation is tense and we're waiting for news.

"The General himself was a chess-man, and I spent many happy hours skirmishing with him over the chessboard in pitched battles conducted in absolute silence: a wonderful memory.

"So in view of all I have said, my personal knowledge of both of them, and the the rather charming history of their marriage - a stage-door romance of a dashing young officer and a glamorous chorus-girl - you can imagine my consternation when I realized that this must be destined to end in tragedy, following our discovery that Madge was involved in some dubious activity and had been observed in covert contact with Antonov. For me, these reports were especially disquieting because of my fears for the General, who was by this time quite frail and totally dependent on Madge in every way. Our observations showed that she had adopted a life-style well beyond her means, with lavish entertainments frequently laid on for all the "right people," so to speak.

She was also spending a great deal on clothes, including the very best from Botticelli's - nothing else was good enough for Madge! It appeared that she had her sights firmly set on the office of Lord Mayor. After all, she had all the right qualifications. She was on everything and into everything which might be useful to her for achieving her ambition, except for one thing she lacked. She needed money, and lots of it, in fact, in order to create the ambiance essential for this exalted position. The General was not a rich man and had little left, after a long life financing Madges' extravagances, so the situation was pretty desperate and corresponding measures were required."

"Needs must when the Devil drives," murmured John Spry in Brenda's ear, endeavouring to lighten the sombre mood of this account of cruelty and crime.

'D', however, had picked up the quiet comment, and remarked on its appropriateness:

"Yes, indeed, perfectly apt in this case, and the devil was, as it happened, conveniently at hand to drive at exactly the right moment."

He paused again, blowing another smoke ring, and watched it float in the air and slowly disperse, assuming as it did so shapes suggesting the contortions of a dying star.

"Antonov," he breathed, sotto voce, "Antonov."

John Spry was once more moved to comment facetiously and this time somewhat ineptly:

"Rupert, come home, and bring the pawn-tickets with you," quoting the well-known entry from the personal column of the first edition of The Times. This was too much for Brenda; she spluttered into her drink and collapsed in an uncontrollable fit of giggles, tears of mirth welling up in her eyes. 'D', however, did not appear to notice anything amiss, and went on with his account of events.

"Antonov wanted revenge. Oxford had effectively robbed him of his ultimate ambition: the attainment of academic distinction. Those irresponsible young wags had succeeded in making a complete fool of him, and it did not pay to make a fool of Antonov; someone would have to pay for it, and pay a high price. That price was to be the destruction of Oxford, and this is the ingenious way he set about it.

"He set up a small network of local people to act as his agents: Number one was Madge Spragnell, as his coordinator. Number two was Jasper Philberd, blackmailed because of his hidden sexual proclivities and his desperate need for more money to finish his ornithology thesis, and also to finance the extravagances involved in purchasing the transvestite paraphernalia of expensive women's clothes and wigs, and the best French perfume, not to mention the heavy expenditure required for his excursions into the night-life of Oxford, at all the very best venues. Now, a propos of Philberd, we are quite certain that Antonov did not know at the time that the former was in fact the villain of the piece, who had spiked his drink that momentous night at The Turf Tavern. A strange trick of fate, shall we say.

"Number three was Erica Trondheim, who as of course a tailor-made factotum: she was quite mad and a perfect tool for Antonov, soft as putty in his hands; it is also of interest to note that he and she, poles apart in every other aspect of personality and background, shared two dominant characteristics: they were both utterly ruthless and obsessive people, and nothing was allowed to stand in the way of achieving their ultimate aim, and this included people. Anyone who might obstruct them must be annihilated.

"And now, dear friends, at this point in our sombre tale I shall hand you over to Inspector Vardon for his summary of events from the police point of view which will, I am sure, fill in the details of this extraordinarily complex business."

So saying, 'D' then retired to Lord Westhoe's table and the Inspector took his place, standing by the open fire, which glowed orange as the pine logs crackled and sparked gently, while dying down. He smiled benignly at his audience and placed his whiskey glass carefully on the mantelpiece next to Joy's beloved Staffordshire figure of Robert Burns. Turning to address the company with a genial air contrasting with his formidable reputation, he congratulated the happy couple warmly on their engagement, and then got down to business, starting with thanks to his hostess for her hospitality:

"First of all, Professor Hetherington, on behalf of all my team and, I am sure, on behalf of all those gathered here, thank you for a wonderful evening, wonderful party fare, and great company with whom to enjoy it."

There were murmurs of assent to this.

"I observe that one of our principal witnesses is not here with us tonight, so I feel that I can say certain things I would not have been able to say, had she been here. That witness is Miss Dacre."

Some eyebrows rose at this statement and Inspector Vardon smiled.

"Yes, you may well be surprised, but in fact Miss Dacre had turned out to be of invaluable help to us in this investigation, as indeed has Professor Pyper. Their personal observations of the activities around St. Julie's Road have provided vital pieces of evidence assisting us to unravel the complex pattern of events. The sightings reported by these independent witnesses of all the comings and goings have helped us enormously. Believe me, Miss Dacre took a lot of persuading over the matter of the impersonation of yourself, Professor Hetherington. She was absolutely convinced that you were the person who went into Elise Trondheim's house that night and killed her; indeed, she was quite adamant about it, as some old ladies can be, insisting that it could only have been you wearing that tweed cape and hat, and there was no question about it.

It was only when we arranged a meeting between her and Professor Pyper that we made any headway at all over the matter, and got her to come round to the idea that in view of all the circumstantial evidence, it simply could not have been you. Professor Pyper managed to get her to change her mind, and I am happy to report that subsequently we had a positive flood of invaluable information from her about her observations from behind her lace curtains. In fact, she was quite pleased with my suggestion, made more or less in jest, but she took it quite seriously, that she should become an honorary special constable attached to the C.I.D. She loved it! So after that it was plain sailing and she cooperated fully with us throughout the whole investigation. Once we had got rid of that bee-in-her-bonnet, she was ours. But it's a strange thing how the human mind works, for she came up with some observations which she considered were quite unimportant, but which supplied us with vital clues towards understanding what exactly was going on during the time preceding Elise Trondheim's death.

"On her shopping trips around Oxford Miss Dacre noticed a good many things which have proved to be of great use to us in various areas of our work, but in this case we were particularly interested in her reports of sightings of Erica Trondheim and a young man, sitting together in a coffee-bar in New Inn Hall Street usually on market day. Miss Dacre's comment was that Erica seemed to be nagging the lad, wagging a finger at him and saying "Do this - do that" kind of thing, and he looked miserable and brow-beaten, so to speak - really nervous, and chewing his fingernails all the time, a sure sign of stress.

Miss Dacre knew him by sight and had seen him pedaling off on his bike down the Woodstock Road, but that was more or less all, and it was not enough for us to establish a link between the two, although Jasper Philberd - for that's who it turned out to be - evidently seemed to be under some kind of threat. Miss Dacre herself, however, attached no importance at all to this, saying that Erica was an argumentative nuisance at the best of times and, to quote her own words: "Erica could even pick a fight with my gatepost if she was in the mood, and she was a perfect pest best avoided in any case."

Inspector Vardon paused to take a sip of the Laphroaig, replacing his glass carefully alongside Robert Burns on the mantelpiece, then continued:

"So now we come to the connection between Philberd and Cledwyn. Our observer was Percy Chadlow, who usually worked until dusk on his allotment in the Trap grounds. He knew that Cledwyn often slept at night in the big shed by the bottom gate when he wasn't able to stay with his girlfriend, so Percy kept a fatherly eye on him and they would often have a brew-up in Percy's shed, as he had a little stove in there for making soup or boiling a kettle, etc., so they had a good friendship going on there, and it was company for Percy, who was a widower, quite recently bereaved.

"Well, one night, Percy packed up at dusk, but when he got to the Jolly Sailors for his usual pint of beer, he found he'd left his pipe and baccy in his shed back on the allotment, but he couldn't go back straight away, as he was involved in a game of cribbage, so it was well after dark when he went. He told us that a dense white river mist had risen, spreading over the ground but there was a bright full moon above, so even though he hadn't a torch with him, he could see everything clearly above the level of the mist, although it was up to his neck as he entered the allotment gate. However, he got to his shed and found his pipe and baccy, and came out to lock up. He stayed for a short while to light up and have a puff, as pipe-smokers do, and then became aware of voices not far away, up by the big shed at the meadow gate. He listened and soon identified one of the voices as

Cledwyn's. The other voice, that of an educated man, he did not recognize, but because the mist over the meadow deadened all extraneous noise, Percy could hear quite clearly what was being said. Cledwyn sounded scared and kept on repeating: "No, no! Honest, it wasn't my fault! On my grandmother's grave, it wasn't my fault, honest, it wasn't!" The other voice then spoke in a very menacing way, but lowered its tone, so Percy couldn't pick up much more, but he realized that Cledwyn was definitely being threatened, for at the end of the exchange the other fellow raised his voice a bit, saying: "You stupid fool! You bungling idiot! Get it right this time or your number's up - do you understand?"

"Fortunately Percy couldn't be seen by the pair, for his fruit bushes served as cover, so he stayed a bit longer and heard what seemed to be orders to pick something up, and "You be there or else!" He also got a good look at the other fellow, and could see that he was tall, with short dark hair and wearing glasses. After that, Percy slipped quietly away and went back to the Jolly Sailors. A bit later, he saw Cledwyn come into the public bar and hide away in a corner, "looking like a lost dog," as Percy put it. The girlfriend did not appear to collect him, so Percy concluded that Cledwyn would have to sleep rough that night, probably in the big shed. Feeling sorry for the lad, he bought him a bottle of Guinness, but all he said in return was "Thanks, Percy," and quite clearly he was scared out of his wits, and shaking like a leaf.

After the cribbage game was over, Percy went back to talk to Cledwyn, but he'd vanished and Tony, the barman, said he'd seen him making off in the direction of Aristotle Bridge, probably going to the allotments to sleep the night there;Tony, who never missed a trick, observed all from his vantage point behind the bar, looking out of a conveniently placed window.

"So that was that, and Percy went off home. He now says he'll feel guilty for the rest of his life for not going after Cledwyn that night, as he might have been able to help the poor lad in some way, even perhaps save him from the terrible disaster which followed not long afterwards.

"And now for the really interesting development. When Cledwyn was found dead in the well, the pace of events began to hot up. We have to thank our good friend Dick Ballard and his merry company of 'winos' and other vagrants for providing us with invaluable information on what actually happened. First of all, to cut a few corners, Cledwyn did not in fact drown in the well at all: he was already dead when he was unceremoniously dumped in it, feet first, having been, as it were, force-fed with vodka, best part of a bottle, it appears, administered by Philberd in the big shed; then he was given a lethal injection of heroin to finish him off - simple as that. Our witnesses to much of these proceedings were our wino friends who were camped out for the night on the dumps close by.

"Now Dick Ballard himself is absolutely drug-clear nowadays, and is just following his private pursuits - a little poaching and so on, but he also keeps an eye open for any unusual goings-on, and reports back to us if he sees anything suspicious. He's very useful as an informer, but that's not his only activity. His good deeds include looking after his wino friends; he'll go down to the dumps at night and knock-up a stew of some kind for these old lags. He's always got plenty of swag-in-the-bag, so they get rabbit stew at the very least, and sometimes even muntjac or pheasant, as available.

"Cledwyn was of course a good mate of theirs, and although he wasn't on the meths, he'd often join them for a bowl of stew, and would hand round his magic mushrooms. It was well known that he was the great authority on fungi, and made a kind of an income from selling then round the pubs. He knew exactly how much to take, and how to keep them fresh in small plastic bags. He had an extraordinary amount of knowledge about fungi in general and hallucinogens in particular. But he also had aspirations to live a respectable life, and had a little job at St. Clothilde's as a part-time kitchen porter. And he had a steady girlfriend, who was a cook at the same place. He wanted to make good, and get right away from the drop-out brigade.

"This, however, was not to be, for Antonov had spotted him and he became his victim, the errand-boy carrying out the master's orders. Since Antonov's lady-friend was a tutor at St. Clothilde he had dinner there quite often, and spied Cledwyn coming and going, and then saw him at the Jolly Sailors and heard about his reputation. So the pieces of his plan began to fall into place for implementing his scheme of vengeance for the devastating humiliation he had suffered over the exams."

"Inspector!" - Professor Peterson had raised his hand.

"Sir, may I put a question at this point?"

"Surely, Professor, fire away."

"Could you explain about the evidence you found to support the witnesses' statements concerning the manner of Cledwyn's death?"

"Ah, yes, of course. Sorry, Professor. This is what happened. On the night of Cledwyn's death the winos had made their way to the dumps to set up camp after dark, as usual. They settled down and got the fire going, and Geoff and Rodge, the two youngest of them, stole quietly into the allotments, nipping over the fence "to pick a few veg and things," as Geoff said, "and to a walkabout round the greenhouses," i.e. to nick tomatoes and cucumbers, or whatever else was available. Then they heard Cledwyn talking to somebody in the big shed with the door shut, so they tip-toed away quietly and went back to get the stew-pot going. About half an hour later, Dick and Hugo appeared with the meat and popped it into the stew-pot. Geoff was then sent over to the allotments again to get water from the tap behind the big shed, which was only a few yards from where they were encamped.

"Geoff was uneasy, and crept quietly round the side of the shed to find out if the other person had gone, but he was still there, talking in a persuasive way to Cledwyn, who sounded slurred in his speech and quite drunk; this was unusual for Cledwyn, who was not a big drinker, being a magic mushroom man. The other voice kept on saying: "Come on, Cledwyn, get it down, it's as smooth as mother's milk." Poor Cledwyn seemed to be trying to say no, but his words were all coming out backwards, as Geoff said. He went back to the camp, but said nothing to Dick Ballard about what he had heard.

"When the stew was ready, about midnight (Geoff knew it must be midnight because all the Oxford clocks chimed one after another for about five minutes) Dick told him to go and fetch Cledwyn if he was still over at the shed, but by now Geoff had really got the wind up, so he took Rodge with him, and told him to keep quiet, as there was "somebody else about with Cledwyn - a posh-soundin' bloke."

"They crept up to the back of the shed and listened for a minute or two. There were no voices to be heard but there was a sound of movement, inside the shed. They both stood stock still waiting quietly, careful to keep in the shadows, for the moon was bright. They heard the shed door creak open and saw the figure of a man emerging stealthily, carrying something heavy over his shoulder, something very heavy indeed. As he walked forward into the moonlight, going away from them in the direction of the meadow gate, they saw what he was carrying - and froze with horror, for it was unmistakably Cledwyn, slung over the man's shoulders, his head and shoulders swinging gently from side to side as the man walked. Cledwyn's long hair hung down over his face, hiding it from view, but Geoff said that he looked quite dead, and it was like watching a funeral procession passing on in complete silence.

"The man went a few paces towards the gate, then he stopped at the well, stood over it for a moment as though thinking, then took off the cover and carefully slid Cledwyn's body, feet first, into it. Geoff and Rodge saw him go down and as he did so, his head lolled backwards, his hair falling away to reveal his dead face, ghastly pale, the eyes wide open and - what really put the fear of God into them - looking straight at them with those dead eyes as he disappeared from view. As they both said: "like he was crying out for help."

"The man looked down the well for a moment or two, then put the cover on again, turned quietly away and made for the meadow gate. Suddenly, he stopped and turned back towards the shed, but unfortunately just then Rodge sneezed and with that the man ran off like a hare towards Aristotle Bridge and vanished.

Terrified though they were, Geoff and Rodge plucked up enough courage to go to the well, but they had no torch and the well was deep, so they listened for a while, calling Cledwyn's name quietly, but of course there was no answer and no sound came from the well, so they went back to the camp with the water carrier filled, and resolved to say nothing. They didn't want any trouble with the police, of course, and with Cledwyn being dead, there wasn't much point in saying anything, anyway, as far as they were concerned. They just told Dick Ballard that Cledwyn wasn't there, and no more was said.

CHAPTER XXII

'What is our life?'

'--- a play of passion -

Only we die in earnest

that's no jest.'

The First Set of Madrigals and Motets of 5 parts:

apt for both Viols and Voices Orlando Gibbons 1612

"However, things changed dramatically when the body was discovered by Percy Chadlow, and as Geoff said later:

"We had to come clean because you'd have found our dabs all over the place when your fingerprint man moved in."

"Good thinking!"

A ripple of laughter went round the room at this, as the fingerprint man himself was there in the midst of them, for he was one of Mrs B.'s four personally invited guests. He was in fact her nephew, and was accompanied by his wife.

"And now," continued the Inspector, "We come to the crunch. As soon as Cledwyn was found dead in the well, Geoff went straight to Dick Ballard and told him what he and Rodge had witnessed that night, so Dick came promptly down to us at St. Aldate's and told us the whole tale. We were well pleased to receive the information, for although Cledwyn was a drop-out and took drugs of some kind, but not normally heroin (according to the pathologist's report), we needed to know more before we rubber-stamped the record, so to speak.

Little did we know what we were about to uncover, for what had looked like an open-and-shut case turned out to be a really complex business. Our forensic team went out, and a thorough search was made of the big shed and the surrounding area, and it was not long before we struck gold.

"It's an indication of Philberd's disturbed state of mind that he was careless enough to leave behind obvious evidence of what he had done. It seems likely that Rodge's loud sneeze gave him a bit of a shock so he wasn't too keen to go back and check the place out. He would have been thrown into a panic about who had sneezed and whether they had seen or heard anything, and from that moment on he must have felt hunted, like a fox with the hounds almost on his tail.

"Now, what we found in the shed was: (a) the empty vodka bottle thrown down behind a straw bale, covered in fingerprints, some of them Cledwyn's, of course, but also a few of somebody else's, so that was of interest to us:(b) an empty syringe, which had been used to give Cledwyn the fatal overdose. This was found outside the shed in a heap of leaves, and the fingerprints on it were not Cledwyn's, but belonged to the other party, whose prints were also on the vodka bottle. However, the prints were not those of anyone on our records, so it seemed we were not dealing with a known criminal.

"The really interesting find was (c): a high-powered electric torch affair, with a red flashing beacon built in, and the fingerprints on it were Cledwyn's; we found this in what we might call his bedroom - a cosy arrangement if straw bales at the back of the shed, rather like a square igloo, well camouflaged by a barricade of rusty old farm machinery.

"And now we come to (d), the booty, or what was left of it! Cledwyn had made himself a kind of secret safe, right at the back of the bales, all very neatly constructed. Two bales deep, behind his bedroom, we found a storage space about three feet square. This had been carefully lined with industrial plastic' sheeting to make it completely watertight. In there were some heavy-duty blue plastic bags, all empty, folded neatly, and a couple of packs, about half a kilo each in weight, containing heroin and cocaine, both unopened. When we examined the empty bags, they were found to have traces of heroin and cocaine in them. Finally, we found the money, in an old tin box wrapped in waterproof plastic. This contained about five thousand pounds in used notes, in various currencies."

Here the Inspector paused yet again, tantalizingly, to relight his pipe. There was a tense silence, the lay members of the audience holding their breath in anticipation, while those in the know sat po-faced, giving away no hint of any foreknowledge of what was to be revealed.

"And so there it was - a major drugs stash, with Cledwyn as store manager, himself not a user yet, ironically, efficiently despatched by a massive overdose of heroin. The conclusive evidence for this was that there was only one needle puncture mark on the body, on the forearm, where the fatal injection had been given. There were no other signs that he had ever injected before. The unfortunate mushroom-man was the fall-guy in the criminal enterprise we were uncovering."

At each pause in the inspector's narration the silence in the room was profound, broken only once by the klaxon of a goods train slowly rumbling under the railway bridge and clanking over the level crossing at the Trap gate.

The question was, the inspector continued, "Who was bringing in this large quantity of top-quality drugs? We had to find out how it was coming in, and why Cledwyn was killed, and who did it? And once again we had a stroke of luck which helped a lot to provide the answers. One night, soon after Cledwyn's death, our men on car patrol observed a young woman collapsed at the foot of the large crucifix outside St. Julie's Church, at two in the morning. She was dead drunk, and was taken down to St. Aldate's police station. When she'd sobered up a bit, we ascertained that it was Linda, Cledwyn's girlfriend. We let her sleep it off in the cells first, then after a light breakfast she came clean and told us much of what we needed to know. The poor girl was in a state of real grief over Cledwyn and gave us her full cooperation. She had a steady job as cook at St. Clothilde's and a bed~sit in Banbury Road, where Cledwyn could stay the odd night without anyone noticing and have a shower and a general clean-up; the rest of the time he slept in the big shed on the allotments. Linda had somehow got him in at St. Clothilde's to do a little, part-time kitchen portering and had hoped to get him taken on full-time, so maybe eventually he could get a place to live with her and they could settle down together. They got on very well and he was quite prepared to make a go of it with Linda, given a chance.

"There was, however, a hitch in their plans. Cledwyn was haunted by spectres in the background. He told Linda that there were 'people on his back', and he didn't know how to get out of it; he said it was more than his life was worth to say who they were. But Linda didn't give up: she sat it out with him night after night at the Jolly Sailors, and she made some useful observations about his contacts as people came and went. She noticed a man who, we now conclude, was Antonov - well disguised. He was there from time to time, sitting alone, deeply absorbed in a crossword and speaking to nobody. Cledwyn, however, always became jumpy when he was around and, as Linda put it, 'kind of clammed up completely' when he saw the man. He simply froze and just sat quiet and hunched up, and didn't want to talk at all. This was uncharacteristic and Linda told us she was uneasy about it.

"However, Dick Ballard used to come and go from the bar and as Cledwyn and he were great mates, laughing and joking together and very much at ease with one another, Linda felt that Cledwyn was safe with Dick and would be 'O.K' when he was around. They talked men's stuff, like fishing and poaching, and Dick even brought his ferret into the bar sometimes, tucked up inside his trouser leg. There was a stifled guffaw of laughter at this from the uninformed, and Inspector Vardon reproved them:

"Gentlemen, you think I'm joking? All the best poachers carry their ferrets up their trouser legs!"

There was further spluttering into drinks at this, but Vardon went on, making no further comment on their ignorance of the method of transporting ferrets.

"Now, isn't it extraordinary," murmured Peterson in Brenda's ear, "how unknowledgeable some people are. I've always carried my ferret up my trouser leg. It's de rigueur!"

Brenda riposted smartly with a quick tweak of his ear. "Don't be provocative," she whispered, "Or I might ask to see it!"

Vardon continued, appearing unruffled by these audible asides:

"Linda told us that Cledwyn had said he was 'getting some dosh together', and that when he'd got enough he wanted them to make a clean break and go right away and set up home in Spain where they might be able to get a little bar or something and 'get away from the aggro'. Linda had reluctantly agreed to this plan, although she couldn't see how he could possibly get hold of money in any quantity while living like the crows on the allotments, apart from the few pennies he appeared to be making from selling his magic mushrooms and things. However, she could see he really meant it, so she stood by him and was saving up as much as possible herself to help the plan along a bit. Cledwyn had said that as soon as he had ten grand, which would indeed be 'soon', they must 'do a runner', so he begged Linda, please, not to let him down, otherwise he'd 'be for the knackers' and no mistake, so as soon as the 'big dosh' came through they'd have to vanish in 'double-quick time', so 'please, please be ready!'

"Now we come to the point where it all went wrong. Once again we have to thank our observers, the winos, for providing us with eye-witness accounts of what happened. They were, truly, the all-seeing eye, hidden away in the dumps. They were all Cledwyn's mates and they kept watch for him when asked. On that particular night Cledwyn had requested them to 'keep an eye', and we had the account of what happened from Geoff, but it was one-legged Willie, the unwitting culprit, who brought about the disaster that overtook Cledwyn as a result of what he did. Cledwyn had joined the winos on the dumps and had told them he was 'on a mission'. He had to 'keep watch' and the boys must cue him when it got to dusk in case he got drowsy. Geoff told us Cledwyn had an electric lamp with him. They all had a drink round the camp fire, and the stove was on in preparation for the meal later. Then, Geoff said, the mist began to come up over the meadow, and all was quiet. And it was at this point that Willie delivered what we might call the 'coup de grace' for Cledwyn. He had procured a bottle of poteen from an Irish friend who had a little still tucked away somewhere in the backwoods.

"Now, Cledwyn had told the boys to watch for a light in the sky, coming over from the direction of Wytham Woods, and to be sure to tell him as soon as they saw it. The wind was from the south-west and the weather was right - so watch! However Willie, being Willie, had other ideas, which at the end of the day were to cost Cledwyn his life. As a joke, as he confessed later, he did a Mickey Finn job with the poteen in their drinks - the whole bottle, it seems. And within a short time they were all drunk, except Willie, who had a high degree of alcohol tolerance, and soon they were all fast asleep; save Willie of course, who was still quietly imbibing. Suddenly, from nowhere, there was a tremendous roar and a bright light showed for a moment or two, like a Roman candle, in the dark sky above the thick white mist lying at ground level beyond the meadow gate.

Willie said he was scared out of his wits at what seemed like a bolt from the blue with no warning, shattering the quiet of the night. He kicked Cledwyn awake and the poor lad, drunk as he was, staggered to the meadow gate, clutching his big torch. Then Willie heard a splash and guessed that Cledwyn had fallen headfirst into the ditch by the gate, which was full of water after a couple of days' rain. Willie then passed out with the rest of them and, in his words, 'knew no more about it'.

"Linda supplied the connecting link at this point, when she mentioned that Cledwyn had arrived late one night at the Jolly Sailors, covered in mud from a fall and in a pitiful state, but when she tried to get out of him what had happened, he wouldn't say anything except that he slipped on the canal bank at Aristotle Bridge and had got a soaking. Linda knew he was lying but she took him home to her place and cleaned him up and he stayed the night with her. As he slept, she said, he had terrible nightmares and kept saying some foreign-sounding name, something like 'Anton! Anton! No, no! Sorry - sorry!' And with this little snippet of information things began to fall into place for us. This was Antonov, without a doubt.

"Geoff told us the rest. After Philberd had threatened Cledwyn, things went quiet for some days. Cledwyn followed his usual routine and came over to the camp for a bowl of stew and a noggin, but not too much, as Geoff noticed. Then he would go to the meadow gate and stay hidden away in the bushes, keeping watch after dark for whatever it was that he expected to happen. And one evening, Cledwyn told Geoff that conditions looked O.K. and maybe tonight would be the night, and would Geoff make sure he was 'on standby' at the big shed if Cledwyn 'tipped him the wink', and he would 'see him right, and the lads as well, over it'.

"Geoff said O.K. and stayed by the shed as twilight came on. He saw the mist come up over the meadow 'bang-on-cue', and he could just see Cledwyn hiding in the hawthorn bushes by the gate. Next, he saw a red flashing beacon-type thing come on where Cledwyn was hiding and then he saw him move quickly through the gate and go a little way on to the meadow, holding the flashing light high above his head. All that was to be seen now was the thick white mist rising rapidly and Cledwyn's head just above it, with his arm reaching up high in the air, holding aloft the red flashing beacon.

"Then suddenly Geoff spotted a light in the sky over towards Wytham Woods, just a short burst, like a Roman candle, away in the distance. 'All of a sudden there it was; an' then all of a sudden-there it was - gawn!' as Geoff said.

The inspector went on:"He couldn't see any more, for the trees blocked the view, so he stayed where he was, watching and listening. All was a 'deathless 'ush', as he put it, with no noise but the rumbling of a goods train somewhere down the line towards Oxford station, while the mist deadened other sounds. Time passed and nothing happened, so Geoff began to think he might just go back to the camp and join the lads, but all of a sudden there was a tremendous roaring sound and a bright light appeared somewhere above and just beyond the trees, a short distance away on the meadow.

"Then he saw what it was. An air balloon, brilliantly illuminated in a moment by its gas-burner firing up as it made a rapid ascent. Next, he heard Cledwyn calling him urgently:

"'Geoff, Geoff! Over here - come quick!'

"Geoff went forward as bidden, but the mist had come on real thick', as he put it, so he just stood stock-still for a bit, then he heard Cledwyn callout again.

"'Where are you?' Geoff called back, 'Put that light on!' A pinkish glow appeared in the mist as the beacon came on a short distance away. Geoff advanced towards the light and came across Cledwyn, who was crouching down by some heavy plastic bags, all tightly wrapped, as he described them.He asked Cledwyn what they were.

"'Ballast:' Cledwyn told him,'from the air balloon.'

"The mist had by now become a dense white fog, and Cledwyn said they must get the bags to the big shed in 'double-quick time'. The big question, however, was how to get there? They were disorientated in the fog. Cledwyn was panicking, pleading: 'Help me, Geoff, or I'm a dead duck. I'll see you right', etc, so Geoff solved the problem by giving his own personal code-signal to the lads on the dumps. He cupped his hands together and did a triple burst of barn owl hoots. He told Cledwyn that Willie would answer with the same call, which would give them the direction where the camp lay. There was no answering call so Geoff tried again; again there was no response and he thought they must all be flat-out with drink.

"By this time Cledwyn was beside himself, shivering and whimpering like a half-drowned Jack Russell. Geoff tried once more, as loud as he could, realizing that the lads must be dead to the world, and knowing that he and Cledwyn might have to stay put till the fog lifted, which could mean all night, and there they would be, like a pair of sitting ducks, for all to see, at first light, maybe, with all this mysterious heavy stuff, marooned in the middle of the meadow! The stuff must be something red hot, for Cledwyn to be panicking like that. It wasn't a happy prospect, and the last thing Geoff wanted was any truck with the police, so in desperation he called again - and the miracle happened, as he put it: he got an answering call, but it was from a fair distance away, not close to, as it should have been.

"Geoff recognized the reply; it was Dick Ballard's own bird-call, a double burst of the barn owl hoot, repeated twice in rapid succession.

"'That's Dick coming over the railway bridge', he said. So with that they knew the way to the bottom gate. He called again and Dick replied, coming nearer along the path by the old stables to the allotments, directly in line with Geoff and Cledwyn, so they dragged the bags that way and luckily came to the gate instead of ending up in the big ditch alongside. Geoff helped with getting the bags to the shed and Cledwyn told him to 'scarper quick' back to the dumps before Dick got there, and to say nothing.

"'Keep it 'stumm", he begged, 'and I'll see you right, Geoff. Best mates, honest!' in his own words.

"Geoff did as he was told and went back to the camp to settle down with the others for the night.

"Cledwyn did not join them as he usually did, but nothing was said, so the secret remained intact, and Dick made no comment about the bird-call business. Geoff kept an eye on the situation and noted that Cledwyn was not seen at all for a while at the camp, but he did see him coming and going from the allotment shed during the night, and obviously wanting to escape notice. However, he kept his word to Geoff; he hadn't forgotten, and a few days later, when Geoff got to the camp at night, he found that Cledwyn had left him 'a fair bit of strong 'baccy'; this, we conclude, probably meant hash, so no doubt Geoff was well pleased.

"That, however, was the last he was to get out of the enterprise, for only a short time later Geoff and Rodge were witnesses of Philberd's disposal of Cledwyn in the well, and that was the end of the poor goose that laid the golden eggs."

As Vardon reached this point, all the lights went out. Fortunately, the candelabrum on the dining table, which had been lit as a centrepiece for the party spread, now came into its own as the only present source of light, shedding a begin glow of warmth round the room.

"Have the lights fused, Mark?" asked Joy.

Mark peered through the curtains.

"No, power cut. All is darkness without," said he, making a school-boyish quote.

Mrs Badger made her way, with the aid of Mr. Badger's cigarette lighter, to the kitchen and returned with four candles, and Mark went upstairs to the landing and brought down the antique brass oil lamp which stood on the window ledge; it was, luckily, full and ready for use. He lit it with his lighter, and returned to the dining-room looking like a character from a romantic film as he came through the door in a pool of light.

"Clark Gable Mark Two," said Brenda.

"Oh, yes, indeed, 'Gone with the Wind'," returned Peterson. There was just a hint of envy in his voice, thought Brenda, smiling to herself.

The soft warm light shed by the candelabrum encouraged a feeling of cosy intimacy among the company, dispelling the sombre impression created by Vardon's narrative, and causing Peterson to remark, as he held up his glass to the light:

"Chateauneuf should only be imbibed by candlelight; any other way is, I consider, almost to commit sacrilege!"

Inspector Vardon, however, unperturbed by the sudden blackout or the irrelevant asides, continued his account.

"We come now to a key point in this investigation: the use made of the air balloon. It seems that Antonov had always been a fanatical balloonist, his ambition being to do a round-the-world flight to get himself into the record-books. He took part in a number of air balloon events round the shires while he was here in Oxford, and James Sadler, whose air balloon ascent at Oxford in 1810 caused such a stir, was a great hero of his."

"Ooh!" whispered Joy to Brenda, "Where's it gone?"

"What?" Brenda whispered back, mystified.

"That print of the event, you know, 'The Ascent of James

Sadler at Oxford, 1810'. It used to be stuck up behind the Westhoes' upstairs-loo door, but not long ago it suddenly disappeared."

"Ah, yes, of course, now I remember." Brenda pondered for a moment. "Livia said it was not suitable for the gentlemen to be ascending in front of the ladies, so she took it down and put up something else she thought was more seemly - that lovely illuminated manuscript print of the Heilige Hildegarde von Bingen in contemplation with all the bees and butterflies whizzing round her head as she blesses them. Don't you think it's charming?"

"Oh, yes, indeed - but then, James Sadler was much more fun to look at in such brief moments of contemplation that one is able to snatch for oneself," murmured Joy regretfully, "Yet another small pleasure denied, but perhaps the design is to lift our thoughts to higher things?"

This was unheard by the inspector, who proceeded with his narrative:

"As already remarked, Antonov was full of resentment and anger at being made to look such a fool by those undergraduates, and he worked out a plan of campaign to blow Oxford apart, skillfully stock-piling his weapons for the purpose, and those weapons were heroin and cocaine, with ample supplies of both. It appears to have been easy for him, through his many contacts, to acquire the drugs and to get them into the country without difficulty, and they were intended to provide the student population of Oxford with good cheap top-class supplies. Cledwyn was the errand boy and Madge Spragnell the sophisticated co-ordinator, well placed as a prominent figure in respectable Oxford society.

Jasper Philberd was Madge's second lieutenant, with Erica Trondheim in the background, cracking the whip over him, driving him to distraction by blackmailing him over his sexual propensities, and commanding him to get rid of her mother, whom she hated; it seems she was desperate to get the house and whatever the old lady had in the way of assets. In fact, it appears that the estate is worth a great deal and Erica was the sole legatee.

"However, when it came to the crunch, Cledwyn and Philberd proved to be the weak links in Antonov's operational chain, and this weakness in the end brought us extremely good luck and led us to the final disclosure at the fair. But that was still to come, and we must go back to the air balloon, which was a typical stunt for a showman like Antonov, a dare-devil scheme designed to show off his audacity and skill, and both would be essential to attempt a huge drop of narcotics on Port Meadow in the dark with the mist rising, a feat which his hero James Sadler would certainly not have contemplated, but we conclude that the disgrace he had suffered had warped his mind and spurred him on to carry out his scheme and drop his deadly ballast on the city he hated. And it worked - he did it!"

"He who dares, wins, perhaps," murmured Peterson to Brenda, with a seductive little wink.

She slapped him sharply on the thigh. "Stop it!" she whispered, "I told you what I'll do - and, moreover, I shall show no mercy!"

"Ooh, I say! Is that a promise?" he asked eagerly, with just the slightest suggestion of a leer.

"Next," continued Vardon, "came the question of storage and distribution of the drugs. It seems that Cledwyn did his job quite well, setting up his network of outlets, with Philberd, Antonov's appointed watchdog, on hand at all times to make sure he got it right, since he was not the most reliable of aides, although in other respects he was the ideal accomplice.

And here Madge Spragnell comes into the frame as overall coordinator and, incidentally, a regular customer. Antonov himself was not, indeed, in the business as a drugs baron, to cream off the profits. He simply wanted to get his own back at Oxford for what it had done to him, as he saw it, so a generous share of these profits went to the troops and they made good money out of the enterprise, but they had to be super-efficient and operate with military precision; any incompetence would be ruthlessly punished - by the firing squad!

"When Cledwyn had got his part of the operation going nicely and things were ticking over smoothly after the first serious hiccup over the aerial drugs delivery, distribution of the narcotics began, quietly and efficiently, round the university. Then Antonov gave the order to eliminate Cledwyn. Philberd was to be the executioner, since Cledwyn had outlived his usefulness and as an unstable character he had to be removed, in case he blew the gaff; that in effect he did when he was so foolish as to warn you, Professor Hetherington, when you unconsciously got in the way, going to and from your allotment."

Sitting quietly at the back of the room, Joy was moved to tears, overwhelmed with sadness at the recollection of Cledwyn pleading with her to keep away from the allotments that evening.

The inspector went on: "Philberd, who was already driven half out of his mind by the pressure brought to bear on him by Erica Trondheim, was a rat in a trap, with no way out. He had to do it, so the deed was done, and Cledwyn's pipe-dream of taking his cut and escaping with Linda never came true. Incidentally, the poor girl is pregnant, which makes it all the worse for her."

"Oh, how sad," said Joy quietly to those around her, "We must raise some money for her. What about an "Elizabethan Day" event at St. James's? That should bring in something to help. Poor little lass, what a terribly hard time for her, with a baby and no father! Tragic!"

All were agreed. Excellent idea! They would all participate.

Vardon resumed: "So the situation was now as follows: Antonov is pulling the strings of his puppets from a discreet distance, playing the "Invisible Man," while Madge Spragnell is in control on the spot and Philberd is the new errand-boy. After his death, when we carried out the search of his room and the garden shed, we found all the evidence, i.e., the drugs, neatly stashed away, much as Cledwyn had them, in Mrs Graystone's disused shed along the party-wall at the bottom of the garden, between hers and the Trondheims'. And finally, more or less by accident, we found the conclusive evidence in his room that Philberd had in fact killed the old lady.

"First, we found the trainers and noted that they matched exactly the footprint on the newspaper in Elise Trondheim's house; the next discovery was the Trondheims' telescope, which was on Philberd's desk in front of the window overlooking the back garden. Then we found Professor Hetherington's washing, that had been stolen from her washing line; the towels all had Hetherington name-tags on them, and they and the underwear had all been properly laundered and ironed and neatly folded in his chest of drawers. It was fairly obvious that he had been wearing these things on his transvestite excursions, for an underslip, bra and pantees were draped over the back of a chair in front of the dressing-table. We did not, unfortunately, find the cape, the tweed hat or the mask. We assumed that at some stage he had prudently destroyed them.

"The most amazing find turned out to be two unlisted French paintings on his bedroom wall, a particularly fine Matisse and a Chagall, both authentic, signed by the artists, and worth a fortune. And here I am happy to acknowledge a great debt of gratitude we owe to Mrs Badger, who came up trumps over this and unravelled the mystery for us, as we could not understand how Philberd could possibly have come by these two hitherto unknown and priceless works, signed and in perfect condition. They did not figure on any list of stolen paintings, and we were extremely puzzled - that is, until Mrs Badger gave us the first clue."

Mrs Badger, sitting with her arms folded across her bosom, smiled graciously; Mr. Badger, seated beside her, remained impassive, puffing gently on his pipe.

Vardon continued: "Mrs Badger remembered that the old lady had told her some years ago that she was very worried about her beloved paintings. She had proudly shown them to Mrs Badger, and told her the tale of how she had come by them, when she lived in Paris many years before. At that time she had known a number of famous writers and painters, and she had bought a Matisse and a Chagall, which in that period before the art market reached its present soaring price levels, were within her means. Mrs Badger identified the pictures for us at once when she was shown them.

"Now, as to how these paintings came to be found in Jasper Philberd's room. It appears that Erica Trondheim hated French paintings of that period, describing herself as a "purist" with extreme eclectic tastes, and the old lady was afraid that Erica might damage or even destroy the pictures in one of her violent paroxysm of rage. In order to protect her treasures she got Mrs Badger to arrange for them to be hidden away in the attic, and Mrs Badger got Frank, the odd-job man, to make a hiding-place for them, and a very ingenious one it was - I couldn't have thought of a better one myself."

There was some laughter at this, which relieved the tension experienced by the uninformed section of the audience on hearing such an unexpected series of revelations.

"Mrs Badger," said Vardon, "showed us the secret hiding-place which was very neat indeed. The old butler's lift is still in place and goes all the way up from the kitchen in the basement to the attic; it is in perfect working order, and at the very top, above the pulley housing, there is a fair space between it and the rafters, just the right size to slide in the two paintings. Frank had made the space into a kind of secret cupboard with a sliding panel at the front which looked as though it was merely the top bit of the pulley housing. We assume that since Philberd's fingerprints were all over this cupboard and there were none on anything else, the old lady must have told him where the paintings were hidden. He hadn't needed to search for them so there must have been a previous encounter between them before she died at the hands of the masked intruder, and we had to do a bit of guesswork about what happened, as there was no hard evidence.

"However, we have a young lady in our team who is very useful to us when we arrive at an impasse, so to speak. Some would call it 'reading the tea-leaves', and even talk about Madame Arcati, but when we're stuck for an answer to a problem like this one, we bring her in and, sure enough, she's usually right. It may be women's intuition, but it seems to work all right."

There were some smiles at this statement, and Peterson was moved to remark: "That old black magic" in a whisper to Brenda, who poked him in the ribs in response.

"Ouch!" he said, as before, but still appeared unruffled and even pleased at having evoked it.

"According to our young lady," Vardon proceeded, "who is with us, incidentally, tonight, what probably happened was as follows: Philberd would have gone up to the attic and found the paintings, being already aware of where to look, a then have come downstairs and left the paintings on the landing.

"Next he had to kill the old lady, and the idea probably crossed his mind that he might 'do a runner' with his booty and make good his escape. But he must have realized that this was impossible: he knew that no matter where he ran, Antonov would get him in the end. Antonov was ruthless and there was no escape - so he had to kill Elise Trondheim.

"When we investigated how it was done, we found no discarded weapon, such as a knife or heavy instrument, so we assume that he chose - quite literally - the soft option, i.e., suffocation. After all, his victim was a lame old lady and it would be the simplest matter just to put a cushion or a pillow over her face to stifle screams and stop the breath.

"So this is how we visualize the possible sequence of events. Philberd creeps quietly into the bedroom, wearing his fearsome mask, picks up a cushion or a pillow, advances slowly from behind her, and comes round in front of her chair. She looks up and is seized with terror at this horrifying ghoul holding a cushion in both hands, raised to bring down on her face. She tries to scream but no sound comes out and she dies instantly of shock. Philberd realizes that she is dead, puts the cushion back in its place and turns to leave. Then he sees the antique brass telescope on the desk and on an impulse he picks it up and departs quickly, taking with him the paintings, carefully wrapped up to avoid detection. He had obeyed Erica's instructions to the letter: he had found the paintings, and Elise Trondheim was dead."

"Oh, my god!" said Petronella out loud, "I can't bear it! How utterly ghastly!"

Vardon paused for a moment and there was silence in the room as the company tried to come to terms with this macabre story, contrasting strongly with the cosy setting of the convivial scene lit by the warm glow of the candles.

"Some explanation is due here," continued the inspector, "of a number of instances of unhinged behaviour. First there is the matter of Mrs Graystone's cat, locked in the Trondheims' disused shed at the bottom of the garden, and its collar thrown into the bushes on the dumps. We have a certain amount of evidence regarding this and other events observed by witnesses. The first of these was the occasion when one-legged Willie and the winos saw Philberd from their camp in the dumps in the act of throwing the cape, tweed hat and mask into the bushes.

Sometime later, they observed Erica Trondheim stealthily approaching across the dumps, and watched her stop at the very spot where the clothing had been dumped and hang a green cat's collar on a branch just above it. This seemed to us at first to be a rather curious proceeding and we were puzzled as to her motive, although we assumed that Philberd must have told her where he had disposed of the garments."

At this point a loud crash was heard from the kitchen, and Mrs Badger exclaimed: "Oh, Chroist Church bells!"

Joy departed with all haste to investigate, preceded by Mrs Badger stomping on ahead.

"'Tis that danged fox o'yourn, that Jenny - the little vixen! She's got in through the kitchen winder an' made a roight an' proper mess, she 'as! She's 'ad the end o' that there salmon mousse - an' broke the dish an' all, she 'as!"

Joy said soothingly: "Never mind, at least they enjoyed the mousse, and the dish was nothing special. It was just that Jenny wanted to join the party. It shows what good taste she has."

Mrs Badger, po-faced, said nothing, responding only with a disapproving sniff; she'd had her eye on that salmon mousse to take home for Mr. Badger's future enjoyment. Beginning the salvage operation, she announced firmly that she must 'take her 'ubby 'ome, "as it was way past 'is beddy-byes," and she hoped that all would be "ship-shape an' Bristol-fashion come the morn" when she returned. So saying, she left quietly with Mr. Badger by the back door, muttering a few imprecations at Jenny and her ilk, invisible at the bottom of the garden save for a row of fluorescent green eyes down by the shed, watching from a discreet distance and missing nothing.

Meanwhile Vardon resumed, after a pause for thought during the distraction caused by the disappearance of Joy and Mrs Badger.

"Now then, where was I? Ah, yes, where is she?" He looked round the room, still only dimly lit by candle-light. "Yes, there you are, Miss Petronella! Remember when you were shot at on your way to the allotments?"

Petronella nodded miserably, remembering it only too well. She could recall, still, the high-pitched scream of the bullet as it passed so close to her cheek - it might have been the kiss of death!

"Well, we may be able to shed some light on this. When we searched Philberd's room, we found something very interesting: a fascinating collection of military souvenirs such as a Royal Artillery cap badge, a bayonet and some medals dating from the First World War, which presumably belonged to his grandfather; there were also a few antique firing-pieces, including a tiny bronze copy of an Elizabethan ship's cannon in perfect firing order, and we have been told that this piece was fashioned in the seventeenth century, so it's a rare piece indeed. Another antique weapon, equally rare, was a double-barreled pocket pistol dating from about 1710. The maker's mark was stamped on the barrel, and it even had three notches cut into the wooden stock, a grim record that the owner had killed three opponents."

Peterson was ready with his whispered comment:

"So three more highwaymen bit the dust. I call that a most unsporting practice on the part of those gentlemen to carry pocket pistols hidden about their person - cruelty to highwaymen, who were after all the gentlemen of the road!"

Brenda responded with a disapproving frown, while Vardon continued, oblivious of the comment.

"Philberd also had on his desk a fine reproduction in miniature of a Royal Artillery carriage gun, dating from Victorian times. But that was not the last of our finds. Our sniffer dogs were eagerly investigating the floorboards and demanding to get underneath so we took them up and discovered what was hidden there: a very nice well-kept Royal Enfield .303 rifle, dating from the Second World War and complete with a case of cartridges. A couple of these were missing and there was clear evidence that the gun had been fired fairly recently. It was also covered with Philberd's fingerprints. Therefore, Petronella, we can only assume that this distraught young man shot at you that day by the dumps in mistake for Professor Hetherington, whom he blamed for the business of the cat. We have of course interviewed the winos and we are quite sure that they know who did it, but inevitably they say they 'know nothin''. "However, we do have a little consolation prize for you after your bad experience, and here it is, with our compliments."

A young policewoman handed him a large bulky black plastic bag.

"What on earth is it?" asked Petronella, as she went to collect it.

The inspector smiled, saying nothing.

Petronella put it on the table and opened it cautiously. The bag fell away, to reveal its contents; and there, sitting mournfully with his head lolling to one side, was the giant teddy-bear from the fair!

"We are sorry," said Vardon, "that he's only stuffed with newspaper at the moment and his head's only held on with safety-pins, but we're sure you'll find someone to restore him to good health with proper stuffing, and a little tender loving care!"

Petronella was speechless, quite overcome with emotion at being reunited at last with her very own much missed teddy-bear. There was enthusiastic clapping from the company, and Peterson shouted "Hoorah!" and called for "three cheers for the cop-shop!"

When the cheers had subsided, Vardon took up his story again with due seriousness, gazing thoughtfully at the bear tightly clutched to Petronella's bosom, that no longer looked orphaned and bereft.

"And now we come to the bizarre events at the fair, starting at the finish, Irish fashion; Madge Spragnell had it seems, been determined to double-cross Antonov - the kitchen was getting too hot for her - but she should have realized that it would never pay to try it on with him. Nobody - but nobody - double-crossed Antonov. "Nevertheless, in desperation, when matters came to a climax she tried to do it. Antonov had already arranged for someone else to take over the operation from Philberd, who was now surplus to requirements; it was time for him to be eliminated, especially in view of his increasingly erratic behaviour, due to mounting pressure brought to bear on him by Erica in her obsessive madness. Meanwhile, the drugs distribution as a whole was going very well, splendidly, in fact, and the insidious cancer of cheap narcotics was beginning to spread through the city.

"So Antonov gave Madge Spragnell her orders about how the change of personnel was to be effected, against the theatrical back-drop of St. Giles' Fair. The plan was designed for the last night of the fair, when the St. James' College consort of singers were performing their madrigals and the stalls were set out to tempt people to buy, all proceeds to go to various Oxford charities, and the raffle tickets would be drawn and the splendid prizes distributed, ranging from the giant teddy-bear here present, to a variety of stuffed toys, champagne, wines and spirits, chocolates etc.

"We know that it was Antonov's intention to have a 'right party', as they say hereabouts, and make a complete fool of Oxford and all it stands for. Unfortunately for him, however, we were in on the action - in force and suitably disguised, of course. Two of our policewomen were up front in the middle of it all, posing as junkies, after some excellent work by our make-up department, nasty bruises and so on, and they still have needle marks on their arms to prove it. Ladies, would you reveal yourselves, please?"

All heads turned to look at the two young women wearing elegant dresses from Botticelli's who stood up together and smiled shyly. Joy looked closely at them and realized that they were Mrs Badger's nieces. How extraordinary, she thought, so that was why Mrs Badger had been so cagey!

"These young policewomen risked their lives in carrying out this extremely dangerous duty," said Vardon. "There can be nothing but the highest praise for their courage and skill in convincing Antonov that they were bona fide junkies. We used the classic ruse of pretending that they were hugely in debt over paying for drugs (via a Soho contact connected with the Triads), and they 'wanted out' from the London scene. Antonov was convinced: he fell for it, hook, line and sinker, and they soon became two of his best agents, excellent in every way and bringing in fresh resources for the great drugs distribution scheme. We set the sprat to catch the mackerel, so to speak."

"And such delectable little sprats, to be sure!" Murmured Peterson, licking his lips and getting another sharp poke in the ribs for impertinence, from Brenda.

"Our two policewomen had gathered that the replacement for Philberd was to be at the event on the last night of the fair and would be identified in the following way: he/she would come forward to claim the first prize in the raffle, i.e., the giant teddy-bear. This "fix" was to be engineered by Madge Spragnell, since Antonov himself, he said, would by then have left the country, leaving the whole operation to tick over in the hands of Madge and the new co-ordinator.

"So we were well clued up to go to the fair, and what a night we had, to be sure! All the fun of the fair, with a vengeance!" "'Vengeance is mine, I will recompense' saith the Lord," whispered Peterson in Brenda's ear. She gave him another hearty thump where it hurt. He belched loudly and hiccuped several times in succession. "Serve you right," she murmured, "You silly old soak!"

This exchange passed unnoticed as Vardon proceeded: "We were, then, all assembled at our posts, ready for action, and as you all witnessed the events, I needn't dwell on them, except to relate what followed on. We realized that things were going seriously wrong from Antonov's perspective, when we spotted him at the back of the crowd. There could only be one reason why he was there, after he had declared his intention to be out of the country before the fair took place: he must suspect a double-cross, and sure enough, he was right. He saw it all for himself first hand, from his vantage-point at the back of the crowd. And when, instead of the new co-ordinator, Philberd went forward with the first prize-winning ticket, then the balloon went up."

"Ah, there now, you see! James Sadler ascends yet again," announced Peterson, with a further hiccup.

Vardon smiled a wry smile.

"Well, when Philberd stepped forward to claim the teddy-bear, the whole operation became a proper dog's breakfast. In an instant we lost sight of everyone: the incoming new co-ordinator, Madge Spragnell, Philberd, and Antonov himself. It was a complete fiasco. We knew that there was no point in pursuing Antonov, since he had many great admirers among the flying fraternity and so could be up and away within the hour from some private landing-strip somewhere over the downs, where there are plenty of them. So we did our best to catch up with Madge Spragnell, but to no avail, for she eluded us completely.

Nevertheless, we do know now how in fact she got away. Her car was missing, and this was our first vital clue, but for a couple of days nothing came through. Then we had a stroke of luck. We had a 'phone call from the Barley Mow at Clifton Hampden, telling us that some anglers had spotted a car in the river at low water, some way downstream. When we went down to retrieve it, we saw it was obvious that it had swerved off the road at speed and gone down the bank so that it was submerged a little way out in the deeper water. The ignition was still in the switched-on position and the keys in situ - but there was no body in the car! However, it was noted that the driver's window was open, so we did a thorough search down river, but found nothing. We had identified the car as hers, but of Madge Spragnell there was no trace."

CHAPTER XXIII

'Come away, sweet love, and play thee...

Songs of sundrie kindes'

Madrigals for five voices

Thomas Greaves 1604

As Vardon paused, the doorbell rang.

"Who can that be?" said Joy, and went to find out.

"Miss Dacre - what a lovely surprise! Do come in."

Miss Dacre was then heard to explain that the P.C.C. meeting had finished earlier than expected, so her nephew had kindly brought her to the party.

While Joy settled her comfortably with the police contingent at their table and provided her with Tio Pepe and smoked salmon sandwiches, there was time for an exchange of ideas and opinions.

"That business of the Big Wheel," said Mark.

"There's a sad piece of news to tell you about that marvellous machine. The owners are selling it, so, alas! we shall see it no more. Apparently it's going to America - actually to Atlanta, where G.W.G. Ferris, the engineer who designed it, came from, so it's going home. It's a sad loss to us, but a big gain for our cousins over the water, who know a treasure when they see one."

"Oh dear!" exclaimed Joy, "I do hope they don't take it into their heads to sell off our beloved Gallopin' 'Orses! What should we do 'without them? I couldn't possibly survive the academic year without my annual canter on my trusty steed!"

"And what about my bumper-cars!" came from Lord Westhoe, who declared: "I simply must have my annual car-crash with our grandsons. It's the only thing that tones me up for the toils of the treadmill! A mini-Monte Carlo Rally to nerve one for the coming term!"

At this, 'D' joined in. "Yes, indeed, I feel the same about my yearly ride in the ghost-train. It's rather a busman's holiday, though, to be honest - horrid surprises confronting one out of the blue, skeletons in every cupboard, not to mention severed heads, dungeons, and 'there-be dragons' lurking in dark corners. Good hardening-off for going back to work at the office!"

"Ah!" said John Spry, "I'm a spectator sport man, myself, so I go for the Wall of Death Ride every time. Great fun - and makes me jolly glad I don't ride a motor-bike!"

Lady Westhoe voted firmly for the gallopin' 'orses, as indeed did the other ladies present, except, surprisingly, for Caroline Grieve, who announced:

"I really couldn't bear to miss my annual visit to the shooting gallery to shoot down all those dear little ducks. It's such fun!"

"You bloodthirsty little besom!" Admonished Peterson, affecting shock and amazement. "And you a dedicated and fully paid-up member of the R.S.P.B.. Disgraceful, Madam!"

Caroline looked crestfallen.

"If I may offer a plea in mitigation," she ventured timidly, "My grandfather was a gamekeeper on the Blenheim Estate and he taught me to shoot. I loved it and he used to take me with him sometimes to the shoot, so I have some wonderful memories!"

"Worser and worserer! Wonderful memories of cruelty to birds." Peterson raised a critical eyebrow.

"But, Professor, didn't I observe you eating some pate earlier this evening, which you appeared to relish," remarked Caroline, driven to riposte.

"Very well, I concede," said Peterson, "Pax - have some Chateauneuf."

Inspector Vardon then proceeded with his narrative:

"Shortly, after finding the car, we had another stroke of luck; the Gods smiled down on us yet again!"

We had a phone call from the Hampshire police who informed us that they had picked up a young man for dealing heroin round Christchurch. He said he had been travelling with a group of hippy types and they had all been to St. Giles' Fair in Oxford, and a woman in some kind of trouble had joined them, begging for help to get away incognito. It seems that she had paid them handsomely with a quantity of drugs, so they hid her away in their convoy and also got rid of her car by driving it into the river somewhere south or Oxford, making it look as though she had probably drowned. She travelled with them as far as Christchurch, and the last they saw of her was when she was down at the harbour in the evening, talking to a man with a sea-going yacht at the jetty. After that, no more was seen of her. Now, when this young man was arrested, he was carrying this."

The inspector then produced a black plastic bag and took a teddy-bear out of it.

"I don't believe it - yet another cuddly teddy-bear!" murmured Peterson.

Cuddly, however, was not the right word to describe this bear. It was a very poor specimen, unhappy-looking and emaciated of medium size but extremely thin, with floppy limbs and, as Peterson later remarked, it had evidently not even seen a pot of honey for many a year. Cruelty to a teddy-bear!

"This," said Vardon, holding up the teddy-bear, "Is the bear Madge Spragnell ran off with at the fair that night. It still had a quantity of heroin in sachets tucked away in its lower limbs when the police seized it."

He sat it down carefully on the table and it slowly toppled sideways, appearing quite literally to lie down and die.

"Cause of death: lack of stuffing," pronounced John Spry in a sepulchral voice, "Coroner's report."

"Oh, the poor thing!" Caroline was quite stricken.

"What is to become of it, Inspector?"

"Would you like it?" he asked with a smile.

"Oh, my goodness - may I really have it?" she asked, picking it up and cradling it gently in her arms, and kissing it lovingly on the nose.

"What is it about teddy-bears," queried John Spry "that makes us all love them so much and go silly at the very thought of them? I've often wondered - by the way I've still got mine. He's called Tim, and I just don't know what I'd do if I lost him - probably drink myself to death!"

"I think perhaps I should tell the truth about my fixation with teddy-bears," confessed Caroline. "My mother washed my teddy one day, when I was just six, and put him in the Aga to dry, and of course my darling teddy was cremated! All that was left of him was a small pile of ashes and his squeaker, which had survived because it was metal. And mother just laughed and bought me a new one, but to me it was a tragedy and I wept and wept for a long time and never really got over it. I can't forget the dreadful moment when she opened the oven door and I saw the tiny heap of smouldering black ashes which was all that was left of my beloved bear. Teddy Mark II never replaced him in my affections - he just wasn't the same bear. So one might say I've been in a state of perpetual mourning to this very day."

"Never mind, dear, your days of mourning are over now," said Brenda. "I'm an expert at stuffing teddy-bears for Oxfam, as a little light relief from toiling over a hot sewing-needle. I'll show you how to stuff him with lots of old pairs of nylon tights to put his flesh back on him, and then he'll be a fit and happy bear and you can love him to bits!"

At this point Joy spoke up: "Inspector, may I ask a question? Just to clarify matters for me. What was the final conclusion reached regarding Erica's involvement in this unhappy business?"

Vardon took his time over his answer, puffing on his pipe, then he said:

"Well, you know most of the story. Erica Trondheim was indeed deranged; she undoubtedly set up the killing of her mother by Philberd, and it appears to us, looking back on events, that Antonov simply played her along, knowing she was quite mad and therefore from his point of view not worth putting down. After all, people don't really take the mad seriously these days, do they?"

"I'm not altogether convinced about that," muttered John Spry to Caroline, out of the corner of his mouth. "Just look at Hitler and Co.!"

Vardon went on: "However, we looked into the matter closely and came up with the following facts: she did not actually go to America, as had been reported. Instead, she hid herself away in mid-Wales for the whole of the time when these things were happening in Oxford. We found all the information we needed about where she had stayed from documentation discovered in her desk relating to the renting of a cottage in an isolated spot up in the Cambrian mountains, only accessible via a narrow dangerous track and miles from the nearest village; somewhere between Carno and Darowen. No electricity or running water - only a mountain stream flowing past the cottage. In fact, no amenities whatsoever."

"Sounds like heaven," commented Peterson. "Let's all go there at once! Just think of all those lovely little brown trout there waiting for us, mouths wide open, longing for us to hook them with a bit of cheese temptingly suspended on a piece of string with a bent pin. Oh, to be a lad again! 'Lie long, high snowdrifts ...' etc.!"

"That was Shropshire, not Wales," said John Spry severely, "And nothing whatsoever to do with mountain streams."

"Your trouble, young man, is that there is simply no romance in your make-up," riposted Peterson, quite hurt. "You're missing out on so much in life, dear boy."

"Don't worry," interjected Mark, "One day soon it'll hit him hard. Just you wait and see! Look at what happened to me, the archetype of the 'gay young bachelor' (in the original meaning of the phrase, of course)."

Marit, sitting alongside him, smiled demurely and quoted a saying in Old Norse that they rather supposed was something like 'It will be all hearts and flowers', but Marit couldn't translate it, so it was unfortunately rather lost on the rest of the company.

Peterson resumed his rhapsody on escaping to Wales, while Vardon relit his pipe with deliberation, to give them time for brief discussion.

"And we could have fresh roast lamb every day!..."

"Capital!" said John Spry, "I'm all for that - and just think the girls could take their spinning wheels and we would have lovely home-spun pullovers in no time at all. No booze, though, lack-a-day! We'll have to think that out - and set up a still, perhaps? We could lug up a few crates of booze to keep us going until we got our distillery up and running."

"What a delightful idea," said Brenda. "We could make some heather wine - if there is such a thing."

Overhearing this, Joy said she wasn't sure about that, and she would consult Mrs Genery-Taylor - if, that is, she could find her in the library, as she seemed to have disappeared from her usual place on the bookshelf. Possibly Mrs Badger had spirited her away into the history section, next door to the cookery books. Anyhow, she would look into the matter when she had time.

"It occurs to me," said Peterson, "that Mrs Genery-Taylor was a bishop's wife. Is that correct?"

"If I remember rightly, she was indeed," replied Joy.

"Oh, what fun!" said Peterson, "Imagine the delightful garden-parties at the bishop's palace, with everyone reeling around, tipsy from the effects of the elderflower champagne or the cowslip wine! That would have shocked the sober folk in the pews, I guess. Oh, that we were there, gently swaying around the velvet lawns, admiring the magnificent floral display in the herbaceous borders, all carefully planned, no doubt, by Mrs G.-T. so that the guests would see two of everything - double flower-beds - through a haze of booze!"

"Oh, yes, I'm all for that," said Brenda.

"Now, what about our idyllic life at the cottage - shall we live in sin, as well? Nobody would know, and we'd be far, far away from all the tittle-tattle of Oxford. 'The pleasures of sin for a season'!"

Cutting short these unseemly propositions, Vardon again took up his account of events.

"We discovered that Erica spoke Welsh quite well. She had some contact with the local farmer and, although he found her quite a strange lady, as he expressed it, they got on well, and he kept her supplied with basic food stuffs: eggs from his wife's chickens, plus milk and cheese and home-made bread, so she fared very well up there in the mountains, far removed from the scene of action in Oxford. She told the farm people she was an Oxford don, writing a book about ancient myths and legends of Wales, and that went down very well, as you can imagine!..."

"The schemin' old bizzom!" a voice exclaimed from the back of the room, sounding suspiciously like Mrs Badger. "Wot a fraud!"

Thereafter there was silence for a minute or two before Vardon continued with his summary of events.

"So now Erica Trondheim remains under section in hospital and it does not seem likely that any charges may ever be brought against her, since it is reported that she would certainly be found unfit to plead. Meanwhile the house and estate of Elise Trondheim, and the paintings by Matisse and Chagall, will eventually be sold, and the proceeds, so we understand, will go towards the financing of Erica's confinement under section 29 in a private secure unit. The legal authorities will presumably finalize the details in due course."

"What about the loose change?" asked Peterson. "We could all do with a shilling or two to compensate us for all our pains, trials and tribulations over this trifling matter."

"You'll be lucky, sir," said John Spry, "You know what those legal eagles are with their artful scheming!"

"Yes, indeed, vultures!" came the reply, "Strip the carcass and then off to the hills in search of more carrion!"

And Peterson polished his glasses vigorously.

"How I do dearly wish that I had read law instead of philosophy when I had the choice - young fool that I was!"

"Well, I do most heartily endorse what you say. Philosophy has always been a howling wilderness of conflicting theories, a kind of non~subject; of no practical use whatsoever in my opinion. You should have read something good and meaty like my own subject, history," said John Spry, with just a hint of self-satisfaction.

"Now how's that for smugness and complacency?" Peterson was incensed. "History is mainly the record of man's brutality, vanity and stupidity - look at the Knights Templars, for example, and all the glorification and misrepresentation of their noble..."

"Boys, boys!" Brenda intervened, "Calm down! Come, come, They're all dead and gone - so settle down and behave yourselves!"

Here, Caroline, looking down at her newly-acquired teddy bear, limp in her arms, changed the subject adroitly with an interesting question.

"It occurs to me," she said, "that no explanation has as yet been given as to why my teddy-bear was second in command to teddy bear number-one?"

There were some puzzled looks at this comment, and Joy asked: "What on earth do you mean, dear?"

"It's quite simple: we were given to understand that there was to be only one teddy-bear stuffed with that dreadful stuff, so why the second one? To me it doesn't seem to add up seeing that there was to be only one star prize, intended for the person taking over from Jasper Philberd."

Vardon for the first time looked a little perplexed. "Do you know," he said, "We've, gone over this a number of times and we just can't come up with a satisfactory answer. There doesn't seem to be any kind of logical explanation."

"And perhaps therein lies, in fact, the explanation," remarked John Spry. "Judging from my casual observations there was not much logic to be seen where Madge Spragnell's actions were concerned."

"You can say that again," murmured Michael Walters to Peter Rumbold. "Totally bonkers!"

"But clever with it!" whispered Mark. "She's actually succeeded in outwitting the opposition simply by being bonkers!"· The inspector, however, had more to say.

"Nevertheless, our own young Madam Arcati has come up with a possible solution to the problem, very neat, but I think only a woman would have thought of it. Since Antonov had apparently left the country, Madge must have thought she had a free hand, so she was going to do it her way - 'while the cat's away the mice will play' of course. As she was already hooked on drugs and so probably euphoric with it; she supposed she had power and control over the whole operation for the future and consequently could do what she liked, with no need to obey orders any more. She was Queen Bee, and nobody was going to tell her what to do. From now on she would call the shots.

"This is only conjecture, of course, but she had been seen frequenting bars around central Oxford and chatting up young men - for what purpose we did not then know, but now with hindsight we conclude that she was probably out head-hunting, hoping to find a suitable victim to act as her personal dogs-body, some nice weak young man who would do her bidding, now that she had full personal authority over the whole enterprise. And his own little reward was to be the smaller teddy-bear, stuffed full of goodies of course. This seems to add up, and looks to be the only plausible explanation, whimsical though it may appear.

"Quite dotty - but dangerous with it," said Mark aside to Marit.

"Lethal," said Petronella, overhearing what he said, and remembering the near-miss when the bullet screamed past her ear. "Just think of all the horrors we've had to endure because of her - and Antonov, of course. Why were we put through all that?"

"Never mind, dear child," said Peterson, "It's all added a little spice to the rather pedestrian and boring academic life of Oxford. It's been quite exciting for us sober citizens, has it not, in the final analysis?"

Opinions were divided on this, and no conclusions were reached. It seemed unsatisfactory but, as Mark observed, "it was not untypical of Madge's general behaviour - a lot of waffle and confusion, causing chaos - and there goes Madge, dancing away in the moonlight, getting away with it completely and leaving all the mayhem behind her."

"Yes, and the General," said Michael Walters, "That was a tragedy."

"Not to mention poor old Wellington and the rest," remarked Joy, heartily wishing she could get rid of Napoleon. As she considered this, she heard a whisper in her ear; it was Lady Westhoe, who said: "Joy, I may have the solution to your problem over the Mynah-bird."

"Really? Oh, my goodness, what is it?"

"Well, one of our students is at present engaged in some interesting research on talking birds, and he would be very pleased to take Napoleon off your hands. He has recently acquired an African parrot for his collection. It is thought to be about two hundred years old, and it comes out with the most extraordinary things in a distinctly Nelsonian style of speech, using nautical terms which would have been current at that time. It also swears and sings sea-chanties, and is reputed to have spent much of its early life on board ship."

"Ooh! Do you think it might have been at the Battle of Trafalgar?" asked Caroline.

"I don't think so, dear girl. A man-o'-war would scarcely be the place for a ship's parrot. Just think of the appalling noise when the guns went off - the poor bird would probably have turned into a deaf-mute, if it hadn't already died of a heart-attack!"

So saying, Peterson gave her a censorious glance over his half-glasses, and then wrinkled his nose appreciatively over his next glass of Chateauneuf. "Really delicious," he remarked. "It might be useful if this parrot could be asked if it knew Captain Morgan's parrot personally, so to speak; surely then it would be quite possible for it to know exactly where he buried the famous treasure!"

"My God, are we all getting drunk?" asked Michael Walters. "Whatever next? This is getting decidedly silly!"

"Ah - I know what's next!"

Peter Rumbold came to life after sitting quietly listening to the others for some time.

"Now, here's a real puzzler for us to tackle. When Madge did her famous vanishing trick, she left her bag and plastic case behind; so, considering how important the contents were to her, why didn't she hang on to them like grim death? Why didn't she have a shoulder strap, for instance? And why were they packed with things obviously prepared for a quick get-away? After all, she was now Queen Bee, and it doesn't seem to me very logical to be preparing to do a runner, just as she was in the process of taking over the great enterprise."

Inspector Vardon looked thoughtful and drew on his pipe again. Then he said: "Now, that's a hard one, but I feel I may have the answer to it, drawing on my own observations with regard to women's handbags which, I believe, are sacred objects to them. My own dear wife, for example, would certainly refuse to have any other type but one with short straps, carried over the forearm, in similar style to that favoured by our present Prime Minister. Shoulder bag? Never! Yet I know some won't wear anything else. It seems to be a matter of taste."

The company considered this, with various speculations on the importance of the handbag as a factor in Madge's flight. Peterson, by now quite soporific, murmured: "Shades of Lady Bracknell, perhaps?" This piece of flippancy was studiously ignored by Brenda.

Vardon resumed his explanation, remarking: "She needed to have both hands free to manage the draw and nothing - nothing at all must go wrong with that, so the bag and the case had to be put down under the stall, at the back, and this proved in the end to be her Achilles' heel. As to why she was packed and ready for lift-off, it is, I think, fair to say that in spite of appearances to the contrary she was a very shrewd woman, who put up a most effective smoke-screen of a Mrs Feather-type character as cover to disguise the ruthless operator she really was. So this was a woman prepared for all eventualities and though she was aware that it was a very dodgy enterprise, she had to go through with it and obey Antonov's instructions. There was no alternative and she had to take over from him, exactly as directed. And then it all went wrong: there was no eruption of drug addiction in the city and we have at least capped the volcano for the meantime, or so we hope, for the last thing Oxford needs is an escalating drugs scene.

"Finally, the crucial questions are: firstly, where is Antonov? We simply don't know. And then, where is Madge Spragnell? Again, we don't know, and only time will tell, on both counts. And so, our thanks to 'D' for coming along this evening in spite of his busy work-schedule, and giving us such a lucid account of the affair.I shall now ask him to say a final word before he goes on his way."

"Inspector!" A voice came from the back of the room; It was Percy Chadlow, who had hitherto sat quietly enjoying the party, with the man from the parachute regiment and his colleague as they swapped yarns about their time in the armed services.

"Yes?"

"Now, sir, Oi was a'wonderin' - sat 'ere enjoyin' these 'ere festivities - about one little thing in particular as Oi don't think as you've a'mentioned. An' seein' as Oi was thereabouts when it 'appened - Oi just got to a-wonderin' about this little tiddly detail..."

The inspector waited patiently for Percy's point to emerge from all this lengthy preamble, and said nothing, asking himself what it could be? He didn't think he'd left anything out of the evidence, surely?

"Twas only a little thing, but it moight 'ave a meanin' in the grand scale o'things. D'you recall about they sniffer dogs, a-sniffin' around the gate by the allotments? They found summat, didn't they? Or so Oi was told. Wot was it?"

Inspector Vardon consulted one of his team; as he had evidently no recollection of the event, it need not have been of any great importance.

"Ah, yes," he said, "Just a small thing but perhaps it tells us a little about Jasper Philberd. The dogs found his wallet buried in the nettles by the gate. He probably lost it when he did a runner from the allotments on the night that he killed Cledwyn. It contained certain items which provide a clue as to what motivated him. There were membership cards for various respectable - and some not so respectable institutions in Oxford, and one for a top gambling casino in London, and we found out from this that he was into gambling in a big way. That of course accounted for his desperate need for cash, and plenty of it, and enabled Antonov to get his stranglehold over Philberd. The wallet also contained a pass-card for his mother, tucked away at the back, with a photograph. Mrs Graystone was a great help to us in identifying these. She told us that his mother had died suddenly about a year ago, and he had gone to pieces afterwards.

He was deeply attached to her and could not cope with the loss; he said he couldn't believe she had left him, Mrs Graystone did her best to mother him as far as was possible, but he was inconsolable. And now for the interesting point; it was at this time that Philberd's obsessive attachment to her cat began. He behaved as though it was his own cat, and literally worshipped it. Mrs Graystone didn't mind, as the cat loved being made a fuss of, and one day she found out why he was so attached to it. He showed her a photograph of his mother cuddling her own cat, with Philberd standing beside her, looking very happy, with his arm round her - a charming picture of a contented family. Now here we have a fascinating coincidence. Now Mrs Graystone told us that this cat was the exact double of her own cat. It seems that the Philberd cat had died not long before Mrs Philberd herself, and apparently Mrs Graystone's cat had become the substitute for it in Philberd's sick mind: it was his cat. So now we see the connection and the meaning behind that crazy business of its abduction by Erica Trondheim. It's an interesting example of interaction in the behaviour of two deranged people, and the trouble and confusion it brings in its wake."

With this observation Inspector Vardon concluded his account of events and sat down with his colleagues.

'D' then stood up and took the inspector's place, standing by the fireplace, and as he did so, all the lights came on again.

"Ah!" he said, "Well timed. 'Dominus illuminatio mea', the motto of the University of Oxford, and may it guide us in illuminating all these dark mysteries."

He paused for a moment, looking out of the French windows across the garden to the twinkling necklace of lights of Lower Wolvercote in the distance beyond Port Meadow.

"It seems to me," he said, "That we have covered nearly all the important points in this complex affair, but there is one aspect which does, I think, deserve a mention, i.e. the rather whimsical choice of an air balloon for delivering the drugs. This dare-devil activity will not in future go unnoticed, since it is proposed to bring helicopter surveillance into operation as soon as it is authorized and funds permit. So there will be no more of these dare-devil escapades and it will be a godsend to Thames Valley Police, who to say the least of it are hard-pressed at the best of times, so aerial surveillance will be a revolutionary means, invaluable in every way, opening up fresh horizons. So it may even transpire that Antonov's actions have produced a positive result in a negative situation, providing the impetus for the police force to press for this facility, costly though it will be, in order to prevent such destructive operations ever taking place again unobserved."

'D' paused again; and then announced genially:

"And now, finally, a personal comment. I think that Madge will return..."

"How on earth can you think that - and why?" asked Joy, startled by this statement.

'D', by now relaxed and mellowed, continued in jocular vein to everyone's surprise. This normally aloof and rather formidable man showed a streak of schoolboy humour and revealed himself as something of a wag.

"Pieces of eight! Pieces of eight!" he intoned, quoting Long John Silver's parrot in a high-pitched voice which perfectly mimicked the bird. In the background, Napoleon responded, muttering in his sleep. "Thank God he was going," thought Joy, "It would be such a relief! At least he would have other birds to show off to, and that would inflate his ego!"

"D's" tone of voice changed abruptly.

"Buried treasure, me hearties," he boomed in a deep bass which resounded round the room and reminded Joy of one splendid Wotan roaring through the Ring cycle in Bayreuth.

"Aar, Jim lad!" he boomed again, raising a hand in a melodramatic gesture which evoked instant laughter all round, as everyone relaxed, collapsing in mirth over this unexpected entertainment.

'D' assumed a stance with his right hand pressed against his breast, which struck them all as very funny, indeed.

"H.M.S. Pinafore," mumbled Peterson, half-asleep, but opening one eye.

Taking a deep breath: 'D' prepared to give voice again, cocking an eyebrow as he began to sing in a fine bass, to the astonishment of the company.

'Fifteen men on a dead man's chest,

Yo-ho-ho and a bottle of rum,

Drink to the devil, have done with the rest,

Yo-ho-ho and a bottle of rum ...'

Isn't that John Masefield? 'Jim Davies', if my memory serves me correctly. Or is it 'Treasure Island'? I really am not sure, but it takes me back to my schooldays at the Dragon. I loved all that swashbuckling adventure - unforgettable!"

Mark was heard to sigh deeply and mutter: "And is there honey still for tea...? Ah! my well and misspent youth! And just look at me now - a disillusioned hardbitten old..."

"One o' them!" admonished 'D' severely, cutting him short with a frown. "'Nuf said! So avast and belay - come along now, Jim lad!," he exclaimed, looking at the grandfather clock as it gave a little pre-strike chuckle, collecting itself to strike midnight: "We must weigh anchor and up and away! The tide is on the turn, so up the crow's nest with thee - and let the cry be 'Westward-ho!"

"Pieces-of-eight, pieces-of-eight," said a voice from the back of the room, mimicking John Silver's parrot: "There be treasure!"

The doorbell rang, and 'D' peered through the curtains out into the darkness.

"Ah, good man, bang on cue!" He gave a thumbs-up, to the unseen visitor. "Our carriage awaits us! Come along, dear boy, are you packed and ready? Belted and buckled?"

"Aye, aye, Cap'n!" With a quick hug and a kiss, Mark apologized to Joy for their hasty departure.

"So long, Auntie Joy, but we've got to fly - quite literally, I'm afraid!"

"Where to, dear?"

"Oh - over the water," he said, pointing vaguely westward in the direction of Wytham Woods.

"Amerikee, I shouldn't wonder!" declared 'D', affecting a rolling nautical gait and focusing an imaginary telescope. "Perchance we'll fetch thee back a doubloon or two if us strikes it rich over yonder!"

"Certainly a necklace of the finest South Sea pearls for my Marit." So saying, Mark kissed her fondly, "Shan't be long, love, only a few days. We've got a meeting to attend." Sailing the rueful smile of one resigned to the inevitable, she held on to him for a brief moment.

"I think this is called 'learning to be an Army wife', isn't it?"

"Is that a promise?" he asked, looking at her intently.

"Yes, I think so - yes, of course - I am resigned to it, isn't it?" She inclined her head gravely, looking solemn.

"Yippee!" Mark was exultant and demonstrated it by picking her up and giving her a quick twirl round in his arms, high up off the ground, then putting her down again gently. "A pearl beyond price," he said.

"That's a weight off my mind! But it's no easy role to play"

"So in that case"; commented 'D', "Forget the pearls – buy the wedding-ring!"

And with that they were gone, whisked away in a trice into the night, in an anonymous black car driven by a fresh-faced youth wearing a dark suit. As they got into the vehicle, he snapped the door shut in distinctly military fashion and gave a half-salute to the party guests watching the departure from the drawing-room windows.

The guests then began to say their goodbyes and leave, with grateful thanks to their hostess. Last to depart were Peterson and Brenda Page-Philips, and as they reached the gate, Brenda noticed a change in Peterson's demeanour and wondered if it was the effect of the cold night air, for all at once he seemed to be reasonably sober; no longer the garrulous toper, so full of himself and always keen to have the last word, he was now quiet, even grave: a completely different character. She eyed him covertly as they walked up the road together.

"May I see you home, Brenda?" he asked, "It's rather late."

"Of course, Tim, that would be kind," she replied with a smile.

As they walked on down Woodstock Road towards Phil and Jim, there was plenty of time to talk, and Peterson opened up in an entirely unexpected way.

"Do forgive me, please, my dear girl, for my silly behaviour, and all that foolish pseudo-academic flippancy and nonsense."

He turned to Brenda with such a straight look of sober honesty that she was quite taken by surprise, having presumed that he must be rather drunk after the evening's jollifications; but no, he was totally compos mentis.

"It's all a big act, you see - a sort of cover-up," he said.

Brenda looked at him enquiringly: "A cover-up?"

"Yes, it's a kind of defence mechanism, calculated to repel all boarders, so to speak." Brenda raised an eyebrow, but said nothing.

"You see, my dear, when my wife died so suddenly five years ago, it seems it was commonly assumed that I was 'in the market', as it were; However, I do assure you, that was certainly not the case."

And Tim Peterson looked at Brenda so earnestly and his voice expressed such obvious sincerity that she was quite taken aback and did not know how to respond, though her feelings regarding him had been somewhat softened as a result of the evening's revelry.

He continued: "We were totally unsuited to one another. It was not - as it was said to be - 'a marriage made in heaven'; on the contrary, it was often absolute hell. We just kept up appearances for the sake of the children, but we simply didn't get on."

"Oh, dear!" said Brenda, with a sigh, "It sounds very much like a replica of my own experience. I was never more relieved in my life than on the day when we were divorced. It was like being let out of prison after serving a long sentence."

"Really?" Peterson was incredulous, "And I thought you were so happy!"

Brenda shook her head gravely.

"No, indeed, we too were unsuited - our characters and tastes were incompatible. Unfortunately we only discovered it too late."

Peterson brightened at once. "In that case..."

He stopped, then took courage and spoke of what was in his mind.

"Dear girl, I have had an idea in my mind which has been plaguing me for some time..." He faltered and glanced at Brenda timidly, like a lost boy.

"Yes?" she said, "What is it, Tim?"

"I am so fed up with presenting an image of a cantankerous old professor, Brenda, which is how I am seen by my colleagues and friends. It is certainly not me, but I have learnt to accept it and act it out, as I'm expected to do. It's quite ridiculous, like a dog going through his tricks to please people. Brenda!" He looked at her with pleading in his eyes. "would you consider the idea of the occasional evening out with me - or dinner, say - at the Randolph?"

"The Randolph?" Brenda went into peals of laughter, which echoed round Church Walk, as they passed by Phil and Jim on the way to North Parade. Then, oh dear! How she wished she had not done that! He looked instantly crestfallen and deflated.

"Tim," she said, taking his arm as a gesture of reassurance, "I didn't mean to laugh" I'm sorry I did, but - the Randolph? I think not my dear, much too up-market I think. Now," she said, looking him straight in the eye, "If you were to say - 'The Opium Den', for instance, I might even weaken and yield to temptation, for I love Chinese food and they do it superbly. Their cuisine is 'sans pareil' and you will love it!"

"Really? The Opium Den - how daring! I've never been there. It sounds like bandit country to me."

Once again the street echoed to Brenda's laughter as they turned into Winchester Road.

"Tim, you are really quite ridiculous! I feel I must re-educate you at once!"

"Please do, my dear," said he, delighted at this unexpected breakthrough. "Tell me more - I am intrigued."

"Well," she said, and paused, then added: "Oh, never mind - we'll leave that until later, but for now shall we make a compromise, say: drinks at the Randolph on .. Sunday? At seven? And dinner at the the Opium Den at perhaps eight-thirty? That's my only free night; as work is driving me mad at the moment. It's literally a never-ending 'Stitch, stitch, stitch' like the 'Song of the Shirt', and I don't seem to have time to breathe!"

"Capital," exclaimed Peterson, "I'll make the booking at once. That will be splendid!"

They had arrived at Brenda's front gate in Winchester Road, and Peterson, elated and acting on impulse, took Brenda's hand and kissed it tenderly.

"My dear Brenda, you have made an old man very happy. I now have something to look forward to beyond the academic treadmill and the drudgery of the daily grind. An evening out with a charming girl who is both witty and intelligent - what more could one ask?"

Brenda turned to him with a very direct look.

"Tim, one should always bear in mind that there are two sides to any story, but as for me, I have told you mine. I find myself in much the same position as yours. My life is all work and no play, except for our weekly sing at St. James'. That's the only recreation I have at present, so why shouldn't we relax for once, kick up our heels and enjoy a little harmless fun together?"

"Precisely, my dear girl. I may be fifty and technically 'over the hill', but 'there's life in the old dog yet', as the saying goes in these 'ere parts."

Brenda laughed again.

"Quite so," she said softly, her eyes twinkling gently. "So, Tim, Sunday evening, seven p.m. at the Randolph? I shall make a note of it."

"I shall be there on the dot precisely, dear lady - have no fear. As Worcester College clock strikes seven, I shall appear instantly!"

"Well, now, that should give us a minute or two each way, shouldn't it?" came Brenda's riposte, but her attempt at a subtle witticism was lost on Peterson, who just smiled uncomprehendingly and said: "Er, quite so, dear lady," doffing his cap as he departed, "The Randolph at seven, then."

As she watched him walking away down Winchester Road, she could hear him singing a little song to himself as he went along~ and she recognized it at once.

'It was a lover and his lass,

With a hey! and a ho!

And a hey, nonny-no...'

A catchy little canzonet of Thomas Morley. How delightful, she thought, Tim must be a true romantic. This was going to be fun! Then, as he went on his way, walking fairly steadily, it may be said, down the road, it occurred to her that he had a really fine bass-baritone voice - a natural soloist. So, as they would be seeing something of one another, it would be rather nice to make music together if the opportunity arose. She must get her old lute-guitar out of mothballs and do some practicing, and she had got her fingers moving again reasonably well and thought herself proficient enough she would invite Tim round for dinner, and if he was agreeable, she would accompany him in some Elizabethan songs. That would be very pleasant, and perhaps when they felt they were ready, they could do a little recital at one of Joy's musical events. That would be lovely!

With this thought in mind she took herself off to bed, feeling much happier than she had been for a long time. Suddenly the world seemed to be a better place somehow, and as she drifted off to sleep she actually found herself looking forward to going to work and being creative with her needle once again, for in recent times work had become a kind of humdrum drudgery. The feeling of release after her divorce had gradually left her after a while, and she felt deadened in spirit. When she came home at night to an empty house with no one for company - however disagreeable that person might be.

But now she felt uplifted - positive, with something to look forward to, as Tim had also said. She knew in her heart that she was not looking for romance, or even an emotional attachment but she knew that Tim Peterson was going to be absolutely right for a good, wholesome relationship, and that was very good for starters! Thereafter we would see what we would see, and play it by ear. And with that reflection Brenda turned over and slept, a deep and dreamless sleep, and awoke fresh and serene, early next morning, all cares blown away.

Meanwhile, at Joy's house Marit had stayed behind after Brenda and Peterson had left, and Petronella had gone discreetly upstairs, leaving Joy and Marit to have a private talk.

Marit's approach was severely practical, and she helped Joy methodically to clear away all the debris from the party, stacking the dishwasher neatly - "We must have all things away and tidy before Mrs B. is coming tomorrow to do the cleaning," said she, switching on the dishwasher with a flourish.

"There, all done and - how do you say?"

"Dusted," replied Joy mechanically, looking out at the night sky.

"Except, not dusted, I think" said Marit. "Washed and polished, is it?"

"Hmmm - yes, maybe," said Joy absently, her mind on other things. "I just wonder what those boys are up to in America? Something dangerous, I'll be bound"

Marit shrugged her shoulders.

"I don't care what he is doing, so long as my future husband is bringing home the meat?"

"Bacon," said Joy, smiling.

"That will do fine - bacon, and as long as he comes home in one piece with no bullet holes through him, I am content. I shall be there, waiting to cook the bacon, and our home will have all the Scandinavian comforts: wood-burning stoves and everything." "Very good," said Joy, "Don't forget to invite me to dinner when you cook reindeer. I've never tasted it."

"Sure, sure!" and Marit nodded vigorously. "The secret is of course the Schnapps, or something else of strong alcohol, but best, of course, is Schnapps, for best results. You are pouring it over the meat when it is going in the oven, and the flavour is becoming ... how do you say it?."

"Outstanding?" queried Joy, "Delicious?"

"Exactly so - standing out. Very good!." Marit paused for thought.

"But, of course, I must be stabbing the meat with a spike..."

"Stabbing the meat with a spike?" Joy was incredulous. What an improbable proceeding!

"Yes, yes, of course - and as I am stabbing it, I am pouring in the Schnapps also. This most necessary for penetration."

Joy's eyebrows rose almost to her hairline.

She went to the kitchen drawer and rummaged around, eventually producing a meat skewer.

"Do you mean one of these ..."

Marit was just a little scornful, breaking into a trill of silvery laughter like a rivulet pouring into a fjord.

"No - no, of course not. That one is a skewer! I am speaking of my grandfather's spike - a long spike with a sharp end for splitting the logs in the forest for the stove. It is an old family tradition in our part of Scandinavia."

"A symbolic ritual, as it were?" asked Joy, "An ancient tradition? Bring home the logs and the reindeer and spike the venison?"

"Exactly, exactly correct. And we are also putting in with the meat many berries and fungi from the forest. This makes a wonderful flavour, quite beautiful,"

"Can't wait," said Joy with relish. "O, hasten the day!"

And then they said goodnight and Marit walked up St. Julie's

Road to her flat, accompanied by Joy's cats, that is, all except Fred, who was prudently fast asleep in the airing cupboard. No nonsense about going hunting as the others were bent on doing, once they had seen Marit through her front door.

However, in spite of his blindness, Fred had been known to go out on an occasional foray round the back garden, and had even brought in a live mouse one memorable evening and, happily, the mouse was quite uninjured!

Next morning, bright and early, not long after dawn, Joy went out into the back garden, wearing her housecoat, and a woolly cap, for there was a distinct chill in the air and a heavy dew had spread the lawn with a jewelled tapestry of tiny rainbow drops shimmering in the early sunlight. Joy's mind, however, was more preoccupied with getting all the washing hung out before Mrs B. arrived for her inevitable morning grumble, which would be especially vigorous and prolonged after the goings-on of the previous night! So she must swiftly tidy up the drawing-room and kitchen, otherwise there would doubtless be fireworks, for Mrs B. liked the house to be 'ship-shape and Bristol fashion' before she began her hoovering marathon. 'Bottoming the place', as she called it, somewhat grimly. But what a treasure she was, our indefatigable, irreplaceable Mrs B.! She must be kept happy, at all costs.

Suddenly, out of the corner of her eye, she caught sight of a movement on the shed roof next door in Harriet Spinster's garden. It was Jenny the vixen, who had brought her cubs out to play in the first light of day, before putting them to bed in their earth. As the cubs played with the vixen's tail, she looked at Joy and Joy looked at her, and they had a magic moment of total trust. Standing stock-still, Joy marvelled at the rare and lovely sight of the frisking cubs, their coats burnished golden brown in the early light, yapping round the vixen, her pale eyes fixed on Joy. For some minutes, it seemed they were allowed to play until, startled as Harriet Spinster's door banged, they vanished instantly beneath the shed. But the moment of mutual trust with the vixen was truly amazing. Jenny had always been a friend of the cats, and was herself en efficient ratter on her nocturnal hunting expeditions, so she really was an asset, and no nuisance at all, and long might she and her brood continue to haunt the gardens and hunt down their prey.

As Joy turned to go in, she saw Iffley sitting at her preferred station on the garden wall and staring up fixedly at the old lady's bedroom window at the back of the Trondheims' house, empty now and up for sale. She, too, looked up and saw that the window was open, and there, sitting in her usual place, looking down at Joy, was Elise Trondheim, smiling benignly.

Iffley's great golden eyes, wide open as she sat still on the wall, continued to stare intently at the window. Then she uttered a deep-throated miaouw, not a worried sound, but a warm and comforting one, almost a purr. Joy looked at her, and said, "Iffley, what is it?" Iffley's reply was a knowing and reassuring cat-blink. Then she closed her eyes for a cat-nap. Joy looked up again at the old lady's window, but now it was firmly shut and dark within, the vision gone. Nevertheless, Joy was left with an inward glow of confidence in the feeling that she had not after all lost her old friend, but had seen her once more, and that sometime, somewhere, she would see her yet again. She felt tears rising and looked up at the sky, where she saw the vapour trails of aircraft on their way westward, beginning the early morning flight to the Americas, and an echo sounded in her mind:

"Something strange in the sky..." - Elise Trondheim's voice resounded, sonorous and sepulchral.

"And I'll see you again," said Joy quietly.

A loud bang of the front gate announced the arrival of Mrs Badger, at least two hours too early, and she had done nothing! "Miss 'Etherington!" A voice proclaimed, rising half an octave to a commanding contralto: "Where be you, moy duck?"

"Ah, well, on with the day," thought Joy as she made all haste to the kitchen door. The taskmaster had come to crack the whip. Snatches of music echoed in her mind - 'Haec dies quam fecit Dominus...', from a Byrd motet - or should it rather be 'Dies irae' - probably the latter!

"Oi'll put the kettle on - a noice cup o' tea, an' then you can tell me all the gossip..."

Then, after a moment or two's silence, the verdict:

"Oh' dear, oh lor' an' Chroist Church bells! - Wot an awful mess. It looks as 'ow a bomb's 'it it in 'ere! Oi'll 'ave to bottom the place an' no doubt about it!"

Mrs B. of course, with a peremptory declaration of intent that would brook no denial.

So, as she approached the kitchen, where stood the Avenging Angel, arms folded across her bosom in judgement, Joy crept forward, mentally on her knees and presenting abject apologies, but she still thought that no matter how Oxford might change in the future, as it surely must, nevertheless, as long as Mrs Badger and her like remained to exercise their quiet commonsense control behind the scenes, keeping a straight course in spite of the warring elements, for after all, life only runs smoothly thanks to the efficiency of the college servants and supporting staff. So God bless them all and long may they continue to be the backbone of this strange entity of pulsating inspiration which is Oxford, the global village.

CHAPTER XXIV

POSTLUDE

'Non vos relinquam orphanos alleluia

vado et veniam ad vos alleluia'

William Byrd 1542-1623

At last Joy prepared to leave for college and most untypically she was really late for her first tutorial of the day. Mrs B. had of course had a great deal to say, and had exacted her pound of flesh - an ample measure, for when she finally departed her bicycle basket groaned with the weight of left-overs from the previous night's celebration, consisting mainly of Joy's epicurean creations and none at all of Mrs B's navvies' delights, which had all been devoured to the last crumb, except for one small pickled onion left solitary in the pungent vinegar. Well, thought Joy philosophically, there was no accounting for tastes.

She took a last look at the back garden. Jenny and the cubs had gone to earth for the day. But then a movement caught her eye. Jasper Philberd's window was wide open; evidently there was a new tenant in the room, for a young man was standing at the window, stripped to the waist - a fine figure of a lad. He appeared to be performing some kind of training exercises, possibly martial arts. Joy retrieved her binoculars from the kitchen window-sill, and focused on the window where the young man was disporting himself with so much vigour. She must get Mrs Badger to pop round to Mrs Graystone and enquire about him - and soon she would invite him to tea!

It began to rain - a sudden squall coming over from the direction of Wytham Wood.

"Hell's teeth!," She must get down to college at once, without further delay - this loitering was disgraceful and her personal standards were certainly slipping - it simply would not do! So hastily donning her waterproof cape and sou'wester, Joy went out to do battle with the storm. She pedaled determinedly down the Woodstock Road, blown sideways by the gale and wobbling violently as the wind caught her cape. By the time she had struggled as far as St. Anthony's her glasses were totally blurred by the rain; she could no longer see anything and came to a halt unceremoniously outside the Royal Oak, opposite the Radcliffe Infirmary, bicycle brakes squealing in protest.

The old inn sign creaked dolefully as it blew backwards and forwards in the wind, and taking off her glasses she looked up at it. There he was - King Charles the Second, his face superimposed on the ancient Boscobel oak in which according to legend he hid from his pursuers - beautifully painted on the signboard. As she gazed at it, Joy felt a sudden shock of recognition: the face in the portrait might have been Cledwyn's, it was so like him; and Cledwyn had been so fascinated by the Siege of Oxford and the fate of Charles the First, and the Restoration of the Monarchy.

As she studied the portrayal of the king on the signboard, Joy decided that it must have been copied fairly faithfully from the marvellous miniature Samuel Cooper, painted in 1665. And there was a definite resemblance to Cledwyn in the long dark wavy hair, the pale face, aristocratic nose, dark brown eyes, and finely pencilled moustache tracing the line of the upper lip. Perhaps Cledwyn was a throwback? After all, Nell Gwynn, the king's mistress, was Welsh by distant origin, and so was Cledwyn, so there might be a connection.

Saddened by the recollection, Joy remounted her battered steed, a venerable machine inherited from her mother and dating from the 1920's, but still going strong. She battled on through the continuing squall, beginning to make headway as she passed St. Giles' Church, but there she was overtaken at speed by the Wolvercote bus, which recklessly drenched her with the contents of the water splash at the corner of St. Giles by the war memorial. Blinded again, she dismounted and cleaned her glasses once more.

At that moment the tempest abated, the wind dropped instantly and blue sky appeared to the south beyond St. Mary Mag's tower, from which a silvery peal of bells rang out, seemingly greeting the end of the storm. A vivid rainbow arched itself against the indigo sky which loomed menacingly above Shotover, forming a perfect frame for the range of buildings from Keeble College Chapel to St. James' College and St. John's, and appearing to end beyond the Martyrs' Memorial. So could the pot of gold possibly lie within the covered market, at the rainbow's end?

But that passing fancy only reminded Joy that she must pop into the University Butcher for some venison later on, to make a venison pie with mushrooms and quince jelly. Mrs Graystone's quince bushes had borne well last year, and her preserves were always excellent.

With this resolve at the back of her mind, she arrived at last at the ancient gateway to St. James College, hoping she had reached a safe haven after the struggle with the tempest. She locked her bike on to the stand outside the gate and after divesting herself of her dripping cape and sou'wester she stepped through the small door set within the great oak double doors into the cloistral quiet of the quad, where all was peace and tranquillity. She smiled wryly at the head porter, warmly ensconced in his cosy little porter's lodge, reading the racing page of the morning paper. He looked up at her through the glass partition.

"Professor!" he called, waving the paper with somewhat uncharacteristic animation, for he was normally undemonstrative and rather solemn, even taciturn in demeanour; however, today he was positively excited.

"Just a minute!"

"What is it, Mr. Bradwell? I'm terribly late ~ I really must dash ..."

Extricating himself from his swivel chair, he stood up too quickly, banging his head on one of the oak beams in the ceiling.

"Ouch!" he exclaimed, although this must have happened many a time before, since he was reportedly six foot seven in his socks and the beams no more than six feet from the floor. It was rather a tight fit for the ex-Regimental Sergeant-Major of the Grenadier Guards, who, as he once confessed, stood seven-foot eleven in his bearskin. He must have been an awesome sight at the Trooping of the Colour.

"Now," he said, "You remember you picked three 'osses the other day for an each-way bet?"

"Did I, Mr. Bradwell?" Joy had of course forgotten all about it.

"Well, now, the big news is that you won - thirty-three to one outsider, first race; then twenty to one on the second race, and five to one on the third."

"Oh, dear - what does that mean, Mr. Bradwell?"

"It means you won a tidy old sum o' money at two pound each way, that's wot!"

He produced a fat brown envelope from a drawer in his desk, "An' 'ere it is!"

"Oh, Mr. Bradwell, what do I do?" she asked desperately, throwing on her gown and looking at the clock behind him on the wall. "Can't I leave it with you? Could you perhaps get the staff drinks all round at the Lamb and Flag, and if there's any loose change I'll do another bet in due course. Would that be in order?" "Fair enough," he replied, beaming with pleasure at the prospect. "There'll be plenty of loose change, don't you worry yourself. Looks like your luck's in at the minute, Oi'd say, good thinkin'!"

With the seal of approval now stamped on the agreement, Joy hurried across the quad, gown billowing in the breeze and somewhat impeding her progress, but she was determined to reach her goal. In this she showed some of the quality of toughness inherited from her forbears. Her mother, when a young don, had first met the bluff young son of a Lancashire sheep farmer in May Week, and it was love at first sight! Joy's father had left the high Pennines to settle in the flat-lands of Oxford, and had set up house in St. Julie's Road, and Joy and her brother had been brought up in the traditions of an academic family, but with an inner core of sound Lancashire commonsense - a very good combination.

Joy was halfway across the quad when Lord Westhoe appeared, coming out of the door to the President's Lodging. He raised his hand in a quick salutation and hurried off, evidently late as well, with his gown flying out behind him like a loosely flapping sail as he was so tall.

As she passed the chapel, Joy heard an ethereal sound coming from within. It was the college choir rehearsing, and she paused for a moment, entranced by what she could hear through the open door - simply lovely!

'Non vos relinquam orphanos: Alleluia!

Vado et venio ad vos: Alleluia!

Et gaudebit, cor vostrum: Alleluia!"

The pulsating rhythm of this wonderful motet, the sudden surge of excitement as it reached 'Et gaudebit', and the final climax of sheer joyful exultation with the last triumphant Alleluias were breathtaking - William Byrd at his very best! There was a wonderful dance rhythm in it, rather like the tarantella beat of 'Nisi Dominus' in the Monteverdi Vespers of 1610. Perhaps she could write something up about it, time permitting - it was haunting her - 'Except the Lord build the house: their labour is but lost that build it. Except the Lord keep the city: the watchman waketh but in vain' Well, the Lord had indeed kept the city through the late peril which had menaced it, and the watchmen had been alert, the danger had been averted and the city preserved to follow its guiding light: 'Dominus illuminatio mea.'

So - what was it; the spirit of Oxford, without a doubt! "If ever the silver chord be loosed..." The biblical quote came into her head for some reason. The silver chord - the meaning of life? Death? The sorrows, the joys, the euphoria, the high achievement: failure - despair, even, but the silver chord running straight through the middle of everything going on in the place, binding it all into a togetherness of purpose at all levels - perhaps that was it?

Here, however, her exalted musings were broken by the arthritic sound of the clock striking ten. There was work to be done and it was high time she got on with it, but as she walked down the cloister she seemed to hear her mother's gentle encouraging voice, saying: "Always remember our magpies, up there in the tree: one for sorrow, two for joy; so let it always be for joy for you, both in your life and in all that you are." Uplifted, she walked on and saw, standing under the archway at the end of the cloister, an anxious brown face belonging to a young man, waiting there in the shadows. It was her first tutorial victim of the day, looks very nervous, and no wonder; it was certainly her fault, for she was very late and the poor boy was looking really worried, so she smiled reassuringly and waved her hand in greeting. In return, he too smiled, a little smile of relief, and raised an uncertain hand in acknowledgement. So that was all right, she thought, and resolved to put the young man at his ease after such a bad start; she must do her best ,to set this young undergraduate on his way to achieve all he could, and gain as much as possible from his life and work in Oxford.

"Good morning," she said, "I'm so sorry to be late!"

"G'day, ma'am," he replied in a broad Australian drawl. "I thought I was down the gurgler regardin' the time. Was I OK?" he asked anxiously.

Joy looked at him more closely and thought: 'What an extraordinary face!' His complexion was dark mahogany, and he had the square face and broad nose of the pure aboriginal Australian, and dark, dark eyes whose gaze one could imagine ranging over the vast desert of the outback - or so it appeared to Joy's fancy.

"You were fine," she assured him. "It was my fault for being so terribly late. Let's go inside."

Joy noted that he was carrying in one hand a long narrow leather case which, he told her later, was made of kangaroo hide. Judging from the shape, she thought the instrument was probably one of the woodwind family - perhaps a bassoon?

"What's that?" she asked, raising an eyebrow enquiringly. "Oh," he smiled fondly at it as he took it from its case with great care. "Down under they call it a 'Borogine nose-flute thingy' - an Aboriginal nose-flute from the outback - a didgeridoo by name. It came down to me through the family, handed down by my dad, and going back as far as my great-grandfather. It's really old, but nobody knows quite how old it is. I was rather hoping I could give you a quick demo, and maybe do something with it while I'm here in Oxford - kind of make my mark in someway, you know?"

He was so touchingly earnest that her heart warmed to him instantly and nodding her head in acquiescence, she sank back gratefully in her leather chair at the desk as he began to play this primeval instrument, standing silhouetted against the mullioned window; statuesque, with his square athletic build and strong determined features. An unearthly sound came from the instrument, pulsating, sombre bass tones, like echoes of ancient caverns.

As he played, Joy became aware of other sounds in the background. In the distance was the exhilarating cacophony of the bells of St. Mary Mag's, as they whipped themselves up into a wild frenzy as they approached the climax of Grandsire Triples. And from the college chapel more music sounded, for the choir was practicing a psalm to organ accompaniment - 'Deprofundis': Out of the deep have I called unto thee, O Lord: Lord, hear my voice'; the chant was by Henry Purcell, in F minor, a sombre passage from the beautiful setting of 'My Beloved

Spake', from the 'Song of Songs', the words of this passage being: 'And the voice of the turtle is heard in our land.' So very sombre and yet so beautiful, this chant.

It felt exactly like a requiem for Oxford, somehow; but - as the strange symphony progressed and the bells rang out so wildly, going faster and faster, suddenly the whole chaotic tide of sound come absolutely together, like some Great Passacaglia and Fugue. There was a strong flavour of Pachelbel about it, rather like the musical ploddings of some magnificent shire horse - quite unstoppable, going determinedly on and on and on... destination - eternity, no less!

The choir and the organ went on grandly in the steady rhythm, with the bells cascading along at nearly double the speed, with the deep, sonorous ground bass of the Aboriginal nose flute binding it all together, as though in total command of the whole unruly orchestra. Quite, quite marvellous!...

This was indeed most truly representative of the spirit of Oxford and all it meant. Pure creativity at all levels - and full of fortuitous accidents of discovery in the process.

The bells with a final triumphant peal, thundered along in a veritable waterfall of sound: then suddenly and unexpectedly, at the solitary 'ding - ding - ding' at measured pace of the five minute bell, heralding the beginning of the matins. The college clock joined in as it struck an enthusiastic eleven antiphony. Simultaneously, the nose flute ceased to play, as though the Grand Fugue had ended as the deep, sonorous notes died away. The player, however, had probably been unaware of any other music sounding through the sonorous tones of his instrument. The chapel was now quiet, the choir practice over, and the choir emerged, crossing the quad and laughing and talking among themselves, evidently exhilarated by an excellent rehearsal. The young man looked at them through the window, then turned and gazed solemnly at Joy, who was sitting at her desk. He seemed apprehensive.

"Well, now, 'Ma'am, what do you think? Do I stand a chance?"

Taking off her glasses and polishing them vigorously, she paused for a moment or two's consideration of what to say, looking down at the score of the Monteverdi Vespers lying open on the desk in front of her. She had been working on the section 'Nisi Dominus' for her proposed performance of the work at the end of the academic year. This exciting section is in the style and rhythm of an Italian dance, the tarantella, and it occurred to Joy that here there could be a part for the Aboriginal instrument. It could play the first beat in every bar throughout the section and the same at the end of the work, in the Great-Amen. Yes - that was it! The deep tones of the instrument would come through very well in the general texture of the music. So she said:

"Fair dinkum - you sure do!" and smiling at him, she told him what she proposed to do. She would take him to the chapel shortly and play through the section on the organ, with him playing his part on the nose flute, adding:

"We can most certainly do something with that!"

At this a beaming smile lit up his dark countenance and laying down his instrument tenderly on the desk before him, he sat down and his first tutorial began, accompanied - perhaps, too, inspired by the distant roll of thunder as the storm moved far away over the downs towards Newbury.

END

Made in the USA
Charleston, SC
01 July 2013